Tide Over

Cover Designer: Disturbed Valkyrie Designs (@disturbedvalkyriedesigns)

Proofreader: Melissa DaSilva

Contact: eveholmesauthor@gmail.com

TIDE OVER

NORTHERN ROOTS: ATLANTIC
NOVA SCOTIA

EVE HOLMES

To those who weather the storms within.
Even with the darkest skies and fiercest waves, the sun will always rise.

BEFORE WE BEGIN

Tide Over is an MM romance, and part of the series *Northern Roots: Atlantic*. Each book in this series is a standalone, set in one of the four provinces of Atlantic Canada, featuring a new MM couple in each book. These books do not need to be read in order.

Northern Roots is a larger series featuring five sub-series, each dedicated to a region of Canada.

I'm so excited to share Tide Over, as it takes place in Nova Scotia, which is my home. There's something special about this little province, with its coastal charm and natural beauty, and I'm so excited to bring it to life for you. The story takes place in Torrin Cove, a fictional fishing village inspired by the real, picturesque villages along the South Shore of Nova Scotia. Though Torrin Cove exists only in this story, all other locations mentioned in the book are real. If you'd like to see where they are, I've included a map following this note.

You'll also notice a sprinkle of Nova Scotian dialect throughout this story. For instance, we often skip the "s" for plurals on words like beer or lobster, and use words like "right" and "some" to describe how we feel. Such as, "That was right some good!" It's just one of our little quirks, so if you see phrases such as this, or some odd grammar here and there, they aren't mistakes — they're just part of life in this little corner of the world.

Scottish Gaelic, another important part of Nova Scotian culture, also plays a role in this story. You'll find translations for any Gaelic phrases listed in the back of the book.

This story explores heavy themes of grief and mental health, and we're not shying away from the difficult, messy parts of healing. Grief can make us act in ways we don't always understand, and healing is often full of ups and downs. These boys go through a hard journey to find their happily ever after, but when they do, it's all the more beautiful for the battles they've fought and the love they've found with each other.

There is some content in this book that may be unsettling to some, so please review the following content warnings:

- Grief and loss
- Mention of death of parent and close friend
- Self-harm (cold water and light burning)
- Suicidal ideation (without plan or action)
- Serious, non life-threatening injury
- Explicit sex scenes

I hope you love Theo and Liam!

Eve xo

ATLANTIC
CANADA
NEWFOUNDLAND
PRINCE
EDWARD
ISLAND
NOVA
SCOTIA
NEW
BRUNSWICK

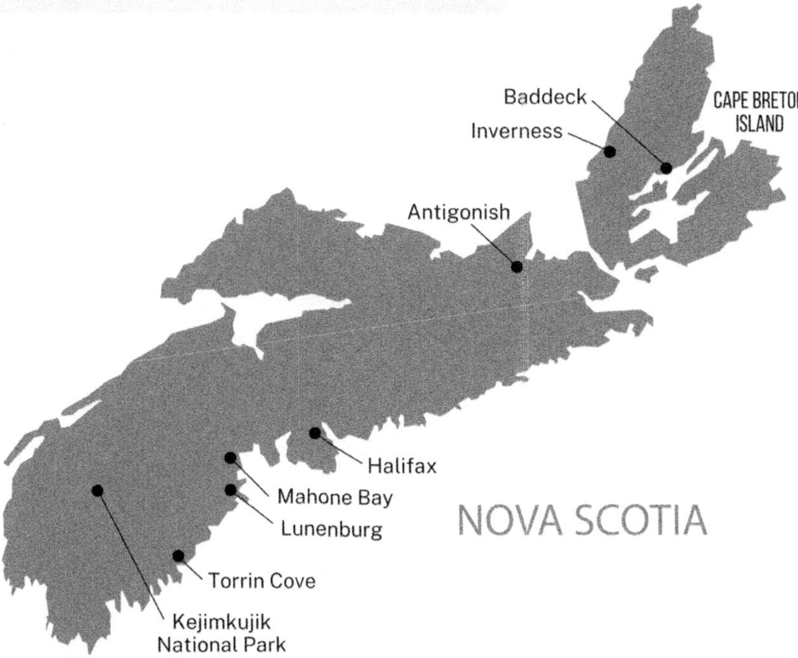
Baddeck
CAPE BRETON
ISLAND
Inverness
Antigonish
Halifax
Mahone Bay
Lunenburg
NOVA SCOTIA
Torrin Cove
Kejimkujik
National Park

ONE

LIAM

I'M NOT sure what I thought I would feel when coming home, but this isn't it.

My eyes follow the ferry as it crosses the harbour in the distance, until it disappears behind the buildings obstructing my view. But I keep staring out the window, sliding my gaze to the sailboats further down the water.

"So, what do you think?"

I nod, watching the boats as they lazily make their way around the harbour. "It's nice." But as my gaze drops to the busy street below, and I watch the morning rush towards downtown Halifax just a few streets over, disappointment settles. "You don't have anything a little less... central, do you?" I ask, turning to face the owner of this apartment.

She stands in the doorway of the empty bedroom, leaning against the doorframe as she shakes her head sadly. "No, sorry. This is my only available unit."

I nod, returning my attention to the harbour. "That's alright."

"If you like this one though, I can give you an application," she says. "I have a couple more showings this afternoon, but it's first come, first serve for qualified applicants."

The muffled sounds of the traffic and chatter from people on the street below fill the empty space, and I tear my gaze away from the sailboats to glance around the room. It's a decent-sized one-bedroom apartment, on the top floor of an older home with only two other units in it. And even though it's close to downtown, the building itself seems quiet. The price is a bit much, but everywhere in Halifax is expensive these days, so I guess that doesn't really matter.

"Yeah." I offer her a small smile. "Sounds good."

"Excellent." She beams as she opens a folder and hands me a piece of paper. "It's pretty straightforward. Current and last address, work information... the usual."

My eyes skirt over the application in my hands. "I don't have a current address. I just got into Nova Scotia this morning."

"Oh, that's fine." She waves her hand in the air. "Just your last address. Where are you moving from?"

"Alberta," I say, glancing up at her.

She chuckles. "Usually it's Nova Scotians moving *to* Alberta, not the other way around."

I release a breath of laughter. "Yeah, I did that already. Moved out there to work in the oil sands, just like everyone else. Now..." I pause for a moment and take a deep breath. "It was just time to leave."

She observes me with a soft nod. "I know a few people out west living that life," she says. "Most of them would love to move back to their hometown. Good for you."

A knot tightens in my stomach, and I swallow thickly as uneasiness settles within me at the simple thought of my hometown. "I'm actually from Cape Breton."

Her eyes light up. "I'm a Caper too! Grew up in Baddeck. Where abouts are you from?"

"Inverness," I reply, a feeling of comfort and familiarity trying to push its way in. I've lived in Calgary, Alberta, for ten years, and as friendly as it can be there, it's nothing like the immediate connection you find with someone in Nova Scotia. Especially when they find even the slightest similarity to bond over, like being from the same large island.

"Oh, I love Inverness," she says. "Such a beautiful place. I bet you're happy that visiting will be much easier now."

My eyes drop to the application in my hands as that comfortable feeling is quickly snuffed out. I nod, pressing my lips together for a moment before holding up the piece of paper. "So, I just fill this out and bring it back to you?"

There's a beat of silence as her brow furrows slightly, then she smiles softly with a nod. "Or you can just snap a photo and email it. Either works."

"Ok." I roll up the paper and hold my hand out. "Thanks for showing me this place on such short notice." Considering I just got into town this morning, and didn't yet have a plan for where I was going to live, I do appreciate that she was able to squeeze me in right away. I figured it would be a few days until I was able to see anything.

She reaches out to shake my hand. "No problem at all."

As I step out of the house and onto the sidewalk, I take a deep breath of the cool, saltwater air. I've come back to Nova Scotia regularly to visit my family since moving away, but breathing in this air now, knowing I am actually *home*... I'm afraid to admit I've missed it. It almost feels like it cheapens my last ten years living in Calgary, and everything I loved about my life there. Even though that life doesn't exist there anymore, and everything has changed.

I look up at the old, colourful houses that line the street as I walk towards my truck, each one holding so much character and history. This city is warm, vibrant, inviting and friendly, and it's everything I've always wanted. Growing up in such a small town in Inverness, I couldn't wait to move to Halifax. Whenever I came here with my parents when I was little, I loved looking at these houses and dreamed of living in one someday, close to downtown, and being a part of everything big and important. And when I ended up in Calgary instead, I thought that was even better.

Was I ever wrong.

Once I reach my truck, I get in and immediately roll the window down, once again taking a deep breath of the fresh air as I lay my head back against the seat and close my eyes. But it's not hope, relief or happiness that fills me. Instead, heaviness settles into my chest and the knot in my stomach tightens even more.

This is all wrong.

I wasn't the only one who wanted to live here.

And now I'm here, alone.

As my eyes open and land on the colourful houses once more, my heart beats faster and dread flows through me. The noise of the busy street seems to grow louder as the passing traffic and happy chatter from people on the sidewalk echoes in my head so loudly it's almost painful.

I tightly close my eyes again and rub a hand over my face. "Fuck," I mutter, leaning forward to press my forehead against the steering wheel.

Then I look down at the rental application in my hand, crumple it up into a ball, and let it fall to my feet.

I can't do this. I don't deserve it. Not after the mistake I've made that cost me everything.

Without another thought, I put my truck in drive and find

myself back on the highway. I have no idea where I'm going, but I know I can't stay in Halifax.

I *should* go home.

I should go to Inverness. I should see my parents. But I can't bring myself to do it. They don't even know yet that I left Calgary and quit my job in the oil sands. Because if they found out where I was going to work now, I don't know how well they would take it.

The weight in my chest grows heavier as Halifax disappears behind me, and the pain and guilt I carry every day surges to the surface. I deserve these feelings... but I'm also desperate to escape them. I don't know where I'm supposed to be, what I'm supposed to be doing, or how to outrun this pain.

The exit for South Shore comes into view, and a voice somewhere inside me urges me to take it. I just drove across Canada, barely stopping the entire way here with a desperate need to get away from the reminders of my mistakes and the loss that broke me.

But I somehow ended up in Nova Scotia. Where the good memories of my childhood and my family, and the reminders of everything I could have had, hurts just as much.

I need to keep running.

Before I know it, I'm taking the exit to South Shore. And I keep driving in the complete opposite direction of home, taking myself further and further away from everything and everyone I know I should be facing.

I just can't do it yet.

TWO

THEO

"YOU'VE GOT to be kidding me," I mutter under my breath as I read over the slip from the buyer's station.

"What?" Mitch asks, peering over my shoulder.

I lift the slip so he can see how much we were paid for the eighteen hundred pounds of lobster we caught this morning. It's almost a two dollar per pound decrease from yesterday.

"Fuck," he says, his features twisting in disgust. "I say we go back to the Frayed Knot tomorrow. They usually buy at a higher rate."

"Yeah," I mumble, shoving the slip into my pocket. Who knows what tomorrow will bring... but it better not be another decrease.

We head over to our boat, where the rest of my crew have finished loading up the buckets, bait, and ice we bought for tomorrow.

"Let's get out of here," I say as I hop into the boat and head to the wheelhouse. As I start up the engine, the crew happily jumps into the boat after me, and I try not to let my frustration dampen their mood. We had a great catch today, and I should also be happy about that. Catches have been plentiful lately, but that also means the demand is lower. And a lower demand equals a drop in price. Which usually wouldn't be a problem, but the cost of fuel, bait, rope, lumber, and everything else I need to keep this boat running is skyrocketing. So the more we catch, the more I have to spend on repairing the wear and tear on the equipment.

It's all just a vicious circle...

I steer the boat into the marina and pull up to our spot at the dock. The crew jumps out as I kill the engine, but as I grab a rope, Sarah yanks it from my hand.

"We got this," she says, kneeling down to tie the boat to the dock. "You go. Your sister is going to be livid if you're late. Again."

I check my watch and wince, because I already am late. "Yeah, alright. Thanks."

As I head down the wharf towards my truck, I wave to a few other boats pulling in and pass Sheila, the marina manager.

"Good haul today?" she asks, stopping outside her office.

"Yup," I say, nodding at her and continuing to walk by.

She chuckles and shakes her head at me. "You need to learn how to shut your mouth, boy."

I turn around with a smile, walking backwards so I can face her. "Alright, then you can tell my sister why I was late."

She snorts, waving a hand towards me. "Get. And tell her I say hi."

With a wave, I turn around and continue to my truck. I told Heather I would be at the store ten minutes ago. It's only a couple minutes' drive away since Torrin Cove is tiny, but still... I was late the last time she needed me to cover for her too.

As I park in front of the general store my family owns, I'm greeted with the familiar sight of the town's retired fishermen sipping coffee on the front porch. The old man crew meets here every afternoon, watching the boats come in and catching up with the current fishermen as they stop into the store. They say it's to "stay social", but we all know it's so they can keep tabs on us.

As my mother says, once a fisherman, always a fisherman.

"How was the water this morning?" my grandfather asks as I climb the few steps onto the porch.

"Decent," I say. "Good haul, calm water. Brought in eighteen hundred pounds."

Jack, one of my grandfather's old crew members, lets out a low whistle. "More than decent, I'd say."

Grandpa leans back in his chair with a smirk. "Still haven't beat my biggest catch then," he says with a wink.

I roll my eyes. He claims his biggest catch was twenty-three hundred pounds. But when he was fishing, the number of traps allowed was lower than our two hundred and fifty, and they didn't have the technology we have now. So there's no fucking way.

"You going to come back out then, old man?" I huff out an amused breath and nod my chin at the mug in his hand. "Or you just going to keep sitting on your ass drinking coffee and reminiscing about things that never happened?"

He tips his head back with a deep laugh, and the other men do the same.

"Nah, I'm not going to put my only grandson to shame," Grandpa says with a sly smile. "And you wouldn't even have a boat or a licence if it wasn't for me, so shut your trap." He winks and takes a drink of his coffee.

I shake my head and turn to open the door to the store. "Put your money where your mouth is and maybe I will."

The door closes behind me as I enter the store, the sound of laughter from the group of men fading away as I'm met with the smell of freshly baked bread and coffee.

And a wild-eyed Heather.

"Finally." She stands from her stool. But she stops and scrunches her face up as I join her behind the counter and pour myself a mug of coffee. "You smell nice," she says.

I shake my head, placing the coffee pot back on the burner. "You're the one that needed me here *right* after I got the boat in."

"Could have allotted some time for a shower," she says as she shrugs her sweater on and makes a dramatic show of side-stepping around me to avoid the smell of fish and sea water.

I roll my eyes at her and she chuckles.

"Smell aside, thanks for coming in today. I know it's not ideal." She grabs her bag from under the counter and slings it over her shoulder. "But I have to pick the kids up from school then drive to Lunenburg for their dentist appointment."

"It's alright," I say, leaning back against the counter and taking a drink of my coffee.

If there's one thing I can always count on, it's Heather being frazzled. And honestly, I'm surprised at how well she *does* hold it all together, considering everything she has on her plate. She runs the business end of the store, has two kids aged five and seven, is actively involved in their school and all their sports and interests, and her husband, Chris, is often travelling for work. And she's my older sister, so she's usually trying to take care of me too. She doesn't ask for help often, but when she does, I want to be able to support her as best I can.

"Ok." She blows out a breath, and looks around the store, like she's making sure everything is in place before she leaves. "Text me if you need—"

"I've been doing this since I was fourteen." I rest my elbows on the counter and gesture with my head towards the door. "Go."

She smirks at me and turns, waving over her shoulder as she heads for the door. "See you later."

"Bye," I say, watching as the door bangs shut behind her. Once she's gone, I let out a long breath and drop my head between my shoulders. Then I stand up, drain my coffee, and pour another one.

"Rough morning?"

I turn my head as Mom exits the kitchen, wiping her hands on her apron.

"No," I say, starting another pot of coffee. "Just need to refuel."

She nods as her eyes slowly trail down my dirty shirt and pants with a small smile tugging at her lips.

"I didn't have time to go home first," I say. "It took longer than anticipated at the buyer's station today."

Mom tilts her head with a smile. "You know I don't mind. Your father used to come in here all the time right off the boat. In a way, I kind of like the smell."

"That's weird," I mutter, dropping down to sit on the stool behind the counter and wave to Melinda, one of our regular customers, as she enters the store. "I can only stay for a few hours today though," I say to Mom. "I have to finish installing cabinets at the Campbells' this afternoon."

"That's fine," Mom says, turning to head back into the kitchen. "I'm almost done baking for the day then you can go."

"Ok, thanks," I call to her as she retreats into her happy place.

That woman could bake all day and night, and never get tired of it. And the town definitely appreciates it. We sell out of freshly baked bread, rolls, muffins, and more every day.

Melinda approaches the counter, setting her regular Wednesday order of milk and bread on the counter. "You're a busy boy, Theo. You shouldn't work so much."

I huff out a laugh as I pour her usual cup of coffee to go and slide it over to her. I've known Melinda since I was a kid, and she was our neighbourhood watch as we played on our bikes in the streets. And even with a new crop of kids in town to look out for, she still keeps an eye on all of us as we've grown up.

"I don't really have much of a choice," I say, as I ring up her order. "Fishing doesn't pay bills in the off-season. Carpentry at least fills that time."

She hands me cash to pay for her order, then dramatically peers out the window. "Looks like *on* season out there to me."

I chuckle, putting her items in a bag and passing it to her. "Yeah, but also, if I didn't do it, who would have built your bookshelves?"

She tsks at me as she takes her bag and coffee. "You're young, you should be having fun."

I shrug and slap on a smile. "Who says I'm not?"

With a playful roll of her eyes, she heads to the door. "Bye, Cynthia!" she calls out as she pulls it open.

"Talk to you later, Melinda!" Mom calls back to her.

When the store is quiet again, I drop down on the stool again and listen to the faint sounds of Mom's mixers in the kitchen, and the old man crew chatting out on the porch. And I finally take a moment to just breathe. I lean back against the wall and look out the window, watching as a few more boats return to the cove. But my gaze slides past them, where the cove opens to the wide expanse of the Atlantic ocean.

A sigh escapes me as I keep my eyes on the massive body of water that I go out in every day. Where I work my ass off and hope it's all going to be worth it. It could lead me anywhere... but I always come back here, to my tiny hometown of Torrin Cove, with a population of about three hundred. Because I always knew I'd be here forever. My grandfather and my dad worked too hard to build up the fishing business, and it was always the plan for me to inherit the boats, equipment, and fishing licences. But lately... I feel like I've been starting to question it all.

Every morning, I wake up at the ass crack of dawn and take myself and my crew into potentially dangerous waters to complete a dangerous job. Then we unload our haul to be paid an amount determined by market demands, and not based on the insane amount of fucking work it takes to actually complete this job. The cost to keep the crew and boat running increases every year, and it all just seems so... pointless.

Except it's not.

I rub a hand over my face and sigh again.

I like what I do. I like fishing, I like carpentry, I like helping out at the store with my family. So why the fuck do I feel so... empty? Stuck? Unfulfilled? I don't even fucking know... it's an unsettling feeling that I can't make sense of. Every day, I do the same thing. Fish, build, sleep, repeat. And it seems like the payoff for all of this is getting to be less and less. And I'm not talking about the money.

But there's no point in even thinking about it. As mundane as it might feel, and as frustrating as it can be, this is my life.

My eyes slide to the retired fishermen on the porch as they drink their coffee and watch the boats come in, and I blow out a breath.

I guess that's what I have to look forward to.

THREE

LIAM

IT'S BEEN ALMOST two hours since I left Halifax, and I don't want to stop. I need to keep going, and get as far away from everything as I possibly can. But I'm almost out of gas, which forces me to take the next exit in search of a gas station. Once I'm fuelled up again, I'll keep going.

I need to keep going.

The exit takes me onto a long and winding road, passing farmland and quaint houses nestled among large trees, until I finally reach the main street of a little town. And I mean *little*.

There's not much here as I drive through in search of a gas station, passing a community hall, a small pub, a little church, an art studio... and that's about it. Just when I start to think it's a lost cause and I should turn back to the highway, I spot a sign up ahead for gas.

It's a log cabin with the name "MacKinnon's General Store" over the entrance, with two gas pumps outside. I pull up to the pump and hop out, and I can't help but chuckle to myself when I try to pre-pay at the pump. It's a fucking log cabin in the middle of nowhere, of course it doesn't take payment out here.

I stick the nozzle into the fuel tank of my truck and look across the street to the water as I wait for it to fill up. The store has a clear view of a cove, and I watch as several fishing boats make their way in. My mind starts to wander as I keep my eyes on them, and I finally start questioning what the fuck I'm doing. In just a couple hours I'll be at the end of the province, surrounded by ocean with only two options. Turn around and go back the way I came, or keep going and let the highway take me along the western loop of Nova Scotia... which will bring me to Cape Breton.

Or the third option.

Continue on into the ocean.

If only I had the courage to accept that I should be running from myself, rather than the consequences of my actions.

Laughter from the front of the store pulls me back into reality, and I glance at the porch where a group of men are sitting, talking amongst themselves as they look over the water. With a sigh, I shove my thoughts back down into the depths of my darkness. I'll deal with them eventually. But not right now.

Once my truck is filled, I put the pump back in place and head up the steps to the store to go pay.

One of the men turns his head to me with a nod and a smile. "Good afternoon."

I nod back at him as I reach for the door. "Hi."

A few of the other men eye me curiously, clearly wondering who this stranger is in their tiny coastal town hidden away from the rest of the province. But they all smile and greet me regardless.

As I enter the store, I'm not at all surprised to see it looking exactly how I imagined it would. It's a homey market-style store, with baskets and shelves of bread and other baked goods on one side, and shelves everywhere that make up aisles and areas for grocery and household essentials. The wooden floorboards creak as I walk towards the cooler in the back of the store, and the smell of freshly baked bread and coffee immediately gives me a sense of comfort I haven't felt in a long time.

A man about ten or so years older than me smiles in greeting as he passes me on his way to the front counter, and I give him a nod as I pull open the cooler door and grab a bottle of water. There's chatter at the counter as an older gentleman buys a cup of coffee, and he talks to the guy who served him as if they know each other well. When he heads out to join the other men on the porch, the other man takes his place and they start chatting away too. For such a small town, this little store is busy. But I didn't see much of anything else on my drive in, so I guess that makes sense. And it's not like I have anywhere to be in any hurry, so I wait and hang back by the selection of local crafts, admiring the wood carvings of whales, pottery mugs, and sea glass art. But since the store is so small, I can't help but overhear the conversation between the two men.

"How's it going today?" the man asks as he sets his items down on the counter.

"Not bad, how are you doing?"

I glance over at them, and I'm surprised to see the guy working here looks to be about my age. I'm not sure why, but I expected someone older, not in his late twenties.

"Can't complain." The older man tosses a pack of gum onto the counter, and the guy behind it rings that up too. "I know you're busy with fishing and other jobs," the customer says, "but whenever you get some time, I'm hoping to have you out to the farm to either fix my barn door, or build a new one. Whichever you think it needs. It's going to bite the dust soon, I think."

The guy nods. "Yeah, I can do that for you this weekend."

The other one chuckles. "Knew you'd say that. No rush,

you've got a lot on your plate, and it's working well enough for now."

The guy working shakes his head and slides the stuff across the counter. "I'm up your way Saturday anyway to finish putting down some flooring for Paul. I can do it after that, it's no problem."

I watch as the older guy picks up his items and slowly shakes his head with a smile. "Just like your father. Thanks, Theo. I appreciate it."

The guy, Theo I guess, gives him a lopsided smile, and the customer heads towards the door with a wave. "Have a good one!"

Once he's gone, I approach the counter, set my water down, and pull out my wallet. "And gas." I tilt my head towards the pump outside.

He punches a few buttons on the register and glances out the window to my truck. "Long way from Alberta."

I look out the window as well, where my Alberta licence plate is visible. "Yeah. Just got into Nova Scotia this morning."

His eyebrows lift with surprise. "Quite the drive."

I nod, taking my bank card out. "Moving back."

He chuckles lightly, flipping the card reader towards me. "Don't hear that too often."

"I know," I say with a breath of laughter as I tap my card to pay. "I just couldn't do it out there anymore."

As the receipt prints, he seems to observe me for a moment. Then he rips it off the machine and holds it out to me. "I can understand that."

I reach out to take it and can't help but observe him as well. From his conversation earlier, I know he's a fisherman... and he certainly looks the part. He's dressed in a dirty black hoodie with holes all over it, and his short, light brown hair is windswept and messy, like he just stepped off the boat. I'm not sure what he's doing working in a general store as well, since he apparently also installs floors and fixes barn doors.

"You from here?" I ask him as I shove my wallet back in my pocket. I don't know why I'm even asking him this, or why I'm apparently lingering. I'm not usually one to strike up a conversation with strangers, or anyone, really. But he doesn't seem to mind.

He nods and sits on the stool behind the counter. "Yeah." Then he chuckles. "Not sure why anyone would choose to live here if they weren't."

I smirk as I look out the window at the boats on the water. The view is beautiful, and even just the vibe in this store is cozy and inviting. Everyone I've encountered so far in the five minutes I've been here seem nice and welcoming, and a brief wave of longing washes over me as it all reminds me of Inverness. Being right on the water, and in a small town where everyone knows everyone... it's just like home in some ways. But completely different in others.

My eyes land on a bulletin board on the wall, and I scan the various flyers and ads pinned to it. Most are just what I expected, selling items like furniture and fishing equipment, and offering services like lawn care. But disappointment settles when I don't see what I'm apparently looking for.

"I don't know..." I say slowly, still scanning the board. "Seems like a nice place."

"It is," he says. "There's just nothing here for anyone unless they're coming for seasonal work."

I glance at him, and he tilts his head towards the cove. "Lobster fishing," he says.

I nod in understanding and bring my attention back to the bulletin board. "Any rentals around here?"

There's a beat of silence before he answers me. "There's a couple around, but this time of year they're already full from regular seasonal fishermen. So, in a few months, once fishing season is over in June, there will be." He eyes me for a moment. "You looking for work?"

"No," I shake my head. "I'm starting a new job in a couple weeks, on an oil rig in the Gulf of Mexico. Three weeks on, three weeks off, so..." I trail off, bringing my attention back to the boats in the cove. "Just looking for a quiet place to live while I'm not working."

When I look at him again, he nods thoughtfully. "Intense job."

I huff out a breath and nod in agreement. "Yeah." I take one final look around the store and try to ignore the disappointed feeling in the pit of my stomach. "Anyway, thanks. I'll keep looking around. Have a good one."

But as I turn to head for the door, the disappointment only grows. There's something telling me I want to be here, which I don't understand. But maybe the next town will be like this one, and will be somewhere I can call home for a bit.

"Well, actually..."

I stop, turning to face him as he stands from his stool.

He hesitates for a moment before he shrugs one shoulder. "I... I don't know if this would be a good option for you but... I have a room available in my house. I just bought it last year and have slowly been fixing it up, so it's kind of rough. But it's bigger than anything I need. I could rent you a room if you wanted to stay here, and if you don't mind living in a bit of a construction zone." He shrugs again. "And it's on the water, so it's nice and quiet."

The look on his face is almost hopeful, which surprisingly mirrors how I'm feeling. I let the hope and excitement bubble up for a moment, providing me with a sense of relief from the darkness, shame, and guilt I carry every day. And even though I know I don't deserve to feel that relief, I'm not sure I can ignore it right now. Because the hope I see in him is somehow making it easier for me to feel it too.

I glance around the store again, letting that feeling take over for a moment. I need to stop running at some point. And while I'm not ready to go home just yet, this could be the next best thing.

His soft brown eyes meet mine as I bring my gaze back to him, and I can't help but let out a small smile. I don't even know him, but something about this place, and talking to him… it just feels like what I'm supposed to do.

With a nod, I step towards the counter. "Works for me." I hold my hand out to him. "I'm Liam, by the way."

He grabs my hand in a firm handshake. "Theo." He smiles softly. "Welcome to Torrin Cove."

FOUR

THEO

I TOSS the last of my tools into the back of my truck, finished for the day and ready to head home. And just in time too. I'm meeting Liam at my place in about five minutes, and I wasn't sure if I'd actually get the last of these cabinets installed before then.

As I head out of the Campbells' driveway and onto the road, I let my thoughts wander back to this morning when I met Liam in the store. I'm not quite sure what the fuck I was thinking, inviting him to live in my house after talking to him for two minutes, but he seems normal enough. And he has a job on an oil rig, so he can't be a criminal or anything. Unless he's on the run and looking for a place to hide, which is why he's in Torrin Cove of all places.

But hey, maybe that's the excitement I've been looking for. So... fuck it.

A few minutes down the road, I turn off and follow the long, winding driveway lined with tall trees. As I round the final bend, the view opens up to reveal my house tucked among the trees, facing the ocean.

And *this* is why I bought this house. It may be too big for just me, and needed a shit ton of work just to make it somewhat habitable, but this view gets me every night when I come home. It's completely private, away from the rest of the town, and has everything I need. So far, it's been a good project to fill my free time and keep me busy when my mind wants to wander.

I park next to Liam's truck and make my way down to the dock, where he's looking out over the water.

"Hey," I say as I step onto the dock, and he turns to face me with a nod in greeting.

"Not a bad spot," he says.

I smile softly as I stand beside him, my gaze following his over the water. It's a secluded stretch of ocean, away from all the boat traffic. And right now it looks beautiful with the orange sky reflecting off the waves as the sun dips low. "This is what sold me on this place."

He huffs lightly. "I see why."

I turn my head to look at him, but he keeps his eyes on the water, seeming to get lost to his head for a moment. My gaze lingers on him a beat longer as I take in the emptiness in his eyes and the heaviness that seems to cling to him.

Until his gaze drops to my speedboat in the water before us, which I have set up for fishing. He nods towards it. "Get out much?"

I look down at it as well and sigh. "Not as much as I'd like. We don't fish lobster on Sundays, so I try to get out on my own then." I shrug slightly. "Otherwise, I just try to go out whenever I find the time and I'm not working too late."

"Building barn doors?" he asks with a small smirk.

I chuckle. "Carpentry and a bit of everything else thrown in." I tilt my head towards the barn on the other side of the driveway. "I have a workshop in there where I build tables, chairs, cabinets, you name it. But it's evolved into house calls for repairs and installations of various kinds." I huff out another laugh. "Like barn doors."

He gives me a lopsided smile as the breeze blows his shaggy dark hair over his icy blue eyes. He lifts a hand to push it back, and I let my gaze run over the tattoos covering his hand and forearm. Then it continues to run up his muscular arm, before I quickly turn my head away.

"You fish?" I ask, looking back down at my boat.

"I did quite a bit growing up in Cape Breton. Not quite the same in Alberta."

I chuckle, turning to face him again as he looks at me, his smile still in place.

"I bet." I tilt my head towards the house. "I'll show you around."

Liam follows me up the dock and onto the small stone patio off the side door.

"I bought this place a year ago, and I was hoping to have more done with it by now." I push the door open and step into the entryway. "Probably shouldn't have sold my other place until I had more of it done, but... it's liveable now." We head into the kitchen, and I gesture to the large kitchen island. "I did finally install countertops, so at least there's a functional kitchen."

Liam walks around the island, silently taking in the space. He stops in front of the sink and peers out the small window which has a view of the water.

"I have a bigger window I'm going to put in there," I say, leaning against the island. "Just... need to find the time."

He nods, turning away from the window and glancing around again. And immediately, I feel uneasy. I don't think he expected this. I told him it was a bit of a construction zone, but... it's more than just a bit. The wall between the kitchen and living room is only partially torn down, since I haven't had the chance to finish taking it out yet. Even though I started it months ago. I still haven't put the tiles up for the backsplash after tearing the old, broken ones out, and the walls throughout the entire house are still full of holes after updating the electrical.

Liam heads through the partially torn out wall into the living room. It's a large space with wood beams across the ceiling and exposed brick on the far wall, where a TV I never watch is hanging. A wood stove sits in the corner, and the original wide, wood plank floors creak as we walk across them.

"It's a drafty house," I say as Liam looks over the wood stove. "It keeps it warm in the evenings without having to turn the heat on this time of year."

Liam nods again and that uneasy feeling grows. What the fuck was I thinking inviting someone to live here? This place is a disaster, and he's probably trying to find a polite way of telling me thanks but no fucking thanks.

And why do I feel so disappointed by that?

But Liam pauses as his gaze lands on the doorway leading into the next room. And that feeling lets up a little bit. Because that room is the best part of this house.

I watch him as he makes his way into the small room and stops in the middle of it, looking out the large bay window that takes up almost the entire wall, with a view of the ocean.

I cross my arms and lean against the doorframe, looking out over the water as well as the sun continues to go down. "I had this idea that I would sit in here and enjoy coffee in the mornings."

He looks over his shoulder at me, then down at the couch and small wood stove in here. "Not a reality?"

I shrug one shoulder with a shake of my head. "I'm a fisherman. Not enough time."

Liam holds my gaze for a moment, then turns to face the window again. "You should make it."

An involuntary sigh escapes me as frustration settles inside me. And not at him... at me. Because I know I should make time to actually enjoy things, such as this house. But time alone with just my thoughts is also something I've been trying to avoid.

"There's another good view through here." I point to another doorway on the adjacent wall, into a small hallway.

Liam heads through the door and into the bedroom across the hall. It has a large window with a view of the woods surrounding the house, opening to the water. The room is bathed in warm, orange light from the setting sun, and I try not to let my gaze rest too long on Liam as he stands before the window, the soft glow highlighting his features in a way that makes it hard to look away.

"There's two other bedrooms upstairs besides mine, if you'd rather be up there. But this one has the best view out of all of them. And your bathroom is right next door." I put my hands in my pockets as I linger by the doorway, watching as Liam just stands by the bed, looking out the window.

As I glance around the room, I shake my head at myself. What the fuck. I haven't even done anything to this room, except put a bed and a dresser in here. The trim needs to be replaced, the floor needs to be refinished, and it definitely needs to be painted.

I swallow and lift a hand to rub the back of my neck. "I know this isn't the best place to live... it still needs a lot of work. It's quiet though, and private. There's no traffic, even on the water—"

"I can move in right now."

My brows lift in surprise as Liam turns to face me.

"Ok," I say, glancing once more around the room. "I can take this bed out, if you have your own...?"

He shakes his head, looking down at the queen-sized bed I put in here for who knows what reason. "I have everything I own with me in my truck. So, the bed works for me."

I nod slowly, observing him for a moment. I'm not sure what he has going on, but maybe I wasn't that far off when I thought he could be on the run.

But fuck it, right?

"Beer?" I ask.

He nods, and I turn around, heading into the kitchen. He doesn't seem like the forthcoming type, and I'm not about to ask for his life story. So, we can at least somewhat get to know each other over a beer if we're going to live together.

I grab two beer from the fridge and pass him one as he takes a seat on a stool at the kitchen island.

"What do you do on the rig?" I ask, twisting the cap off my beer as I lean against the counter opposite the island.

"I'm a welder," he says, then takes a drink.

I nod, fiddling with the label on my beer bottle. "And this is your first time working offshore?"

He nods as well, looking down at the bottle in his hands. "Yeah. Did my training for offshore last week, so my first shift starts next week."

Before I can say anything in response to that, he looks up at me. "I can help with your renos while I'm here."

I glance around the kitchen and shake my head slowly. "You don't have to. There's quite a bit left to do, and probably not how you want to spend your time off."

He shrugs, sitting back and looking around as well. "Not like I have anything else to do."

An urge rises to ask him why he's here in Torrin Cove, when he's from Cape Breton. He's on the complete opposite end of the province, and from what he said in the store, I don't think he actually planned on living down this way. But I don't ask him, and instead I point at the partially knocked down wall behind him. "I guess I wouldn't say no to some help tackling that beast."

He turns to look at it and chuckles. When he turns to face me again, his bright blue eyes meet mine and I can't help but stare directly into them.

The corner of his lips tilt up in a soft smile. "I can help with that." Then he gestures around the kitchen with his beer bottle. "So, you fish, work in a store, and have a carpentry business, all while renovating a house. Quite the life you got carved out for yourself here."

I suppress a sigh and take a drink, trying to ignore the familiar feeling of frustration as it rises to the surface. But I simply nod. "Yeah. My family owns the store, and I inherited the fishing business. Quite the life..."

I immediately regret the way that came out, and Liam eyes me curiously. Thankfully though, he doesn't dig any deeper into that response.

And as we shift our conversation back to the house and renovations, there seems to be an unspoken understanding between us. We don't ask each other anything personal. Nothing more about work, family, home... nothing. We just talk about tile, support beams, and wiring.

Liam is a mystery, and I have no idea what he's doing here. But I know all about hiding parts of yourself from others, so... who am I to judge?

FIVE

LIAM

THE STAIRS CREAK softly as Theo makes his way downstairs, and I listen while he quietly passes my closed bedroom door and heads into the kitchen. But I continue to lie in bed and stare up at the dark ceiling, just like I have been all night. And it has nothing to do with the room or the house... I just can't get my mind to settle.

The faint smell of coffee drifts into my bedroom, and I hear the soft clink of a spoon against a mug as Theo gets ready to go to work. I turn my head and look out the window, taking in the darkness of the early morning. A long breath escapes me as I listen to the waves gently lapping against the shore, and once again think of everything that happened yesterday. I don't know if I should be here. I also don't know where I'm supposed to be. But this place, Torrin Cove... it feels right. The quiet simplicity of this little town might be just what I need right now.

I hear the door to the house close, and a moment later, Theo's truck starts up. And I can't help but think about how my presence here might impact him. From the sounds of it, he's an integral part of this small community. His family runs the only store in town and he's the captain of a seemingly successful fishing business he inherited. Plus owning a house like this and having a carpentry business on the side... everything seems so certain and safe for him. So what will this town think of some random guy suddenly moving into his house?

The sound of his truck fades away and I stay here in bed, looking out the window until the sky begins to brighten. When the sun peeks out over the water, I sit up in bed and watch as the yellow rays spread across the gentle waves.

This is all just so perfect, isn't it...

With a sigh, I stand up and pull on a t-shirt and a pair of sweatpants and head out to the kitchen. I find some coffee pods in a cupboard, and as I take one out, I make a mental note to replace it later. While my coffee brews, I look around the kitchen as the sunlight starts to stream in through the windows, highlighting the small details I didn't notice last night. This house may be a work in progress, but Theo has made it his home in some subtle ways.

There's an oil painting of a fishing boat on the wall near the entryway, and above the island is a driftwood pot rack which looks handmade. But what catches my eye is some children's artwork on the fridge. I step closer, scanning the colourful pieces of paper. Does he have kids? And if so, where are they? But as I look over the drawings, I see *To Uncle Theo* scrawled across the pages. And I can't help the small smile that tugs at my lips as I take in the pictures of rainbows, fishing boats, and what I'm assuming is Theo with two kids.

The coffee machine sputters as it finishes brewing, so I take my mug and wander into the living room, taking in the quiet and inviting space. Until I find myself in the room with the large bay window looking over the water.

I stand in the middle of the room as I take a drink of my

coffee and watch some boats fade away in the distance. But guilt burrows deep inside me the longer I stay here, and my eyes drop to the couch. I feel like I'm taking something from Theo by being in here, doing exactly what he said he wanted to do with this room. And as my gaze shifts to the wood stove in the corner, then back out to the beautiful view before me, I take a step backwards.

"Fuck," I mutter, turning around and leaving the sunroom, heading back into my bedroom.

The familiar weight of guilt continues to press down on me for taking something from Theo, and I let it serve as a reminder for everything else I've done as I sit on the edge of the bed and drag a hand over my face. Until the tightness in my chest becomes overwhelming.

I need to feel this guilt. I need to hold it in my hands, and I need to let it hurt me.

Without thinking I grab my bag and dig out my phone, turning it on for the first time since I met Theo yesterday. I've kept it off for so long, shutting everyone out to protect them, and me... but I don't deserve to be protected. I deserve the pain.

But when I watch the texts roll in, and my eyes land on one from my mom, the heaviness in the pit of my stomach grows and tears sting my eyes.

I stare at her name, leaving the text unopened as I let the hurt settle deep into my soul. She doesn't deserve any of this. She doesn't deserve a selfish son who caused our family so much pain, heartache, and loss.

I turn my phone off and toss it back into my bag. Suddenly, I'm walking towards the door and putting my shoes on. And when I end up on the dock, looking down into the dark water below me, I finally take a breath.

But I can't take my eyes off the water.

I lower myself down to sit on the edge of the dock, remove

my shoes, and slip my feet into the water. It's freezing since it's only April, and pins and needles quickly spread up my legs. But I keep my feet submerged, staring down at them as I welcome the pain from the icy cold water and the cold air on my bare arms. The sensation is biting and sharp on my skin, and I close my eyes as I urge the hurt to grow bigger than the pain inside me.

But it's not enough.

My hands land on the dock on either side of me, and I push myself off, and slide in. The water engulfs me, wrapping me in a heavy blanket of cold and quickly stealing my breath as my head goes under. I'm completely submerged, letting myself fall as deep as I can as my body begins to feel heavy, my chest tightens, and my arms and legs turn numb, making it difficult to move. I squeeze my eyes shut as tight as I can, and focus on this feeling. The pain, the numbness, the need to take a breath... I need to stay right here. I need to finish this, and make everything right.

But as I rise out of the water, gasping for air... all I feel is disappointment.

I grab the edge of the dock and hoist myself up, then lie back and close my eyes as I catch my breath. The sun is creeping higher into the sky, growing brighter with each passing minute and providing just the faintest touch of warmth to my icy skin. Seagulls call out in the distance, and a cold breeze brushes over me, making me shiver.

I'm so fucking weak.

My feet are still in the water, and I can barely feel them as they're completely numb from the cold.

I wish the rest of me could feel that way too.

With a heavy sigh, I push myself up and start walking back up the dock, the numbness fading with each step as feeling returns to my feet. And I hate that.

Once I'm in the house, I get a shower and change into dry clothes. But I feel restless, and I have no idea what to do with myself. Until I'm back in the kitchen, staring at the wall between the kitchen and the living room. Theo has a small section of drywall removed and he's disconnected the electrical to it, but that's all he has done so far. I look around the space for tools, but since he said he hasn't touched this in a while, I'm assuming they're not in here.

My gaze slides to the kitchen window, across the driveway to the barn which houses his workshop. I stare at it, wondering if I should even go in there. It's his space, and I already feel like I'm taking this house from him by simply being here while he's out working. It's obvious he doesn't get to enjoy much of this place, so who the fuck am I to waltz in here and take what he's worked so hard for? But the longer I stand here in front of this wall, the greater the need is to tackle it. Because I need to do *something* to avoid being alone with just my thoughts and urges.

The air is a bit warmer now, and the midmorning sun shines on my face as I walk across the gravel driveway. The crunch beneath my feet, the gentle lapping of waves, and the distant cries of seagulls fill the air... which would all be such soothing sounds if I let them in. But as I push open the door to the old wooden barn, a calm feeling tries to slip past my defences. My eyes adjust to the dimly lit space before me, where sunlight filters through the dusty windows, casting soft beams over Theo's workspace. I can't help but breathe in deeply, taking in the scent of sawdust and fresh lumber, and step closer to the large workbench on the far side of the barn.

The other side of the barn appears to be storage for Theo's fishing gear, with broken lobster traps piled up in a corner, and ropes, buoys, and nets hanging on the wall and from the high ceiling. But my focus is on the workbench before me, with a partially built shelving unit sitting on it. I slowly walk along the bench, taking in the pristine work, and find myself taking in another deep breath. That peaceful feeling I've been trying so desperately to keep out is attempting to take over, and for a brief moment, I consider it.

But I don't. I can't.

I close my eyes and run my hand along the workbench, letting the sharp wood pieces in the sawdust poke at my skin and bring me back to reality. When I open my eyes, I'm facing the wall where Theo's tools are hanging. There are some scattered on the workbench as well, so I scan the space until I find a hammer and a pry bar. I take them, making note of where they were, and head back into the house.

I get to work right away on the wall, not letting myself stop and think as an intense need to destroy something quickly builds inside me. And as I swing the hammer into the drywall, something almost like relief flows through me.

As I continue to tear down the wall, pulling large pieces of drywall off and dropping them to the floor, I finally give in... just a little bit. I don't *want* to feel good, because I know I don't deserve to. But with each swing of the pry bar, I can't help it. I may not have the courage to tear myself apart the way I need to, but I guess this is the next best thing. And even though I try to resist, the more I tear down, the more something inside me begins to crack open. It's wrong, but I can't stop. Each piece of the wall I destroy feels like a release I shouldn't want but can't turn away from.

Eventually, I hear the door open, and I turn around to see Theo enter the kitchen.

His eyes widen as he takes in the wall, the entire left side of it now down to the studs. "Holy shit."

"Yeah." I wipe my forehead with the back of my forearm,

looking down at the mess all over the floor. "Sorry, I'll clean this all up. I just figured I could do something with it today."

Theo shakes his head as he tosses his keys onto the kitchen island and observes the wall. "No need to apologize. You did more with this than I did in three months."

He shrugs out of his jacket, and I take in the dirt on his clothes and the tiredness in his eyes. He turns towards the coffee maker to start making himself one, and I keep my eyes on his back.

"Hope you don't mind I borrowed some tools from your workshop," I say, watching as he reaches into a cupboard and pulls out a mug.

"No problem, help yourself." He then holds up another mug and glances over his shoulder at me with raised eyebrows.

I nod, and he makes me a coffee as well.

As it begins to brew, he walks over to the wall and picks up the pry bar. He looks down at it for a moment, then slams it into the drywall on the side I didn't get started on yet. I watch him as he rips a large piece out and it falls to the floor, and I swear I see the same thing in him that I felt.

Relief.

I step closer and swing the hammer into the drywall as well. We work together, and within minutes, the entire wall is down to the studs.

Theo sets the pry bar on the island and heads over to the coffee machine, handing me a mug.

"Thanks," I say as I take it, and he nods, picking up his own.

"I'm heading out to the barn to finish a set of shelves, then I have to deliver them later on," he says, turning towards the door to head outside.

"Ok." I pick up the pry bar, ready to start taking out the studs, but Theo stops and turns to face me.

He eyes me for a moment, like he isn't quite sure what to do or say. Then he releases a small breath and diverts his gaze from mine. "One of my buddies is playing at the pub tonight. He plays guitar and his girlfriend is a fiddler. I'm heading down to watch them, if you want to come?" He meets my eyes again. "You can get to know the town a bit."

That last sentence makes me pause, as I know I shouldn't get too comfortable here. This isn't my home, and I don't know how long I'll be in this town. But as I look into his warm brown eyes, that same hopeful spark I noticed in the store yesterday morning flickers back to life, and I can't help but nod.

"Yeah. Sounds good."

SIX

THEO

THE SOUND of music and happy chatter washes over me as I step into the pub, and Liam follows close behind me. The familiar warmth of this place immediately puts me at ease, as it always does, and I smile and nod at everyone who greets me as I step further into the pub to an empty table.

"Here ok?" I ask Liam, stopping and pulling out a chair.

He nods, pulling one out as well. "Yeah."

We take our seats and Liam's eyes dart around the room, taking in the bustling space. The table next to us laughs loudly and my friends, Caleb and Emily, get set up to play. Liam shifts in his seat, looking a bit uncomfortable.

Just as I'm about to ask him if he's alright, Allison appears at our table, dropping two coasters down with a bright smile.

"Hey, Theo. What can I get you guys?"

I look up at her, returning her smile. "Hey. I'll take a Storm Surge."

She chuckles with a slight shake of her head at my predictability. But I know what I like, and I'll continue to get my favourite pale ale from the local brewery every time I'm here. "Should have known." She turns to Liam. "And you?"

He glances towards the bar and gives a slight shrug. "Same."

"Coming right up," she says cheerfully, then takes off behind the bar.

I bring my attention back to Liam, but some of his discomfort seems to dissipate as his eyes wander over the old photos, paddles, signs, ropes, and maps covering every inch of the wood walls and ceiling.

"This is a cool place," he says.

I chuckle, leaning back in my chair. "Yeah. The owners of this place are collectors. Most of this stuff they got from local fishermen over the years." I point to a buoy hanging from the ceiling near the bar. "That's my most recent contribution, when they cornered me at the marina because the pub was apparently lacking a 'MacKinnon touch'."

Liam turns to look at the buoy and smiles with a soft laugh. And I try to ignore the flip in my stomach at the sight and sound.

"Hey, bud." A hand lands on my shoulder, and I look up to see one of my crew members, Mitch.

"Hey," I say, nodding a greeting to his wife, as she takes her seat across the pub and waves to me. "Didn't think you'd make it out tonight."

"Dropped the kids off with my mom, so we're getting a couple free hours," he says, then his eyes slide to Liam. He reaches across the table, extending his hand to him. "Hey, I'm Mitch. I work with this asshole."

Liam huffs out a laugh and shakes his hand. "Liam."

I shake my head and roll my eyes at Mitch. "Liam is staying in town for a bit, at my house. He just got in yesterday."

"Oh, nice." Mitch smiles between me and Liam. "How do you guys know each other?"

Liam looks at me, the unease flickering back into his eyes.

I shrug a shoulder. "We just met yesterday."

Mitch's brows lift slightly as he glances between us again. Then he smiles widely, tossing his hands in the air. "Hey, always happy to welcome a new friend! Hope you enjoy your stay here." He quickly glances over his shoulder as Allison starts talking to his wife. "But I gotta go before she orders me a sugar-free vodka soda or some shit. Nice meeting you, Liam."

"See ya," I chuckle as he hurries over to his table and grabs Allison before she can go fill their order.

"He's nice," Liam says, watching him as he mindlessly rolls the coaster on the table.

I nod. "Yeah, he's been on my crew for years now."

Liam's eyes snap to me, and some questions seem to swirl within them. And surprisingly, I want him to ask them.

But if he was going to, he doesn't get the chance.

"Here you go." Allison plops our drinks down in front of us, her usual smile in place.

"Thanks, Allie," I say.

"Of course. Anything else?" she asks, looking between us.

Liam shakes his head, and I do the same, looking up at her. "No, we're all good. Thanks."

"Sounds good. Let me know if you need anything." She squeezes my shoulder as she leaves, greeting some people as they enter the pub.

We each take a drink of our beer in awkward silence, the sounds of everyone laughing and talking around us seeming to get even louder. But even though it's a bit awkward... it's not uncomfortable.

Caleb and Emily settle onto their stools in front of the mics, and the pub fills with excited whoops and cheers from the surrounding tables. I turn to Liam and lean in a bit closer to him, gesturing to them with a tilt of my head.

"Caleb and Emily play here often. They live in Mahone Bay, but Caleb grew up here."

Liam nods, shifting his gaze to them as they laugh and chat with some people at a table close to them. "Seems like a pretty tight crew here."

I huff out a laugh. "Tight is an understatement."

"Hello, hello." Caleb says into the mic. "Happy to be back here in The Thistle, with a view of all your ugly mugs."

A ripple of laughter and taunts flows through the crowd, and Emily chuckles with a shake of her head, leaning in to speak in her mic. "He's just jealous he can't be as beautiful as all of you."

I smile as I watch them introduce themselves and begin their set. If soulmates exist, they're definitely it. The love they have is evident in every glance and note they play together, and I knew from the day they met that they were meant to be. But as happy as I am for them, a quiet sadness settles inside me. Because I know I'll probably never have that.

Caleb and I were best friends growing up, along with a few others who have moved further away. And while we're all still close, I'm the only one still here in Torrin Cove, doing the same thing day in and day out, while they start a whole new life. And whenever I see them, happy and living life just how they want it, I feel like I'm missing out on something... or maybe everything.

My eyes slide to Liam as he watches them play, Emily's fast fiddling getting everyone stomping their feet and yelling out their praise. And I smile as I see Liam softly tapping his fingers on the table to the beat. The tension that's been present in him since we arrived appears to be melting away as he relaxes into his seat and contentedly listens to the music.

And once again, I start to wonder what his story is...

But I'm pulled from my thoughts as the pub door opens and my sister enters with her friend, Marie. They take a seat at the bar and she glances around, her eyes landing on me. She immediately looks at Liam, then back to me and points at him, mouthing, "Who's that?"

And she just continues to expectantly stare at me, like we're going to have this conversation across a noisy, crowded pub.

I roll my eyes and shake my head at her, then lean in to Liam so he can hear me. "I'll be right back."

He just nods, bringing his attention back to Caleb and Emily as they rip into a fast reel.

I grab my beer and head to the bar, where Heather is still watching me.

"Who's that?" she asks, before I even reach her.

"Hi, Heather. Nice to see you out tonight."

She flashes me a forced smile. "Hi, Teddy." Then she gestures to Liam. "Who's that?"

"Liam," I say, leaning against the bar next to her. "He lives with me."

She cocks an eyebrow. "That's it? Just Liam who lives with you?"

I sigh, knowing how weird this all sounds. Because it kind of is. "Yeah. He came into the store yesterday and was looking for a place to live. I offered a room in my house since I have the space, and I'm never there anyway."

Her eyes widen and she smacks my chest with her hand. "Theo! You don't even know him!?"

I rub my chest and shoot her a look. "No."

Heather rubs her forehead, like this is a huge bother to her. "My god. Ok, well..." she glances over at him again. "Bring him to Sunday dinner at Mom's then."

I draw my brows together as I eye her. "Why?"

"Do you have some screws loose or something?" She sighs. "So we can meet him. If someone is going to be living with you, we should know who he is."

I don't know what to say to that, because I don't even know who he is. All I know is that he's from Cape Breton and he's a welder going to work on a rig offshore.

So I change the subject.

"How did you manage to get a night off, anyway?" I ask, knowing this will get her riled up.

"Because I fucking deserve it," she says, not missing a beat. "Chris got home this morning after three days away for work, relaxing in hotels in the evenings, so it's my turn."

Allison appears on the other side of the bar. "Hey, Heather. What can I get you?"

"Shot of tequila and whatever IPA you have on tap," she says, and I give her an assessing look. She rolls her eyes at me. "Stop it. It's been a week."

"And you guys want a couple more?" Allison asks me.

I glance over at Liam to see his beer almost empty, like mine, then nod to her. "Please."

She heads down the bar to grab our drinks, and Heather watches her for a moment before turning back to me. "When are you guys going to give it another go? I liked you two together."

I shake my head, draining the last of my beer. "We're better off as friends. We both agreed."

She shrugs one shoulder. "Alright. But it's been over a year. I think it's time to get back out there."

"With all the free time I have?" I ask.

Heather tilts her head and gives me a knowing look. "You do that to yourself, and you know it."

"Whatever," I mumble, as Allison slides our drinks across

the bar. "Thanks," I say to her as I pick up mine and Liam's beer and turn away from Heather. "Don't get too drunk."

She chuckles. "No promises."

I head back to the table and place a beer in front of Liam. He looks up, surprised, as if he'd been lost in thought. Then he smiles softly. "Thanks."

"Sorry about that," I say as I take my seat. "I was just talking to my sister."

Liam glances at the bar, and Heather waves at him with a smile. He huffs out a light laugh and holds up his hand in a wave back to her.

"Careful," I say, taking a drink of my beer. "Give her an inch, she'll take a mile."

He flashes a genuine smile, and his eyes light up in a way I haven't seen yet. I find myself wishing he would show that smile more often, even though I've only known him for two days. And I also can't help but feel a sense of satisfaction knowing I caused that smile.

What the fuck is wrong with me.

I take a deep breath in and turn back to Caleb and Emily as they finish their set and announce they're taking a break.

And Caleb heads right for our table with a huge smile.

"How's it going?" he asks as he takes a seat with his beer.

"Pretty good," I say. "You guys sound great."

"It's all her," Caleb says, then he smiles at Liam. "Hey, I'm Caleb."

"Liam," he says, shifting in his seat. And I'm starting to see he's not exactly a fan of attention.

"Liam is going to be living here when he's not working away," I say, attempting to make him feel a bit better by explaining this situation for him.

Caleb's expression morphs into one of intrigue, and he turns back to Liam. "Rotation? Offshore?"

Liam perks up a bit. "Yeah."

"Sick," Caleb smiles. "I know a few people who do that. What do you do out there?"

"I'm a welder," Liam says, leaning forward a bit. "Just starting offshore after working in Alberta."

Caleb lets out a low whistle. "Shit. That's fucking intense, man. Underwater welding and hanging from ropes over the raging sea... damn."

Liam smirks, and I swear I see a sparkle in his eye. "Should be an adventure."

"I could never." Caleb leans back in his chair and looks between me and Liam. "You guys got balls. I can just manage to get in a boat to casually fish close to shore, and you two just head out there to battle the sea. You're both insane."

I laugh. "Battle the sea?"

He shrugs. "Basically."

Liam laughs as well, and I can't help but sneak another look at him, my eyes immediately falling to his smile.

"I gotta make my rounds though, before I head back up there," Caleb says as he pushes his chair back and stands up. "I'll catch up with you again soon."

"Talk soon." I bump the fist he holds out for me, and he gives Liam a wave as he heads off.

And as I turn to Liam, a sense of disappointment settles as I see him looking relaxed and comfortable.

"Sorry to be lame," I say with a wince. "But I have to cut this night short. Four AM comes early."

He shakes his head. "No problem. I'm ready to go."

"You can stay," I say. "You know your way back?"

Liam shakes his head again. "It's fine, I'd rather go back now."

"Ok." I nod and finish off the last of my beer, turning around to wave at Allison for the bill.

When she brings it over, I grab it before Liam can and give him a look. "You took out my wall. Don't even try."

He huffs out an amused breath of laughter, but looks uneasy as he watches me pull my wallet out. "I don't mind—"

"It's best not to argue with him," Allison says with a smirk. "He usually gets his way."

I shake my head with a chuckle as I tap my card to the machine. "Not quite how I remember it."

She laughs as she takes the machine back. "See ya later, guys."

We stand to leave, and I wave to Heather as we head towards the door.

"Sunday dinner!" she yells, and points between me and Liam.

I roll my eyes and push the door open, heading outside into the cool darkness.

Liam doesn't say anything about Heather's comment as he falls into step beside me, and we walk in silence along the road towards my house. It's not too long of a walk, and the sound of the ocean gently lapping against the shore creates a peaceful backdrop. The muffled sounds of music from the pub fades away behind us as we continue down the dark road, and I release a breath. I know I should just get this over with, since there's no getting out of it.

"So..." I say slowly. "We do Sunday dinner at my mom's every week."

Liam nods. "Nice."

"Yeah." I hesitate. "And... you're invited this weekend."

He turns his head to look at me, and even in the dark I can see the question in his eyes.

"And it's actually not even an invitation, it's more of a... demand." I wince as I look away from him. "Because I'm willing to bet my sister has already told my mom you're living with me. So, there will be a phone call in the morning asking if you have allergies and preferences." I run a hand through my hair. "But I get it if you don't want to, and I can get them to back off."

Liam is silent for a moment as we continue walking, and worry burrows in the pit of my stomach. I just *know* he is wondering what the fuck he got himself into by coming here. So far he's been set up to live in a construction zone, set to work on said construction zone, just met people who asked him more about himself than I have in the two days I've known him, and now he's being forced into a family dinner with people he's never met. And I know I'm not the most welcoming person. This definitely isn't what he signed up for, and I wouldn't be surprised if he just up and leaves in the morning.

But he lets out a light chuckle. "Ok," he says softly. "I get it. They want to know who this random person is living with you. Works for me."

I turn to look at him, taking in his dark hair blowing in the breeze, and the moonlight highlighting his gentle smile.

And the worry is replaced with something I haven't felt in a long time.

Excitement.

Because I haven't scared him off just yet.

SEVEN

LIAM

I SIT at the kitchen island, restlessly sipping a third cup of coffee as I look around the space. It's somewhat early in the afternoon, and I already have most of the studs out of the wall. There's a few more to take out before I can patch up the holes on the external wall. Then... I'll need to find something else to do.

With a sigh, I rub a hand over my face. Theo mentioned he's doing another job somewhere after fishing today, so I'm not sure when I'll see him back here. Which means I'm not sure what else I could work on without stepping on his toes. But I need to do something. I can't just sit here.

And I can't deny that going out last night to the pub piqued my curiosity about this town. I'm not sure what I expected when I decided to stay here, since my plan was to hide myself away. But something about the strong sense of community, and the welcoming vibe I got from everyone, surprisingly has me wanting to see more of this place.

So I stand, refusing to let myself overthink this as I shove my shoes on, pull on a jacket, and head out of the house.

I walk down the long driveway lined with tall, mature trees, and turn left when I get to the road. Eventually, I see the pub in the distance where we walked to just last night. As I pass by it, I see people in the windows as they eat and laugh, enjoying each other's company and the slow way this town seems to work.

As I continue down the road, I pass a couple little shops and some people out walking. They all smile and say hello as if they know me, extending the same warm welcome I received in the pub last night.

Eventually I find myself walking by MacKinnon's General Store, and I can't help but pause outside of it for a moment, taking in the old log building that Theo's family owns. And once again I think of just how important he seems to be to this town.

"How's it going today?"

My eyes flick to the front porch of the store, where two older men are sitting.

I give a small wave and back up a step. "Hey, how are ya?"

"Oh, just dandy," one of them replies with a nod.

I nod back, then quickly turn around to continue my walk.

The road curves gently along the shoreline, and I pass several homes with coastal cottage vibes that look out over the ocean. A few side streets travel up a hill off the main road, leading to what looks like the main residential area of the town. Theo wasn't lying when he said his house was separated from the rest of the town.

At the end of this residential area, I find a small gravel parking lot with a few cars in it. And as I look up, I see the marina.

It looks like all of the boats are in, which makes sense since it's later in the afternoon. I scan the row of cars and don't see

Theo's truck, so I guess it's safe to assume fishing is done for the day.

I watch the marina for a bit as I stand here in the parking lot and observe the quiet area, imagining what it looks like in the early hours of the morning, when all the crews are getting ready to head out. I tentatively step onto the wharf, feeling like I'm maybe crossing some kind of boundary, and let my eyes roam over the boats lined up in the water.

The sounds of seagulls and the smell of salt water take over my senses as I walk along the wharf, and I look over the boats, reading the names of them. Some are what I would expect, like *Celtic Rose, Lady Lilly* and *Siren's Sorrow*. And others make me chuckle, like *Blazing Buoy* and *Plunder and Lightning*.

My gaze roams over the piles of lobster traps on the wharf and gear in the boats, unable to even imagine how much work this all must be.

"Liam?"

I turn my head to see Mitch standing on the wharf by a boat on the opposite side of the dock.

"Oh, hey," I say cautiously, glancing around. There's no one else here, except another man and a woman in the boat, and I'm not sure if I'm allowed to even be here.

Mitch smiles as he coils up a rope. "How are ya?"

"Uh, pretty good," I say, shoving my hands in my pockets and stepping closer. "Just out for a walk." I let my eyes roam over the boat, assuming this must be Theo's. And I can't help but chuckle when I see the name. *Can't Sea Me*.

Mitch points to the woman as she hoses down the boat deck. "This is Sarah." Then he points to another man stacking large buckets. "That's Glen. Guys, this is Liam. He's new in town and staying with Theo."

"Hey! Welcome." Sarah smiles warmly at me and Glen gives me a salute.

"Thanks," I say with a smile and then quickly glance out at the water. "How was it today?"

Glen lets out a small groan. "Not the best. It may look calm in here, but the water out there was not cooperating today."

Mitch tosses the rope onto a pile of other ones and shakes his head. "Yeah, it sucked. I'm fucking beat. I'm looking forward to getting the boat to sleep so I can do the same." He then looks at me with a sly smile. "Don't be surprised if you encounter a bit of a cranky captain this evening."

Sarah smacks him and rolls her eyes. "Stop it."

Mitch shrugs. "Just speaking the truth."

An uneasy feeling settles inside me, and I take a step backwards with a nod. "I'll let you finish up then. Good seeing you again," I say to Mitch and then nod to Sarah and Glen, "and nice meeting you."

"You too!" Sarah smiles, and Glen gives me a wave. "Have a good one!"

I turn around, put my head down, and walk straight home. I don't look up at anything, or anyone, and just focus on the road under my feet.

This wasn't supposed to happen.

I already feel enough uncertainty and fear on my own. And now the thought of things not going well out on the boat for Theo and his crew, seeing Mitch feeling frustrated and tired and knowing Theo is too...

I can't get close to anyone, and I can't get comfortable. I can't lose it all again.

Yet here I am, going to a family dinner tomorrow...

Once I'm back at the house, I head straight for my room and grab my phone out of my zipped bag.

My heart pounds against my chest as I turn it on and wait as the screen lights up.

I look at the notification for the unread text from my mom,

and try my best to ignore the voice in my head screaming at me not to do it.

But with a shaking hand, I tap it, and her words appear on my screen.

MOM

Checking in again and hoping to hear from you soon. I know you need some time, but I just want to let you know that Dad and I are thinking of you, like always. I love you, mo mhac.

My vision blurs as tears form in my eyes.

Mo mhac.

Gaelic for *my son*.

My mom has called me that for as long as I can remember. But I'm not sure she would want to call me that anymore if she knew the truth about what I've done, and that I'm the reason why we're all hurting.

But this is the reminder I need. *This* is why I can't get close to anyone.

With a sniff, I blink back the tears and turn my phone off again. I slide it back into my bag and zip it shut, then I take a breath and shove it all back down where it belongs. Because I can't deal with it yet, as I continue to just hide away like a fucking coward.

Heading into the kitchen, I immediately pick up the tools I was using earlier and set to work removing the last of the studs from the wall. I keep my mind empty, and my focus on the task before me, not stopping until the wall between the kitchen and the living room is completely removed. And as I set the hammer down and look outside, I'm surprised to see the sun setting.

My eyes scan the sky as I step out onto the front patio, then drop to the yard before me. Two Adirondack chairs sit on the lawn facing the water, with a firepit before them. As I head down the stairs and get closer, I see ashes in the firepit, and wood piled up next to it.

I lower myself onto a chair and sit back as I gaze up at the sky, watching it slowly change colour with the setting sun. And when the sky is ablaze with red and orange hues that resemble flames, I lean forward and arrange some wood in the firepit. There's a bucket with some kindling and matches, so I start a fire and sit back, watching as the flames grow and mirror the sky before me. And I can't shake the thought that Theo may appreciate a quiet fire to relax, now that I know about the day he had.

As I watch the flames envelop the logs, heating them until they crumble, I lean forward and feel the heat against my face. The wood slowly turns to ash, disappearing before my eyes as the flames grow bigger, destroying everything in its path. And an urge rises as I wish these flames would destroy more than just the logs before me. I wish they would rip through me as well, and destroy everything broken inside me. I don't even realize what I'm doing, before I pull my hand back with a hiss.

"Fuck," I mutter, shaking my hand out with a wince. I look down, the light from the fire illuminating my red fingertips from where I touched a burning log.

But I can't ignore how good the pain feels.

"Hey."

My head snaps up as Theo approaches the firepit and stands next to the empty chair beside me.

"Hey," I say, resting my hand on my thigh and hoping he didn't see whatever that was.

But he clearly did, as he gestures with his chin to my hand. "You alright?"

"Yeah." I wave that hand in dismissal. "Just... log slipped."

He nods, shifting his gaze out over the water, which is now almost completely dark. "Mind if I sit?"

I shake my head, and he grabs another log to toss onto the fire before he takes a seat. I glance at him, taking in the now familiar tired expression on his face as he gazes into the flame.

"You make these?" I ask, gesturing to the chairs we're sitting on.

He looks between them and nods. "Yeah."

"They're nice," I say, appreciating the immaculate work.

And then we fall into silence as we sit and just watch the fire, and listen to the sounds of the water. The fire in the sky has now completely faded away as the one before us shines bright in the quiet darkness. And that feeling from earlier that I pushed away, forces its way back in... and this time, I'm able to name it.

Comfort.

And I don't know why I'm not wanting to push it away this time...

"How long have you been captain?" I ask Theo, surprising myself as I break the silence with this question. It's been on my mind since Mitch said he has worked under Theo for years. I thought he was young at his age to be a captain of a crew, and I've been curious to know when he started.

Theo turns to look at me, his expression also one of surprise. But also intrigue, as a small smile tugs at his lips.

"Five years," he says.

My brows lift in shock, as I wasn't expecting it to be that long. But I just nod.

And Theo smiles in return. "I didn't expect to be captain of a crew at thirty, let alone twenty-five. But when my dad passed, it all came to me." He pauses for a moment. "I'd been on the boat for as long as I can remember though, so... I guess I was as ready as I was going to be."

I observe him for a moment as he absent-mindedly picks at his thumb with his finger and gazes into the fire, a heaviness settling over him. Much like the one I've become so familiar with over the past couple months.

Maybe everything isn't so certain and safe for him after all.

"That's a lot," I say.

Theo just nods. "Yeah," he says, so softly I almost don't hear him.

We're quiet for a bit longer as we watch the roaring fire, the crackling of the logs the only sound filling this space between us. But a feeling quickly bubbles up inside me and takes over. Something almost like an urge to give him what he just gave me.

"You can ask me something," I say, keeping my attention on the fire.

I feel Theo's eyes on me, so I slowly lift mine to meet his gaze as my heart picks up its pace, and I prepare to open myself up to whatever he's going to ask. I don't feel ready for this... but something inside me wants to let him in, just a little bit. And I don't understand that at all.

But Theo's face softens as his lips tilt up in a soft lopsided smile. "Want a beer?"

And I can't help but laugh. As the smile spreads across my face, the tension inside me fades. Theo keeps his eyes on me as his smile grows as well, and the sense of comfort settles inside me once more.

I shouldn't get close to anyone. But, in a way, it feels like he knows me already.

EIGHT

THEO

THE TABLE LEG I'm working on spins in the wood lathe, and I just stare down at it. I've finished shaping it, and the next piece of wood is ready to go, but I just keep watching this one as the whirring sound fills the quiet morning air in the workshop. Eventually, I flip the switch to turn it off and sit on the stool with a sigh. And as I check the time on my phone, another frustrated sigh escapes me.

It's only six thirty in the morning. I've been out here for an hour, and already I wish this day was over. I can usually fill my Sundays with enough work out here to make the time go by, since it's a day off from fishing and I need to stay busy. But today, something about this just isn't doing it for me.

My eyes travel to the dusty window facing the house, and I find myself wondering if Liam is still asleep. Guilt rises at the thought of him, and how much time he's spent alone since he got here a few days ago. I get the sense he isn't exactly looking for a buddy, but he just seems so... lonely. We've barely spoken and I know nothing about him, but I also can't deny that I've felt an increased pull to get to know him, and to just be around him. There's something comforting about him, and I don't know what it is. After a shitty day yesterday on the water, and then a construction job not going so well, I actually enjoyed sitting quietly by the fire with him last night.

And at that thought, yet another rush of guilt flows through me, and I drop my head to rub a hand over my forehead with a groan. *Fuck.*

Maybe I do know what that comforting feeling is. And if it *is* what I think it is, I can't fall too deep into it. I've been successful so far in keeping that part of me quiet, so I'm not going to let it all out now. He needed somewhere to stay, and I had the room... that's all this is. I'm not going to ruin this for him.

I shift my gaze around the workshop, to the other side of the barn at my fishing gear, and do what I always do when these feelings try to push their way to the surface. Throw myself into my work.

I take in the broken lobster traps and make a mental note to fix those this week before I end up with an even bigger pile. My eyes then lift to the nets and longlines hanging from the ceiling, and I know I should get started on repairing those before tuna fishing season starts in August. I also need to check on the longliner boat in storage down at the marina and make sure it's ready to go when the season opens, and schedule any repairs for before then. This week I have a few jobs lined up at—

Movement out the window catches my eye, and my gaze darts towards the house as Liam steps onto the front deck. He leans against the railing as he looks over the water and takes a drink of his coffee.

And as my eyes rest on him, my mind quiets.

His tattooed hand holds his coffee mug, and his dark, almost black hair blows in the light breeze. But as the early morning sun shines down on him, it only seems to highlight the darkness and sadness inside him.

The feelings I've pushed away and tried to ignore for so long grow louder the longer I watch him. Eventually, it becomes unbearable, and I cautiously let them in. As I grant myself a brief reprieve from the oppression I've imposed on myself, I open myself up to a moment of... what if. As unrealistic as it is, and as much as I know I shouldn't, I can't help it.

I stand from my stool and head out of the barn, crossing the lawn to the front deck.

"Morning," I say as I climb the stairs.

Liam turns his head to look at me and smiles softly. But it doesn't quite meet his eyes. "Morning."

I stand beside him and look over the water as well. But my gaze drops to Liam's hand as he holds his mug, and I see his red, sore looking fingertips. I want to ask him again if he's ok, because I don't believe his answer from last night. Even though it was dark... I'm pretty sure I know what I saw.

But Liam must realize I'm looking at his hand, as he shoves it in the pocket of his sweatpants. "What are you working on?" he asks, keeping his gaze out on the water.

"A table for a family a couple towns over," I say, looking out at the water sparkling under the sun.

He nods, and we stand quietly for a moment as we watch the gentle waves roll over the rocks on the shore.

But those confusing and unbearable feelings are now nagging at me, pushing me further into the *what if.* Because as confusing as they are... it also feels good to give in a little bit. So I turn to face him. "There's no rush on it though."

Liam turns his head to meet my eyes, and his brighten.

I smile, tilting my head towards my boat in the water. "Should we catch some mackerel to take to dinner tonight?"

He smiles, and I try to ignore the flip in my stomach. He

stands up straighter, and I think this might be the most alive I've seen him since he came here.

"Sounds good," he says with a nod.

As he heads inside to change, I make my way back to the barn and grab my tackle box and bait. And with every step I take towards the dock, anticipation inside me grows.

I've never taken anyone out on my boat. While I bought this house to hide away and be alone, it's out on the water where I truly find peace. And I've always kept it to myself. Because out there, I don't have to play a part, meet expectations, and be the Theo MacKinnon everyone knows. Out there, it's just me, the boat, and the open water, where I can let everything go as I release my thoughts, worries, and burdens with each cast of my line. And when I come back in, I leave it all out there, ready to be who I need to be.

But clearly I'm fighting against that need, because I'm bringing Liam into all of my private places.

As he joins me on the dock, and his blue eyes sparkle with excitement, I just smile. Because I have no doubts about sharing this with him. He needs this, and I think I do too.

We get into the boat, and I start up the motor as Liam unties the rope from the dock. He takes his seat next to me as I steer the boat into the open water. There's a spot I like to go to this time of year that's a bit sheltered from the wind by a large island, so I head that way and pick up speed. And I swear I see him take a deep breath in, and release it with a smile.

When we reach the spot, I slow down and steer us into the channel between the mainland and the island, then switch on the trolling motor. The trees are still bare since it's early spring, but it's private and sheltered, and the water is calm.

"Nice," he says with a nod as he looks around.

I chuckle. "Yeah, it's my favourite spot to fish."

His gaze lingers on me for a moment, before he looks down

at the rack holding the fishing rods. "Do you have a preference?"

"No," I say with a shake of my head. "They're pretty much the same."

He pulls two rods out and hands me one, and I subtly watch him as I get mine ready. He clearly knows what he's doing as he selects a minnow lure and cuts the line to tie it on. But he fumbles a bit as he attempts to tie the knot, and he bites back a grimace as the line seems to press into his sore fingers.

I set my rod down and lean forward, gently taking his from his hands. He lets me, and neither of us say a word as I tie off the knot, slide the bait onto the hook, and hand it back to him.

"Thanks," he says softly, and I just nod back, dropping my lure into the water and letting my line out as I sit back in my seat.

Liam does the same, and we sit in silence as we each look out at the water. The only sounds surrounding us are the gentle lapping of water against the side of the boat, and the soft hum of the reels letting out line.

Once we each let out enough line and have closed the bail arms, I glance at him.

"So, you fished a lot back home?" I ask, even though I know the answer already, since he told me. But I wonder if I might be able to get a bit more out of him.

He nods. "Yeah. Not a whole lot on the boat though," he says, gently pulling his rod back to spin the lure under the water. "I'm from Inverness, so we're close to the Margaree River. We fished off the bridges, and it has the best fly fishing."

I smile as I take in how relaxed he looks right now. "I actually haven't done much fly fishing, believe it or not. But I've heard great things about fishing on Margaree River."

He turns his head to look at me. "Never been?"

I shake my head. "I've been around Cape Breton lobster

fishing with some crews growing up. Other than that, life keeps me anchored here."

Liam is quiet for a moment as he slides his gaze out over the water again. "Hopefully you get a chance to soon."

I don't say anything as I try to suppress my sigh, thinking how I could actually do that. We fish six days a week during lobster season from November to June, and we're just as busy during tuna season from August to November. But during the offseason... I just can't make myself do anything I want to. Like I'm afraid to enjoy myself. So instead, I fill my time with carpentry work to stay busy.

We're both quiet as the boat slowly moves along the channel, and the cool breeze nips at my skin. The sun provides a slight warmth in the cool April air, and I release a breath into it, letting go of all my thoughts and allowing this place to bring me the peace it always does.

"I can see why you like it out here so much," Liam says, eventually breaking the silence.

I chuckle lightly. "Yeah, it's pretty damn nice."

"You should do it more."

I look at him, letting my eyes roam over his soft features and relaxed posture as he continues to gently move his fishing rod back and forth.

"Maybe I will," I say softly.

He turns his head, giving me a smirk. "And if you know of any good fly fishing spots around here, maybe I can show you how it's done."

A laugh bubbles out of me, and Liam's face breaks out in a grin. And when he also laughs, I think that might be the best sound of all.

Suddenly, the end of Liam's rod bends and he sits up straight, his hand quickly moving to the reel. As he pulls his line in, I secure my rod and lean forward to open the livewell in the floor of the boat. He effortlessly pulls the mackerel out of the water and stands up to grab the line, pulling it into the boat. As he grasps the fish, I lean forward and undo the hook from its mouth to save his fingers.

Liam tosses it into the livewell with a smile, and when his eyes meet mine, they are alive with pure joy.

And all I can do is stare back at him with a smile of my own.

He sits down again with a chuckle and casts a playful glance at me. "Maybe I'll have to show you how this is done too."

I laugh, opening the bait bucket and grabbing a worm from it for his hook. "Lucky catch. Just wait, I'll be reeling them in soon."

He laughs as well, and once the bait is on his hook and his attention is back on the water... my smile falls.

Because I can't deny this anymore. This thing about myself that I think I've known for a while now, but kept buried deep, never allowing myself to even try to understand. But out here, with him... it's so obvious.

I've been afraid to admit, even to myself, that I think I might be gay. But the more time I spend with Liam, the feelings I've pushed away for years are surfacing and overwhelming me. And I'm finally starting to listen.

He's here, in my boat, in a space I've always kept for just myself. And I can't continue to ignore the feelings I get when I'm around him.

I'm attracted to him. And I want him.

Fuck.

NINE

LIAM

I WATCH the tiny town pass by through the passenger window of Theo's truck as he drives us to his mom's for dinner. My sore fingertips press into my thigh, the rough fabric of my jeans sending a jolt of pain through them. I welcome the sensation, taking in a sharp breath as the pain courses through me, letting it serve as a reminder not to get too comfortable.

Even though I did let myself get comfortable today.

I glance over at Theo in the driver's seat as he turns off the main street, and confusion replaces the pain. I know I shouldn't be doing any of this. I shouldn't be enjoying myself, going to family dinners, and laughing with him about who can catch the most fish. But today, out on the water with him... I effortlessly let it all go. I actually felt like the old me, and it felt good.

But I don't think that's a good thing. The old me fucked everything up.

Theo pulls into the driveway of a charming coastal home with weathered wood siding and a seafoam green front door. As I step out of the truck, I take a moment to appreciate the view of the water from up here on the hill, overlooking the marina below.

"Uncle Theo!"

A little boy runs towards Theo as he pulls a cooler out of the truck bed.

"Hey, little man," Theo says with a smile, as the boy stops before him.

He's a mini version of Theo, probably about four or five, with a soft sprinkling of freckles over his nose and cheeks, messy brown hair, soft brown eyes, and dirt smeared all over his shirt. He immediately pushes up on his tiptoes, peering at the cooler in Theo's hands and tries to open the lid. "What did you bring?"

Theo chuckles, opening the cooler for him. "Mackerel."

I can't help but smirk as mini Theo peers into the cooler, his forehead scrunched in concentration. After a moment, he solemnly nods and looks up at his uncle. "Six."

Theo smiles. "That's right." Then he glances at me and narrows his eyes slightly, the competitive spark between us still present. Because four of those are mine, and only two are his.

And of course, I gave him some shit about it. Because I outfished the fisherman.

The boy suddenly turns to look up at me. "Who are you?"

My eyes flick to Theo, then back to the curious boy before me. "I'm Liam."

"Liam lives at my house," Theo says, closing the cooler lid. Then he ruffles the boy's hair. "This is my nephew, Mason."

Mason observes me carefully with a furrowed brow. "You live with my uncle?"

I nod slowly as I get a small taste of the potential scrutiny I'm about to face inside the house with the rest of Theo's family. "Yeah... I just moved in a few days ago."

He continues to stare up at me as a moment of silence

passes between us, and my nerves start to grow. If I can't make it past this kid, how the fuck am I going to manage in there?

But Mason just nods. "Ok." Then he turns to Theo. "Me and Isla are playing in the backyard. Will you come play with us?"

Theo chuckles. "In a bit. We're going to go say hi to everyone first."

"Ok, but don't take too long. Isla won't dig for worms with me," Mason says, then turns to run around the house to the backyard, yelling, "Isla, diggers are for worms, not dolls!"

I release a breath of laughter as Theo shakes his head.

"He takes bait catching very seriously," he says, walking towards the front door.

As I follow him, I take a deep breath, trying to prepare myself for whatever this is going to bring.

He pushes the door open, and immediately we're met with warmth, the smell of baked bread, and laughter from within the house. As Theo leads me around a corner towards the voices, my heart beats faster, and I rub my thumb over my blistered fingertips, urging the pain to override the nerves.

The room that opens up before us is cozy and inviting. An older man and a guy about mine and Theo's age are sitting on the couch, chatting in front of a crackling fire in the wood stove. The room opens into the kitchen, where I recognize Theo's sister sitting at the island with a glass of wine, talking to a woman who I assume is their mother as she mixes something in a bowl.

"Hey," Theo says as he steps further into the living room, and I cautiously trail behind him.

All eyes turn to us, and as they land on me, the nerves take over. I'm on full display, and those feelings quickly rush in again, telling me I shouldn't be here. Every muscle in my body tenses, as I get ready to turn around and run.

But as Theo turns to give me a soft smile and I look into his eyes, I stay right where I am. The safe and content feeling I had today rustles beneath the apprehension and fear, and the tension inside me slowly fades away. I'm not sure why I feel this sense of ease around him, and I'm confused about why I'm not fighting it. But it doesn't seem to matter as I let his smile pull one from me as well.

"This is Liam." Theo gestures to me, and I give everyone an awkward wave.

The older man smiles, pushing to his feet and holding out a hand. "Welcome, Liam. I'm Jimmy, Theo's grandfather."

I shake his hand. "Nice to meet you."

Theo's sister steps forward with a big smile. "Hi! I'm Heather, the sister. Nice to *finally* meet you."

Theo rolls his eyes and heads into the kitchen, but she ignores him and continues, gesturing to the other guy on the couch. "This is my husband, Chris. And my kids are around here somewhere..." she trails off, glancing out the window.

"Mason already introduced himself outside," Theo says as he sets the cooler on the counter. "They're in the backyard. He's digging for worms."

Heather lets out an exasperated sigh. "I knew it." She rushes for the back door and whips it open. "Mason Cameron, I asked for *one* day without any mud!"

She disappears into the backyard, and I cautiously step further into the room as Jimmy and Chris take their seats again with a laugh, and Theo snorts, opening the cooler.

Theo's mother smiles warmly, wiping her hands on a towel as she steps closer to me. "Hi Liam, I'm Cynthia. Come in and make yourself at home."

I smile at her, but it feels forced. The internal war inside me starts up again, as I take in how lovely and welcoming these people are. Since arriving in Torrin Cove, I've felt like I'm on a roller coaster. The highs, allowing me to feel the peace this welcoming town and Theo's home brings me, then the lows, when I remember why I can't have that. Because this isn't my home.

My fingers twitch at my side as I continue to stand near the doorway, not sure what to do. But Cynthia notices my discomfort, and gently places a hand on my elbow, guiding me into the kitchen.

"So, what did you bring us?" She peers over the kitchen counter, where Theo is preparing the mackerel to cook. "Oh, lovely!" She then smiles at me. "We're having lobster as well, so looks like Theo caught our whole meal tonight."

Theo lifts his eyes and smirks at me. "Yup. The *whole* thing."

I huff out a laugh, shaking my head at him. "You wish."

Suddenly the back door crashes open, and Heather comes in, dragging a mud-covered Mason with her.

"Don't touch anything," she says with a sigh as Mason smiles widely while he wiggles his fingers. "Chris, please tell me we brought more clothes."

"On it," Chris says as he stands, grabbing a bag from the corner of the room. Then he follows them down the hall as Mason shrieks with delight and Heather lets out a groan of disapproval.

"Unbelievable."

I look down at a little girl standing beside me, with her hands on her hips as she shakes her head. And I can't help but let out a laugh at the drastic difference between this girl and her wild little brother, with her hair in perfect braids, clothes clean and pristine, and not one bow out of place.

"Isla," Theo says, picking up the plate of fish, "this is Liam."

Isla holds her hand out to me, and my brows lift in surprise as I reach out to take it.

"Nice to meet you," she says with a polite nod. "Now excuse me, I have to help Nanny make dessert."

I look at Theo, not quite sure how to respond to this well-mannered and intelligent little girl. Theo just laughs as Isla joins her grandmother in the kitchen and he gestures for me to follow him to the back patio. I close the door behind us as I step outside, taking in the big backyard with huge trees. There's a peaceful, babbling brook running through it, and Mason's toy trucks are strewn about in the mud where he was digging for worms.

Theo fires up the barbeque and I take a deep breath of the crisp air. So far... this isn't so bad.

I turn around as the door opens again, and Jimmy steps out. He smiles and hands Theo and I each a beer, holding up his drink in a cheers. "Didn't think you'd barbeque without me, did ya?"

"Never," Theo mutters with a sly smile. "How would I ever get it right if you weren't here to tell me what to do?"

"Atta boy." Jimmy laughs and takes a seat on one of the chairs on the patio. "So, Liam. How are you liking Torrin Cove so far?"

I lean against the patio railing and give him a soft smile. "It's nice. Kinda feels like home." And suddenly my smile falters and panic rolls through me. I didn't mean to say that, and I don't even know where it came from.

But Jimmy just smiles back at me. "And where's that?"

"Inverness," I say with an uncertain edge to my voice, as I try to just keep my shit together and get through this.

"Ah," he says happily. "I know some folks up that way. Or knew, anyway. It was many years ago. What's your last name?"

My heart pounds as I stare back at Jimmy, frozen as I face a possible connection to back home I'm not ready for. What if he knows my family, and knows what happened... and I have to explain why I'm here, and not with them.

I consider giving him a fake last name so I can continue to hide away, but as Theo glances at me over his shoulder, I realize he doesn't know it either.

"Fraser," I say, telling the truth and keeping my eyes on Theo for a moment longer, letting my heart slow down a bit.

Jimmy smiles as I shift my gaze back to him. "I can't say I knew any Frasers up there," he says, and relief immediately rushes through me. "I fished with a few men out of that area though, way back in the day. I actually purchased my first ever lobster boat from Inverness."

Theo looks over at him as he flips one of the fish on the barbeque. "Yeah?"

Jimmy nods. "Indeed. It wasn't much, but it got me started. And your father was quick to learn to drive it." He chuckles. "Wasn't an easy drive either."

A smile spreads across Theo's face as he quietly listens to his grandfather reminisce about teaching his son, Theo's father, how to drive the first lobster boat he ever owned. And I take this moment to watch Theo. Because even though his smile remains, there's a sadness in his eyes as the light in him slowly fades away.

"And now, with the technology you guys have on those boats, and the size of them," Jimmy waves a hand in the air with a shake of his head, "they're basically doing the work for you."

Theo scoffs and cocks an eyebrow at him. "Offer still stands, old man. Come on out tomorrow morning and show me how it's done. I'll gladly step back for a day."

Jimmy laughs and looks at me, tilting his head towards Theo. "Smartass, isn't he?"

I chuckle as the door opens and Cynthia pops her head out.

"How's the fish coming?" she asks. "Everything else is ready."

"All done," Theo says, turning the barbeque off and loading the now cooked fish onto the plate.

We head inside to find the table set with various salads, rolls, and a centrepiece of lobster. Mason runs around the table as he tries to grab a lobster, while Chris chases after him, his hands snapping like claws as he playfully pretends to be a lobster trying to catch him.

I stand back and watch the chaos with a smile as Chris finally wrangles Mason into a seat, and everyone else follows suit. As I take my place next to Theo, my eyes roam over the gallery wall behind the table, filled with family photos. But one picture in particular catches my attention. Theo, as a young boy, with a man who I can only assume is his father. Theo is holding up a lobster with a huge smile, and his dad is crouched beside him, smiling proudly.

"Here."

My attention is brought back to the table as Theo places a lobster on my plate.

"Hope you like lobster... you kind of have to in this house," he says with a smirk.

I chuckle. "I do."

I quietly sit and listen to everyone talk as they fill their plates and pass bowls around the table, and before I know it my plate is overflowing. And everything looks delicious.

"So, Theo," Heather says, setting her wine glass down and smiling at him. "I was thinking about it a bit more."

"Uh oh," Chris says from the other side of Theo, and Theo huffs out a laugh as he takes a bite of his salad.

"I just don't get why you and Allison aren't together," she says, and I look up at her. Allison... from the pub?

"I told you," Theo says, keeping his eyes down on his plate, tension seeming to enter his body as he pulls the claw off his lobster. "We're better off as friends."

Cynthia hums thoughtfully, observing her son. "I still don't know why you two even broke up. You were so cute together. And she is so sweet."

Theo shakes his head, shifting in his seat. "It just wasn't working. Like I said, we're friends. That's it."

I observe him for a moment, wondering why he seems so bothered by them asking this. And as Heather shrugs and turns her attention to helping Mason and Isla with their lobster, I can't help but notice I'm also feeling uncomfortable at the thought of them together. I don't know why though. She seems nice, she's pretty, and they appear to get along well. And actually, she's the type of girl I typically go for. But I'm definitely not looking to pick up girls while I'm here, so this uncomfortable feeling isn't jealousy that he's been with her, and I haven't... Is it?

But I shake it off, pushing those feelings away as the conversation at the table shifts and Theo visibly relaxes next to me. I listen quietly while I eat, as they talk about Isla's dance recital, the store, and Chris' recent work trip. I find myself laughing along to Jimmy's stories and Mason's antics, and Cynthia hushing my protests as she scoops seconds onto my plate. I join in conversation with ease as they effortlessly include me, even when they ask me questions about my job. They don't dwell or put any pressure on me when my answers are short and I try to deflect. And whenever I do feel the tension creeping back in, one look into Theo's soft brown eyes pulls me right back out of it.

On the drive home, I lay my head back against the seat, looking out at the water in the darkness, feeling content, relaxed, and the complete opposite as I did on the drive there.

"So how many worms do you think Mason has in his pocket?" I ask with a smile.

Theo laughs at the memory of him subtly showing us his dirt and worm filled jacket pocket before they left. "Enough to give Heather a stroke, I'm sure."

I chuckle as Theo pulls into the driveway, and I let the peaceful view of his house pull me deeper into this relaxed state. And as we head inside, each carrying containers of food that Cynthia sent home with us, I'm surprised that the feeling continues to linger.

Theo takes the containers from me when we reach the kitchen, and places them in the fridge. When he closes the door, he turns to me and a beat of awkward silence passes between us.

"Uh," he runs his fingers through his hair as he drops his gaze from mine, "I gotta get to bed."

I nod. "Ok."

He gives me a lopsided smile, but as soon as he starts to turn away from me, my hand snaps out to grab his arm and stop him.

Theo's eyes widen slightly as they meet mine, and we stand in silence with my hand grasping his arm.

I don't even know what to say, or why I did that. I just... need him to be here, with me, for a moment longer.

I just feel safe with him.

"Thank you," I say quietly. "For today."

Theo nods softly, and his eyes briefly drop to my lips, before they flick back up to look into my eyes again. "Anytime."

And I don't know what to make of the sudden lurch in my heart at that small movement.

I reluctantly drop my hand from his arm and step backwards, keeping my gaze locked on his as his eyes flick between mine, and his chest rises and falls with a breath.

"Night," he says in a soft voice.

"Night," I say, and it comes out almost in a whisper.

As he disappears into the dark hallway, I stay where I am, listening to the creaking of the steps as he heads upstairs.

Eventually, I release a sigh, and head into my room to lie on the bed and stare up at the ceiling, like I do every sleepless night.

I have no idea what that was. And I have no idea why it felt so good.

But I don't get to explore that thought any more, because the next thing I know... I'm asleep.

And it's the best sleep I've had in months.

TEN

LIAM

THE RAIN BATTERS the large bay window of the sunroom as I linger in the doorway, watching the outside world through a watery haze. The fog is thick over the water's edge, obscuring the view just beyond the shoreline. But I continue to stare at it anyway, urging the rhythmic drumming of the rain against the glass to drown out the noise in my mind, and the questions swirling around inside it.

But as a chill ripples through me, I turn away from the window and retreat into the living room. I open the wood stove and light a fire, letting the flames gradually warm me up. But as the fire flickers and grows, the thoughts and questions grow a little louder in this quiet room.

I slept last night. For the first time in months, I fell asleep with ease, and didn't wake all night. Not until I heard the soft creaks from Theo coming down the stairs and leaving for work. I'm still surprised by how relaxed I felt yesterday, going out fishing with him and spending time with his family. But I think it's because of *him*. There's something about him that seems to be drawing me in, and I don't know what it is, or why. Even now, sitting here alone and staring out the window, I almost feel like I miss him. And I think that's because the only times my mind has been quiet, has been with him.

But he's not here now. And the noise is getting louder, and louder.

I shouldn't be feeling good. I shouldn't be spending time with a family that isn't mine, enjoying myself and pretending like nothing happened. Because something awful did happen, and it was my fault. And nothing will ever fix it. For me, or my family.

As I sit on the couch, I shift my gaze out the window and allow the heaviness to settle over me. The rollercoaster dips low once again, dragging me back into the depths of my sadness and pain. And the deeper it goes, the stronger the urge becomes to *feel* that pain.

My burnt fingertips push into the fabric of the couch, sending small bursts of pain up my fingers. But it's not enough. My gaze drifts from the window to the fire before me... but despite the overwhelming urge to feel more, a voice deep within me begs me not to give in.

Which is the most confusing fucking feeling.

I don't even register what I'm doing as I head for the door to the front deck, and step outside in my sock feet, sweatpants and t-shirt.

The rain falls on me in cold sheets as I just stand here, staring out into the fog.

What the fuck is wrong with me? Why am I doing any of this? Why can't I just end this, once and for all? To finally put myself out of my misery, do the right thing, and get what I truly deserve.

It should have been me.

My family should be mourning *me*.

The rain continues to beat down on me, cold water soaking

my clothes and seeping into my bones as I begin to shiver. As I blink away the raindrops clinging to my eyelashes, warmth suddenly rolls down my cheek. And a new kind of pain takes hold of me, as tears mingle with the rain streaming down my face.

The deep, hollow ache inside me finally takes over, and waves of emotion crash over me. A heavy weight presses on my chest as I desperately wish for things to be different, and to go back to how it all was before. But it never will. I've never had to face anything alone before, having someone by my side from the very beginning to help me navigate this life. Now, all I have are memories and pain. And I'll forever live with the regret for the mistake I've made.

A sob escapes me, this pain greater than anything I've ever inflicted upon myself as it completely takes over. I can't keep it out any longer as it forces me to feel everything I've tried so hard to keep out, and have been too scared to let in.

I collapse to my knees on the deck as my body folds in on itself, and I continue to sob. The cold, hard rain relentlessly pours down on me, refusing to let up. It just keeps coming, all at once... the rain, the cold, the grief, regret, anger, loneliness... It's overwhelming.

I want it all to disappear... and I also wish it would never stop.

I don't know how long I stay here in the pouring rain, but eventually I find myself blankly staring out into the foggy ocean. I continue to sit on the deck as I shiver uncontrollably, my body and mind frozen from both the cold, relentless rain and the intensity of my emotions.

But my mind wanders to Theo, as I try to see through the veil of muted grey blocking my view of the ocean, and anxiety stirs in my stomach. He's out there right now, in the pouring rain and dense fog.

Another tear slowly trickles down my cheek as I take a deep breath, and swallow down the fear. I don't want to have to go through this again...

"Please come back," I whisper into the rain.

I close my eyes and take another deep breath before I push to my feet. But as I turn to go back inside, I stop. As I look through the glass door at the warm, cozy living room, the fire roaring in the stove... I'm not ready for it.

I'm not sure where I'm even going as I step off the deck and onto the grass, still shivering and in my sock feet. But as my eyes land on the barn, I head that way.

The heavy rain drums steadily on the barn roof as I push the door open, stepping inside. I shiver as I flick on the light over the workspace, unsure why I even came in here. But as I glance around the space and take in Theo's tools strewn about on the workbench, a subtle sense of calm washes over me. His presence lingers here, and I find myself taking in a deep breath. I move towards the tools as I once again try to bury the weight of everything I've been carrying. Working on the house has been helping with that, and right now, I need it more than ever.

There's still some spackling left to do in the kitchen, so I grab the putty knife and spackle, and turn to head back to the house. But before I reach the door, I hear rustling from the dark corner of the barn where Theo stores his fishing gear.

I groan, eyeing the shadowy area. Please don't let there be mice in here...

But as the rustling sounds again, I also hear a soft, little meow.

I carefully set the spackle on the workbench, squinting into the darkness. I don't hear anything else, so I take a step closer. And as a bobber rolls across the floor, I see little eyes peering out at me from a tangle of bobbers and rope.

"Hey..." I kneel a few steps away from the kitten and

extend my hand, but it remains huddled in its hiding spot, eyeing me warily.

"Who are you?" I ask softly, settling onto the floor and observing the frightened kitten. It can't be any older than a couple of months and is all black and barely visible in the dim light.

As I sit here, watching the kitten watch me, I stay quiet and don't make any sudden noises or movements. The rain continues to patter on the roof, creating a soothing backdrop to our quiet, tentative stare down. It looks like the kitten might have a sore eye, and I'd like to get a closer look. But I stay where I am and wait.

Eventually, a tiny black paw emerges from the rope and bobbers, stepping towards me. But a bobber rolls off the pile, and the sudden movement startles it as it retreats into its hiding spot.

"It's ok," I say gently, extending my hand again, slowly. "You can come closer."

The kitten cautiously steps out again, approaching my hand and sniffing me. Then it rubs its nose against my finger, and I hear a soft purr.

I smile as the little kitten grows braver, inching closer and rubbing against me. It's all black with a tiny white tip on its tail.

"Where did you come from?" I ask quietly, turning my hand over to gently pet its little head. The kitten purrs louder and presses even closer, rubbing against my leg. "Why are you here all alone?"

And as I sit here on the floor of Theo's barn, surrounded by ropes and fishing gear with a lost, lonely kitten, I let just one more tear fall. "It's ok. We don't have to be alone."

ELEVEN

THEO

I SLAM the door to my truck as I get out and head towards the house, the rain continuing to drench my clothes like it has been all fucking day. The never-ending downpour and thick fog made for a horrible day on the water, and I'm soaked, cold, and in the worst fucking mood. It took all day to haul in our catch, get it to the buyer's station, and get back to the marina. Now it's almost 5:00PM, which means I've run out of time to tackle the other jobs on my list. So it looks like I'll be spending the evening in the workshop.

A wave of warmth washes over me when I enter the house, and I close my eyes and release a breath as I finally get some relief from the cold rain. As I kick off my boots and shrug out of my jacket in the entryway, I peer into the kitchen and notice a soft glow coming from the living room. I move further into the house and see a fire crackling in the wood stove, and Liam sitting on the floor in front of the couch.

My brow furrows as I pause in the kitchen, taking in his slumped posture. His head is down and his back is turned to me as he leans against the couch, which partially obstructs my view of him. My heart quickens as I step closer, flashes of him reaching into the fire flickering in my mind, until he lifts his head and our eyes meet.

"Hey," he says, then quickly glances to the floor in front of him with a guilty expression. "Um, so... I probably should have checked with you first..."

It takes me a moment to catch up to what he's saying as relief floods through me, and I step into the living room. Then I look down at the floor where he's sitting, and see a tiny black kitten swatting at the toy Liam is dangling.

Liam looks up at me again, and I cock an eyebrow at him. This is not at all what I was expecting.

"I found her in the barn when I was getting spackle," Liam says, eyeing me as he waits for my reaction.

I step closer, and the kitten looks up at me. One of her eyes is red, and looks like it has some sort of ointment on it.

"Is she ok?" I ask.

"Yeah." Liam nods, turning his attention back to her as she starts playing with the little toy mouse again. "I took her to the vet. They confirmed she is a girl, and probably about eleven or twelve weeks old. She has an infection in her eye, but we got some drops to clear it up."

I watch him as he picks up another toy that has a ribbon hanging from it, and she goes into attack mode, dramatically falling onto her back and reaching up with her little paws to grab at it. Liam chuckles, smiling down at her as she kicks her back legs at the ribbon, and I can barely hold back my own smile at the sight.

Of both of them.

"I didn't know what to do with her," Liam says, looking up at me again. "I don't know if you want a cat in the house, but, with the rain..."

I lower myself onto the floor across from Liam, and the

kitten watches me curiously. Then she bravely walks over to me, and playfully attacks my fingers as I wiggle them for her.

I smile down at the ferocious little beast. "It's no problem."

We're both quiet for a bit as we watch this tiny cat chaotically play with anything and everything in her sight. And as I sit here in peaceful silence, feeling the warmth from the fire and listening to the rain on the window, with Liam and this little terror... the frustration from today starts to fade away.

"I wonder where she came from," I ask, chuckling as she does an epic somersault while trying to catch the little mouse toy Liam tosses across the floor.

"I don't know," Liam says, glancing up at me. "She was just sitting in the pile of ropes and bobbers. I don't know how long she was there."

"Probably made for a nice little hideout," I say, watching her as she climbs up on Liam's knee.

He pats her head, and she nuzzles against his hand. "Did you like it in there?" he asks her softly, and my heart damn near explodes.

Watching him with her, I feel like I'm seeing the real Liam. He's been showing more of himself the longer he's been here, but a big part of him has remained hidden. Right now, though... I don't think it is. And he's exactly what I expected. He's sweet, caring, gentle, and unguarded, displaying a vulnerability that has my attraction for him growing by the second.

"But I'm leaving for work in a couple days, so... we'll have to find her a home," Liam says, his smile falling as he keeps his eyes on her while she purrs and rubs against his knee.

And my heart sinks.

I watch the kitten for a moment before I shake my head. "No."

Liam looks up at me and I smile as I see a flicker of hope in his eyes.

"She looks pretty comfortable here. And..." I shrug, reaching out to pat her, "I'm getting used to not coming home to an empty house every night."

A gentle smile forms on his lips as we continue to hold each other's gazes for a moment, and something passes between us. I'm not sure what it is, but it feels like some sort of unspoken connection, and a comforting warmth lingers between us.

Until we both bring our attention back to the kitten between us.

"She needs a name," Liam says.

I nod, subtly blowing out a breath and trying to ignore the need to look into his eyes again. "She does."

We watch her as she starts playing again, and Liam chuckles, gently poking at the little white tip of her tail. "She looks like a little bobber."

I laugh, taking in the cute marking as she swishes her tail back and forth, ready to attack the ribbon Liam slowly drags across the floor. "Bob doesn't quite work for her, does it?"

"No," he laughs. "It doesn't."

I lean back on my hands, watching as Liam continues to drag the ribbon around, and the kitten chases it. "I'm not the best at naming anything, let alone an adorable kitten. Leave it up to me and she'll end up being Miss Bobber, or something."

Liam's eyes meet mine, bright with amusement and joy as his smile lights up his entire face. "I think Miss Bobber suits her quite well."

I smile back at him, taking this moment to study his face and the happiness written all over him, hoping I'll get to see even more of it. "Miss Bobber it is then."

Liam lowers his gaze from mine as the kitten heads over to the water and food dishes he's set up for her, and I look around to take in everything he bought for her today. Dishes, food, toys, litter box... She's all set.

But then I feel his eyes on me once again, and I shift my attention back to him.

His gaze roams over my wet hair and down to my damp shirt, where the rain leaked through my jacket. "How was it today?"

A small sigh escapes me as I look out the window behind him, where it's still pouring. "Honestly... it fucking sucked."

I bring my gaze back to Liam, his forehead creased with concern. But a smile tugs at my lips as I look into his icy blue eyes, alive with emotion, and so much behind them that I wish I could understand. Yet on some level, I feel like I already do. There's no denying it now that I have a thing for him. And as much as I know I need to fight it, I can't fight this moment of weakness as we sit here with a rescued kitten that now belongs to us... and with him looking at me like that.

"But... it's better now," I say quietly.

The concern in his face fades, replaced by a soft smile as he keeps his eyes on mine. "Same."

TWELVE

LIAM

MY LEG BOUNCES restlessly as I stare out the airport window, watching as the plane pulls up to the gate. The ground crew is busy loading luggage and preparing for passengers, but my mind is miles away.

I want this job. I *need* it. But the guilt that is gnawing at me is impossible to ignore. I'm about to board a plane headed to a dangerous offshore rig, and my parents have no clue. They don't even know I'm in Nova Scotia right now, let alone that I'm about to leave. As far as they're concerned, I'm still in Calgary, working my old job in the oil sands. And they don't know the truth because they've been giving me the space I didn't even have to ask for — because I shut them out. Which I know is wrong, but it's just easier this way. For now, they can go on believing their only child is still good, safe, and whole.

Until I tell them the truth, and they see me for what I really am. Selfish, reckless, and broken.

My family has already lost one person they love. And they'll be losing another once they learn what part I played in that. So as cowardly as I am, hiding and keeping the truth from them... it's also so they can heal a bit before I break their hearts all over again.

With a shaking hand, I pull my phone out and turn it on. As the screen lights up, I rub a hand over my face and blow out a breath, trying to slow my racing heart.

My eyes take in every letter of every word of my mom's last text to me, especially those last five words... I love you, mo mhac.

I swallow thickly as I tap out a text to her. But my thumb hovers over send, unable to bring myself to tap it. The words are true, and I want her to know... but I can't. Because it was always my response to her, whenever she told me she loves me.

Gu bràth

Forever.

My thumb continues to hover over the screen for a moment longer until I exit out of her texts, the message still unsent. But before I shut my phone off, my eyes land on Theo's name in my messages from when he texted me his address over a week ago, when we first met.

My gaze lingers on his name, slowly tracing each letter as calm begins to override the anxiety and sadness. The same calm I felt when I was at his house, going out fishing together, sitting by the fire with him and Miss Bobber... just being with him in that big, quiet house.

A voice sounds over the speaker, jolting me back to reality as the flight attendant announces boarding for my flight. I sigh, shutting my phone off and sliding it back into my bag. And as I make my way to the gate, I hold onto the peace and comfort I found in Torrin Cove.

I'm going to need it.

Waves crash against the rig below as I lean against the railing, staring down at the deep, dark water. The water I was just in earlier today. It's only my first full day here, and already I've had to dive for underwater maintenance on a pipe. It was hard work with the water being as wild as it is, but... it was the danger I've been looking for.

I watch as the waves continue to pound against the legs of the rig, and the water swirls and churns as the light fades from the sky. The darkening ocean is mesmerizing as I keep my eyes on it, thinking how easy this water could swallow me whole.

My heart picks up its pace as the wind whips my hair around and I lean a little further over the railing.

How easy it could be...

But I push myself back with a sigh. As tempting as it is, I can't. Not here.

I continue my walk back to the workshop and when I get there, the electrician, Jesse, is cleaning up his area.

"Hey," he says, looking over his shoulder at me as I enter the space. "Good day?"

"Yeah," I say, dropping my tools onto one of the workbenches. "Ready for bed now."

He laughs. "Surprising how much maintenance is needed on the rig, huh? That salt water erodes everything so fast."

I huff out a laugh, putting the welding gun back on its shelf. "Really though."

"I think some of the guys are getting ping-pong fired up. You in?" Jesse asks, grabbing his hoodie and slipping it on.

"Next time," I say, checking the time. It's 9:00PM, so while it's still early, I'm fucking exhausted from flying all day yesterday, getting the helicopter onto the rig, working a partial shift with orientation, and then a full twelve hours today. "I really am ready for bed."

Jesse chuckles with a nod. "The first couple days of shift are always brutal. Well, we ping-pong pretty much every night, since there's not much else to do here. So, next time for sure."

"Sounds good," I say, giving him a smile as he heads out of the workshop with a wave.

I'm not long getting everything put away, and by the time I get to my room, I'm really looking forward to lying down and hopefully sleeping. I didn't get much, if any, last night and I'm going to need to sleep tonight if I have any hope of being able to function tomorrow.

My roommate is one of the roughnecks on night shift, so he's already gone when I get here, and I'm selfishly happy about that. I don't know if I have it in me for more small talk tonight.

But the second my head hits the pillow, my mind is racing.

It's been busy enough since I got here that I've managed to avoid thinking too much, and feeling the weight of it all — of being back to work for the first time since everything went to shit. But now, as I lie here and rub my eyes, the emotions overwhelm me as they all hit at once. Guilt, sadness, and anger crash into me as images flash through my mind — fire billowing out of the work bay, my family's tear-stained faces, a funeral that should have been mine. The reality of it all, and the fact that I am here, working a new job, without my best friend... it's too much.

My heart thunders in my ears while my breath slips away from me, and I try not to completely lose it here in this tiny room, on a rig in the middle of the Gulf of Mexico. My fingers tangle in my hair and pull tight as I squeeze my eyes shut, willing myself to push through this and get my shit together. I desperately try to bury everything and put it back where it belongs, but it just keeps coming.

Until a picture of wild, windswept hair, gentle brown eyes, and soft freckles appears in my mind.

My hands release my hair and lower to my chest as I take a deep breath in, hanging onto the image of Theo in my head. I'm not sure why he's the one I'm picturing, but the calm he brings is exactly what I need right now. So I hold onto it and remember how I felt back in his house... even if I don't understand why.

I open my eyes and turn my head, eyeing my bag. He would probably still be awake...

I get up to grab my phone out of my bag and turn it on, almost with desperation. My heart picks up its pace again as I tap out a message to him, and I hesitate as my thumb hovers over send. But I tap it.

Hey. How's Miss Bobber?

I lie back down on the bed, watching the screen as I chew my bottom lip. Waiting.

THEO

Hey, she's good.

Then he sends me a photo of her, curled up on the couch, sound asleep. I smile, letting the photo of Theo's home, and this little kitten, soothe my soul.

Her eye is looking better already.

It is. She's a trooper.

She was asleep in your bed when I got home tonight.

I chuckle, remembering how she made herself right at home on my pillow. But as I think of Theo finding her, my heart skips a beat as I picture him in my room, sitting on my bed. And I have no idea what that means.

My fingers hover over the screen as I think of what to say back to him, but I don't know. This feeling can't be what I think it is...

How's the rig?

I release a breath and shake off those thoughts and feelings, tapping out my response.

Good. A steady stream of work, and a lot of maintenance and repairs.

Get a good catch today?

I watch the bubbles dancing as he types, and feel the anticipation rising, hoping he had a good day.

It was decent. Average, considering our last few weeks. And calm water, which we were overdue for.

A smile tugs at my lips as I read his message, relieved he finally had a good one. The past week was tough for them, and even though he hides it and I don't know him all that well, I can tell it was getting to him.

That's good.

Hope you got out on your boat for some fishing too then.

Unfortunately not. I had to install some flooring today.

I huff out a breath. Didn't think so. He works too damn much.

You probably should. You need the practice...

The bubbles appear immediately, and I smile as I can practically feel his eyes narrowing from here.

You were lucky. And you had the better rod.

I laugh into the empty room.

I thought they were pretty much the same?

Yeah, *pretty much*. Not the exact same.

All I hear are excuses.

Re-match when you're home, and you'll be crying into the livewell.

Yeah, tears of laughter because you never even got a nibble.

Big talk for a fly fisher.

It's ok, I can show you how to do that too.

How to stand in water and fling a string around? I think I got it.

I let out another laugh, now absolutely needing to find a fly fishing spot around Torrin Cove.

It's on then.

My eyes flick to the corner of the screen, and when I see it's getting late, I also realize my eyes are finally feeling heavy.

I should get to sleep though. I'm pretty beat.

Yeah, same.

Then he sends another photo of Miss Bobber, still lounging in the same spot on the couch, mid-yawn with her mouth wide open like she's letting out a tiny roar. I smile and save the photo.

Thanks. Night.

Night.

I turn my phone off and toss it back into my bag, then sink back into bed. And this time when my eyes close, different thoughts and questions swirl through my mind. The chaos that had me in its hold earlier is gone, replaced by something quieter, and something... almost peaceful. And I can't help but wonder, once again, what this feeling is. It's almost like... I'm into him.

But why, and how? I've never been into a guy before. And if that is what it is... why him? The guy I *live* with. What the fuck?

I don't know... I don't know what this is, what it means, or how I feel about anything, let alone him.

All I do know is that he provides me with a sense of calm and comfort that I haven't had in a long time. And as I drift off to sleep, brown eyes and freckles lingering in my mind, I just let it happen.

THIRTEEN

THEO

"MY SPAGHETTI LOOKS LIKE WORMS!"

Heather sighs and gives Mason a cautious look across the dinner table. "Please don't tell me you put worms in your spaghetti."

Chris leans over, peering into Mason's plate. Then he shakes his head. "We're good."

"Oh, thank god." Heather lets out another breath, then turns back to Mom to continue their conversation. "So, anyway, the new ice cream display freezer will be delivered tomorrow. It was a tragic day yesterday when tourists came through looking for moon mist ice cream and I couldn't deliver."

"Oh good," Mom says. "Would you happen to have some time tomorrow, Theo, to get that hooked up?"

I look up from my plate to my mother's hopeful expression and nod. "Yeah, I'll come after we get in off the water."

"Thanks, honey," Mom says with a smile.

They keep chatting about the store, throwing around ideas about expanding the farm market side of it, and I find myself zoning out while I mindlessly pick at my dinner. Until the sound of a name snaps me out of it.

"How's Liam making out?"

I look up at my grandfather as he watches me, waiting for my answer.

"Uh, good," I say, shifting my weight in my chair.

"Informative as always, Teddy," Heather chuckles. "Care to elaborate?"

I shoot her a look. "He's just over halfway through his shift now. He'll be back in a little over a week."

Mom smiles. "And he'll be coming to dinner when he's home, I hope?"

All eyes are on me, like I know the answer to that.

"I can ask him." I shrug. "I'm sure he will."

Grandpa chuckles, leaning back in his chair. "So, how exactly did he end up here anyway, and not back in Cape Breton?"

I shrug again. "I don't know. He said he wanted a quiet place to live."

Grandpa tilts his head slightly, brows furrowing. "Cape Breton is pretty quiet."

"Does he still have family there?" Chris asks, effortlessly catching Mason as he almost falls off his chair trying to reach for his toy truck on the counter.

Isla rolls her eyes and reaches behind her, sliding the truck further out of reach. Then she points at Mason. "Sit down and eat."

I shake my head as everyone keeps their eyes on me, waiting for my answer to Chris' question. "I don't know."

"What *do* you know?" Heather says with exasperation. "He lives with you! Do you guys talk at all?"

"Yeah," I say, furrowing my brow at her. "But I'm not grilling him for his life story. If he wants to share, he can."

Heather sighs with a shake of her head and Mom huffs out a little laugh, cocking an eyebrow at me.

"He's not a big talker, ok?" I say, bringing my attention back to my plate and taking a bite, hoping this is the end of the questions.

"Just like someone else we know," Grandpa says with a chuckle.

I lift my eyes to him. "Guess it works out well then."

He laughs, and then thankfully changes the subject, asking Isla about her next dance recital.

As she excitedly commands the attention of the table, eager to share every detail of her butterfly dance routine, I quietly pull my phone from my pocket. And my own excitement stirs as I see a missed text from Liam earlier — a photo of several dolphins in the water beneath the rig.

With a smile, I tap out a response.

Damn, that's crazy they get that close.

I slide my phone back into my pocket, knowing Liam won't see the message until he's off tonight. Still, I can't ignore the familiar rush I get whenever I get a text from him, which has been daily this past week. We've been keeping in touch over small things throughout the day, such as Miss Bobber updates, swapping photos of the rig and some chairs I built, and talking a bit about tile for the bathroom. It's been a steady, ongoing conversation as we trade messages whenever we can, and most nights, in those couple hours before bed, we get some uninterrupted time to text. And despite what my family may think, we're actually getting to know each other a bit more.

Once dinner is over and I've helped clean up, I say my good-byes to everyone and head home a bit earlier than usual to tend to Miss Bobber. As soon as I open the door, she trots over to me with a soft meow.

"Hey, Miss." I bend down to pick her up, and she immediately starts purring. "You hungry?"

I carry her into the kitchen as she purrs into my ear and rubs her face against mine, making me chuckle.

"Here we go, gotta do these first," I say as I pull out her eye drops.

She squirms as I put them in, and as I set her down and toss out the now empty bottle, I think we're both relieved that's over. For good. And thankfully, her eye is looking perfectly healthy now.

"There," I say, looking down at her. "All done."

Just as I put some food in her dish and she starts eating, my phone buzzes. And that rush flows through me once again as I pull it out to see Liam responding to my text from earlier.

LIAM

They stuck around for a while underneath me as I was working on the platform.

I drop down to sit beside Miss Bobber on the floor as she eats, tapping out my reply.

Not a bad view while working. Done now?

Miss Bobber happily crunches her food beside me in the quiet kitchen, and I look down to take a photo of her as I wait for him to text back. And curse myself for being so eager.

Yeah. And bowing out of ping-pong tonight.

I huff out a breath of laughter. Apparently the guys on the rig play every night, which makes sense... what else do they have to do on a rig in the middle of the Gulf of Mexico when not working? But from his replay of their matches the other night, it sounds like it can get pretty intense.

Afraid of losing?

He starts typing immediately, and I smile.

I've won more than I've lost.

May have to challenge you when you're home then. See what you're so afraid of.

Fuck no. No ping-pong on land. I can't take any more.

I laugh, pushing to my feet as Miss Bobber leaves her dish and starts playing with her toy mouse.

Fair enough. We'll stick to fishing then.

Which is also not on land...

So ping-pong on the boat?

Logic is there, but still no.

I chuckle again and head upstairs, into the bathroom off my bedroom.

So what are you doing tonight if not dominating?

As I start brushing my teeth, I set my phone on the counter, screen still open to his texts as he types back.

I'm in my room, in bed. I had to get up last night for an emergency fix on a drilling pipe, so only slept a few hours.

My heart skips at the thought of him lying in bed, texting me. *What the fuck.* I close my eyes and sigh, disappointed in myself for entertaining those thoughts. Again. Because this isn't the first time.

That sucks. So you're just always on call?

Yeah, I'm the only welder on the rig. Some have two, but this one doesn't.

A typical 9-5 sounds pretty damn good right about now.

I strip down to my boxers and leave the door to my room open for Miss Bobber. She's still playing downstairs, and once she's finished she usually sneaks in and curls up with me for the night. I climb into bed and lie back against the pillows, tapping out my reply to Liam.

I hear ya. 4:00AM six days a week is brutal. Probably wouldn't have been my first pick if I had the choice.

But as I hit send, I wince. Fuck, I shouldn't have said that.

It wasn't your choice?

With a sigh, I rub my hand over my face. I've never said this out loud to anyone before, and I'm not sure why I'm telling him this now. But being behind a screen makes it a bit easier to say, and for some reason, I find that I want to share it with him.

No. My grandfather put so much into building this business, and then my dad did too. It's impossible to get into lobster fishing now with the price of the licence and the equipment. Everything I inherited is now worth $1.8 million, so it would be a dick move of me to sell it off after they built it all up. It was always expected I would take over, so… I did.

But it's not what you want to do?

I think on this for a moment, unsure how to respond. If I didn't want to fish, I know my grandfather would understand, and my dad would have too. But I also know they worked their asses off so I could easily walk into this business and be set for life. Not many people my age can even get a lobster fishing licence, let alone own both a lobster and tuna licence with all the equipment. But it's hard fucking work, and I didn't think I'd be taking it over in my twenties.

But the usual guilt rises with these thoughts, as it always does. I'm lucky to own a thriving business in a lucrative trade, and I'm even luckier to never have to worry about money, so I shouldn't be thinking this way. And I do enjoy the work. But... sometimes I can't help but wonder what my life might look like, and who I could be, if I did something else. If I got out of Torrin Cove and experienced something different... if I might know and understand myself better than I do now.

I do like it, and I can't see myself doing anything else now. I guess I just wonder sometimes what I would have done if I didn't have it all laid out for me.

Any idea what that would be?

Million-dollar question.

I smile as I realize how comfortable I am sharing all of this with him... even if I don't have the answers to his questions.

Full-time carpenter.

Ha. You already are. On top of full-time fishing.

Should have seen that coming.

True.

So, what about you then? You could do the 9-5 thing with welding.

Liam doesn't text back right away, and I start to worry that I shouldn't have asked that. Eventually the typing bubbles appear... then disappear. My brow furrows as I watch this happen a few more times. I'm about to tell him he doesn't have to answer when his message comes through.

I could. I've worked away in oil since day one though so... this is also all I know.

Just as I'm about to start typing out a response, he starts again. So I wait.

Came close to changing careers entirely though.

My brows lift as I read his text, surprised that he's offering up this information. While he's been opening up more since we've started texting, he's never shared anything this personal before. I'm not sure if I should ask any more about this, but... it feels like he's inviting me in.

Something to do with your switch to offshore?

He's silent again for a moment until he sends a simple text. But even with that one word, I can tell there's an emotional weight behind it.

Yeah.

I stare at his text, feeling his sadness through the phone. There's a reason why he left Alberta, and why he ended up here instead of Cape Breton... but I think that reason is a heavy one for him. And I'm not going to push him on it. If he ever wants to share it with me, he can.

I can always use another deckhand if the rig doesn't work out.

He starts texting immediately, and I smile.

You paying oil money?

Better. You get lobster and sunrises. But... no dolphins.

Well, talk to me again when there are dolphins.

I chuckle, then pause, looking at the time. As much as I want to keep talking to him... it's getting late, and 4:00AM will be here before I know it.

I'll keep you updated. But for now, I need to get to sleep.

Same.

I send him the photo I took of Miss Bobber earlier, just like I do every night. Liam hearts it, and mine flutters.

Night.

Night.

I set my phone on the bedside table and let out a sigh as I lie back and close my eyes. But as I lie here in my quiet bedroom, listening to Miss Bobber play downstairs, I can't get Liam out of my thoughts.

Our conversation tonight keeps replaying in my mind, and the confusion I've felt for so long suddenly feels overwhelming as a question lingers. Who would I be if I experienced something different?

For so long, I've felt disconnected from myself, as if I'm hiding a significant part of me deep down where no one can see. I never thought I was ashamed of possibly being gay, but I don't know why I couldn't bring myself to face it. Now, as I lie here, staring up at the night sky through the skylight in my ceiling, it's all starting to make sense.

My life is firmly anchored to Torrin Cove, dictated by everything that has been decided for me. And I think this is why I've hidden so much of myself away. Because living in a tiny town where everyone knows everyone, I'm not able to explore this side of me. I don't know anyone here who is gay, and most people my age have left. Even if I did find an opportunity to be who I truly want to be, I'm terrified that some people might not accept me. And in such a close-knit community, that wouldn't just affect me... it would also affect my family. And now I'm realizing this fear is why I shove these feelings down, keep to myself, and work my ass off to distract myself from wanting more.

But Liam is stirring something within me, and bringing those feelings to the surface. While I've dated a few girls before, I've never felt for them what I feel for Liam. I've never had this urge to be with them, to know them, to touch them... to just see them smile and be close to them. It felt like something I was supposed to do, and not something I wanted.

I *want* Liam.

And right now... I want to give in.

Images of Liam flood my mind as I close my eyes again and release a breath. Heat builds within my chest as I picture his icy blue eyes, and his dark hair softly blowing in the breeze. My skin tingles as my hand slides down my abs to the waistband of my boxers, and my pulse quickens as I slip it in to grasp my hardening cock.

As I slowly stroke myself, and grow even harder, warmth spreads through my body. The edges of my mind turn hazy, as if the rest of the world is fading away, leaving just him. Liam's eyes are locked on mine, and a soft smile plays at the corner of his lips, drawing me in even deeper.

A groan escapes me as I stroke myself faster, and my senses sharpen. I take in everything I can about him, wishing he was here so I could touch him, smell him, *see* him...

"Oh, fuck," I moan as my other hand moves to my nipple and I imagine what it would be like to have his mouth on me.

My heart is racing, and the pressure inside me is quickly building, begging for a release. But I want more. I need more. I need *him*.

I continue to jerk myself, staying in this moment as I finally allow myself to let out everything I've kept buried for so long. To fully embrace my feelings and acknowledge who I am, and what I want. For the first time ever, I'm not holding back... and it feels so fucking good.

Tingles spread up the back of my neck and in my balls, and the pressure inside me is pulsating as I near the edge.

With a groan into the quiet room, and the image of Liam's smiling face in my mind, the pressure peaks with a rush of ecstasy. I come over my hand and stomach, and an intense feeling washes over me that almost feels like relief, leaving me feeling lighter than I think I ever have.

But as I open my eyes, breathing heavy as I stare up at the skylight, that lightness starts to fill with darkness. The reality of my situation sets in once again as I remember all my reasons for hiding this part of me.

Yet here I am, jerking off to my roommate who probably isn't even into guys.

Fuck.

I'm in deep.

FOURTEEN

LIAM

"IF YOU DON'T HURRY up and get this game started, I'm going to paddle your ass. And I bet you'll fucking like it."

I chuckle from my seat on the couch as Raúl shoots Colin a look across the ping-pong table and holds up the ball.

"Aw, so excited to get my ball," he says with a smirk, bouncing it on the table.

Colin laughs, settling into an intense stance on his side of the table. "You only got one? Well, that actually makes a lot of sense."

"Fuck off," Raúl says, finally serving and getting this game started. The amount of trash talk these guys all do with fucking *ping-pong* is ridiculous.

I stay seated on the couch, watching the game with a few of the other guys. It's the last night of our three-week shift, and they are definitely making the most of it. The intensity of this game might be the highest I've seen yet.

But while they're all amped up, I'm fucking exhausted. I'm used to the three-week rotation schedule since I've done it in Alberta, but this is my first time being the only welder on a rotation. And offshore, there are a lot more emergencies to tend to outside my shift.

The guys all cheer as Raúl earns himself a point, and I slap on a smile. I'm also not used to this much social interaction. In the larger camps in the oil sands, it was easy to find quiet solitude when I needed it. But here, living in such tight quarters, there's no escaping the social aspect of rig life. I do genuinely enjoy spending time with these guys, but putting up a social front day after day, even with people I like, is tiring. And in these last few days of rotation, I've been craving the peaceful quiet of Torrin Cove more and more.

My phone buzzes in my pocket as the game, and the trash talk, picks up again.

THEO

Late day, just finishing.

He sends a photo of a large window he installed in an older home today, and holy shit. He did an awesome job. The photo he sent earlier this afternoon before he started showed an absolute disaster. The old window was broken, and the wood around the frame was rotted. Now, after he replaced both the frame and the window, it looks flawless.

Damn, that's awesome.

Then I smirk down at my phone as I tap out another text.

But you do know there are seven days in a week, right? Not every job has to be finished in one day. Poor Miss Bobber, all alone...

As I wait for him to respond, I scroll up in our texts to another photo he sent early this morning. A photo from the lobster boat at dawn, the sky over the water a mesmerizing blend of colours as the clouds catch the early light of the rising sun. It looks like a painting, with everything looking so perfect and still.

"You up, Liam?"

I look up from my phone to see Colin holding his paddle out to me.

"I'm good," I say, shaking my head. Then my phone buzzes in my hand, and I quickly glance down at it.

> Seven days, seven jobs. No rest for the weary.

> And I actually went home before coming here and put a fire on for her. So… I'd say she's doing alright.

I smile at the thought of him lighting a fire for Miss Bobber, and a flicker of excitement stirs inside me knowing I'll see them both tomorrow. But I quickly lift my eyes to Colin again.

"I'm actually going to head to bed," I say, pushing to my feet.

He cocks an eyebrow at me, then glances down at my phone in my hand with a smile. "Got a girl back home? Bet she's excited to see you."

I huff out a laugh and shove my phone in my pocket. "No, I don't. And I'm going to bed because I'm tired from being on call for three weeks," I say as I playfully push him out of my way.

Colin chuckles, waving his paddle at me. "Tell her I say hi."

I flip him off as laughter erupts around us. With a wave goodnight to everyone, I turn and make my way down the hallway to my room. Once I'm inside, I pull my phone out again.

Maybe the weary should take a page out of Miss Bobber's book and sit by the fire once in a while.

I set my phone down, leaving the screen open to his texts as I change into sweatpants and a t-shirt. As I pull the shirt over my head, I glance down at the screen and pause as realization sets in. Since I've been on the rig, I've actually kept my phone on... something I haven't done in months. I've kept it off for so long to avoid emotions and reminders of home, but since I started texting with Theo... I keep it on.

My eyes linger on it for another moment before I reach out to pick it up. I exit Theo's texts and tap on my mom's name, the unsent message I typed out to her staring back at me.

Gu bràth.

It's been over three weeks since she sent me her message. I can't even imagine what she must be feeling, or how much my parents must be hurting with each day that passes without hearing from me. They're respecting my wishes, even though it's causing them pain. A war begins to brew inside me, as I want to protect them from knowing what I've done, but I also want to ease their suffering and make them feel better.

Theo's text appears at the top of the screen, and I quickly tap it, not ready to make that decision yet.

Just got home, and that's exactly what she was doing. Climbing my legs now.

I lie back on my bed, letting out a breath as the sadness over my parents lingers, and I try to push past it.

Because she was lonely. You work too much.

You're one to talk.

Yeah, but you have a choice.

Theo is quiet for a moment, and as I stare at the screen and wait for his response, I let my mind wander to what he told me before. How he feels like he didn't have a choice in his life. But outside of fishing, he does. So I can't help but wonder why he works himself so much.

Not as much as I'd like. I just do better when I'm busy.

I furrow my brow as I read his text again. Not as much as he'd like? So, there is something else he'd rather do? I can relate to the need to stay busy — I need it to drown out the noise in my own mind. Does he also have something he's trying to escape?

But I don't ask. Because I know what it feels like to try to run, and try to escape something that clings to you no matter how far you go.

Same.

We're both quiet for a little bit as I take a deep breath in and the familiar, uneasy sensation builds inside me. But this time, I don't push it away. I let it grow just enough to push me forward, and give me the courage to share a bit more of myself with him. The part I've been trying to escape.

I guess I have a choice too. But I stay busy, even on my weeks off, because it just makes everything a little easier to manage. I'm sure it's obvious that I didn't exactly plan on ending up in Torrin Cove. But... I couldn't make myself go home. So even though I need to keep my mind busy, I also know how important it is to slow down and enjoy what you have before it's all gone. But that, I'm not so good at.

My fingers tremble as I hit send, and I rub my thumb over my now healed, slightly scarred fingers. I'm not sure why I felt the urge to share this with him, and anxiety grows as I worry what he might think of it.

Of me.

I'm not either. And I know what it's like to hide yourself away behind work so you don't have to be alone with your thoughts. And even after losing my dad and seeing how quickly it can all change, I still can't slow down.

The anxious feeling softens as I read his message. I appreciate that he never pushes or asks for more than I'm ready to give. He just... understands. And while it's unfortunate that he does understand, there's also a comfort in that. I don't know what he's hiding, or what happened to his dad, and I won't ask. I won't push him either.

Before I can respond, another text from him comes through.

I guess living in my disaster zone of a house is a good thing then.

A smile spreads across my face as I chuckle.

Perfect way to stay busy.

Perfect way to get my house finished.

And now I can't help but laugh out loud.

You're right though. I should spend more time in this house and enjoy it.

A soft flutter rises in my chest as I think of him spending more time at home... with me.

You do have a whole ass room to drink coffee in.

Haha I do.

Sounds like we need to get started on renos in there.

I smile, liking the sound of that.

Sounds like it.

But as I look at the time, my heart sinks a bit. It's getting late, especially in Nova Scotia, and I know he should be heading to bed.

Shouldn't you be asleep?

I will be soon. Someone already is.

Then he sends a photo, and I freeze.

Theo is lying shirtless in his bed with a soft smile, and Miss Bobber is curled up on his chest as she sleeps.

I don't know why... but I can't stop staring at it.

At him.

But I quickly tap out a text and hit send before he thinks I'm ignoring him. Or slightly freaking out... which I am.

She looks comfy.

She is. And she's snoring, which is actually adorable.

I chuckle, trying to keep my eyes away from the photo of him. But they keep snapping back to it as I tap out my message.

Well, you better do what she says then and go to sleep.

Agreed.

Have a good night. See you tomorrow.

My heart seems to skip a beat as I read those last three words.

See you tomorrow.

Night.

But I keep his texts open and tap on the photo, making it bigger.

My eyes trail over his soft freckles on his cheeks and nose, his warm eyes and gentle smile... his hard pecs...

What the fuck.

I close my eyes and release a breath, once again wondering how this happened.

How I managed to develop a thing for Theo. My roommate... a *guy*.

But as I open my eyes again to the photo of Theo, his warm eyes looking back at me, I focus on the calm and comforting feeling they bring. The same feeling I get each night after talking to him. I never would have anticipated the effect he has on me, but it's one I can't ignore. Because somehow, he's managing to slowly open me back up, despite my efforts to shut down and give up.

My heart thumps as I exit out of his texts and tap on my mom's name again.

And send the message.

Gu bràth.

FIFTEEN

THEO

THE ATTENDANT at the buyer's station hands me today's slip, and I'm relieved to see the price has held steady from last week. With a slightly above-average haul today, this return is a welcome sight.

"Thanks," I say, shoving the slip in my pocket. He gives me a nod and moves on to the next in line.

I make my way back to the boat, where my crew is loading the last of our bait and ice.

"All set, Captain?" Mitch asks, tossing the last bucket to Sarah, who stacks it with the rest of them.

"Yup." I hop into the boat and whistle across the wharf to Glen where he's chatting with another crew. He shoots me a look and flips me off, but I just chuckle. He hates being whistled at, but if he doesn't want to be treated like a dog, he should stop wandering off like one.

He grumbles as he jumps into the boat. "Could have just said my name."

I shrug, starting up the engine. "Could have just stayed with the boat."

Mitch laughs and pats his leg. "Here, puppy."

"Fuck off." Glen takes a seat on the bench, shaking his head. "I'm too old to be working with you shits."

"Stop sookin'," Sarah says with a chuckle as I pull away from the wharf.

Their continued bickering fades into the background as I drive us back to the marina, and my anticipation grows. Because Liam gets home today. I glance at my watch as we near the marina, a bit surprised that we managed to make it back earlier than usual since it's only 2:00PM. But that surprise quickly shifts to excitement, knowing his flight landed at 1:00PM. And now I have to roll my eyes at myself for feeling like this just because he's back in Nova Scotia.

I guide the boat into our spot at the wharf, cutting the engine as the crew hops out to tie us off. Everyone quickly falls into their usual routine to clean up and get the boat ready for tomorrow, and I toss some broken traps onto the wharf to add to my growing pile at home. Lobsters thrive in rocky areas, and luckily for us, our traps are set on a large rocky ledge which leads to high catch rates. Unfortunately, those same rocks take a toll on the traps.

As the crew works on the boat, I start fixing what I can with the tools I have here, and stack the rest to take home. But I keep glancing at my watch, as my mind drifts to a pair of blue eyes.

"Got somewhere to be?" Sarah's voice pulls me from my thoughts.

I shake my head, ripping out a torn net from one of the traps. "No."

Mitch pauses mid-hose and looks up at me from the boat deck. "What job do you have this afternoon?"

A mental list of tasks flashes through my mind as I realize I didn't schedule anything for today. There are a few loose ends I could tie up and some other jobs I could start, but none of it is urgent. Looking down at the pile of traps needing attention, I realize that's probably my plan for the day.

"Just heading to the workshop, I guess," I say, tossing the last trap onto the platform to haul to my truck.

"You guess?" Glen laughs. "You don't have the entire rest of your day booked? Who are you?"

Mitch laughs and starts hosing the deck again. "Give him an hour. He'll end up building a patio somewhere or something."

I roll my eyes at them and Sarah chuckles, patting my shoulder.

"You go, I'll whip these two into shape," she says with a smile.

"Thanks." I shake my head at Glen and Mitch as they start taking bets for what I'll end up doing this afternoon.

I manage to slip out of the marina before Sheila can corner me and talk my ear off, as she often does. Luckily, she's busy chatting with another crew while I haul the lobster traps to my truck, avoiding any delay. So I quickly load them into the back, hop in, and head towards home. As I pass the store, I wave to my grandfather and the old man crew on the front porch, opting not to stop in today. I'm too eager to get home.

My heart leaps as I pull into my driveway and see Liam's truck parked by the house. I park next to it and take a deep breath as I get out, letting the excitement roll through me for a moment. But it only grows as I push the door open and step inside the house, hearing a faint rustling from the kitchen. I peer around the corner as I kick my boots off and shrug out of my jacket, smiling as I see him at the kitchen counter, illuminated by sunlight streaming in through the window.

"Hey," I say, entering the kitchen.

He turns to look at me, and the smile on his lips sends a rush of warmth through me.

"Hey." He glances at the clock on the microwave. "I didn't think you'd be home so early."

"Yeah." I rub the back of my neck, also glancing at the time. It's 3:00PM, which might be the earliest I've been home since lobster season started in November. "I have some work to do in the workshop today."

Miss Bobber meows at my feet as she walks back and forth between me and Liam, looking up at us like she is expecting all the attention.

Liam nods, his eyes briefly roaming over my face before he quickly drops his gaze to Miss Bobber. "She got bigger."

I chuckle as he bends down to pick her up, and she purrs as she rubs her face against his nose.

"She did," I say quietly, watching them.

We're both silent for a moment as Miss Bobber's purrs fill the space between us, and a quiet comfort settles inside me. One that I've been missing for three weeks.

"Want a coffee?" I ask, heading for the coffee maker.

"I just made one," Liam says, setting Miss Bobber down and taking a seat at the kitchen island before a fresh cup of coffee.

I glance over my shoulder at him while I get my own started, and take in how tired he looks as he runs a hand through his hair. "How was your flight?"

"It was ok," he says, looking out the glass patio door to the water. "Long."

I nod, leaning against the counter as my coffee brews. I can't help but watch him as he gazes out the patio door, the sunlight casting a soft glow on his dark, almost black hair, with his blue eyes sparkling like crystals in the light. But as my mind wanders to what I did when I was imagining those eyes on me, I quickly avert my gaze and turn back to the coffee maker.

"Um, it's a nice day out..." I say as I take my coffee mug and stand awkwardly in the middle of the kitchen. But when he looks at me, I give him a soft smile. "I might actually take your advice and slow down for a minute."

He cocks an eyebrow at me, a small smile tugging at his lips. "Really..."

I laugh. "Yeah." Then I tilt my head towards the patio door. "Coffee outside?"

The smile spreads over his face and he nods. "Yeah."

As we head out onto the patio, and down the steps to the Adirondack chairs, anxiety mixes with the excitement I've been feeling. I've been looking forward to him coming home, especially after how well we seemed to connect while he was away. But during this time, I've also come to realize just how into him I am. And now that he's here... I'm not sure I know how to manage these feelings, which are quickly overwhelming me.

We take a seat on the chairs overlooking the calm water, and I take a moment to feel the warm sunshine on my skin. With just a couple days left in April, the spring air feels crisp and fresh. I take a subtle deep breath in to calm my nerves and cast a sideways glance at Liam.

"So, should I make some ping-pong paddles?"

His eyes widen as he turns his head towards me. "Do *not*. For fuck's sake, no, please."

I laugh and take a sip of my coffee with a slight shrug of one shoulder. "You'll miss it eventually."

"I guarantee I won't." He smirks, letting out a soft laugh. "Three weeks is hardly enough of a break from it."

I chuckle and steal another glance at him as he takes a sip of his coffee. He seems more at ease compared to when he first came here, though I'm unsure if that's because he's been away working for so long or because we have come to know each other better. The familiar heaviness still lingers, but overall, it feels like I'm seeing more of him now than I did before he left.

"Three weeks doesn't even seem like enough of a break for all the work you do on the rig," I say. "You must be exhausted."

He nods, looking out over the water. "Yeah. The work itself isn't so bad. I'm not a good sleeper anyway." He shifts a bit uncomfortably in his seat and pauses for a moment. "But I missed this. The quiet. Rig life is loud and busy."

I nod. "I can imagine," I say quietly, glancing around at the peaceful, secluded home I built for myself, happy I can share this with him.

So that's what we do. We both sit in silence as we drink our coffee and listen to the seagulls and the gentle lapping of the ocean against the shore. I don't remember the last time I took a moment like this for myself in the middle of the day... and I'm surprised at how much I like it.

Liam sets his mug down and pushes his sleeves up, the warm sun coaxing him to roll them higher. As he does, my eyes land on the tattoos that cover his right hand, fingers, and forearm. It's completely covered in ink, but one in particular catches my eye. It looks fresher than the rest of them, and I recognize it as the Triquetra — a Celtic knot with interwoven lines and endless loops, symbolizing the eternal bond between friends.

I divert my eyes as Liam catches me looking at it, and I shift my gaze out over the water. But before I can scold myself for checking out his ink, Liam surprises me.

"I got it for a friend," he says.

I turn my head to look at him, but he keeps his eyes fixed on the ocean.

"He died."

My heart sinks as I take in the emotion written all over his face.

"I'm sorry to hear that," I say quietly.

His text to me yesterday flashes in my mind, as I remember

what he said about knowing how quickly everything can change, and that he ended up here because he couldn't make himself go home.

Liam just nods stiffly, still looking out over the water. His fingers fidget in his lap as his jaw tics, and it looks like he's just barely holding it together.

I know that feeling.

"I thought my life was over when my dad died," I say, dropping my eyes to his hands as he picks at his fingers.

He turns to look at me, his eyes full of sadness.

"I learned everything from him," I continue, releasing a breath. "He was my best friend. We did everything together, and I wanted to be just like him. I know I've said it felt like I didn't have a choice, and this was all decided for me, but... I also wanted to walk in his shoes. Because to me, he was everything." I pause for a moment as emotion swells and catches in my throat. "And then all of a sudden, he's gone, and I'm doing it all without him. It's a heavy weight, and a lot to manage."

Liam nods, his eyes flicking between mine. "How did you do it?"

I release a sigh and shake my head slightly. "I don't know if I'm the right person to ask."

He nods again and brings his gaze back to the water.

But I keep mine on him.

"Time does help," I say softly. "And... I'm here if you want to talk. I think my biggest mistake was keeping it all in." I pause as Liam looks at me, and warmth rushes through me once again. "Keeping everything in."

His brow furrows a bit as he keeps his eyes locked on mine, before he gives me a soft nod. "Same."

A soft breeze rustles his hair as we sit here, side by side. And as we look into each other's eyes, another layer of understanding passes between us.

And I want nothing more than to reach out and touch him. To comfort him and take away whatever pain he's feeling.

But then his eyes soften as they gently roam my face. "Thank you."

All I do is nod, because more words feel unnecessary. In this moment, the quiet between us says it all, and the connection we share speaks louder than anything we could put into words.

SIXTEEN

LIAM

MISS BOBBER POUNCES on her toy mouse, her little paws swatting it towards me. I bat it back, chuckling as she scrambles across the kitchen floor in hot pursuit. The smell of coffee fills the kitchen as I stand and look out the window, watching the gentle waves lap against the shore.

I managed to sleep in for the first time in what feels like forever. After yesterday's long flight and the last three weeks of intense, non-stop work, I needed it. Though I woke when Theo came down the stairs this morning, the comforting sounds of him getting ready for work eased me back into a deep sleep. I can't remember the last time I slept that long, or that well.

As I gaze out the window at the wide expanse of the ocean, my thoughts remain on Theo. I keep thinking of yesterday, and the conversation we had where we each shared something so deeply personal. Telling him about Nick's death almost broke me right there in front of him... but as usual, he understands. And like always, he didn't push for more. He remained a calm, comforting presence, and shared more of himself as well.

Even now, as the familiar ache of grief begins to swell again, it feels different. The need for pain isn't as demanding, and the thoughts urging me to punish myself aren't as loud. It still hurts, and I still want to hurt, but it almost feels... manageable.

And I have no idea how to feel about that.

But what I do know is that I don't feel so alone in those feelings of sadness and grief anymore.

And with every moment spent with Theo, I'm realizing just how strong the pull towards him really is. Yesterday, every time I looked at him, I couldn't stop myself from tracing every detail of his face — the soft spattering of freckles across his nose and cheeks, the way his eyes soften when he listens, and the quiet intensity behind his gaze. I didn't realize how much I missed simply looking at him. While there's an emotional connection and understanding forming between us, I'm also realizing that I'm physically attracted to him. The feelings are deeper than I expected, and I don't know what to do with them.

"Fuck," I mutter as I rub a hand over my face, then grab my coffee from the machine. Seriously, what the fuck? At twenty-nine, I'm suddenly into guys? And a straight one at that, since he's apparently got a thing going on with the waitress at the pub. I guess I need to fuck up everyone's life, don't I...

As I sip my coffee, trying to clear my mind, I watch Miss Bobber bat her toy around the kitchen, her playfulness a welcome distraction. But still, a restlessness stirs inside me. My eyes wander around the room, searching for something to ground this unsettled energy, until they land on the nearly empty container of coffee pods on the counter.

And I think of Theo again.

"Argh." I run my fingers through my hair and head into my bedroom to change. Fuck it. If I'm going to be thinking about him, I might as well do it on a walk to get out of the house and pick up more coffee pods.

He'll need them for tomorrow.

Miss Bobber watches me curiously as I slip my shoes and a hoodie on, and I furrow my brow at her.

"Don't judge me," I mumble, then bend down to pat her. "I'll be back soon."

It's a nice day, and after spending weeks out on the rig, it feels good to get outside and take my time as I walk along the main street. The sun feels warm on my face, and I take a deep breath of the fresh spring air as I watch the seagulls floating on the sparkling ocean. The town is quiet mid-afternoon, and I don't run into anyone until I near the general store.

"Well, well, welcome back!"

I look up at the front porch of the store to see Jimmy with a bright smile, sitting with a few other men.

"Hey," I reply, managing a small smile as I climb the steps. It's the MacKinnon's store, so I'm not sure why I'm feeling anxious or surprised to see Theo's grandfather. Obviously his family are going to be here.

"How was the rig?" Jimmy asks, gesturing to a vacant seat beside him.

I hesitate for a moment before I sit and give him and the other men another awkward smile. "It was good. Not that different from the oil sands, just... with water."

The men laugh, and one of them leans forward. "Underwater welding?"

"Yeah," I nod.

"What's the weather like out there?" the man sitting across from Jimmy asks, setting his empty coffee mug down on the table between them. "Jimmy says you're in the Gulf of Mexico?"

My eyes snap to Jimmy, and he smiles warmly at me. He told them about me? Why?

"Uh..." I shift in my seat, unable to decipher exactly how I feel about that. "It's hot, and really humid. And we get a lot of wind."

"Hey, Liam!" The door to the store opens, and Heather comes out with a big smile and passes me a mug of coffee. "Happy to have you back. Do you take anything in your coffee? I can get you cream, milk, sugar...?"

I shake my head, glancing down at the coffee in my hands. "Um, no, thank you. This is fine," I say, looking up at her. "Thanks."

She squeezes my shoulder and smiles, then glances around at the other men. "The rest of you can get your own."

They all chuckle as she heads back inside, and Jimmy huffs out a laugh. "Enjoy the hospitality while you can, Liam. It doesn't last long with that one."

I let out a light laugh and take a sip of my coffee, glancing out at the water as some fishing boats make their way into the marina.

"Theo's already in," Jimmy says, watching the water as well. "Pretty early for them."

My heart flips at the sound of that, remembering how early he was in yesterday too. And even though I enjoyed having him around yesterday, I worry if him coming in early again means the catch wasn't great, something went wrong, or if they just made good time.

I just nod, keeping my eyes on one of the boats.

"So, Liam," one of the men says, drawing my attention to him. "What kind of certifications do you need to work offshore?"

The man is watching me intently, like he is genuinely curious, and I can't help but smile.

"Quite a few," I say. "I already had all the welding certificates needed to work in oil and gas, and my diving and underwater welding certificate. But I had to do a lot of safety and rope access courses for offshore."

The man lifts his eyebrows with a nod. "Hard worker."

I huff out a laugh, looking down at my coffee. "It's not too bad."

Then a black truck pulls up in front of the store, and my heart rate quickens.

Theo hops out and jogs up the steps, then stops in surprise when he sees me. "Oh, hey."

"Hey," I say, giving him a soft smile as I take in his wild hair and dirty grey hoodie.

"I was just going to grab coffee for home," he says, stepping closer and nodding a greeting to the men.

I chuckle. "Same."

He smiles, sitting in the chair across from me. "So, you a part of the old man crew now?"

"Oh, shut your trap," Jimmy says with a laugh. "You'll be here someday, and you won't like that name so much."

Theo's smile briefly falters as he shifts in his seat, but his attention is then quickly pulled to one of the other men.

"How was the catch today?" the man asks.

Theo nods, leaning back in his chair. "Nothing to complain about," he says.

"We got some nasty weather coming in this evening," Jimmy says. "High wind and heavy rain."

"Yeah, I know," Theo says, blowing out a breath and running his hand through his hair. "We got the boat tied in in case it's bad. Looks like it might go into the morning." He then checks his watch and sighs again. "Well, I should get up to the Murphy's and finish their fence."

Jimmy laughs and shakes his head. "And why would you do something as foolish as that?"

Theo shoots him a look. "Foolish as what? My job?"

"Work on a fence before a rain and wind storm? Let the storm do what it's going to do and then finish the job in one go."

My eyes slide to Theo, as he nods thoughtfully. "Yeah... I guess."

Jimmy smiles, a bit smugly for having told his grandson what to do. "It's the calm before the storm. Enjoy the nice day and live a little. And stop leaving Liam alone in that house until the sun goes down."

Theo slides his gaze to me and a small smile tugs at his lips. "I mean, unless you want some private ping-pong practice time?"

A laugh escapes me as I shake my head. "Why, so you can get some private fishing practice in?"

His eyes light up with challenge as he stands and points at me. "Alright, it's on. Fishing rematch. Let's go."

The sound of the water lapping against the boat is soothing as I sit back in my seat, and we quietly wait for the fish to bite. We each caught one mackerel already, and I can't help but smile at the intensity in Theo's gaze as he guides his lure through the water, determined to catch more than me this time.

Too bad that won't be happening.

I glance at the trees around us in the same spot Theo brought us to last time. Even though it's starting to cloud over as the storm begins to roll in, it's still so peaceful out here.

"Motherfucker," Theo mumbles as he jerks the rod back. "Had a bite and lost it."

I chuckle, casting a sideways glance at him. "Mm hm."

He rolls his eyes at me, but I see the smile peeking through.

We sit in silence for a bit longer, slowly trolling along the channel while we wait for another bite. But the longer we sit here, that pull I feel towards Theo grows stronger.

"So, what do you want to do with your sunroom?" I ask, keeping my eyes on the water, trying to once again get my mind off my apparent attraction to him.

I hear him blow out a breath. "I'm not sure. I've been so focused on the kitchen I haven't thought much about the rest of the house."

I just nod, giving the rod a little nudge to keep the lure moving.

"What do you think?" he asks.

I turn my head to look at him as he gazes back at me. "It doesn't matter what I think. It's your house."

His brow furrows as he keeps his eyes locked on mine. "It matters to me. You live there too."

My heart skips a beat, but I swallow hard and quickly look away. "Yeah, but... I won't be living there forever. Eventually, you'll want your own space. Especially if you want to start a family someday."

Theo falls silent, and I glance back at him. He's looking down at the boat floor, but when he meets my eyes again, there's something in his expression I can't quite figure out.

"I don't think that will happen," he says, shifting his gaze out over the water.

I watch him for a moment longer, unsure what that means. There seems to be a shift in him, and I can't help but worry I've said something wrong. But also, it's true. I won't be living here, in his house, forever. I'm slowly coming to terms with the fact I have feelings for him, but from everything I know about Theo, he's straight. And while I try to figure out this mess in my head, the last thing I want to do is get in the way of him building the life he wants.

"Why not?" I ask quietly, the words slipping out before I can catch them.

Theo's gaze flicks towards me, but he quickly looks away as his posture tightens, almost like he's bracing for something. His fingers fidget, and his jaw clenches. But it's not frustration or anger that crosses his face… he looks sad.

"I'll never be able to find what I'm looking for here," he says, his voice heavy with quiet resignation.

My pulse quickens as a flutter builds in my stomach. A strange mix of curiosity and courage stirs inside me, pulling me closer to the question that's now burning in my mind.

"What is it you're looking for?" I ask, once again unable to stop myself.

Theo exhales, his breath slow and deliberate, before he cautiously turns to face me. His brown eyes lock onto mine, and it looks like he's trying to hold something back. But I hold his gaze, and the tension in his expression gradually fades. His eyes soften, and something between us shifts as an unspoken energy seems to take over.

But just as his lips part, raindrops start to fall.

Theo pulls his bottom lip between his teeth and glances up at the sky. "Should I put the cover up?"

He doesn't meet my eyes again, almost as if he's relieved by the interruption, which only fuels my curiosity. What was he about to say? Questions swirl in my mind, and a hopeful feeling flutters in my stomach as I wonder if whatever he's holding back might be something I've been quietly wishing for.

But as the rain starts coming down harder, drumming against the water around us, I shake my head. "We should probably just go back in."

Theo nods, casting a hesitant glance my way. And I think I

see disappointment in his eyes. But I'm not sure if that's because we didn't get to finish fishing... or because he didn't get to say what he wanted to.

And as we put away our fishing rods and Theo brings us back to shore, the unspoken disappointment lingers in the air between us.

By the time we pull up to the dock, the rain is pelting down in thick sheets, and the wind has picked up, whipping across the water to rock the boat beneath us. I hop out onto the dock as Theo tosses me the rope to tie us off and he shuts off the motor. I tie the boat snug against the dock as Theo secures everything on board, and the water grows rougher as the rain completely soaks through our clothes.

When Theo moves to step onto the dock, the boat lurches with a wave, causing him to stumble. I quickly reach out to grab his arm as he works to catch his footing, and I pull him onto the dock. But even when he's safely standing before me, I don't let go.

That same quiet energy from earlier hums between us, stronger this time. He stands before me, the wind whipping around us and the rain pounding against the dock as my hand remains on his arm. And all I can feel is the warmth of him under my fingertips, despite the cold.

Our eyes are once again locked, and as I search his, the questions continue to swirl in my mind. I don't even know what I'm asking... but I'm hoping for an answer.

And the next thing I know, our lips meet.

An electric tingle races up my spine as my heart pounds wildly, my breath catching in my throat the moment his soft, rain-soaked lips meet mine. I don't even know who moved first, who crossed that final inch between us... but it doesn't matter. My fingers tighten around his arm as my lips part, and the taste of rain mingles with something unmistakably him. He steps forward, closing the small distance between us, and my heart thumps even faster. And when I feel his tongue against mine, and his rough stubble scraping my skin, a heat rushes through my body that has me feeling confused, yet so good.

Until Theo suddenly pulls back, eyes wide with panic.

Well, fuck.

SEVENTEEN

THEO

LIAM'S EYES flick between mine, reflecting the same panic I feel as my chest tightens.

Fuck. What have I done...

I just ruined everything.

"Sorry," I breathe out, my voice barely cutting through the pounding rain.

Shame quickly rises and takes over as I turn away from him. But the anger I feel towards myself for doing that to him is even greater. My heart races as I head towards the house, rain pelting down on me with every hurried step. I know I'm eventually going to have to deal with what I just did, but right now, I can't.

I can't believe I just fucked everything up by kissing him.

I reach the door to the house and hear Liam's footsteps crunching on the gravel behind me. But I quickly kick my wet boots off in the entryway and rush inside, desperate to get upstairs so I can try to calm the fuck down and sort my shit out.

Fuck, fuck, fuck.

"Theo," Liam's voice calls out, but I don't stop. Which I'm sure makes me an asshole, but I'd say I'm already there.

"Theo." Liam's voice is closer this time, his footsteps quickly approaching me as I make it to the bottom of the stairs.

Just as I take the first step, his hand lands on my arm to stop me.

"Just... wait," he pleads, his voice tight with emotion.

I pause on the stairs as he keeps my arm in his grip. But I can't bring myself to look at him.

"I'm sorry," he says softly.

My brow furrows, and I turn to face him. Liam's eyes are wide as he looks up at me with an expression that looks like... guilt?

"I shouldn't have done that," he says, a slight shake to his voice. "I'm sorry."

What the fuck?

"*You're* sorry?" I ask, my heart thumping wildly.

He nods as he drops his hand from my arm and takes a step backwards. "Yeah. I don't know what I was thinking. I just... I don't know..." he trails off as he runs a hand through his wet hair and his eyes dart away from me.

I step down off the stairs to stand before him, my head spinning as I try to piece together what the hell is happening.

"You wanted that?" I ask, trying to add strength to my voice as doubt lingers.

His eyes meet mine, and I search his face as I wait for confirmation that this is real, and this is really happening.

Then he nods slowly. "Yeah."

We stand silently before each other as the rain beats against the window, and an intense energy hums between us. My heart races as I stare at him, and I'm unable to catch up with my thoughts to form any words.

Liam shifts uncomfortably and looks down. "I really didn't mean—"

"I did too."

His head snaps up and his eyes widen as they search mine. We stand before each other, dripping wet from the rain and staring into each other's eyes as something shifts between us.

I wanted it… and he did too.

It's real.

His blue eyes shine in the dim light of the hallway, piercing through the shadows. And the longer I hold his gaze, the more my courage swells. I'm not alone in this feeling, and he's not running away from me.

"I've been wanting that for a while," I say, my words coming easier now despite the way my heart is rioting and my hands are shaking.

Surprise flickers across Liam's face before his throat bobs, and he nods softly. "Same."

I step closer, and Liam's chest rises and falls with a deep breath. But his eyes stay glued on mine, and I see the same anticipation in him that I'm feeling. The second his hand finds my hip, I press my lips to his. And this time, I let myself *feel* it. No hesitation, no doubt, no worry. Just the undeniable pull between us that has been simmering beneath the surface, waiting for this moment.

My hand lifts to cup the side of his face as our lips part, and my tongue glides against his. His grip on my hip tightens as our kiss deepens, and every one of my senses is overwhelmed by him. The scent of the rain clinging to his skin, the feeling of his hard muscles under my hands, the contrast of his soft lips and the roughness of his stubble… I can't get enough. And as his hands slide up my sides, pulling me closer, it feels like he can't either.

The fear and doubt inside me melts away with every stroke

of his tongue against mine, every pull that brings me closer, and every touch of his hands on my skin. For the first time ever, I feel like I am exactly who I'm supposed to be. No hiding, no pretending, and no holding back. This feels right, in a way that nothing ever has.

Eventually, our kiss slows and we gently pull back from each other, remaining close as we catch our breath.

"Now what?" Liam asks, his breath on my lips with each word.

I exhale deeply and slowly shake my head. "I have no idea."

A soft meow sounds, and we both look down at Miss Bobber sitting at our feet with her tail curled around her. She watches us expectantly, like she's also curious about what happens next.

"Maybe some dry clothes..." Liam says, his gaze lifting to meet mine again.

"Yeah," I murmur with a nod.

As his hands fall away from me, I immediately miss the feeling of him, and nerves start to rise once more. But a small, reassuring smile from him calms any fears I may have, that this is all going to come crashing down around me.

He wants this.

Liam heads into his room to change, and I go upstairs to do the same with thoughts and questions endlessly swirling in my head.

How long has he felt this way? Have I been so in my own head that I couldn't see it? Is this fucking *real*?

What does this mean for us now?

I pull on a t-shirt and sweatpants, forcing a deep breath and trying my best to push all those thoughts and questions aside for now.

He *wants* this.

The welcoming smell of burning wood fills the air as I head

down the stairs. Liam looks up from the wood stove as I enter the living room, and he adds another log of wood before closing the door. Miss Bobber scurries across the floor as she chases a stray piece of bark, and Liam pushes to his feet.

For a moment, we just stand here looking at each other as the soft crackle of the fire and the rain against the windows fills the quiet space between us.

"Hungry?" I ask, breaking the silence.

Liam nods. "Yeah."

He follows as I head into the kitchen, and although there is a new awkwardness between us, it's not uncomfortable. The quiet comfort remains, lingering despite everything else changing. The silence is just a part of who we are, and the questions that hang in the air between us aren't urgent or heavy. They're patiently waiting for their time as this shift between us settles, and we allow ourselves to take our time with it.

I glance out the window at the boat rocking in the waves at the dock and chuckle, remembering the fish we caught that are still in the livewell. "Could have cooked our fish."

Liam leans against the counter and crosses his arms with a chuckle of his own. "All that work for nothing."

I cock an eyebrow at him. "All that work? It was so hard to catch *one* fish this time, huh?"

The corner of his lips tilt up as he shakes his head. "Remind me, how many did you catch?"

Just as I open my mouth to fire back, because I *know* I would have caught more than him this time, the lights suddenly cut out. The room falls into shadows, dimly lit from the fading evening outside, and just enough for me to make out Liam's features. The soft glow from the fire in the living room casts a quiet mood over us once again, as the world outside rages against the calm inside.

"So... sandwiches?" I ask with a shrug.

Liam laughs softly. "Looks like it."

The quiet between us lingers as we make some sandwiches, the soft sounds of slicing bread and rustling wrappers filling the space. I grab a couple beer from the fridge, and we settle on the floor in front of the fire, pulling cushions from the couch to sit on.

The flames cast the room in a soft, golden glow, and as we sit here and quietly eat, calm washes over me. The warmth from the fire seeps into my bones as I settle further back on the cushions, and Miss Bobber plays among the pillows and blankets.

Once we've finished eating, I add another log to the fire, watching the flames twist and grow as warmth spreads through the room. I take a long drink of my beer as I let the courage build inside me.

"So..." I start, picking at the label on my beer bottle. "Are you..." I trail off, not quite sure how to ask the question I'm dying to know.

Liam turns his head to look at me. "Into guys?" he finishes for me.

I nod, swallowing hard as I meet his eyes.

He holds my gaze as the reflection of the flames dance in his eyes, and everything seems to slow. Then he shakes his head softly, almost hesitantly. "I don't know... I never have been."

My heart skips a beat with both hope and uncertainty as I consider what that means.

"Are you?" he asks quietly.

I pause, keeping my eyes on his and forcing myself not to look away and hide again. I finally let that part of me out, and I'm surprised by how much I want it to stay.

And the longer I look into his eyes, I swear I see hope.

I nod. "Yeah," I say, my voice barely above a whisper.

He nods as well, his eyes flicking between mine as a question brews behind them. "Why did you run?"

I release a breath and drop my gaze from his, bringing my attention to the fire. "Valid question," I murmur, then take a drink of my beer as I think about how to answer that.

Liam just waits, his presence quiet and steady as I gather my thoughts.

"I thought I crossed a line with you," I say. "I think I've known for a while that... that I'm gay." Those words hang in the air as I shift against the cushions, pushing my fingers into Miss Bobber's fur as she stretches out between us. My heart races as I say this all out loud for the first time, and even though it's unnerving, a heavy weight lifts. "I've never done that before. With a guy. And I thought you'd freak out." I huff out a light laugh. "Instead, I did."

Liam chuckles lightly. "Don't worry. I did too."

I turn to look at him, but I'm surprised to find his eyes soft and encouraging.

"But not because of you," he says gently.

"So, you've never been with a guy?" I ask, my brow furrowing a bit as I try to make sense of all of this.

He shakes his head. "No."

Silence settles between us for a moment as rain pelts the window, and Liam sighs.

"I've been asking myself all these questions," he says, looking down at Miss Bobber. "How, why... and I don't know. All I do know is that something has been drawing me to you. And out on the dock, it just finally took over and I couldn't stop it."

I huff out a laugh and Liam looks up at me with a confused expression.

"Pretty sure I kissed you," I point out.

His brows draw together, and he slowly shakes his head. "I don't think so."

A smile tugs at the corner of my lips, and his eyes soften with a smile as well. Even though we may not even know, or agree on who started it... it doesn't matter. What does matter is that we're both here and having this conversation now. Because it could have been a very different one... a devastating one.

"So, Allison...?" Liam gives me a cautious look.

I nod with a sigh. "Yeah. We dated for about six months." I turn to look into the flames again. "She lives a couple towns over, and we met when she started working at the pub. It just felt like what I was supposed to do. But I didn't understand why I was always holding back, and why I always felt like I was forcing myself just to be present with her. Eventually, we both realized we were better off as friends. I feel bad, because she really is great, but... there was nothing there." I swallow, picking at the label of my beer bottle again. "There's no way there could have been."

Liam is quiet for a moment as I keep my eyes on the fire.

"And you've never explored these feelings with another guy before?" he asks.

"You're the first..." I say, hesitantly shifting my eyes to meet his again. But the softness in his eyes immediately puts me at ease. "I don't think I really knew, or understood, what all those confusing thoughts and feelings were," I continue. "And when they started to make a bit more sense, the fear grew."

Liam's brows draw together as he listens, and I see the question in his eyes.

"Torrin Cove is too small," I say with an exhale and a shake of my head. "Everyone is up in everyone's business, and my family relies on the support from this town. I can't fuck that up for them."

His expression shifts, the confusion melting away as understanding settles. "Not as much choice as you'd like," he murmurs, echoing the words from my text, when we talked about having choices in our lives.

The fire crackles softly as I stare back at him, and just nod. "Yeah."

We both bring our attention back to the fire, the quiet settling over us once again as the heaviness of my reality hangs in the air. Until Liam breaks the silence.

"I've always kept people out," he says in a quiet voice, almost hesitant.

I glance over at him, but he's still staring into the fire, his gaze distant.

"Even in relationships... not that there have been many," he continues, his fingers tracing the edge of his beer bottle. "I don't know what it is, but I think it might be fear. Maybe fear of letting people really see me, opening myself up to potential hurt, or maybe because I shared *everything* with my family and my best friend, and I was afraid of that changing." His jaw tightens as the firelight flickers across his face. "But then I lost them anyway."

My heart sinks at the pain lacing his words, and the silence that follows feels even heavier.

Then he turns to look at me, a vulnerability in his gaze. "And even with the fear and hurt... I want to let you in."

My heart thumps as I look into his eyes, and those words hit me somewhere deep. "Same."

We stare at each other as the firelight flickers between us and an intense need inside me grows. And before I know it, I'm leaning into him and our lips meet. Every unspoken word is shared as our tongues push past our lips and hands roam, the energy between us seeming to crackle in time with the roaring fire. There's an understanding between us that I've never experienced before, and I don't think this is something I could find with just anyone. We're both broken in our own ways, but we're also slowly helping each other piece it all back together.

Our beer bottles clink as we set them aside, and our kiss deepens with a growing urgency, becoming something that speaks of shared fears and trust. Something neither of us fully understands yet, but that we both want to explore.

Miss Bobber scurries out from between us before she gets squished, her little paws crawling over our legs instead as we move closer and chuckle against each other's mouths. But our lips stay locked, and hands continue to roam.

Liam slides his hand up my chest, wrapping his fingers around the back of my neck as the heat between us continues to build. I give him everything as I let my hand slide down his side, feeling the hard lines of his abs, and I find myself eager to give him even more of me. More of what I've been holding back on for my entire life.

Because right now with him... I finally feel *free.*

Eventually, we pull back, breathless and reluctant to let go as we sink into the cushions together. He stays close as I breathe him in and listen to the rain beat against the windows and the crackles from the fire fill the room.

I close my eyes as I feel his breath on my shoulder, and an unfamiliar, yet welcome, easy feeling settles inside me. The storm may be raging outside, but inside, the chaos I've carried for so long has finally faded away.

And it feels *good.*

EIGHTEEN

LIAM

MY EYES open to the sound of Theo's voice, and I slowly take in the dark living room. The fire in the wood stove has burned low, reduced to a faint glow of embers, and Miss Bobber is curled up on Theo's empty pillow beside me.

"Not this morning," Theo says, his voice drifting in from the kitchen.

A chill settles over me as I sit up, looking around at the nest of cushions and blankets on the floor where we fell asleep. The wind and rain is still going strong, creating a gloomy atmosphere outside with the predawn light just starting to peek through the darkness.

"Ok, see you Monday," Theo murmurs, lowering his phone from his ear. I can just make out his silhouette, shadowed and blurred by the darkness. But I can read the frustration on him.

He looks up and catches my gaze.

"Sorry," he says, setting his phone on the counter and rubbing a hand over his face.

"No work?" I ask, pushing to my feet to grab a log for the fire.

He shakes his head. "No," he says, voice tight and sounding frustrated as he walks back into the living room.

I glance at the window, watching the rain stream down the glass. "Seems like a good thing."

Theo sighs, sinking into the couch while I settle back onto the floor. Miss Bobber lifts her head to eye us both before stretching out again on Theo's pillow with a satisfied sigh.

"To not go out in this, yeah," he says, watching the fire grow as it casts a warm light over his face. "I'd never take my crew out in this weather."

"So what's the problem?" I ask, taking in the tension etched into his features.

He shakes his head with a sigh. "Tomorrow is Sunday, so no fishing. Traps are probably full now, so we'll miss a haul, and the catches have been good. And it just sucks when my crew misses a day's pay."

I observe him as he gets lost to his head for a moment... always thinking of others.

"This storm came at the worst fucking time too," he continues, frustration building in his voice. "I have so many jobs I need to finish. I'm falling behind, and now everything is going to be pushed back while people are left waiting even longer. If the power comes back on this morning, I can at least get some work done in the shop. But most of my jobs are—"

Suddenly I reach out my hand, letting it rest just above his knee. Theo falls silent, his eyes dropping to my hand on him before lifting to meet mine.

Silence stretches out between us, the fire softly crackling as my gaze falls to his lips. The memories of last night flood my mind as I think of the way his mouth felt on mine, and how we shut out the world around us for those quiet, focused moments.

And I want that again.

I want to pull him out of his head, just like he does for me.

And I want to make him feel good. I want to touch him, hold him, and stay in this moment we created for ourselves, away from the stress, anxiety, and fear. The questions I've had about my apparent feelings towards Theo are slowly making more sense the longer we stay here, and now... I feel an intense urge to find the answer to another one.

I tug at his leg, and the corner of his lips twitch as he slides off the couch onto the floor with me.

"Would it really be so bad if you took a morning off?" I ask, looking into his eyes.

The corner of his eyes crinkle as he smiles, and I find myself tracing the freckles on his nose as they're illuminated by the soft glow of the fire.

"I guess not," he murmurs, his voice low as he leans in closer.

My lips press against his, and my heart stumbles at the feel of him against me. I move with him as he sinks back against the cushions and my tongue slips past his lips. And when his hands trail up my back to pull me even closer, I give in to him completely. We stay locked in a heated kiss as I take in everything about him, and I allow myself to feel the unexpected comfort and ease in his touch. With every brush of his hand against my skin and every sweep of his tongue against mine, I find myself wanting more. And before long, I feel myself hardening in my sweatpants.

The feeling of being turned on by a guy is still a foreign one, but something about being here with Theo just feels right. I'm surprised at my lack of hesitation when I pull his hips into mine as he rolls into me, and at the desperate way I want to take more from him.

But when I feel his hard cock pressed against mine, I'm suddenly very aware that I have no idea what I'm actually doing, no matter how much I want it.

He's hard for me, I'm hard for him, and I've never touched a dick that wasn't my own.

But I want to make him feel good, and I want to explore this with him.

I just hope I don't fuck it up.

My heart thunders as I trail my lips down his neck and slide my hand under his shirt, feeling the muscles of his abs. My breath catches in my chest as I bring my hand higher over his pecs, the hard lines a complete contrast to everything I'm used to. I can feel his heart racing, and his breath quickens as I bring my lips back up to his, grabbing the hem of his shirt and pulling it up, urging him to remove it.

Theo pushes me back so he can sit up, removing his shirt in one swift motion and tossing it aside. My eyes trail over his arms and chest, and I swallow hard as I take him in. The firelight dances over his muscular torso, and I reach out to lightly trace my fingers over the soft freckles splashed over his shoulders.

When my eyes lift to meet his, my emotions reflect back at me. Heat, need, and hunger... but also uncertainty and hesitation. Neither of us have been here before, and for a moment we just stare into each other's eyes, silently waiting for the next move.

The look in his eyes urges me to drop my hands to the hem of my t-shirt and pull it off. Theo's eyes immediately drop to roam over my bare chest, and he takes a deep breath.

"Fuck," he breathes.

Our lips meet again, and as his hands run over my chest, he moans softly against my lips. He lowers his head to press his lips against my chest, and a groan escapes me as I sink my fingers into his thick, wild hair, and grow impossibly harder.

Fuck... I want this. I need this.

I push him back against the cushions again and lie beside

him as I push my tongue past his lips, tasting him and feeling his muscles under my touch. My hand slowly runs up his arm and down his chest and abs, as his finds the back of my head and tangles in my hair. My heart riots as my fingers reach the waistband of his sweatpants, and I pause. But only for a moment.

Theo's breath catches and he exhales against my lips as I push my hand into his sweatpants and boxers, my fingertips grazing the head of his hard cock. But then he grips my hair tight and forcefully shoves his tongue into my mouth, giving me the permission I need to go for it.

I wrap my hand around his cock and slowly move it up and down his length. He moans softly against my mouth, urging me to do it again.

"Fuck," he breathes, and my cock is now so hard it almost fucking hurts.

I continue to slide my hand up and down his dick as I kiss down his neck, his moans and heavy breathing competing with the sound of the wind and rain outside. I'm completely lost to everything Theo as I feel his rough stubble against my lips when I kiss his jaw, his fingers gripping my hair, and the sound of his groans as I stroke him. Until his hand drops to push his sweatpants down over his hips to free his cock, and my eyes lock onto the sight of my hand wrapped around him.

Holy fucking shit.

The sight somehow makes this feel even more real, and my stomach flips as I watch my hand slowly stroke his dick. The soft glow from the fire illuminates his muscles as shadows dance along his body, and I'm absolutely mesmerized by him.

My lips fall to his again as I increase my pace on his cock, and he holds me tighter against him. He slowly unravels under my touch, groaning and panting as I work him. The sounds he's making are driving me fucking wild, and the way he grabs at me and writhes as he rides closer to the edge urges me to give him even more.

His fingers dig hard into my shoulder as he pushes me back from his lips. "I'm going to come," he pants, and excitement stirs inside me.

I nod, brushing my lips over his. "Come."

His fingers pull my hair tight as my lips meet his again, and his hips jerk as I stroke him faster. He lets out a low groan as he presses his forehead to mine, and his entire body tenses.

I look down to watch him come, my cock twitching with need as he shoots cum over his abs. "Fuck," I breathe out.

Theo pants and groans through his release, and the second he's finished, he rolls me onto my back and devours me in an intense kiss. His sticky abs press against mine and my hands land on his ass to pull him closer to me, needing everything I can get. The more he gives me, the more I take, and everything else has completely faded away. The why and how of this whole thing are distant thoughts as I hold him against me, and the only thing that matters is just this, right here.

Just Theo.

Eventually he sits up, pushing himself back onto his knees between my legs. He looks down at me like I'm a meal he wants to devour, pulling his bottom lip between his teeth as he runs his hand up my thigh, and over my rock-hard cock in my sweatpants.

A groan escapes me at the feeling, but that's not the only thing that feels good. Watching him right now, I feel like I'm really *seeing* him. He's hidden himself away for so long, closed off to even himself for fear of what his true self would mean for him and his family... but here, with me, he can finally be himself. And watching him take in this moment, and feel the way he's been wanting to for so long... I'm thankful I can give that to him.

His eyes lift to meet mine as his fingers hook the waistband of my sweatpants and I give him a playful smirk to urge him on.

"Let's see if you're better at this than fishing," I say, giving him the encouragement he needs to take everything he wants.

His eyes flare as his grip on my waistband tightens, then he pulls my pants and boxers down to free my cock. His throat bobs as he looks down at me, and his chest rises and falls with a deep breath. But the fire is in him now, and even though he seems a bit nervous, he goes for it and wraps his hand around my cock.

I let out a soft moan of approval, and his eyes flick back up to mine. He slowly strokes me as he watches me, looking into my eyes with an intense heat. The roughness of his hand feels so fucking good on my cock, and as he increases his pace and pressure, I can't help but close my eyes and groan, letting the pleasure take over.

Until he removes his hand and leans over me, pressing his lips to mine in a soft kiss.

My hand lands on the back of his head to keep him here for a moment. As much as my cock is aching for his touch again, his soft lips taste so fucking good, I can't let go quite yet.

But his lips then drift from mine to kiss along my jaw and down my neck. My fingers slide into his hair as he continues to kiss further down my chest, and my heart thunders as he reaches my abs.

His eyes flick up to mine as he presses his lips to my lower stomach, and a question swirls in the depths of them. Like he's checking in to see if I want this, if I like it... And my answer to all of his questions is yes.

So I just nod, and press my hand to his shoulder, pushing him down.

He smirks up at me, challenge igniting once again in his gaze, and I can't help but let out a light chuckle.

Until he wraps his lips around the head of my cock.

"Oh, fuck," I groan at the warm, wet sensation of his mouth, and watch him slowly slide his mouth down my cock and back up.

He looks up at me as he takes me in again, and I swallow hard at the sight. My hand grips his shoulder tight as I try to keep my composure and not bust right here and now.

Any uncertainty in his eyes is quickly replaced with hunger as I moan and move my hand from his shoulder to his hair. "Fuck yeah," I pant.

I'm unable to keep my eyes off him as he grips my cock with one hand, sliding it up and down my length in time with his mouth. He licks and sucks me, and the feeling of his soft moan around my dick almost sends me over the edge. Watching him go all in, and completely let go, feels almost as good as what he's doing to me.

It doesn't take long for the pressure to build within me, and I'm quickly moving closer and closer to my release. When I can't hold back any longer, I tug at his hair to lift his head off my cock and pull him up to me. I shove my tongue into his mouth, tasting me on him as he adjusts himself over me to bring his hand back to my cock. He strokes me with need as we fall into a messy kiss, and within seconds, I'm coming with a grunt.

"Oh my god," I groan as he jerks me through my release, cum coating my abs.

Eventually I release my grip on him, and he removes his hand from my cock as he falls onto his back beside me.

"Fuck," I pant, my breaths heavy as I come down from a pretty fucking intense high.

"Yeah," he says with a light chuckle.

We lie here in silence for a few moments, staring up at the

ceiling, naked and covered in cum, listening to the rain and wind outside, and the warm crackling fire inside.

"Maybe we're tied now," I say, breaking the silence.

He turns his head to look at me. "What?"

I roll my head to meet his gaze with a soft smirk. "I'm clearly the better fisherman. But you... you can suck cock really well."

Theo huffs with a smile, shaking his head as he turns to look up at the ceiling again. "I'll still be catching more fish than you next time."

I smile, my eyes tracing the outline of his face in the dim firelight. "Does that mean I need to suck your cock?"

He turns to me again, eyes sparkling. "If you think you can rise to the challenge, I wouldn't complain."

I chuckle, and we both fall into comfortable silence once again as we watch the fire and listen to the rain.

"She slept through that whole thing," Theo says.

We both turn to look at Miss Bobber, sound asleep on the pillow beside me.

I huff out a laugh, lifting my hand to rub a finger over her little paw. "Thank god."

NINETEEN

THEO

THE SMELL of coffee greets me as I descend the stairs and pull a clean shirt over my head. The power is still out, so I had to clean off the evidence of mine and Liam's morning with a cold shower, shivering through every second. We set a pot of water on the wood stove to boil for coffee, and it smells like Liam's already got it brewing.

I enter the living room and see Liam standing by the glass door to the front deck, staring out at the rain falling in relentless sheets, and the gloomy, oppressive grey clouds that hang low over the angry ocean. The muted morning light barely touches his face, but I can tell he's miles away and lost to his thoughts. The raging storm outside seems to mirror something inside him, and he looks weighed down by something heavy.

He turns to look at me as I step closer, and he quickly offers me a small smile. But it looks forced.

Panic settles as I take in the drastic shift in him, the Liam standing before me nothing like the one from the cushions in front of the fire just minutes earlier.

"You ok?" I ask hesitantly.

Thoughts and questions swirl in my mind as I look into his eyes, and I try not to give them any attention. But I can't help it. He *told* me he wanted it. But now... maybe he has regrets.

Fuck.

Liam just nods, but nothing about him looks like he's ok. The familiar sadness that's always present in him, the one he managed to escape last night and this morning, is back. And it seems stronger than ever.

I try to swallow down my fear and accept that maybe this was all just too good to be true.

"If you didn't want to do that..." I trail off, my anxiety rising as I replay everything about this morning in my mind, wondering if I somehow forced him into any of it.

But he initiated it.

And he seemed to like it...

I sucked his fucking dick.

Jesus Christ.

His eyes widen and he shakes his head. "No. No, I wanted it." He releases a breath and steps towards me, eyes roaming over my face. "I *do* want it."

Relief washes over me, but it's fleeting. I swallow hard as I look into his eyes, because there's something else deep inside him that seems to be causing him pain. There's a dark cloud hanging over him, and I'm not sure where it came from.

"What's going on?" I ask softly, hoping he'll take the opportunity to share whatever it is that's weighing so heavily on him.

His eyes flicker with uncertainty as they search mine, like he's trying to find the right words. Then he exhales slowly. "How can happiness bring so much guilt?"

My heart sinks, because I know exactly what he means. I've been there too. Those feelings still creep up on me sometimes.

I nod in understanding. "Moving on without someone... it's one of the hardest things you'll ever have to do."

Liam's gaze drops, his jaw tight as he gives a small nod. It looks like he's barely holding it together, and like he wants to let it all out, but doesn't know how.

The rain beats steadily against the glass door overlooking the ocean, filling the silence between us as the dull morning light casts shadows over us.

"Feels like your own storm, doesn't it?" I murmur, breaking the silence.

His eyes lift to meet mine, full of a storm all their own.

"It's like riding a massive wave, at the mercy of angry winds," I say quietly. "You don't know how long you'll stay high, feeling good and happy... until it all crashes down on the other side. And you're drowning again, waiting for something... anything... to pull you back up."

He holds my gaze for a moment until he gives a small nod, a silent acknowledgement that he's been caught in that endless cycle.

I shift my gaze out the window, watching the waves crash against the shore. "Grief is hell," I murmur. "But it passes. It always comes back, usually when you're not ready for it. But each time, its weight feels a little less... because eventually you're able to prepare for it."

When I glance back at him, he's staring out at the ocean too, his profile etched with sadness.

"I don't deserve to pass this storm," he says, so quietly that the sound of the rain almost swallows his words.

His words tear through me and a deep ache settles in my chest. Before I can even process how to respond to that, Liam turns abruptly and heads towards the kitchen.

I follow, reaching out to gently grab his elbow and force him to turn and face me. "What does that mean?" I ask, trying to add strength to my voice.

He shakes his head with a heavy sigh. He avoids my eyes as

he stares past me with a distant look. Then he closes his eyes, rubbing his face with his hand like he's trying to push away the emotions that are threatening to spill over.

"It's ok," I say, letting go of his arm and stepping back slightly to give him the space he seems to need. But I can't shake the urgency building inside me, and the need to know what he meant by that.

He draws in a breath, eyes still glued to the window. "Nick died at work. There was an accident, and... I..." His voice falters, and he shakes his head.

"You were there?" I ask gently.

Liam nods, and the weight of his silence is a heavy one. "We grew up together," he says finally, his voice thick with grief. "We were the same age, and our parents are best friends. He was my brother." He swallows hard, each word a struggle. "We did everything together. We went to welding school, moved to Alberta... we even worked in a lot of the same camps up north."

I watch him, my heart breaking with every word he forces out.

"I haven't been home or talked to my family since his funeral three months ago," he says quietly.

My brow furrows as I think on that for a moment. "Why not?"

Emotions flicker across his face, his eyes still not meeting mine as he shakes his head again. "I just can't do it," he says, his voice hollow like he's trying to detach himself from it all.

I watch him for a moment as his hands fidget, his eyes still refusing to meet mine as the tension in his body grows.

"And now, I just..." He sighs, rubbing his forehead in frustration. "How am I supposed to feel happy, to feel *anything* good, when..." He exhales sharply, cutting himself off and seeming to struggle for words. "Last night... it's the longest I've gone without thinking about him. About what should've happened if..." His jaw clenches, his unfinished thoughts seeming to shift to carry an apparent anger. "I shouldn't be living my life when he's supposed to be here. I'm supposed to be the one..." His voice cracks, and he trails off, overwhelmed by emotions he can't quite put into words.

There seems to be more he wants to say but can't. And I get it. Grief has a way of warping everything and twisting emotions until nothing makes sense. I know that feeling. How the intensity of it builds like an unstoppable wave, crashing over you until you're desperate for any kind of release, even if it's not the healthiest.

When I lost my dad, I bottled it all up and stuffed it down with everything else I didn't want to face, letting it build until I couldn't take it anymore. And the only way I was able to cope was to throw myself into work, burying the pain under endless tasks. I know it's not the best solution... but it's something. It's a way to let the pressure out as I figure out how to carry the grief, pain, and confusion about how I can fit into this life I'm living.

I let out a breath and glance around the room before turning back to him. "I think the sunroom needs new drywall."

His eyes finally meet mine with confusion, but curiosity swirls under the surface.

I walk over to the stack of tools in the kitchen and grab a pry bar. Liam watches me as I move to stand before him again and hold it out.

"I don't know much," I say quietly, "but I do know pain. And you need to let it out."

Liam drops his gaze to the pry bar and reaches out to wrap his hand around it. My eyes fall as well, and I take in the slight scarring on his fingers. My heart skips a beat as I remember him reaching into the fire... and I think what I had suspected is true.

He was hurting himself. He wanted to feel the pain and let it out.

"While I may not have done much with this house... it has been a good outlet." I look up at him again. "I think you need it too."

Liam reaches out with his other hand, grabbing my arm and pulling me into him. His lips meet mine in a soft, yet desperate, kiss. I let him hold me here for as long as he needs, until he slowly releases me with a soft nod.

"Yeah," he says, in almost a whisper.

I pour us some coffee, the comforting scent filling the air as we head into the sunroom. The rain continues to beat steadily against the large windows, creating the perfect backdrop for Liam to release the storm inside him.

We push the couch away from the wall and stand in the middle of the room, staring at our target. It looks like it's been patched and painted so many times that it's barely even drywall anymore. We're quiet as we take it in, and I wait for Liam to make the first move.

Suddenly, he steps forward, swinging the pry bar into the wall with force. It crashes into the wall with a satisfying crack, creating a large hole right in the middle of it. He yanks it out and slams it in again, harder this time, sending pieces of drywall and plaster falling to the floor. Each swing is heavier and more desperate than the last, and I just stand back and watch him, letting him release everything he's been holding onto.

Miss Bobber peeks around the corner to see what the commotion is all about, but quickly scurries away as chunks of drywall come crashing down before her.

Eventually, I step forward, swinging my own pry bar into the wall. And with every piece I rip away, I also release some of the emotions I've kept buried for so long.

The sadness that lingers, always there when I think about my dad and how I'm navigating life without him. This life he created for me, and how I thought he'd be around longer to show me how to live it right. Anger boils over as my thoughts shift to the job he passed down to me... and that this job I love is the same one that took him away. And then frustration simmers underneath it all, because I've also carried a different kind of pain. I've finally figured out who I am, and why I've felt so oppressed and trapped for so long. But outside these walls, I don't know if I can be that person.

Even as I tear them down.

But alongside the sadness and anger, there's something else... something lighter. Because Liam is here with me, behind these broken walls. And with him, I've felt more like myself than I ever have before.

When the last piece of drywall falls to the floor in dusty, crumbled pieces, Liam turns to face me. His ice blue eyes meet mine, and I watch as a single tear streams down his face.

I step towards him, lifting my hand to the side of his face. And as I press my lips to his, I give him a silent promise to help him the best I can.

TWENTY

THEO

ALL I CAN DO IS stare at Liam, asleep beside me, in my bed. The early morning light casts a soft glow on his features as he sleeps peacefully, absent of the usual tension he carries. As I let my eyes trace his face, and I listen to his soft breaths, I can't help but once again replay our conversation from yesterday morning. We didn't talk about it anymore as we worked on the sunroom, instead just falling into a peaceful quiet as we tore out the old drywall and installed new panels I already had in the workshop. His mood lifted as the day went on, but I know he'll continue to carry those feelings for a long time. This is just the beginning for him, and if he wants me to, I'll be here through it all. As long as it takes.

Miss Bobber lets out a soft meow when she notices I'm awake and starts her little journey from her spot at our feet, climbing the hills and valleys created by our bodies under the blankets. Liam stirs as she climbs his legs, and he looks down at her as she makes an adorable leap into the space between us.

His dark hair falls over his face, and I smile as he brushes it aside, revealing his bright eyes in the dim light. He glances at my lips before a small, sleepy smile tugs at his own.

"Your bed is comfier than mine," he mumbles groggily.

I chuckle, running my hand over Miss Bobber's head as she purrs and nuzzles into my palm. "Well, yeah. Why the hell would I take the less comfortable bed?"

He rolls his eyes, letting out a soft huff before turning onto his back to gaze up at the skylight, as the sky slowly brightens with a new day.

We lie here for a bit, Miss Bobber's purrs the only sound filling the space between us as she climbs onto my chest. But my thoughts are stuck on him. Liam Fraser... this random guy I invited into my house just over a month ago. And he's in my bed. Just by coming into my life, he put so much into perspective, and gave me the answers to questions I was too afraid to even ask. And he barely even had to say a word.

Even after everything we've done together over the past two days, I still can't believe this is real.

"Thank you," he says quietly, breaking the silence.

I turn my head to look at him, tracing the lines of his face with my eyes as he continues to look up at the sky. I know he's referring to yesterday, for pulling him out of the spiral he was in. I don't think he's had anyone to do that for him. Until now.

"Anytime," I reply softly.

I let my eyes linger on him for a moment longer, noticing that he does seem lighter today.

Like his storm might be passing.

"What jobs do you have today?" he asks, turning to meet my gaze.

I think for a moment, running through the never-ending list that's been piling up. Now that the rain and wind has passed, my phone will probably be blowing up with calls for help with various tasks. I'd like to get as much done as possible before dinner at Mom's tonight.

I rub a hand over my face. "Probably just working around town on storm cleanup. There are a few elderly people a little ways out of town that I like to check in on after bad weather. Make sure their yards are clear and that everything's alright."

A soft smile spreads across Liam's face, his eyes warm as they meet mine. "I'll help."

I chuckle with a smile of my own. "You want to work on your time off?"

He lets out a quiet laugh, turning back to gaze up at the skylight. "I've been working on your house pretty much every day, and you're more than capable. Better use of my time to help someone who isn't just trying to get free work from a roommate."

I laugh, jostling Miss Bobber where she lies on my chest. "Asshole."

He turns back to me with a smile. But it slowly fades as he looks into my eyes, and the sparkle in his is replaced with desperation. "But... it's an outlet," he says quietly.

I nod, lifting my hand to run my fingers along his jaw. "Let's go to work then."

I pull into Mom's driveway just as Mason comes around the corner of the house, dragging a large bucket with a rope slung over his shoulder, heading towards the tree in the front yard.

"What..." Liam starts, watching Mason as he surveys the tree before him.

I put the truck in park and shake my head. "Who knows."

As we climb out of my truck, Mason immediately drops the bucket and rope, grabs a toy truck, and runs over to us with wide eyes and excitement. "Liam! You work on a metal island?? Does it sink? Do you sleep underwater?"

I wince, glancing at Liam, who looks at me with amused confusion.

"I did my best to explain the rig to him, but..." I shrug. He's five with a wild imagination and a short attention span. I did the best I could.

Liam chuckles and turns back to Mason. "It's held up over the water by big poles that go all the way into the ocean floor."

Mason's eyes widen even more as he processes this, and I can almost hear the gears turning in his head. He looks like he's on the verge of a mental overload.

"So... how do they get the poles out there? Does the metal island float all the way to the middle of the ocean? Does a submarine carry it? Or does a plane bring it there? How deep is the ocean?"

Liam and I share a glance, and I wonder how deep we should try to go into this explanation. I gesture for Liam to take the lead, and he rolls his eyes at me with a smirk.

"Those are good questions," Liam says, nodding at Mason. "I'll ask, and let you know."

Mason nods in approval, then proudly holds up his toy truck, filled with dirt. And probably worms. "I got bait, Uncle Theo."

I bite back a laugh and nod. "Awesome, bud. Keep up the good work."

"Oh, I will," he says seriously, then turns and drops back into the dirt with his trucks, apparently forgetting about his rope and bucket adventure.

I wonder if Heather has any idea what he's up to...

As we turn to head inside, my heart rate picks up. The idea of being around my family with Liam, after everything that's changed between us, has been building in the back of my mind all day. And now that we're here, it's hitting me hard. I have to try to play it cool, like I didn't have my lips wrapped around his cock yesterday morning.

I push the door open, stepping inside as Liam trails behind me. We didn't actually talk about how each of us are feeling about coming to spend an evening with my family after what we've been up to the past couple days. But I can feel the apprehension in him. He's still getting to know my family, and now... well. We're dealing with a whole new dynamic that only we know about.

A fire crackles in the wood stove as we enter the living room, the cozy warmth of the room mixing with the comforting smell of supper in the air. Grandpa is sitting on one of the couches with Isla reading a book, and Mom, Heather, and Chris are in the kitchen.

"Hey," I say, and all eyes land on us.

And my heart thunders.

Fuck. I hate that I feel nervous and on edge in front of my own family. This is exactly what I've been trying to avoid by ignoring my own needs and pushing everything down. The fear that they won't accept me, and that I'll never be able to be myself around them if they knew I was gay.

Even though I *know* that's not true, and I know that won't happen. But I can't stop those thoughts from creeping in, whispering *what if*. What if I lose everything I love?

"Hi!" Mom greets us brightly, placing rolls into a basket. "You're just in time. Dinner's almost ready. Busy day?"

"Yeah," I say, trying to shake off those feelings as I sit on the couch across from Grandpa and Isla. "Just some storm cleanup around town."

Liam sits beside me, his posture stiff as he nods a greeting at Grandpa.

"I was talking to Marie today," Grandpa says, his gaze

flicking between Liam and me. "She mentioned you two were out there clearing that old dead tree that fell on her fence. The wind really did a number on it." He smirks at Liam. "Theo's putting you to work now, eh?"

I scoff, shaking my head, while Liam chuckles softly. "He offered," I say.

Grandpa smiles and winks at Liam. "Good man."

Heather looks up from the salad she's making in the kitchen. "Mason still outside?"

"Yeah," I say, glancing out the window at him as he fills his bucket with dirt. "Hope you brought extra clothes."

She sighs loudly. "Always," she mutters.

Chris appears before us, handing us each a beer.

"How was the rig?" he asks Liam.

Liam takes the bottle and looks up at him. "It was good. A lot of work."

"I bet," Chris says, sitting down on the couch next to Isla. "You must do a lot of gas tungsten arc welding out there."

Liam perks up and eyes him curiously. "Yeah, I do. Are you...?"

Chris chuckles. "Not a welder, no. My uncle is, though. He's retired now, but he worked in the mines. He's a talker, so while I don't know much, I've picked up more about welding than any accountant probably should."

Liam smiles, his tension immediately easing. "Welding in the mines, that's quite a job."

Chris nods and takes a sip of his beer, relaxing into the couch as Isla dramatically flips the page in her book. She gives him a pointed look and they share a silent exchange before he sighs, shifting further down the couch.

"Yeah," Chris continues, nodding at Liam. "He's got some crazy stories. I don't think I could ever work underground." He pauses, eyeing Liam with a smirk. "Or underwater."

Liam chuckles. "Luckily I don't have to dive too often."

Chris cocks an eyebrow at him. "Once would be too many times for me."

I sit back, letting them settle into their conversation about welding, feeling a quiet relief as Liam visibly relaxes. He looks comfortable and at ease talking with Chris, and Grandpa whenever Isla allows him to take a break from their reading.

Eventually, I slip away to the kitchen to join Mom and Heather as they begin setting the table.

Mom smiles as I grab a stack of plates. "Did you manage to get everything done today?"

I shrug. "Kind of. I have a lot of jobs piled up that I need to get to. But I got to everyone that needed help today."

She reaches out and squeezes my arm. "Thanks for doing that. I know they all appreciate it."

I grab a cherry tomato off the counter and pop it into my mouth. "They better."

She chuckles and swats me with her dish towel, pulling a laugh out of me as well.

As I bring the plates to the table, I glance over at Liam. Isla is now sitting beside him, and he's still comfortably talking to Chris and Grandpa.

Heather sets the salad down on the table and follows my gaze. "It's nice to have him back. You two seem to be getting along really well."

Warmth flows through me as I watch Liam laugh at something Grandpa said, and he patiently holds his arm still while he lets Isla colour in his tattoos with a marker.

You have no idea...

TWENTY-ONE

LIAM

THE TRUCK IS quiet as we drive home from Theo's mom's, and a warm feeling lingers in my chest. Theo's family is so welcoming and easy to get along with, I think it's impossible not to have a good time with them. They've invited me in as if I'm one of their own, and tonight I felt like I truly belonged there. Even with the nerves that twisted inside me before we arrived, since I was now walking into their safe family space sharing a secret with Theo. And even though I still don't know what this all means for us, there wasn't one moment I felt out of place or uncomfortable while we were there.

But now, the storm is creeping back in. I once again feel at the mercy of angry winds as the wave feels like it's about to crash and pull me back underwater.

Because his family reminds me of mine.

Guilt rises as Theo pulls into the driveway, and I keep my eyes out the window to watch the trees pass by in a blur. I haven't talked to my family and can't even bring myself to turn on my phone again to see if Mom texted me back. Yet here I am, having dinners with someone else's family, pretending like I'm whole.

I miss them.

A lot.

"Hey."

Theo's voice breaks through the silence, and I blink as I turn to look at him. The truck is parked now, and he's watching me with a furrowed brow and concern etched in his features.

"Sorry," I mumble, rubbing my hand over my face.

"What's up?" he asks cautiously.

I blow out a breath and shake my head, letting my gaze drift out the window again as my chest tightens. My mind whirls as I try to find the words to express what it is I'm feeling, but it's all just a jumbled mess.

"Your family is great," I say eventually, desperately trying to hold onto the last bit of warmth and happiness from the evening. The comforting smell of leftovers Cynthia sent with us fills the truck, but it also makes the ache in my chest grow.

Theo stays quiet as memories of my own family flash through my mind. Nick and both our parents sitting around the dinner table, laughing, talking, and taking life for granted. It hurts, but there's something else there too. Something that feels like comfort, even though it's wrapped in loss and pain.

"Mine is too," I say quietly before I turn to meet his gaze.

His eyes are soft and steady as he watches me in the darkness, like he knows there's more under the surface. And I want to let him in. I tried yesterday, when the grief was all consuming... but I couldn't get the words out. I'm not brave enough to say it yet. But even just being here with him, looking into his eyes... it calms the storm inside me and pulls me out of the water.

My hand moves before my mind can catch up, reaching across the console to grasp the side of his face. His warm skin beneath my fingers reignites the warmth inside me, and I lean in to press my lips to his. His hand lifts to lightly hold my arm as I keep him here against me, and everything else falls away. The guilt, the pain… it all moves into the distance, muted by the simple fact that he's here with me, and feels like home in a way I didn't expect.

When I pull back and look into his eyes, he smiles softly.

"Let's go in," he says.

I nod, grateful as always that he never asks for more than I can give. He just… gets it.

As we step into the house, Miss Bobber greets us at the door and I smile down at her.

"Hey, little one," I murmur, bending down to lift her into my arms. She purrs as she rubs her head against my nose, her soft fur warm against my skin as I follow Theo into the kitchen.

He opens the fridge to put the leftovers inside, but one of the containers falls and lands on the floor with a loud *thud.* Miss Bobber startles in my arms, her purring coming to an abrupt stop as her wide eyes lock on Theo.

"Shit," he murmurs, bending down to pick up the fallen container, inspecting it to make sure it's ok. Once he's satisfied and puts it in the fridge with the others, he closes the door and turns towards me.

I watch him, brow furrowed as I hold Miss Bobber tight against my chest. He looks down at her in my arms, then up at me in confusion.

"You scared her," I say, instinctually tightening my hold on her.

He presses his lips together to hold back a smile as he looks down at her again. "I didn't mean to." Then he steps forward, lifting his hand to gently scratch behind her ears. His gaze softens as it sweeps over her, like he's checking to make sure she really is ok. He smiles when her purring starts back up again. "You're alright."

I watch him as he continues to scratch her ear, and her purrs vibrate against my chest. And I can't help but take a moment to appreciate him. So thoughtful, gentle, and always making sure everyone around him is alright.

His eyes lift to meet mine and the corner of his lips tilt up in a soft smile. "I need to get to bed. You coming?"

My eyes flick between his as my heart skips a beat. And I just nod.

I set Miss Bobber down and she trots over to her food dish, settling in for a snack before her usual routine of playtime before she curls up in one of our beds.

Well, I guess now it's just one bed.

We each head to our bathrooms, and I watch Miss Bobber bat her toy mouse around the living room while I brush my teeth. I chuckle at the sounds of her scurrying around and chasing her toys as I turn off the lights and head upstairs. Theo is still in his bathroom, and the soft sounds of running water fill the quiet space as I pull off my shirt, slip out of my jeans, and sit on the edge of his bed. The lamp on the bedside table casts a soft golden light over the room, and as I look around, I realize just how comfortable this whole thing feels. This is only the third night we've spent together, and the second in Theo's room. But in a way, it almost feels like it's always been like this, and exactly how it's supposed to be.

Theo steps out of the bathroom, pulling off his shirt as he heads towards his dresser on the other side of the room. My eyes track his movement, watching the hard lines of his muscles as he slides his jeans down over his hips and tosses them in the hamper, and the way his bicep flexes as he runs his fingers through his hair. Until Theo, I've never looked at a guy like this before. But now that I've given in to those urges I've been feeling around him... I can't seem to stop.

As he turns towards the bed, I drag my eyes up his abs and chest to meet his. He's standing before me in just his boxers, and this is the first time I get to really *see* him and take him in, free of the obstructing shadows from the dim firelight.

A breath escapes me as I push to my feet and slowly cross the room, my gaze falling once again to his chest. My hand lifts when I reach him, my fingers lightly tracing the freckles scattered over his shoulders. He exhales as I drag my fingers up his neck and rub my thumb over his freckled cheekbone.

He watches me quietly for a moment until he takes my hand in his, holding it between us as his fingers trace the tattoos Isla coloured in earlier this evening. A smile tugs at his lips, then he lifts his gaze and leans in, pressing his mouth to mine. His kiss is soft, yet laced with a quiet hunger that I find myself desperate to meet. I push my tongue past his lips, and he walks me backwards, guiding me until the back of my knees hit the edge of the bed. He gently pushes me onto my back, and my heart riots as he crawls over me, finding my lips again. And before long, I'm clawing at his back and pulling him closer to me as the need in us only grows.

My hips press into his, and the feeling of his hard cock against mine sends a thrill straight through me. He lets out a soft moan against my lips as I grind into him and that's all the encouragement I need to give him even more. My hands trail down his back and over his ass, gripping him tight to hold him against me as I roll my hips again. The stark contrast in the feeling of his hard cock and the soft fabric of my boxers is so fucking good, all I can do is release a breath and give in as he takes over. He kisses down my neck as he grinds his cock against mine, and I tilt my head back with a moan.

But I need more.

I roll him over so I'm on top of him, and his arms wrap around me as I rock my hips into his. We're both so fucking hard, and this feels so good we're panting and moaning as we fall into a heated, messy kiss while grinding against each other.

Eventually, I push myself back and straddle his hips, looking down at his flushed face. His glassy eyes drop to my dick in my boxers, and he starts to reach for it. But I grab his wrist to stop him.

Theo furrows his brow as he lifts his eyes to me again, but I just give him a little smirk. As I nudge his knees apart so I can settle between them, the tension in him quickly fades away, and his eyes fill with anticipation.

But as I kneel between his legs and look down at his hard cock in his boxers, nerves flutter in my stomach. He was so good at this for his first time. And I need to be too. Because I want to do this for him, and make him feel good.

I try to calm my racing heart as I grasp the waistband of his boxers and pull them down, freeing his cock. As he kicks his boxers off, my eyes stayed glued to him, roaming his completely naked body before me. Fuck...

My hand trails slowly up his thigh, and I feel his eyes on me. My gaze travels up his body, watching his chest rise and fall with heavy breaths of anticipation. Mine does the same with a mix of nerves and excitement as my hand gets closer to his dick. But the groan he lets out as I wrap my hand around him pushes away any nerves I had. My hand moves up and down his hard cock as he continues to moan softly, but I want to hear even more.

I lower myself onto my elbows between his legs, and his breathing increases as he looks down at me. As I meet his gaze, I swallow, preparing myself to just go for it. And I'm immediately rewarded with a perfect groan from him as I wrap my lips around the head of his cock. I take a moment to manage the sensations in my mouth, as it somehow feels both hard and soft against my tongue, and I can taste his salty precum. As I slide my lips a little further down his length, I keep my eyes on him, and he slides his fingers through my hair to push it out of my face.

"Fuck," he breathes as he watches me slide back up his cock and take him in my mouth again.

His moans of encouragement urge me on, and I move my hand up and down the base of his cock as I suck him. I let my tongue explore the ridges of his dick and watch him as he completely lets go. His grip in my hair tightens as I work him, and the sounds coming from him are driving me fucking wild. And I just want to make him moan even more, and even louder.

"Oh my god," Theo pants, "your mouth feels so fucking good."

My eyes fly up to him as his head tips back with a groan, and I watch the muscles in his chest flex as he tightens his grip on my arm and my hair.

Holy fucking shit.

His words push me to give him even more, and I increase my pace on him. My hand glides up and down his cock with the wetness from my mouth as I continue to lick and suck his head, and I feel him getting closer and closer.

Until he suddenly pulls my head back and I release him from my mouth.

"I'm going to come," he says, his chest rising and falling with deep, fast breaths.

And I just stare back at him.

Because as hot as that is, and as much as I want to make him come, I'm not sure I know what to do to finish him with my mouth.

Theo seems to read my mind and pulls me up to him, pressing his lips to mine. As my tongue slides against his, I push my hips into his again and pull a delicious moan from him. I'm so fucking hard, and he feels so fucking good against me that I have to do it again, and again. Theo wraps his arms around me to keep me tight against him as we moan and groan against each other's lips.

Eventually I push myself back just enough to slide a hand between us so I can grasp his cock, but he quickly grabs my wrist to stop me.

My eyes meet his and he just shakes his head, releasing my wrist to shove my boxers down over my hips. "Keep doing what you're doing."

My heart skips a beat as I roll my hips again and my cock, now free from my boxers, rubs against his. Theo's eyes flutter closed, and a groan escapes him as I drop my lips to his neck. Heat spreads through me as I thrust my hips and feel his hard body against mine. His fingers digging into my skin only adds to the overwhelming sensation as a tingle spreads up my spine, and I grind into him even harder. He's groaning and clawing at me as every move I make seems to bring him closer and closer, and I feel like I'm not far behind him.

Until he suddenly presses a hand to my chest to push me back and guides my hand to his cock.

I can't help but let out a small smile as I look down at him. Theo… usually so quiet, reserved, and subtle, has finally found his voice. He's telling me exactly what he wants, how he wants it, and with the confidence I knew was in there.

And I'm more than happy to give it to him.

I wrap my hand around his cock and stroke him as I straddle his hips. Immediately, he grunts, and his muscles tense.

"Fuck," he mutters, "I'm coming." His hands land on my thighs in a bruising grip and I continue to stroke him, watching his skin flush and his head tip back as he groans, coming over his abs and my hand.

I'm impossibly hard as I stare down at him, watching him in awe as he moans and writhes beneath me. When he's almost down from his high, his eyes open and he looks up at me. He exhales and sits up, wrapping his arm around my back and flipping us over so he's on top of me.

The feeling of his weight on me, his lips moving against mine, and his tongue in my mouth is enough to unravel me. I'm so close, and feel like I'm going to tip over the edge at any minute. But I need to hold on. He feels so fucking good, I need to savour this.

Theo kisses down my body, and I hold my breath as I watch him. But when he takes my cock into his warm, wet mouth, a rush rolls through me and the pressure starts to build. His soft brown eyes watch me as he takes my cock further into his mouth, and I can hardly fucking stand it.

"Jesus Christ..." I murmur as he slides his mouth up and down my length. I swallow hard as the sensation becomes almost unbearable, and when his hand cups my balls I bite my lip hard to keep from coming in his mouth right here and now.

But I can't come yet. Because as I watch him, so confident, comfortable, and free, I want to give this to him. I want him to take everything he wants, and as much of it as he wants. Seeing him so uninhibited is like watching him come to life. Everything just seems so natural, and it's like he's completely weightless. Because he's finally found his freedom.

A strangled moan escapes me as his tongue runs up the length of my cock, and I close my eyes to try to keep myself together just a little bit longer.

But I can't. He feels too fucking good.

My hands land on his shoulders as I lift my head to look down at him and try to pull him up. "I'm going to come," I say.

But he doesn't move.

He stays right where he is and keeps his mouth on my cock.

Holy. Fucking. Shit.

There's no way I can hold back any longer.

One more glide of his tongue and my release quickly rushes to the surface. I groan loudly as my head tips back against the mattress and my fingers slide into his hair, gripping and pulling tight as I come in his mouth.

My cock pulses as I come harder than I think I ever have, and as I look down at him, I damn near lose my breath. He keeps his lips around my cock, his brown eyes glued to mine, and sucks every last drop of cum out of me.

When he releases me from his mouth, he pushes back onto his knees and his throat bobs as he swallows.

All I can do is stare at him and remind myself to breathe.

His eyes are on fire as he stares back at me, looking fucking *alive.*

And this might be the most alive I've felt in a long time too.

TWENTY-TWO

THEO

AS I QUIETLY EXIT THE bathroom, my gaze drifts to Liam in bed. I can just make out his sleeping form in the predawn darkness, with Miss Bobber curled up beside him, where she'd slept between us all night. His dark hair is a tousled mess, and the soft rhythm of his breathing is the only sound breaking the stillness of the early morning. For a moment, I just watch him, letting my eyes adjust, and soaking in the quiet calm that surrounds him.

I step closer and lean down to press a gentle kiss to his forehead. He stirs as his eyes open, and he sleepily looks up at me.

"Hey," he mumbles groggily.

"Hey," I whisper back, smiling softly. "Sorry, just heading to work."

He rubs a hand over his face and yawns. "And after?"

"Just need to finish up some stairs on a front deck in town."

Liam nods, looking up at me again. "Need help?"

I shake my head, a small smile tugging at my lips. "It won't take long."

His gaze drops to Miss Bobber as she stretches, and he rubs

her belly. But even in the darkness, I can see the disappointment in his eyes.

"But," I sit on the edge of the bed beside him, "you asked if I knew any good fly fishing spots around here."

His eyes light up as they shift back to me, and I can't help but chuckle.

"I do." I nod.

A smile breaks out on his face, and warmth spreads through my chest.

"So," I say, unable to take my eyes off his smile, "you'll have to dig out all the fly fishing gear from the barn today. It hasn't been used in who knows how many years, because fishing on a boat is better."

Liam scoffs with a playful roll of his eyes. "You can't even catch fish on a boat."

A light laugh escapes me as I shake my head. "You'll eat your words tonight."

"Sure," he says sarcastically. Then he gently runs his hand down my forearm. "But... sounds good."

I lean down to kiss him, and he holds me against him for a beat longer, lingering like he doesn't want to let me go. When I reluctantly sit back, I stare into his bright blue eyes, wishing I could just stay with him all day.

"See you later," I say, reaching out to give Miss Bobber a pat before pushing to my feet. I close the door behind me, leaving him and Miss Bobber to enjoy a few more hours of sleep since it's just after 4:00AM.

After I make a coffee to take with me, I head outside into the crisp, chilly air. The headlights cut through the darkness as I start up my truck, illuminating the side of the house. I take a sip of my coffee as the engine rumbles to life, the peaceful silence of the morning interrupted by its low hum. And as my eyes drift over the weathered wood siding, a sigh escapes me.

Grey and worn from years of coastal weather and salt air.

But underneath it all is something strong and resilient. Something that protects everything inside, keeping it safe, warm, and comfortable.

And people try so hard to recreate that weathered look. To put on the armour without facing any storms, like they want the scars without earning them.

That's fucked.

I make my way through the still sleeping town to the marina, where a few captains have already arrived to start preparing their boats for the day. I give them a wave as I head towards my own, and sneak past the office so Sheila doesn't catch me and give me an earful about the happenings of the wharf. As our marina manager she doesn't have to be here this early... but she always is. She's the self-proclaimed mother of everyone here, and says she needs to keep an "eye" on us. If I didn't need to be up at 4:00AM, I wouldn't be... but whatever makes her happy.

And she does make a damn good marina mom.

I step onto my boat and head straight for the wheelhouse, flipping on the engine to let it warm up. Just as I get the bait hauled out, Sarah arrives, hopping onto the boat deck with a grin and a salute.

"Morning, Cap," she says cheerfully, taking the bucket from me.

"Morning," I reply, always in awe of her cheerfulness no matter what time of day it is. I let her take the bucket and turn my attention to the GPS in the wheelhouse as she sets to work readying the bait. It's been two days since we emptied the traps, so they're likely all full. I don't want this to be a long day, so I spend some time looking over trap locations so we can just get in and out and focus on the haul.

"Some chilly out this morning, eh?" Glen says, coming up behind me and peeking over my shoulder at the GPS.

"Hm," I agree with a nod, keeping my eyes focused on the screen.

He pats my shoulder with a chuckle. "We're ready for a big haul. Let's get at 'er."

Once everything is loaded and ready, I steer us out of the marina, the boat slicing through the calm water as the first hints of dawn streak the sky. I take a deep breath of the salty air, listening to the rumble of the engine and the gentle laps of the water as the soft glow of the wheelhouse screens light up the dark space around me.

But even as we head into what could be a long, gruelling day, I feel oddly at peace. And I know why.

Liam.

The thought of him drifts through my mind, bringing a calm that I don't often feel at work.

Or ever.

But even with this unfamiliar feeling of peace, I can't ignore the familiar questions that are creeping in. I glance back at Sarah, Mitch, and Glen, and wonder what they would think if they knew. If I told them I was gay, would everything change? Would it be weird and awkward between us? Would they leave my crew? Would everything be ok?

I'm afraid to find out the answers to these questions, because I love this crew. They're like family, and the last thing I want to do is lose them, or anyone else.

But the more time I spend with Liam, the more the urge rises to confront these questions, and consider what it would be like to stop hiding. To feel this peace all the time, and not just in stolen moments behind closed doors.

But I'm not sure I can afford to find out. Because the thought of possibly losing the life I've built with this crew and with my family… and potentially hurting the people I love… I can't do that.

I don't know what to do.

With a sigh, I push those questions aside and try to hang onto the calm and peaceful feeling I started my morning with. But I'm not sure how much longer I can keep all these parts of my life separate.

I cast my line into the middle of the tranquil river, watching as the fly drifts on the surface of the water. After a moment, I slowly reel it back in and cast it out again. Once it lands on the water, I glance at Liam further down the river, laser-focused as he effortlessly casts his line. And a smile forms on my lips. While I'm far from a seasoned fly fisher, Liam clearly is. Each of his casts are smooth and precise as his fly floats gracefully downstream before he pulls it back in for another go, and I find myself just watching his motions.

I've never fished here before, but I knew about this river from a hike years ago. It's about thirty minutes from Torrin Cove, and a decent trek off the road, so it's quiet, secluded, and is perfect for fly fishing. And after a tough haul today, this is very needed. Not only because of how peaceful it is… but because I get to see Liam smile and enjoy himself.

Even though we haven't caught any fish yet.

"So," I say, casting my line again, watching the shimmering water as the sun dips low, "when was the last time you went fly fishing?"

Liam doesn't answer right away, so I abandon my fly on the water for a moment and glance over at him.

He remains quiet for another moment as he watches his fly

drift downstream. "Last year," he says eventually. "When I was home visiting."

There's a tension in his voice, and a sadness that reminds me of the other day. When he almost broke down talking about home, and his guilt for feeling happy. I still don't know why home is such a difficult topic for him, but I've pieced together enough to know that Nick's death has left a deep scar, and it seems to have reshaped his relationship with his family in some way. I wish I could do more to help, but I also think he knows I'm here for him whenever he's ready.

But right now, I want to keep him feeling relaxed and happy, so I shift the conversation.

"Well, I hope you did better than you're doing now, because..." I trail off, raising a questioning eyebrow as he casts his line.

He huffs with a side-eye aimed my way. "I'd say my chances are still better than yours, with that technique," he says, gesturing to my fishing rod with a nod.

"Hm," I hum thoughtfully. "Didn't you say you were going to *show me how it's done*?" I turn my head to him again and sweep my hand towards the river. "Let's see it then. I'm waiting."

His eyes light up as he smirks at me. "And what do I get if I do?"

I smile as I pull my line in. "Winner's choice."

"Deal." He nods.

We fall silent as our focus shifts back to the water, keeping our eyes peeled for trout. Neither of us has seen a single fish since we've been here, but we keep casting, pulling the lines in, and casting again, hoping for a bite.

Until Liam's rod bends, and he pulls his line tight.

Motherfucker.

I pull my empty line in with a huff as he works on pulling

in his fish, which puts up a decent fight. But he fights back and successfully lifts it out of the water. And it's a big one too.

Of fucking course.

He unhooks the fly from the trout's mouth and holds it up with a triumphant smile. And I try really hard not to smile back at him, because it's damn near impossible to resist the joy radiating from him.

With a sigh, I open the cooler and Liam drops the fish inside. Then he shuts the lid and turns to face me with an expectant look.

I raise an eyebrow, picking up my rod again. "Need something?"

He nods. "Yeah. I won the bet."

I roll my eyes as I straighten out my line, ready to cast it into the water and level this out. "Looking for praise?"

"Something like that," he says, stepping closer to me.

I look up at him, and his eyes burn into mine with an intensity that sends heat flooding through me. I slowly lower my rod, and the fly slips from my hand into the water at my feet.

"You said winner's choice," he says in a low voice, taking another step closer.

My heart rate spikes as I watch the corner of his lips tip up in a sly smile, and anticipation rises.

Liam lifts his hand and slips his fingers into the front of my waistband, pulling me closer so my lips brush his. "I'm redeeming my prize right now."

TWENTY-THREE

THEO

OUR EYES REMAIN LOCKED, his reflecting the shimmer of the setting sun dancing on the river's surface, while my heart pounds like it's trying to break free from my chest. His fingers brush against my stomach as he grips my waistband, and that single touch feels more powerful than the rush of the river beside us.

So all I can do is swallow and nod, giving him permission to take anything he wants from me.

Liam smirks, the small stones on the riverbank shifting under his feet as he steps closer and slides his fingers past the waistband of my pants and boxers. As they brush the tip of my hardening cock, a breath catches in my chest.

My eyes dart around, but I know we're completely alone. We've been out here for over an hour, and we haven't seen a single person. And we won't, with the sun starting to set and being three kilometres away from the road.

"I can stop..." Liam murmurs, his gaze catching mine.

I meet his eyes, then shake my head and slide my hand to his hip, pulling him closer. "Fuck no."

Our lips meet, and the rush that rolls through me as Liam slips his hand out of my pants to slide my zipper down is almost unbearable. And as he pushes his tongue past my lips while he palms my now hard cock, my entire body lights up.

I let out a moan as he slowly slides his hand up and down my cock, and his stubble scratches my chin. My hand lifts to grasp the side of his face as I kiss him with everything I have, needing to taste him, touch him, *devour* him. He fills every one of my senses as my fingers slip into his hair, his tongue slides against mine, and he moans softly against my lips. And when he rubs a thumb over the head of my cock, slicking my length with precum, a tingle runs up my spine and I pant against him.

"Oh my god," I murmur into his lips, and he strokes me again, pulling another groan from me.

I need my hands on him. I need him to groan for me, feel his hard muscles, stroke his cock, and make him feel the same pleasure he's giving me.

My hands drop to his pants, and I pull back from his lips to look down as I take his hard dick in my hand. My heart thunders as I take in the sight. Liam, hard for me as he strokes my cock... I still can't even believe this is real.

Liam drops his lips to my neck with a nudge of his head, and I tilt mine to give him the access he wants. He kisses the skin under my ear as he continues to jerk me, and I close my eyes as I take in the feeling of him in my hand, and the cool evening air nipping at my skin. I rub my hand up and down his cock and listen to his heavy breaths mingling with the soft murmurs of the water, and the gentle breeze in the fir trees.

"Fuck," I mutter, gripping his hip tight with my other hand as I take everything in, and let the wave of pleasure build.

Liam hums against my neck, and the added sensation damn near drives me fucking wild.

I bring my lips back to his and take him again in a heated

kiss as I increase my pace on his cock. He does the same on me, and soon we're both panting and moaning against each other.

"Oh my god," I mutter, feeling my release rising quickly to the surface.

"Hm," Liam hums again, pressing his forehead to mine as he looks down between us. "Fuck, you're hot," he murmurs.

My entire body stutters as his words drive me over the edge, and my hand falls from his cock as I come with a groan. I hold onto him tightly, watching my cum spill over his hand as pleasure crashes over me and my dick pulses.

Liam moans as he keeps his eyes on my cock, pulling every last ounce of ecstasy from me. And when his gaze lifts to meet mine, his eyes are gleaming with desire as they trace every feature of my face.

I exhale softly, taking in the way the setting sun glows in his clear blue eyes, and casts a warm, orange hue across his face.

Keeping my eyes on his, I take his hand and run my fingers through my cum. Then I wrap my cum-covered hand around his cock, and slide it up his length.

"Jesus Christ," he stutters, his hips jerking and his eyes fluttering closed. His hands land on my hips, squeezing tight as he drops his head to watch me pump his cock with my cum.

My other hand lifts to tangle in his hair as I watch him quickly come undone in my arms and I'm suddenly very aware that we are out in the open, in the middle of the woods, where anyone could find us.

But I don't fucking care.

I stroke him faster and bring my lips to his as the thrill settles inside me, and I let it fuel this moment between us. As I take everything I've ever wanted, and give him everything he deserves.

He tenses under my touch, and grunts against my mouth as

his fingers dig into my hips. The thrill inside me only grows as he comes, and I can't get enough of him.

I eventually release him, dropping my hand from his hair to step back and take him in. His breaths are heavy as he stares back at me, eyes glassy and cheeks flushed with pleasure. And I feel like I have to pinch myself.

He's fucking perfect.

I tug a piece of carpet free, and Miss Bobber darts after a loose string. I laugh, teasing her with it as she pounces. Liam huffs out a laugh when she suddenly gets distracted by a dust ball and bolts after that instead.

It feels like we've been pulling up the old carpet in the sunroom for hours since I got home from work, the seemingly easy task taking longer than expected. And not just because of an adorable kitten who wants to play. Whoever laid this carpet down must have been preparing for the fucking apocalypse with the amount of nails and staples in this ugly thing. And underneath this mess, is another mess.

Beautiful hardwood... covered in plaster.

"What the fuck are people thinking when they cover hardwood," I mutter, yanking up another strip of carpet and finding more plaster caked on the wood. This is going to take a ton of work to refinish, but it'll look good when it's done.

Liam looks over and shakes his head. "I don't know. Kids?"

I shrug. "Aren't kids messy? Wouldn't hardwood be easier to clean?"

He thinks on that for a moment and nods thoughtfully. "Yeah... no idea then."

We fall back into our rhythm as I pull up carpet and Liam

follows behind me with a hammer and pry bar, pulling up the endless strips of nails and staples in the floor.

By the time we have half of it done, we sit on the floor against the wall and crack open a beer. Which is frustrating... the room isn't even that big. It should have been done two hours ago.

Liam takes a drink of his beer as he leans back against the wall beside me, looking out into the room. "Nick and I pulled carpet out of his parents' entire house once," he says quietly, his voice sounding distant.

I turn my head to look at him, surprised he's bringing this up. He's staring off into space, like he's lost to a memory. I stay quiet and let him work through whatever it is.

He eventually releases a breath and blinks out of his thoughts. "It was a fucking disaster. Worse than this," he says, his fingers fidgeting with his beer bottle.

"Yeah?" I ask softly, giving him the space and permission to continue if he wants to talk about it.

A small smile gently tugs at the corner of his lips. "He thought it was hilarious. I was ready to give up after three steps."

I chuckle. "He sounds great."

He nods as his smile fades. "Yeah. He was."

Silence settles over us again as the weight of his words linger.

"*Is*," I say softly.

Liam turns to look at me, his eyes searching mine with a question.

"He may not be here now, but he didn't cease to exist," I say, thinking of how I felt talking about my dad after he passed. "The memories are still real, and he'll always be a part of you. What you shared with him is still alive, and always will be."

His eyes fill with emotion, and he blinks a few times as he nods, lowering his gaze. "It's still hard to talk about him."

I nod. "You don't have to do anything you're not ready for."

His eyes shift out to the room again, and a distant look takes over him once more. "There's a lot I'm not ready for." I watch as tension enters his jaw, and he absentmindedly picks at the label on his beer bottle. "Sometimes I feel like I'll never be."

I can't help but think again about everything he's told me so far, and wonder just how deep this pain goes. I know there's more, but I'm not going to push him for it. I remember what it felt like when my dad died, and how every time someone asked me questions or pushed me to talk before I was ready, it shoved me back instead of helping me forward. So I'm not going to do that to him, especially when he's starting to open up, just a little bit.

But as I think about having questions, needing to talk, and opening up... my mind drifts to the nagging thoughts and questions that have been trying to push me in a direction I also don't feel ready to go in.

"I've been wondering lately what it would feel like to come out," I murmur, breaking the silence.

Liam turns his head and I meet his gaze with a sigh.

"I have no fucking idea what to do about it," I say.

He nods as he looks into my eyes. "You don't have to do anything you're not ready for."

I smile at him with a little chuckle. "Wise words."

He shrugs one shoulder with a soft smirk.

Then I sigh, my smile fading as I lean my head back against the wall. "But I also feel like I'll never be ready." I keep my eyes on his, hesitating before I quietly add, "But if I do... it could affect you too, if..."

His eyes soften as I trail off, unsure how to finish that thought as the words get stuck in my throat.

If you'll still be here? If you want people to know that side of you?

...If you'll still have me?

"The only thing I care about is you," he says softly. "Whatever you want, I'm here."

A fluttering feeling forms in my chest at the thought of him wanting to be with me during this massive change in my life... and just wanting to be a part of my life. It's big for him too. And I can't help but wonder what his family would think. He said he's never been with a guy before, but he doesn't seem to share the same fears I do.

A question bubbles as I watch him. I feel like it's an important one, for both of us... so I go for it.

"What would Nick think?"

Liam shifts his gaze past me, his eyes distant again as emotion flickers. He seems to lose himself to his head again for a moment, and I worry I pushed too hard, too soon.

"He'd give me a hard time," he says eventually.

Fuck.

My heart sinks, and I brace myself for the moment this all unravels. Where Liam realizes his best friend, the most important person in his life, wouldn't have approved of us.

Liam's gaze slides back to mine and his lips tilt up in a soft smile. "In the best way."

My brow furrows, and he chuckles lightly.

"He'd love it. But I'd be hearing awful dick jokes for the rest of my life." He lets out another soft huff before he drops his gaze, and his smile fades.

I watch him for a moment, until he lifts his eyes to meet mine again. The sadness has returned, but with it is something else. Something a little softer.

"He'd really like you," he says, his voice barely above a whisper.

I smile softly. "Sounds like I'd really like him too."

He holds my gaze for a moment longer. "And I think your family would support you, no matter what."

I nod, taking a deep breath in. "I know."

Liam's eyes roam my face, then he lifts a hand to brush his thumb over my cheekbone. "Mo chridhe," he murmurs.

My brow furrows. "Is that... Gaelic?"

He smiles softly with a nod.

I huff a laugh as I stare back at him in disbelief. "You speak Gaelic?"

He just nods again, still looking into my eyes.

"What does it mean?" I ask.

He leans in to kiss me softly, holding me against him for a moment. Then he pulls back just enough so his lips lightly brush over mine. "Just something to describe what you are to me."

TWENTY-FOUR

LIAM

I GLIDE the paint roller over the final section of the sunroom wall, the first coat of coastal blue sweeping across the drywall. I step over Miss Bobber playing at my feet so I can paint the last spot of wall, and it's a miracle she hasn't turned into a little blue furball. Painting with her at my feet has been quite the challenge.

The first coat is finally done though, so I set the roller down in its tray and wrap it up to keep it fresh, then give Miss Bobber all of my attention. I drag her favourite toy across the floor, and she immediately pounces on it. Her little paws bat at the furry mouse before she pulls it to her mouth and rolls onto her side, kicking her back feet at it in a ferocious attack. I can't help but laugh at her fierce determination as I push to my feet, letting her finish her work until she's ready for me again.

My gaze turns towards the bay window, and I sweep my eyes over the view. The pale blue ocean stretches out towards the horizon, blending into the midmorning sky until it's hard to tell where one ends and the other begins. It's a perfect morning. There's not one cloud in the sky, and the water is calm as seagulls glide gracefully overhead, occasionally dipping low to scan for fish below the surface.

Theo should be having a good day out there today. I hope he is.

I take a deep breath in, just the thought of him making my heart feel light.

I'm completely falling for him.

I've been drawn to him since I first came to Torrin Cove and met him in his family's store, but the more time I've spent with him, the stronger that pull has become. And now that I've finally given in to it, my feelings for him are growing at an alarming rate. It feels good... but it's terrifying too.

I've let him in, and shared things I haven't even allowed myself to fully process yet. Memories of Nick, and how much I miss him... even attempting to tell him what really happened, and what I've done.

And I still haven't even spoken to my family.

My eyes drift to the sunroom door, towards my bedroom, where my phone is buried at the bottom of my bag. It's still switched off, like it has been since I got home two weeks ago. The usual guilt settles inside me as I think about the messages likely waiting for me, especially from Mom after the text I sent her. I haven't had the courage to check, and read her response.

But right now, I'm tempted to look... and I don't know what to do.

I know I'm hurting my family by staying away and keeping them in the dark about everything. About what really happened with Nick, how I'm feeling about everything, and about where I even am right now. I'm in the same province, a five-hour drive away, and they have no idea. And I only feel worse knowing they're respecting my silence, giving me space to work through it all. But really, I'm not working through anything.

I'm hiding.

I ran away.

If I can't face myself, how can I face them?

I look out at the water again, and a familiar memory creeps into the edges of my mind. The one that is always threatening to resurface, that I've been desperate to keep out so I don't have to relive it.

But this time, I let my guard down... just a little.

A vivid image of the camp up north in Alberta flashes before me. Nick stands beside me as our supervisor tells us he wants one of us to finish maintenance on the oilfield skid. It should have been me, since I was working on it all day the day before, but I wanted a change. So I convinced Nick to do it instead.

My chest tightens as I see Nick walking towards the bay where the skid was housed, and I quickly squeeze my eyes shut to make the replay stop.

No. No, no, no, I can't. Make it go away.

The weight of it all crashes over me, as every emotion I've been running from hits me all at once. Sadness, anger, guilt, regret... It's too much. I can't do it.

I can't do this.

A sudden urge rises to *feel* this pain. To control it, use it, and escape the intense pressure building inside myself. This feeling I can't name, but is so overpowering it drives me to act on it. The desperation grows the longer I stand here, eyes closed and fists clenched, the need to control the pain and take it into my own hands is overwhelming... the need to hurt, feel, and punish.

Before I realize what I'm doing, my feet are moving, taking me to the front deck. I look out over the ocean and wrap my hands around the railing, gripping it so tight it hurts.

Don't... don't...

My eyes stay glued to the water as I fight the urges growing inside me, the storm quickly picking up in intensity. Until another image pushes its way into the forefront of my mind.

Freckles scattered across cheekbones, soft brown eyes, and wild, windswept hair.

The chaos inside me settles as I keep him in my mind, taking in a deep breath and slowly blowing it out.

Theo.

He's always here for me, and I want to be here for him.

I need to be here for him.

The pain slowly pulls away, lessening just enough so I can close my eyes to feel the sun on my face, listen to the gentle sound of water lapping the shoreline, and the seagulls calling from the air above me. My heart eventually slows its pace, and my grip loosens on the railing. It still hurts... but with Theo, I feel like I can still live. Even with the pain.

I stay here for a while longer, looking out to the ocean and wishing Theo was here with me. But because he's not... I can't be here alone with my thoughts.

I head back inside, pat Miss Bobber as I pass her, and grab my hoodie. I shove my feet into my sneakers and step out of the house again, getting into my truck with no plan for where I'm going.

But when I pull up in front of MacKinnon's General Store and see Jimmy sitting on the front porch with some other men, an immediate comfort washes over me.

Jimmy smiles as I step out of my truck. "Well, hello! How's she goin' today?"

I give him a nod in greeting and climb the steps. "Not bad," I say, sitting in the empty chair he gestures to.

"Working on the house again today?" he asks after the rest of the men give their greetings and return to talking about one of their boats.

I nod, leaning back in my chair. "Painting the sunroom. We finished putting up the drywall yesterday."

Jimmy huffs a laugh and shakes his head. "I thought Theo was crazy for buying that place. The property's something else, but the house... it was in rough shape. I haven't seen it in a while though, sounds like it's come a long way."

I smile, thinking of Theo buying that run-down house, knowing he would see past the scars to what could be beautiful underneath. It's what he does. "It really has. He's done a good job."

Jimmy grins. "I'd say both of you have."

He's pulled back into a conversation with the other men about boat motors, so I sit and listen, looking out over the water. Now that it's May, it's warming up quite a bit as we near noon. So I push my sleeves up and feel the warmth on my skin from the sun, falling deeper into this feeling of comfort.

The screen door bangs shut, and I turn to see a guy around my age exit the store. I've never seen him around town before... not that I'm out that much. But as he looks at his phone, then up and down the street in confusion, it's obvious he's not from here.

"Can I help you find something?" I ask, drawing his attention to me.

His eyes dart to me, then back to his phone. "I'm not getting service."

I nod, giving him an assessing look as he seems kind of skittish and awkward. He's wearing hiking boots and outerwear, and by the looks of the gear strapped to the roof rack on his car, he either just was, or is going, camping.

"Need directions?" I ask as he squints at his phone.

He nods tightly, glancing quickly my way before dropping his gaze again.

I gesture down the street. "Straight that way will take you to the highway."

He looks down the street and nods again. "Thank you," he says.

But before he can leave, Jimmy leans forward. "Coming or going? Long way from Newfoundland."

I glance over at his car parked by the gas pump, noticing the Newfoundland licence plate.

The guy turns back to us, fidgeting with the receipt in his hand. "Going," he says, his eyes travelling over the storefront. "I was in Kejimkujik Park to see a scarlet tanager, and I found it, so now I'm going home."

A smile tugs at my lips as I take in the awkwardness about him, that is also somehow endearing. "A scarlet tanager?"

His eyes meet mine, and they light up. "A small songbird, and one of the most difficult to spot because they forage in dense, leafy, high canopies. They come here in summer to breed and return to South America in the fall, and in spring they are sometimes forced out into the open to search for insects which increases the chances of spotting them. I did, I saw one, a summer male that is brilliant red with black wings and a tail, and I saw him before he will molt into winter plumage in late summer. Then he'll be greenish with black wings. He's red because he's a breeding male so that's really good that he's here." He nods, looking more confident than when he first came out here, as we all stare back at him in silence.

"Cool," I eventually say with a smile, not quite sure what else to say. He's obviously super into birds, and I know absolutely nothing about them.

His confidence falters again as he forces a tight smile and lifts a hand in an awkward wave. "I need to go. Bye."

"Bye," I chuckle as he heads down the steps.

Jimmy waves to him as he gets in his car, then turns to me, drawing his brows together. "A scarlet tangler?"

I laugh, watching the guy drive away. "Tanager, I think."

He shrugs. "Well, he sure sounded excited about it."

"I'd say."

"Hi, Liam." Cynthia steps out of the store with a smile. "I thought I saw you out here."

I look up at her with a smile as she wipes her hands on her apron. "Hey," I say.

"And what are you up to today?" she asks.

"I was working on the house... but," I shift my weight in my chair, "I just needed to get out for a bit, I guess."

She observes me for a moment then smiles brightly. "Well, perfect timing. I need some help, and these old fellas aren't going to cut it."

The men all grumble in protest and Cynthia waves her hand in the air with a roll of her eyes.

"I need muscles," she says. "Any of you want to move a freezer for me?"

And suddenly, the protests all stop.

"Thought so," she says with a shake of her head and motions for me to follow her. "Let's go."

I chuckle, pushing to my feet and following her inside the store. She leads me to the kitchen in back, and I wave to Heather on the way as she helps a customer at the counter.

"I dropped my favourite dough whisk behind the freezer," Cynthia says as we enter the kitchen, pointing to the large deep freezer against the wall. "That's what I get for doing too much at once and not just using the counter space." She laughs softly. "Would you mind pulling the freezer out so I can grab it?"

"Sure." I step forward and grab the edges of the freezer to shift it forward enough for her to slip behind it and retrieve her whisk.

Cynthia holds it up triumphantly. "Thanks, honey. The day this one goes will be tragic."

I chuckle and glance around the kitchen. It's a big space with multiple ovens, fridges, freezers, and shelves crammed with bowls. The counters are dusted with flour, and there's a few bowls and stand mixers out.

"Ever baked before?" Cynthia asks, heading to the sink to wash her whisk.

I nod, the smell of baked bread pulling me back home for a moment, igniting a sharp pain deep inside me. "My mom likes to bake."

She looks over her shoulder, observing me for a moment before she smiles softly. "Well, I'm on my last batch of bread and could use a hand." She turns away from the sink, drying the whisk on her apron before holding it out for me.

I look down, and cautiously reach out to take it.

Her tone is softer when her words cut the silence between us. "I'd love to spend some more time with you."

My heart lurches as I meet her warm brown eyes, so much like Theo's. And despite the ache inside me, I find myself wanting to stay.

I nod, and her smile widens.

"Good. We're making sourdough." She gestures to two bowls on the counter. "We're at two different stages here, so you'll get to see it all."

I step closer, peeking into the bowls. One is empty, and the other filled with a soft, fluffy dough.

"The thing with sourdough, is it's so much more than just a recipe. You have to *understand* it," she says, pulling the empty bowl closer to her. "That's the secret."

I raise an eyebrow at her. "You may have the wrong person to help you then..."

She laughs, pushing the bowl towards me. "I'm a good teacher."

I chuckle, appreciating her confidence and hoping I don't screw this up for her.

Cynthia pulls out the ingredients and walks me through the process of making sourdough. She tells me all about the starter and how it needs to be "fed"... which completely weirds me out. It's kept in a jar and it looks like some kind of alien slime thing that could come alive at any moment. But I do as she says and measure out ingredients, mixing it all together while she pours brownie batter from one of the stand mixers into a pan, and slides it into the oven. And while we work, she tells me all about the store's history.

Jimmy and his wife, Marie, both grew up in Torrin Cove, and were together since they were teenagers. Marie always wanted to own a store, and when they were just in their twenties, Jimmy made her dream come true.

"She passed about fifteen years ago, after a tough fight with cancer," Cynthia continues, her voice softening as she closes the oven. "We all keep this place running for her. Theo's dad, Lloyd, put so much into it before he passed, too. He absolutely adored his mother." She sighs, looking out into the store as a weight seems to press down on her.

I slow my whisking as I watch her for a moment, knowing how that weight feels. "I'm sorry for all the loss you've had."

She turns back to me and smiles sadly. "Thanks, honey. It's been hardest on Theo. He was close to his grandmother, and even closer to his dad. They were more than just father and son, they were best friends." She moves to stand beside me again at the counter, dumping the dough from the other bowl onto the floured counter. "And I know it's still hard for him to be working in the job where his father died."

My head jerks up and I look at her, trying to process what she just said.

She looks up at me with a furrowed brow. "He didn't tell you?"

I shake my head. "No..."

Cynthia sighs, turning back to the dough. "I guess I'm not surprised. It's still hard for him to talk about." She pauses for a moment. "Lloyd died in an accident on the lobster boat. Thankfully Theo wasn't with him to see it, but... losing his father like that, it just destroyed him."

She releases a breath as she cuts the dough, and I just watch her and listen, frozen to the spot.

"I worried about Lloyd out there on that boat every day," she says quietly. "And now I worry about Theo every day too. But just like we are doing in this store for Marie, he's doing for his dad. And I can understand that."

My heart pounds as I take this all in, and everything Theo has shared with me suddenly makes so much sense. How he feels this deep responsibility to continue lobster fishing, and like it wasn't really his choice... and I see now why it wasn't. His father died doing something he worked so hard for, so that Theo could be set for life and his family would be cared for. And Theo stepped up, continuing to build their business and confront the same danger that took his dad's life. Every day.

This family has faced unimaginable loss. But instead of breaking them, it brought them even closer.

"Mom."

Cynthia and I turn to see Heather standing in the doorway, tapping away at her phone looking frazzled.

"Chris is heading to Antigonish tomorrow to help his parents with their yard. He was going to take the kids, but it looks like he'll stay overnight. Any chance you can take them in the afternoon?"

Cynthia winces. "Oh, honey, I'm sorry. I'm delivering a cake to Lunenburg tomorrow for a baby shower."

"Oh, right." Heather sighs. "I forgot about that. Maybe Grandpa can keep them entertained if I take them here for the day."

"We can take them," I say, the words coming out of my mouth before I can even think about what I'm saying.

Both of their eyes land on me, and I'm suddenly aware I may have crossed some line I wasn't sure was there. But Theo loves those kids, and tomorrow is Sunday. He won't be fishing, and we have time...

"We were just going to work on the house for the day," I say slowly, wiping flour off my hands and trying to avoid their gazes. "They can play with the kitten."

Heather chuckles lightly, and I lift my eyes to meet hers.

"I still think it's adorable you guys have a kitten," she says with a smile.

I huff out a laugh, but then Heather eyes me curiously.

"The only reason I didn't ask Theo is because his house is a death trap and he's always working... and last time Mason was over there he almost fell through a hole in the floor."

I let out a small laugh, shaking my head at the visual. "No holes now."

Heather nods slowly, a smile spreading across her face. "Ok, then. I'll drop them off in the morning."

A warm feeling settles over me as I smile back at her.

Helping this family feels like the least I can do, after everything they've given me.

TWENTY-FIVE

THEO

THE SMELL of freshly brewed coffee fills the kitchen as I lean against the counter, watching the sky slowly change colour over the ocean outside. A soft orange glow spills over the counters, bathing the room in warmth as steam billows from the coffee machine and curls into the stillness of the early morning. It should feel peaceful, but my mind won't stop racing through the endless list of tasks waiting for me.

The kitchen counter I need to build for the MacNeils', which I haven't even started yet. And I wanted to have it finished and installed by the end of the week. Then there's the set of kitchen chairs for Donna that need to be fixed and refinished, still sitting in my workshop, untouched. And Frank Gillis is building a new barn and I said I'd help with his stall doors. And shelves in the feed room...

Not to mention the work around my own house, which Liam has been doing most of.

I rub a hand over my face and blow out a breath. But the creaking stairs pull me from my thoughts, and I turn to see Liam step into the living room as he makes his way towards the kitchen. He's wearing just his sweatpants hung low on his hips, and my gaze automatically drops to trace the lines of his abs and chest before lifting to meet his blue eyes.

"Morning," I say, my voice quiet as I try to shake off the tension I'm feeling.

"Morning," he replies, rubbing his eyes. Then he stops before me and his brows draw together. "You're overthinking."

A hollow laugh escapes me. "Yeah. I have too much to do."

Liam observes me for a moment, then moves to the coffee machine. He hands me my now filled mug and sets another pod to brew. "Who's nagging you?"

I furrow my brow as I stare at the back of his head. "No one."

He glances over his shoulder with a confused expression. "No one's been rushing you for their jobs?"

A sigh escapes me as I see where he's going with this. "No..."

He nods thoughtfully, turning to face me as he crosses his arms and leans against the counter. "Hm. So, no one needs anything right now, and everyone understands your busy schedule..."

My eyes narrow as I stay quiet, not wanting him to win this one.

But he smirks, because he knows he already did. "And don't you want to spend time with your niece and nephew today?"

"Of course I do," I say, rubbing a hand over my face as guilt stirs with the realization I've only been seeing them for Sunday dinner at Mom's. Which definitely isn't enough.

Liam takes his coffee from the machine, watching me carefully. "It's ok to slow down sometimes. You don't always have to be working."

I lean back against the island opposite him, the warmth of the coffee grounding me as I take a sip. And I know he's right.

"Yeah," I murmur, nodding slowly. "I know."

We stand in the quiet stillness as the warmth of the sun filters through the windows and wraps us in its soft glow. We sip our coffee in comfortable silence, and I slowly let go of everything that was on my mind earlier.

"Your mom said something yesterday..." Liam says softly, breaking the silence.

I look up to see him watching me carefully, the sun shining in his dark hair, making his blue eyes seem even brighter. While I was initially a bit surprised to hear he went to the store yesterday and spent the afternoon with Mom, it actually seems to have been good for him. Since I got home last night, I've noticed a quiet shift in him. A subtle lightness, like something deep inside has loosened or lifted... though I can't quite put my finger on what that is.

"Yeah?" I ask.

He nods slowly. "She said your dad died on the boat."

My heart skips a beat, and my eyes quickly drop to the coffee in my hands. I pause for a moment as I watch the steam curl upwards, until I nod. "Yeah."

"That's why you stayed," Liam says softly. "Why you do all this."

I swallow hard, feeling the familiar ache in my chest whenever I allow myself to think about Dad. When I lift my eyes to Liam's again, he's watching me with understanding. Because he knows exactly what this feels like.

"Yeah," I say, nodding again.

He sets his coffee on the counter and steps forward, pulling me into his arms. He says nothing as he holds me, and my arms wrap around him as I take a deep breath in, finding comfort in his touch.

And he's right. Staying here in Torrin Cove and taking over the family business was never my choice... it was my promise. I couldn't even consider leaving to pursue anything else, and selling off everything my grandfather and my dad worked so hard for. Dad loved it on the water, and I do too... even on the hard days when all I can think about is him.

So I stayed. And I continue to put everything I have into his passion, our town, and our family.

For him.

After a moment, Liam pulls back just enough to meet my eyes. His gaze is full of understanding, and a strength I didn't expect.

"Doing what's best for your family is brave," he says quietly. "But being brave means knowing when to think of yourself too."

My chest rises and falls with a heavy breath as I look into his eyes, and he brushes a thumb across my cheek.

"Your family loves you," he says. "And not because of what you do, or how much you give. They love you for exactly who you are." He then drops his hand from the side of my face and rests it over my chest. "Mo chridhe."

The Gaelic words flow over me, soothing even though I don't know what they mean. But the sound of them, and the way they feel coming from him, makes my heart soar. My head drops to his shoulder as I breathe him in, and Liam holds me tight against him.

I know his words are true. I've suppressed myself for so long, burying who I really am, so my family won't have to face yet another heartbreak if everything falls apart. I know they will accept me for who I am... but the fear is for them. If the store crumbles, if the crew leaves... all my family's hard work and passions could be gone in the blink of an eye. Even if I know deep down that won't happen, I can't even let myself consider the risk. The weight of that fear has been enough to keep me silent and hiding.

But Liam's words still echo in my mind. *Being brave means knowing when to think of yourself too.* I've held it all in for so long, pushing down the truth that I'm gay, and afraid to admit it even to myself to protect my family. And finally letting that part of me out, even just here behind these walls with Liam, has released years of relentless pressure. Here, with him, I can finally breathe.

And it feels so good.

I lift my head from his shoulder and find his lips with mine, letting everything fade away so I can appreciate this moment with him.

Because I'm pretty sure I'm in love with him.

His hands slide up my back, pulling me closer as he kisses me with the same need I'm feeling. And as we stand here in the kitchen, wrapped up in each other and bathed in the soft morning light, Miss Bobber rolling around in a sunspot on the floor... it all feels so right.

Liam then chuckles against my lips as I feel Miss Bobber at our feet. He pulls back to look down at her as she goes full attack mode on his foot. We both laugh as she nearly climbs his leg with wide, wild eyes, and he gently shakes her off.

"Wild cat..." he mutters with a smirk. Then he looks up at me. "The kids will be here soon, good thing she has energy."

I huff out a laugh as she darts around the kitchen island and the jingling of the bell on one of her toys sounds from the living room. "I'd say she's ready." My gaze then drops to his bare chest, and I run a hand over his pecs, taking in the feel of him under my touch. "But I don't want you to have to get ready yet."

He draws a slow breath in as his eyes follow my hand on his chest, then lower to my sweatpants. His hands grip my hips tighter as he pulls me against him, his lips hovering over mine. "Same."

He steps into me, backing me up against the counter as he presses his lips to mine again. This time with heat and urgency. His tongue slips past my lips, and I immediately open for him, wanting everything he has to give me. His hips press into mine and I moan into his mouth as I feel him against me. I want to pull him even closer, take more and give him everything I—

A knock on the door brings us both back down to reality, and Liam steps backwards with wide eyes, wiping his mouth with the back of his hand. "Well, shit," he says with a heavy breath.

I shoot him a pointed look and shake my head. "You're the one who invited them over."

He rolls his eyes and exits the kitchen, heading towards the stairs. "Just answer the door."

I watch him for a moment as he disappears into the hallway to go upstairs and grab a shirt, then I head to the door and open it to Heather, Isla, and Mason.

"Uncle Theo! I brought my diggers!" Mason happily holds up his bag full of toy trucks with a big smile on his face, and dirt already smeared across the front of his shirt.

Isla rolls her eyes, clutching a stack of books to her chest. "He crawled into the ditch to get them."

Heather sighs, ushering the kids inside as I hold the door open for them with a chuckle. "I didn't bother changing him this morning, but I brought extra clothes," she says, handing me a bag.

I take it and glance down at Mason as he kicks off his shoes. "I could just dunk him in the ocean."

His eyes widen as he looks up at me. "Can you?!"

"Oh my god," Isla mutters, heading towards the kitchen. But she stops suddenly as she stares into the living room.

I follow her gaze to see Miss Bobber rolling around on the rug with her toys.

"She's. So. *Cute.*" Isla drops her books on the kitchen island and rushes over to her, Mason quickly following. They drop onto the rug with her, and she looks up at them curiously. But once they start dangling her toys for her, she's in heaven.

"She is *very* cute," Heather says, watching with a smile as the kids play.

I hear the creaking stairs through the laughs and giggles, then Liam enters the room, now wearing a t-shirt.

Unfortunately.

He takes in the adorable scene before him and smiles, then looks up at Heather. "Hey."

"Hey, Liam," she says. Then she shifts her gaze around the living room and kitchen. "I see all the work Theo has been making you do has paid off. It looks incredible in here."

Liam's eyes dart to me as he smirks, and I just roll my eyes. "I'm not *making* him do anything."

She gives Liam a knowing look, pulling a laugh out of him. And the sound is so perfect that I can't even bring myself to protest anymore.

"For real though, this is insane," Heather says, running her hand along the kitchen counter, her eyes drifting up to the exposed beam where we took down the wall between the kitchen and living room. "Not only is this place actually livable now, it's beautiful. Good job, guys." Her gaze catches on the doorway to the sunroom, and she heads towards it. But she stops at the threshold and looks back at us with a shocked expression. "Now *this* is going to be amazing."

I follow her to the room, leaning against the doorframe as she steps over the now carpetless hardwood floor, still covered with some plaster, and takes in the newly painted drywall and trim around the windows.

"Perfect place for morning coffee," she says with a smile, gazing out at the view.

I smile too, my eyes flicking back to the living room. Liam is crouched on the carpet with the kids as they play with Miss Bobber. His eyes meet mine, and he gives me a lopsided smile.

That's our plan.

When I bring my attention back to Heather, she's looking through the hallway into Liam's room. Or I guess, what used to be his room. His empty bag is still tucked in the corner, but his clothes are in my room, and every night, he's in my bed.

Her eyes sweep over the neatly made bed, his bag the only sign of him ever being in there.

"Liam's tidy," she says, eyebrows raised.

I freeze, watching her peering into the room.

Fuck.

But Liam chuckles from the rug behind me. "It's just where I keep my bag. I took a room upstairs."

Relief floods through me as Heather laughs. "Well that makes more sense. No man is that tidy."

I force a chuckle as well, trying to get my heart to settle the fuck down. When I meet Liam's gaze, he gives me a reassuring smile, and I take a deep breath.

Randomly finding out the guy I moved into my house has been sharing a bed with me isn't exactly how I want to come out to my sister.

"Ok, I need to go," Heather says, reaching down to ruffle Mason's hair as she walks past them towards the door. "Be good for your uncle, please," Heather says, looking back at the kids. But mostly at Mason.

"I'll make sure he is," Isla says confidently, patting Miss Bobber as she rubs up against her.

Heather chuckles, shaking her head. "And have some fun too, Isla."

But once Heather is gone, Mason jumps to his feet, looking up at me.

"Can we look for worms? Can we fish? Can we use my diggers in the sand? In the *water?* Can I dig a hole? Then fill in the hole? Can you throw me in the ocean like you promised?"

Liam stifles a laugh behind him, and Isla sighs loudly with a shake of her head.

I nod slowly, trying to contain my own laughter. "Yeah, bud. Why not?"

"Yeah!" Mason pumps his fist in the air. "Let's go!"

Isla pushes to her feet with a sigh as Mason runs to the door to put his shoes on. "If you don't mind, I'd like to read."

I nod, placing my hands on her shoulders to steer her towards her books on the kitchen island. "I'll bring a chair down to the dock for you."

She smiles widely and picks up her books, clutching them tightly to her chest. "Perfect!"

Liam grabs one of the Adirondack chairs for Isla and takes it down to the dock while I help Mason bring his bag of diggers. He settles near the rocky shoreline beside the dock and dives into his project right away, digging a hole as if his life depends on it. Within minutes, he's covered in mud and sand, grinning from ear to ear, and the happiest I think I've ever seen this kid.

We sit on the edge of the dock, drinking our coffee, as the warm sunshine offers a comforting contrast to the cool water as we dangle our toes in it. Liam chuckles beside me as we watch Mason play, and Isla lounges in her chair with a book, completely absorbed in her own world.

"You might have to dunk him in here after all," Liam says, taking a sip of his coffee.

I huff out a laugh, watching Mason reach deep into his hole and pull out a handful of dirt. He sifts through it in search of worms, and when he doesn't find any, he wipes his hand on his shirt and reaches in again.

"Or hose him off." I shrug. "Pretty sure he'd be down for either."

"I found one!" Mason says suddenly, jumping to his feet and holding his hand in the air. "I got a worm!"

"Awesome," I say with a chuckle, watching as he runs up the dock towards us.

He holds it out proudly when he reaches us. "Liam, look!"

Liam laughs, leaning in to inspect his worm. "That's a big one. You could catch two fish with that."

Mason's eyes practically pop out of his head. "Can I...?" His eyes dart to me.

"Well," I say, pushing to my feet, "we do need something for lunch. Let's catch some fish."

He lifts both hands in the air and tilts his head back. "Yeah!! Best day *ever*!"

Isla glances up from her book with a furrowed brow. "Do I have to stop reading?"

"No," I say with a laugh. "Read all you want."

She grins, grabbing another book from her stack. "Best day *ever*."

By the time I grab the fishing rods from the barn and Liam helps Mason bait his hook, the kid is vibrating with excitement.

"I'm going to catch *two* fish," Mason declares, beaming as Liam passes him his rod.

"Two more than your uncle then," Liam says, smirking as I hand him his rod.

I shoot him a look. "You're full of it. You only caught a couple more than me."

Liam huffs as he grabs a worm from the bait box. "More than a couple."

Mason looks up at me with a furrowed brow, then to Liam. "Uncle Theo fishes lobster. Maybe he needs help with mackerel?"

Liam's gaze slides to meet mine, a smug smile tugging at his lips. "Yeah," he says. "I'd say you're right."

I set my jaw and bite my tongue, not willing to take the bait this time. Enough is enough. I'm a fucking fisherman. This is getting embarrassing.

We focus our effort on fishing for the entire morning, and by lunchtime, Mason caught his two fish.

Liam also caught two.

And I caught one.

For *fuck's* sake.

But by the time evening rolls around and we load the kids into the truck for Sunday dinner at Mom's, all is forgotten. It was a perfect day, and the worries I was feeling this morning have faded away, replaced by the love I feel for my family.

And Liam.

TWENTY-SIX

THEO

I TAKE a deep breath in as I stare at my reflection in the mirror, then exhale slowly. It's been a great day, and it felt good to let everything go for a while. And now, I want to end it feeling even better.

As I step out of the bathroom, Liam slips into the bedroom, leaving the door slightly ajar.

"She's going wild down there," he says with a soft chuckle. "It's going to be a long night for her."

The bells from Miss Bobber's toy jingle from downstairs, and I can't help but chuckle myself as I hear her running around after it. But as Liam moves towards the bed, wearing nothing but his boxers, my attention locks on him.

My eyes roam over his body, and I watch as the muscles in his arms and back flex when he pulls the blankets back on the bed. But before he can get in, I walk up behind him and slide my arms around his waist, pressing my lips to his shoulder.

A breath escapes him as he tilts his head to the side so I can trail my lips up his neck. My fingers trace the hard lines of his abs, and my cock is already hardening at the feeling of him under my touch.

Liam takes a deep breath in before he turns in my arms, and his lips meet mine. His tongue pushes past my lips, and we fall into a slow and intoxicating kiss. The light and carefree feeling I've had today is quickly evolving into a deep, aching need to feel every inch of him. To be so close to him that there's absolutely nothing at all left between us.

As my tongue slides against his while his hands grip me tighter, his words from this morning float back into my thoughts.

I'm feeling brave. So I want to take something for myself.

I want *him*.

I push him back onto the bed and crawl over him, desperation growing at a rapid rate. Our kiss is now needy and full of heat as his hands slide down my back and over my ass. When I feel him hard against me, I moan into his mouth and grind into him, taking even more.

"Hm," he hums against my lips, slipping his fingers into the waistband of my boxers and sliding his hands over my ass. He grips my flesh tight as I roll my hips against him again, the feeling sending a rush of exhilaration through me.

He suddenly rolls me onto my back and settles between my legs, pulling my boxers down. As I kick them off, the look in his eyes is one of pure hunger. He runs his hand over my hard cock as he rakes his gaze over my body, and as I lie here before him, exposed and vulnerable... I feel completely comfortable and safe. There's no fear with Liam. No danger, risk, or hesitation. I can be entirely myself, free to explore my deepest desires... and he's right there with me.

Liam leans down to take me in his mouth, and a groan immediately escapes me. My fingers slide into his hair, pushing it back so I can watch him and take in every bit of this. His eyes find mine and I keep my gaze locked on him as he sucks me. And it's not long until he has me writhing beneath him and panting his name.

But this isn't where this ends.

I reach out to pull his hand off my hip and push it down... towards my ass.

His eyes fly up to meet mine again, and he releases me from his mouth. He doesn't say anything as he just looks up at me, like he can't quite believe this is happening.

So I smirk down at him and shift my leg, opening up wider for him, and nod.

Liam releases a breath and drops his gaze, slowly running his fingers down the length of my cock, over my balls, and to my hole.

I can't help but moan as he presses a finger to my hole, and he looks up at me, both heat and hesitation in his gaze.

We're both new to being with a guy in this way, but some things... I've tried on my own.

"Lube is in the top drawer," I say, looking into his eyes.

They widen slightly before he nods and reaches over to grab it. When he settles between my legs again, his eyes slide from the lube, up to me. "Have you..."

I just stare back at him with a small smirk, letting him conjure up the image of me playing with my ass.

His eyes light up and a smile spreads across his face. "That's fucking hot."

I widen my legs in response, and his eyes immediately fall as he lets out a breath. I watch him with a thundering heart as he coats his fingers with lube, and tosses the bottle on the bed beside us.

A shiver rolls through me as he presses a cool, slick finger to my hole, and his cool blue eyes peer up at me. He gently swirls his finger, pulling a moan out of me.

"Tell me what to do," he says in a low voice. "Tell me what you like."

I'm already overwhelmed, in the best way possible, with the feeling of him doing this to me... and we've barely even started. With Liam here, in my bed, wanting to make me feel good... it's like everything is magnified. Every touch from him sends my body into overdrive, and my responses are intense, needy, and desperate. This is more than I've ever felt before, and it's all because of him.

And from the look in his eyes, he's enjoying this just as much as I am.

I nod as he stares up at me, waiting.

"Push it in," I say.

He pulls his bottom lip between his teeth as he looks down at his hand, and slowly pushes his finger into my ass. Electricity shoots up my spine from the pleasurable pressure in my ass, and I moan as I grip the sheets on either side of me.

"You ok?" Liam asks as he looks up at me.

All I can do is nod and gently roll my hips, asking for more.

His gaze drops again to watch as he slowly drags his finger out of my ass, and pushes it back in. He does this a few more times, before he gently curls his finger inside me, and brushes against a spot inside me that has every nerve in my body lighting up. I let out a guttural groan as warmth radiates through me, and his eyes quickly lift to watch me as he does it again, and I moan even louder.

"Fuck..." he whispers, his eyes trailing back down my body like he's drinking in every inch of me. When his gaze lands on my cock, he drops his head to take me in his mouth as he rubs my prostate again.

"Jesus Christ," I mutter, my hands moving to grip his arms tight as everything in my body seems to come alive. The sensations of his warm wet mouth on my cock, slowly sucking and licking as his finger continues to slide in and out of my ass... I can barely even form a thought.

Then he pushes another finger inside me.

"Oh my god..." I groan, my head tipping back as he continues to suck my cock and finger my ass.

"More," I say, looking down at him. "Faster."

Those bright blue eyes meet mine as he increases his pace on me, and they sparkle with desire. I feel like I could come from the sight of him alone right now, but he feels so fucking good, I need this to last. I want to savour this moment with him, and I want to make him feel just as good as I do.

Pressure quickly builds deep in my pelvis, radiating through my body as he works me, and I grip his hair tight. I'm barely hanging on, and I don't know how much longer I'm going to last.

When I feel like I'm close, my hands land on his shoulder and I push him back. "Stop."

Liam's eyes widen as he looks up at me. "Did I hurt you? Shit, I—"

"No," I say, shaking my head as I pull him up to me. I sink my tongue into his mouth, taking a delicious taste of him as the urge rises, so strong it's impossible to ignore. The intense need to be as close to him as I can possibly get. To experience this with him and give him every part of me.

I release him from my kiss and look up into his eyes as he holds himself over me.

"Fuck me," I say, my voice almost a whisper.

His brows lift as his eyes flick between mine. "Really?" he breathes out.

I just nod. This isn't the first time it's crossed my mind... but after the day we had today, and the way my feelings towards him have been growing... I want all of him.

"Condoms are in the drawer," I say, my heart thumping.

He nods slowly but doesn't move as his gaze lingers on mine. And a sinking feeling settles in my stomach.

Shit. He doesn't want this...

"I had to go through an insane medical assessment to work offshore..." he says slowly, his eyes falling to my lips. "They tested for *everything*."

My heart riots in my chest as his eyes meet mine again.

"I'm all clear."

I stare up at him for a moment before I nod, willing my heart to settle the fuck down. "I haven't been with anyone since I last tested... also clear."

His lips tilt up in a small smirk, and my hands land on his chest to push him backwards onto his knees. I sit up with him and immediately grab the waistband of his boxers, pulling them down to free his rock-hard cock. As I lick the glistening bead of precum off his tip, his hand lands on the back of my head and he groans. The sound is fucking *beautiful*, so I take him into my mouth and pull another moan from him. I continue to suck and stroke him, desperate to make him feel good as I give him everything I can.

Until he suddenly grabs my shoulders and pushes me onto my back.

He exhales, gripping his dick and staring down at me with a shake of his head. "This isn't about me."

I can't even find the words to respond as he stares down at me, eyes intense and roaming as he runs his hand up my leg and my abs. Then he leans over me, hovering his lips over mine. "You're fucking perfect, mo chridhe."

A stuttering breath escapes me as he kisses along my jaw, then pushes back and grabs the lube. I watch with heavy breaths as he lubes his cock, and swipes more over my ass.

When he lines up to push inside me, he pauses and meets my eyes, his hair falling messily around his jaw, framing the intensity of his bright, ice-blue gaze. In the soft glow of the lamplight, his stare pierces through me as he waits.

And I nod.

I fucking *need* this.

Liam pushes his hips forward, and his cock presses against my hole. I try to keep my muscles from tensing as he enters me, but the more he pushes in, the harder it is to relax. It's both a burning discomfort and a pleasurable pressure, and even though I want it more than anything, my body feels like it's trying to fight it. My hand lands on his arm as I wince slightly, the feeling much more intense than his fingers.

A look of concern crosses his face as he stops, but I pull at his arm and shake my head.

"Keep going," I say.

He hesitates for a moment, but then he continues. And suddenly, he's all the way in, and the pain is replaced by a feeling of fullness that is unlike anything I've ever felt before.

He stares down at me and releases a heavy breath. "Fuck."

I nod, releasing a breath of my own. "Yeah."

We both look down as he gently moves his hips back and slowly thrusts into me again. I take a deep breath and let the sensation roll over me. The pressure feels amazing, and even just hearing his groan as he gently fucks me pushes away every thought and feeling of pain or discomfort, both in my body and my mind.

He slowly and carefully moves his hips again, and I relax more with each thrust into me. I watch his abs flex, listen to his moans, and feel his cock sliding in and out of me as the strange feeling of being filled by him quickly becomes one of intense pleasure. And soon I find myself pulling on him and begging for more.

"Harder," I say, my hand sliding down his side to his hip, pulling him against me.

He leans forward and brings his hands to either side of my shoulders, looking down at me as he buries himself deep inside my ass. I let out a grunt and close my eyes at the feeling of him so deep inside me, and he stays here for a moment longer. My hands run up his sides to either side of his jaw as I pull his lips to mine and kiss him hard.

Then I murmur, "Now *fuck* me."

A rush of air escapes him as he pushes up on his hands and thrusts into me, harder this time.

With a loud moan I drop my hand to my weeping cock, needing to relieve the pressure that's building. Liam's gaze follows my hand as he continues to fuck me, slowly increasing his pace.

"Fuck..." he mutters, then pushes back onto his knees between my legs and bats my hand away to he can take my cock in his. He strokes me in time with each thrust into my ass, as his eyes roam over my body like he's going to fucking devour me.

And I fucking want him to.

Our moans and groans fill the room as we get completely lost in each other, and I feel myself getting closer and closer. Being filled by him, with his hand on my cock, and his eyes all over me... it's a feeling like nothing else. It's both too much and not enough, and I never want it to stop.

Heat flushes through me as I try to hang on longer, and I bite my lip. The sight of him, the feel of him... He's consuming every inch of me, and I'm afraid to even blink in case I miss something.

But his hand reaches forward, and his thumb pulls my lip from between my teeth. Then he leans forward and pulls it into his mouth, biting it himself.

"You need to come?" he mutters against my lips.

I shake my head, not trusting my words right now as I

attempt to hold back a moan while he slowly slides his cock in and out of my ass.

"Looks like you do..." he says in a low voice, his lips dropping to my neck. He slowly licks up my neck to my ear with a low hum. "Tilg a-mach air mo shon, mo chridhe. Tha feum agam ort."

I have no fucking idea what he says... but I can't hold back any longer.

I fucking *come.*

The beautiful sounds of his Gaelic words rattle around in my mind as he fucks and strokes me, and I let everything out. I groan loudly as the pressure releases and pleasure crashes over me, and I come harder than I ever have before.

Liam looks down at me with a look of awe as he fucks me through my orgasm, and I can't take my eyes off him either. When I finally catch my breath, I look into his eyes and run my hand over his abs.

"Come inside me," I say.

His eyes flash with intense need as he pauses for a moment, then releases a breath and slams into me again. His face is flushed and his muscles tense as his hands grip my hips tight.

"Oh, fuck," he moans as he drops his head and his hips stutter in their movement.

As I watch him come inside me, his abs contracting, his hold on me tight... I ask myself a question I've been wondering a lot lately.

How the fuck did I manage to get a man like him?

His eyes lift to meet mine as he takes in a deep breath, a dark strand of hair falling over one eye as we hold each other's gaze.

And now that I have him, how am I supposed to manage when he leaves for work again this week?

I'm fucking obsessed.

TWENTY-SEVEN

LIAM

I SWIPE the sponge over the last of the grout on the kitchen backsplash and stand back to inspect my work. The soft blue, nearly white, tiles give the kitchen a soft coastal feel against the off-white cabinets, and I smile as I sweep my gaze over the space. Theo did a great job picking these out, and I'm happy I was able to finish the last of the grouting this afternoon.

As I drop the sponge into the bucket at my feet, Miss Bobber trots over, her front paws resting on the edge as she peers into the murky water.

"You don't want to go in there," I chuckle, bending down to grab the bucket.

She follows me as I head for the bathroom to dump the dirty water, but darts away as I flush the toilet. Only to reappear moments later when I exit the bathroom, attacking my feet in playful fury.

"Ferocious beast," I mutter, wiggling my toes as she dramatically pounces on them.

As I head back into the kitchen, I let my gaze wander around the space and take it all in. Theo already had quite a bit of the kitchen done before I moved in, but now that the backsplash is in, it's finished.

And it feels like home.

Our home.

My eyes drift to the fridge, landing on the drawings from Isla and Mason. The ones I saw when I first arrived still hang there... but new ones have been added from their visit with us yesterday.

And scrawled across the top of one, in wobbly handwriting, is, "To Uncle Theo and Liam."

My chest tightens as I stare at Mason's drawing of me, him, and Theo on the dock fishing. And the sense of belonging I've been feeling, being accepted into this family, settles over me. This strong, loving family that has weathered so much yet still has so much love to give. Even to strangers who show up needing a place to call home.

Even though I do have a home.

I just can't bring myself to go there.

My gaze shifts to what used to be my room downstairs, where my phone is buried at the bottom of my bag in the corner... untouched for the past two weeks. And before I realize what I'm doing, my feet are carrying me towards it. My hand shakes slightly as I pull it out and power it on, and I watch as text messages flood the screen. Some are from old coworkers and friends in Alberta... but my eyes zero in on the one I knew would be here.

Mom: We miss you, mo mhac. Please call when you're ready xo

I keep my eyes on her words as I head out of the bedroom and onto the front deck. The cool drizzle in the air mists my skin, and the fog rolling off the ocean feels like a heavy blanket around me. But I need to be out here, for space to breathe.

My heart thunders as I stare down at my mom's name. Then I hit *call* and bring the phone to my ear. It rings twice before Mom's voice answers, bright and filled with hope.

"Liam?"

I swallow the lump rising in my throat. "Hi, Mom."

"Oh my god, baby." She chokes up, and then calls out to my dad. "Ross! Come here, it's Liam!"

I hear my dad's muffled voice in the background, and I drop my gaze to the wet railing, gripping it to steady myself. I take a deep breath, trying to get my shit together.

"Liam?" Dad's voice comes through the phone, warm and laced with relief. "It's good to hear from you. How've you been?"

I take a shaky breath and sniff, hesitating for a moment as I try to add strength to my voice. "Alright. How are you guys?"

"We're just plugging along," Dad says softly. Then he pauses. "You at work?"

"No... I go back this week."

"Good, good," he says. "Hopefully you got some time to rest."

"It's been ok," I murmur, closing my eyes and hating how awkward this is.

Silence stretches between us and my mind is both blank and frantic at the same time as I have no idea what to say.

"How are you holding up?" Dad asks gently, breaking the silence.

I rub a hand over my face as the chaos of emotions inside me rises, threatening to spill over. I stay quiet as I try to find the words to answer that loaded question, sifting through endless thoughts and feelings. My parents remain silent, waiting patiently, and giving me the space I need.

"I don't know," I say eventually.

"That's ok," Mom says quietly, her voice tender and full of love. "We know it takes time."

I blow out a shaky breath, overwhelmed by how understanding they are despite the months of silence. My heart pounds in my chest so hard it almost hurts as guilt swirls inside me. But I try to push it down so I can muster up the bravery to ask about the rest of my family.

"How are Phil and Leah?" I ask, the words sounding like they're miles away.

The last time I saw Nick's parents was at the funeral, but even then, I don't think I really spoke to them. I barely even remember being there as I just went through the motions, feeling trapped inside myself and wishing everything would just end.

"They're doing ok, Liam." Dad's voice is gentle as he takes his time with his response. "They ask about you a lot."

My throat tightens as tears burn the back of my eyes, and I lower my head to press my forehead against the railing. I don't say anything as I try to just keep it all together.

"We're always thinking of you, baby," Mom's voice trembles on the other end, thick with her own tears. "We just hope you're doing the best you can."

I draw a sharp breath in as I try to hold back my tears. But hearing her sniffle is breaking me, and I don't know how I'm supposed to do this. Any of this.

"Do you think you'll come visit soon?" she asks cautiously.

My gaze lifts to the fog-covered ocean, and I blink through the blur of tears. "I'll try," I whisper, not sure if she can even hear me.

But she does. "Ok," she says softly, and full of understanding. "We're here for you, my love. Whatever you need."

The familiar ache takes over as guilt once again settles.

They lost someone too, and I wasn't there for them. But they still want to support me... even when I'm the one who caused this pain.

I nod, even though they can't see it, and my voice catches in my throat. "Yeah." Then I wipe my eyes, stand up straight and draw a breath in. "But I should go..." I say, needing to end this call before I completely lose it and hurt them even more.

"Ok," Dad says, seeming to understand. "Call again soon... even if it's just to say hi."

I stare out into the fog as a tear rolls down my cheek. "Ok."

"Be safe," he adds, his voice soft and caring.

At those words, the storm inside me surges.

I hang up without even saying goodbye as the emotion crashes over me like a wave I can't outrun. I collapse onto the deck, resting my head against the cool railing as everything I've been holding inside comes pouring out. The tears, the guilt, the weight of everything I've kept buried... It's too much.

I didn't even tell them I'm in Nova Scotia. I didn't tell them anything.

Why did I do this to them?

I don't know what I was expecting when I called them. But I've been missing them, and the longer I stay here in Torrin Cove, the stronger that feeling grows. This place is starting to feel like home as I build a life here, living in happy moments between diminishing darkness... and falling in love. But I've left my parents in the dark while they manage their own pain. The pain I'm causing.

Every day I experience the strength of the MacKinnon family as I feel how deeply they care, and watch how they hold each other up, even with everything they've been through. And I can't even talk to my own parents. I can't tell them I'm just hours away and that I love them, miss them, and *want* to see them.

I want to hug them and tell them I'm sorry. I'm sorry for leaving like I did, for cutting them out when we needed each other the most. For not letting them in so we could heal together.

I'm sorry for the pain I'm putting them through every single day.

The sobs rip through me, shaking my body as I grip the railing like it's the only thing keeping me grounded. I can still hear my mom's voice in my head... her understanding and loving words, laced with hurt and emotion. They still care about me so much, even when I've done nothing but push them away.

It hurts. It fucking *hurts.*

An urgent need is quickly growing as I let everything out. And the feeling is quickly becoming unbearable.

I fucked up.

And I keep fucking up.

They don't deserve me.

And I don't deserve to be here.

The only thing I deserve is *pain.*

TWENTY-EIGHT

THEO

AS I PARK NEXT to Liam's truck in the driveway, my gaze drifts over the view of the water. The sun is just starting to go down, and the fog that clung to the ocean all day has finally burned off, revealing a beautiful, calm evening. I lean my head back against the seat as I take a moment to let the warm, comforting feeling settle. It was a long day, but it looks like it's going to be a perfect evening with Liam.

I head into the house, and Miss Bobber greets me at the door with a soft meow.

"Hey there, Miss," I say, bending down to pick her up. She purrs as she rubs her nose against mine, tickling me with her whiskers.

I carry her into the kitchen, my eyes immediately landing on the finished backsplash. With a smile, I set Miss Bobber down and observe the pristine grout work.

"Hey," I call out, waiting for Liam to join me in the kitchen. But the house is quiet.

Miss Bobber winds herself around my legs as I peer out the window to the dock, but don't see him there either.

"Where is he?" I ask Miss Bobber as I head into the living room. And then I hear the shower running upstairs.

I fill Miss Bobber's dish with food and make my way upstairs, excitement stirring as I get closer to the bedroom. After a long day on the boat and installing some stall doors, I could use a warm shower with Liam...

But as I enter the bedroom, the excitement fizzles. The bathroom door is slightly ajar, the lights are all off, and the air is cool.

I slowly push the bathroom door open, and catch the reflection of the shower in the mirror. It's running, but I don't see Liam in there.

A chill settles deep inside me as I step into the room and look through the glass shower door.

Liam sits slumped against the wall, fully dressed, as water pours over him.

"What the fuck?" I rush forward and pull the shower door open. I drop to my knees in front of him as freezing cold water sprays over me. As I take his face in my hands, his skin feels icy, and red, vacant eyes stare back at me.

"Liam..." My chest tightens as I search his face, unsure if he's even seeing me. It looks like he's not even here right now.

He blinks slowly as his eyes finally focus on me, and he shivers violently.

I lean over and shut off the water, the cold stream finally ending, and brush his soaked hair away from his forehead.

"Liam," I say again. "What... what's going on?"

He shivers again, giving his head a slight shake like he's trying to reconnect and come back to the present. My brow furrows as I watch him, an overwhelming worry taking over.

"Come on," I say softly, rising to my feet and pulling him up with me. He follows, moving slowly as I guide him out of the shower. I grab a towel and tug at his soaked clothes. "Take these off."

Liam doesn't protest as he fumbles with his clothes, and his hands seem to move on autopilot. I quickly head into the bedroom and grab a pair of his sweatpants and a t-shirt from the dresser, trying to make sense of what I just saw. When I return, he's drying himself off, his wet hair hanging over his eyes as he keeps them cast down.

I hand him his dry clothes, and when his eyes meet mine, the sadness in them has my breath catching in my chest. It's deeper than I've ever seen. And it breaks my fucking heart.

He pulls on his clothes in silence, and I head back into the bedroom to quickly change out of my own wet clothes and try to stay calm. I'm not sure what this is... I've never seen him so distant, and... broken.

But I do know that vacant expression, because I've felt it before.

It's escape. I just don't know what he's escaping.

When he steps out of the bathroom, his eyes find mine, and he searches them like he's trying to figure out what to say and find the right words. But his look says it all. He's hurting, and he needs help.

I step forward and pull him into my arms, holding him close against me. His cold skin presses against mine as his arms wrap around me, and his head falls to my shoulder. A mirror image of us yesterday morning, when he was the one comforting me.

We stay quiet as I hold him, and he hangs on tight.

Until he says, in a soft voice, "I called my parents."

My heart skips a beat. I don't know what this means, but I know for Liam, it's big. "Yeah?" I ask, trying to keep my voice calm.

He holds me a moment longer, then gently pulls back. His eyes are glassy with tears, and he just nods.

I push his hair away from his face, feeling the weight of everything pressing down on him. With his hand in mine, I lead him to the bed and pull him down to sit with me. I've never wanted to push him to talk about this, and I understand why Liam is quiet with his pain... but now, I think he needs to.

"What happened?" I ask gently.

He stares at the floor as his fingers fidget and he picks at his nails. "They still love me," he says quietly.

My brow furrows as I watch him, not sure what to make of that. "Is that a good thing?" I ask cautiously.

He nods slightly, then takes a shuddering breath. A tear rolls down his cheek, slow and heavy. I slide my hand into his and squeeze, urging him to look at me. His eyes finally meet mine, and the raw emotion in them almost breaks me.

"Liam... what's going on?" I ask, some of the urgency I feel coming through in my words.

He holds my gaze for a moment before looking down at our joined hands. "My parents still think I'm in Alberta, and I haven't talked to them, or Nick's parents, since his funeral."

I nod. He's mentioned this before, and I can't say I haven't been wondering why he's been avoiding them.

"I left them in pain," he continues, his voice tightening. "I ran away from everything that hurt me, but I'm hurting them even more by staying away."

I stay silent to give him the space he needs, knowing that this is big. And I think he's on the edge of something he's never fully shared before.

"But if they know..." His voice cracks, and his brow furrows like he's struggling to continue. "I'll hurt them even more."

I squeeze his hand again. "If they know what?" I ask softly. "That you're here?"

Liam shakes his head. His breath catches, and his face crumples as he leans forward, letting go of my hand so he can bury his face in his. "That Nick..." He chokes on his name. "That I made him go..." His words dissolve into a pained cry, his shoulders shaking. "That I was supposed to die," he says, the words breaking out between sobs. "It should have been me. They don't know what I did... I..."

His breath hitches on his words, and he can't get the rest out. His sobs are so raw and deep that I feel my own tears rise as I wrap my arms around him, pulling him against me. He cries into my shoulder, like months of pent-up grief and anguish is pouring out all at once.

"It's ok," I whisper, holding him tight.

I lean back against the pillows, taking him with me and holding him against my chest. The room darkens around us as he lets it all out, and eventually the only light left is the soft glow from the windows. Just enough to make out his face as his tears slow.

He wipes his eyes as he takes in a deep, shaky breath.

"It was you," he says softly, his voice hoarse.

I tilt my head towards him, feeling his hair against my cheek. "What was me?"

He swallows, shifting to lie on his back as he releases another shaky breath and I trace his outline in the darkness with my eyes.

"I felt like... It was too much," he says slowly, and anticipation builds as I wait, worried that I know what he's getting at. "I just... wanted it all to end," he says softly, and my stomach drops at those words, and the ones he said earlier.

I was supposed to die. It should have been me.

My pulse thunders in my ears, and he turns to look at me.

"But then I thought of you." He sniffs, and pauses for a moment. "And I didn't want it to end."

I hold his gaze and take his hand in mine again, gripping it tight. The image of him in that freezing shower, and the blank, hollow look on his face... he was checking out, and trying not to hurt himself. I don't even want to think about what he would've done if I hadn't come home when I did.

There's something about Nick's death that is haunting him, twisting something inside him and making him feel like he was supposed to be the one to die. He's been drowning in guilt, and now I see just how strong that is. It's kept him away from his family, so he can punish himself... alone.

But he's not alone.

I look at him in the darkness and lift my hand to his face, feeling the warmth of his skin mixed with the wetness of his tears. "I wish I could take all this pain away for you."

But I know there's nothing I can do. The only thing that truly eases the weight of grief is time, and holding onto good memories. Those moments that made everything feel brighter when they were still here, that can now add lightness to our dark days.

"Tell me a good memory with Nick," I say, looking into his eyes and wishing I could see them.

He's quiet for a moment, until Miss Bobber jumps onto the bed. She delicately walks over us, and settles on Liam's chest. Her soft purrs fill the room, and the soothing sound seems to reach him, providing him a sense of comfort as he lifts his hand to stroke her fur.

"Last year..." he begins slowly, his voice low and thoughtful. "Our parents came out to visit us in Calgary." He pauses and I see his chest rise as he draws in a breath, like he's gathering the strength to continue. "He had this idea that we would all go out for sushi, because he saw a place near our house that he's been wanting to try. I don't think he's ever had sushi in his life, but... we went." Liam's fingers gently comb through Miss

Bobber's fur as he speaks, and I can hear some of the tension easing from his voice. "He definitely didn't understand what all-you-can-eat is."

I keep my eyes on him and let him take his time, the heaviness slowly lifting, just a little.

"He ordered for all of us, and I still have no idea what he did. But he royally fucked it up." He huffs out a breath through his nose. "It all started ok. We each had a salad and a bowl of edamame beans for the table. But with each plate of sushi that arrived, which was insane, also came another bowl of edamame beans."

A smile pulls at my lips as I picture a table filled with edamame beans.

"Eventually, we had ten bowls on the table, along with more sushi than anyone could ever eat. It was a fucking disaster." He shakes his head with a breath of laughter. "But our parents thought it was hilarious and we spent hours there, laughing until we were crying and trying to eat as much as we could..."

He trails off, and I hear the joy fading in his voice.

"Nick made everything fun. No matter how ridiculous it was."

I give his hand a gentle squeeze. "Sounds like it."

He stays quiet for a moment, and when he speaks again, his voice is soft and fragile. "That's why I can't go back home. He was my brother, and his parents are mine too..." He pauses, shaking his head. "To go back there, without him... and tell them..." he draws a shaky breath in. "It's why I'm here. I couldn't stay in Alberta, and I couldn't go home. I just kept driving, hoping something would take me away, and end this pain..." He turns his head to look at me. "Then I found you."

I lift my hand to his face and gently brush away a tear. As grateful as I am that we found each other, I wish more than anything that his pain wasn't what brought him here. "I'm glad you're here," I say softly.

Liam nods, and I swear I feel something deep inside him release. His pain isn't gone, but for now, at least we have each other.

"Same."

TWENTY-NINE

THEO

"MITCH," I call out behind me, waving him up to the wheelhouse as I steer the boat towards shore. He joins me, and I raise my voice over the hum of the engine. "I'm heading back to the marina first. Drop me off there, then take the haul to the buyer's station."

His brows draw together as he observes me for a moment. "Where you going?"

"I have something I need to do," I say, eyes fixed ahead as the shoreline comes into view. "You good to do that?"

"Yeah, man. Whatever you need," he says with a firm nod.

"Thanks," I reply, bringing my focus back to the wheel, guiding the boat towards the marina.

Once we reach the dock, I hop off and let Mitch take over so the crew can head to the buyer's station. I feel bad that I rushed the crew a bit this morning to make sure we finished at a good time, but luckily, they didn't ask why.

Because it's true. I have something I need to do.

I slip into my truck, successfully dodging Sheila so she doesn't stop me to question why I'm here early without my boat or crew.

And as I pull away from the marina, my thoughts drift to Liam, like they have been all morning. After he fell asleep last night, I stayed awake, unable to take my eyes off him. And I had an idea.

I pull into Donnie Rankin's property, and park by the old barn he's clearing out. I was working here the other day, and my eye caught something when he was showing me around. And he said I could take it.

I pull the steel rods out of the barn and load them into the bed of my truck. They're in good shape, and Donnie has no use for them. But I do.

It's still early afternoon when I pull into my driveway, and I really hope I find Liam taking it easy after the day he had yesterday. It was hard leaving him this morning, and for the first time in years, I considered calling the day off to stay home with him. But he woke up before I could do that, and told me to go. He said he would be fine...

I hope he is.

I step inside the house and kick off my boots by the door, anxiously listening for any sign of him. When I enter the kitchen, I see him sitting on the couch with Miss Bobber in the living room.

"Hey," I say softly, walking over to sit beside him.

His brows draw together as he eyes me. "You're home early..."

I nod, reaching down to pat Miss Bobber's belly as she rolls onto her back, her little paws in the air as she tries to grab my fingers.

"Yeah," I say quietly as I take him in. His eyes are dull, and a darkness clings to him. "I have something I need to work on," I continue. "And I need your help."

His gaze meets mine, and I smile, tilting my head towards the door. "Come on."

We leave Miss Bobber to play with the tassels on a blanket as Liam follows me outside to my truck. I open the tailgate to show him the steel rods, and he looks at me with questions swirling in his eyes.

I pull one out, resting it on the edge of the truck bed. "The sunroom needs a coffee table."

He looks between the rod and me, and I gesture with my chin to the workshop where we've stored his welder. "Time to get to work."

A light flickers in his eyes, pushing his darkness away, just a little bit.

I step closer to him, sliding my hand onto his waist. "I told you I planned to use that room for morning coffee... when I could."

He nods, and I lean in to brush my lips over his. "I think we both need that," I murmur against his mouth. "And I want it with you."

He exhales, his breath warm on my skin, then presses his lips to mine. He holds me tight as I lift my hand to the side of his face and let him take everything he wants and needs. Our kiss is full of gratitude and promise, and I feel some of the tension in him ease. When he pulls back, his eyes are softer, and clearer.

"Let's do it," he says quietly, with a gentle nod.

We unload the steel rods and carry them into the workshop, setting them on the concrete floor. I grab some paper, and we sit side by side at the workbench, sketching out a design. And within minutes, we have a plan. But the lines on the page are more than just a table... it's a piece of the life we're building together.

Liam hauls out his welder as I prep the wood for the tabletop, pulling out the two-by-fours and setting up the saw. But before long, my hands slow, and I find myself just watching him.

He has two of the rods clamped, and his welder ready to go. And when he flips his shield down over his face and the torch ignites with a sharp hiss...

Fuck me.

I lean against the workbench and watch as he kneels on the floor, sparks flying as his torch glides across the steel. The muscles in his forearms flex as he holds steady, welding the two pieces together, flawlessly and effortlessly.

When the torch clicks off and he lifts his shield to inspect his work, I'm still staring at him.

He glances up at me and all I can do is shake my head.

"Fuck," I mutter.

His brow furrows slightly and I just scoff.

"Like you don't know you're hot," I say.

A smirk flickers across his face, and he lifts one eyebrow as I step around the workbench. I lean down and press a firm kiss to his lips, lingering just long enough to feel the heat from the torch on his skin.

When I release him, he chuckles lightly, giving me a playful shove backwards. "Get to work."

I chuckle as well, returning to the workbench and forcing myself to focus on making the top of this table. I finally tear my eyes off him long enough to cut the boards and run them through the planer and sander. Once they're smooth, I arrange them in a herringbone pattern and glue them onto a plywood base. We fall into a comfortable silence as we work side by side, the hum of our machines filling the space. And it feels good.

By the time I have the boards clamped to let the glue dry, Liam's finished welding the base.

"I just need to let this set before I can cut it down," I say, wiping my hands on a rag.

Liam removes his shield, hanging it on the welder before coming over to run his hand over the tabletop. "It looks great."

I watch him for a moment, sensing the shift in him already. A quiet ease is pushing out the tension in his body, and the heaviness from earlier is starting to fade.

And I want to keep that going.

"Beer?" I ask, nodding towards the house.

He nods, his gaze meeting mine. "Yeah."

We shut everything down in the workshop and head inside the house. But when I open the fridge, I groan.

"Dammit," I sigh looking at the nearly empty shelves in the fridge. "I forgot we're out."

Liam shrugs as I turn to him, leaning against the counter. "We could go out."

I hesitate for a moment as I stare back at him, surprised he would suggest that. "You want to?"

He exhales, running a hand through his hair as he glances around the kitchen. "Honestly... yeah. I think I need to get out of the house for a bit."

I nod, letting my gaze linger on him. It's been a hard couple days for him, and I don't blame him for needing a change of scenery.

"Ok," I say, closing the fridge door. "Let's go."

After we change and clean up, Liam fills Miss Bobber's food dish before we head out. I drive us to the pub so we don't have to walk home in the dark, and as we get out of the truck I take in the view of the sky, painted with the soft hues of dusk. The fading light reflects across the surface, giving the whole scene a peaceful glow as a soft breeze rustles my hair.

As we walk through the door to the pub, we're greeted with the soft hum of Celtic music and the low murmur of conversation. It's fairly quiet in here today as it's a weekday evening, so we grab a table by the window looking over the water.

And it suddenly hits me. Besides going to my mom's or working on some jobs in town... we've never really done this. Since we've been together, we've stayed hidden behind the walls of the house, as we quietly make it ours. And even though no one knows the truth about us, sitting here like this kind of feels like we're on display.

But as I glance around, and see that no one is paying us any attention, I feel a spark of hope... and bravery.

Liam glances out the window, then turns to me. "You never told me how the haul was today."

I settle back into my seat, watching the last streaks of colour stretch across the sky. "Everything went well this morning," I say. "I had the crew take the haul to the buyer's station, but Mitch texted that it was a good one."

Liam nods as he looks into my eyes, and some kind of emotion passes through his. Something soft, caring, and... appreciative.

"Hey, Theo."

I look up as Allison approaches our table with a smile.

"Hey." I smile back at her as she sets menus before me and Liam.

She glances between us, her bubbly personality shining like always. "Can I get you guys a drink?" She then looks at me. "I'm assuming the usual?"

I chuckle with a nod. "Yeah."

She turns to Liam with a smile, and there's an intensity in his gaze as he watches her.

"And for you?" she asks.

He blinks and nods, his eyes softening a bit. "Same."

"Sounds good. Be right back," Allison says, leaving the table.

Once she's gone, Liam leans forward, resting his forearms

on the table. "You know you didn't have to leave work early," he says quietly.

I nod with a soft smile and a small shrug. "I know. But I wanted to."

His eyes drop to my lips, and my pulse immediately quickens as I take in the way he's looking at me.

"Mo chridhe," he murmurs slowly, lifting his eyes to meet mine again.

A slow smile spreads across my face, and I shake my head gently. "Someday, you're going to have to tell me what that means."

He lets out a breath of laughter, and simply shrugs one shoulder.

"Alright, here we are," Allison says, her bright voice cutting through the quiet tension as she sets our beer down in front of us. "Anything to eat?"

I sit back in my chair, trying to shake off the feeling of Liam's eyes on me, and the effect of his words. "We haven't looked at the menu yet."

She chuckles. "Right. Like you're not going to get the same thing you do every time?"

I roll my eyes as I pick up the menu and hold it out for her. "Yeah, ok. Fine. The club."

She smirks at me as she takes the menu, then turns to Liam. My gaze shifts to him as well, and his jaw is tight as he looks between us. But Allison doesn't seem to notice.

"Do you know what you'd like?" she asks him.

His gaze flicks up to meet hers as he shifts in his seat, sliding his menu towards her with a small smile. Which looks completely forced. "I'll take the same."

"Good choice," she said cheerily. "Be right up."

Liam's eyes follow her as she leaves, his gaze narrowing and his brow creasing. I lean forward, observing him with amusement.

"Problem?" I ask.

His eyes snap back to me, then he rolls them gently and looks out the window. "No," he mumbles.

I try not to smile as he shifts his gaze back to me.

And I just stare back at him, waiting.

"Fuck off," he mutters, lifting his beer to his lips and taking a sip.

But as a smile spreads across my lips, one forms on his as well.

I lean in close and lower my voice. "She's harmless." Then I tap my chest. "Gay, remember?"

His eyes flick between mine as they soften, and his lips tilt up in a soft smile.

"Hey guys!"

We both look up to see Sarah approaching our table with a big smile. "Finish your job in time, Theo?"

I nod, leaning back in my chair, keeping my eyes on Liam. "Made great progress."

Liam smiles shyly, dropping his eyes to his beer before him.

"I assume Mitch let you know it was a good haul today?" Sarah says, then turns and waves at Allison behind the bar where she's holding up a glass. "Hey, Allie! Yeah, I'll take one, thanks."

"Yeah, he did." I nod. "That's great."

She then turns to Liam with a warm smile. "Good to see you again, by the way! When do you head back to work?"

"End of the week," he says, quickly glancing at me. And disappointment settles at that reminder.

"Aw," she furrows her brow. "That's too bad. We never even got to hang." She glances at her table where her husband and son are looking over the menu, then turns back to us, with a curious expression. "Hey. Liam, why haven't you been out on the boat with us yet?"

My eyes slide to Liam, as I wonder the same thing. I guess I never thought to invite him since he's here to relax after working for three weeks straight, and I get up at 4:00AM every morning.

Liam raises an eyebrow, looking at me with a playful challenge. "I don't know... Captain?"

I chuckle. "Tomorrow?"

"Yes!" Sarah says, squeezing Liam's shoulder. "Amazing. Ok, I gotta go, but see you both in the morning!"

As she heads to her table, I bring my full attention back to Liam. He's looking back at me with sparkling eyes, and a genuine smile.

And I can't help but grin back at him. "Well, this will be fun."

THIRTY

LIAM

A HAND LANDS SOFTLY on my shoulder, gently shaking me awake. My eyes open slowly, and I look up at warm brown eyes, illuminated by the soft glow from the bedside lamp.

"Time to get to work," Theo says in a low, soothing voice.

I breathe out a soft laugh, the blankets slipping off as I sit up so the cool early morning air nips at my skin. Miss Bobber stretches lazily beside me, in the spot she claimed between me and Theo through the night. At 4:00AM, she clearly has no plans to get up, and I don't blame her.

I pull on my clothes and head downstairs to join Theo, where he's making coffee. The house is still and quiet, wrapped in predawn darkness which brings a sense of peace and calm. The smell of coffee urges me to take a deep breath in as I enter the kitchen, and Theo turns to look at me with a slow once-over, and a soft smile. He hands me a travel mug full of coffee, and I take it, slipping an arm around his waist at the same time to pull him close. The kiss I give him is as gentle as the morning, as I take a moment to appreciate him for everything he is.

When I reluctantly pull away, his hand cups my face, his thumb brushing my cheek. "Ready?"

I nod. "Yeah."

We make our way out to his truck, and Theo drives us through the sleeping town towards the marina. Darkness blankets the streets and houses, making everything even more still and peaceful than this town usually is. If that's even possible.

Theo pulls into the almost-empty parking lot, and I chuckle to myself. Of course, he's the first one here.

He glances over as I cock an eyebrow at him.

"Captains arrive first," he says.

"And you're always the earliest of all captains?" I ask.

He pauses as he stares back at me, hand on the door handle of the truck. "I like to be early," he says with a huff then opens his door and hops out. "Come on."

I chuckle as I follow him, and we make our way down the dock towards his boat. As we walk, I listen to the quiet sounds of our footsteps on the wooden boards and the soft laps of water against the hulls of the boats. And when I take a deep breath of the salty air, I let it all settle everything inside me.

When we reach his boat, Theo hops in and pulls out a couple pairs of waders, tossing one to me. Just as we start putting them on, a voice sounds behind us.

"New crew member, Theo?"

We turn to see a woman, I'd say in her fifties, standing on the dock with her hands on her hips.

Theo chuckles. "Just for today, Sheila. This is Liam."

I give her a smile and Sheila smirks at me, nodding with her chin towards Theo. "You've got your hands full with this one, let me tell ya."

I let out a small laugh, glancing at him as he rolls his eyes.

"Lies," he mutters, bending down to unlock a cabinet. "Don't listen to her, she's full of shit."

Sheila tips her head back with a laugh. "That's my boy." She then winks at me. "He might be a handful, but he's a good one."

I smile, glancing back at Theo. "Yeah... he really is," I murmur, just loud enough for him to hear.

He catches my gaze with a soft smile, then there's a gentle thud on the boat.

"Welcome to the crew!"

I turn around to see Sarah's bright smile as she joins us on the boat, and Sheila moving on to talk to another crew.

"Hey," I greet her as she heads for the container Theo pulled out and takes it from him.

Theo crouches down to pop open a floor panel to reveal a motor, and starts to check the oil. And I can't help but subtly keep my eyes on him while Sarah tells me about their morning routine.

"Our fearless captain handles everything about the boat," she explains, placing the container down in the middle of the deck. "We take care of the gear." She flips the lid off the container to reveal a tub of salted herring packed in ice. "This is our bait. We pick it up from the buyer's station the day before so we're ready to go first thing."

Theo steps into the wheelhouse and starts up the engine, the rumble of diesel bringing the boat to life.

"Well, I'll be damned!" Mitch steps onto the boat, clapping me on the back. "No fucking way. About time you came out with us!"

I laugh, turning as Glen hops on board and gives me a playful salute.

"I didn't know we were adding to the crew," Glen says, raising an eyebrow at Theo. "I could've slept in. Liam can take my spot."

Theo leans casually against the wheelhouse, arms crossed as he eyes Glen. "I bet he'd do a better job."

Glen pretends to size me up, nodding thoughtfully. "Yeah. Probably."

I chuckle as he nudges me with his elbow. Theo just shakes his head, pushing off the wall and heading into the wheelhouse. "Let's go."

Mitch and Glen untie the ropes securing the boat to the dock and Theo effortlessly backs us out, aiming us towards the wide, dark expanse of the ocean. The low rumble of the engine mixes with the sound of water lapping against the hull as Glen, Mitch, and Sarah settle onto a bench just behind the wheelhouse, and Sarah motions for me to join them.

"Ever been lobster fishing before?" Mitch asks, raising his voice over the hum of the engine.

I shake my head. "Nope. First time on a lobster boat too."

"Really?" Glen asks with a smirk. "Aren't you a Caper?"

I chuckle with a shrug. "Yeah, but I never really knew anyone in the business."

Sarah snorts, sipping her coffee. "Well, you certainly do now."

Theo glances back at me through the window, and motions for me to join him in the wheelhouse.

I step inside, taking in the screens and controls surrounding him. The soft glow of the equipment bathes his face in dim light, and his expression softens as his eyes meet mine. He holds my gaze for a moment, and I want nothing more than to reach out and touch him and press my lips to his. His eyes momentarily drop to my lips, confirming he has the same thought, before he turns his attention to a screen before him and points to it. "This is where we're going."

I lean closer, taking in the various markers scattered across one section of the screen. "Those are your trap locations?"

Then my eye catches the distance. "Wow, they're pretty far out."

He nods. "Yeah. About forty minutes out."

I glance out the front window at the dark, endless water ahead. There's something unsettling about heading this far out into the ocean in the darkness, but seeing Theo so calm and at ease settles me. I lean against the wheelhouse wall and sip my coffee, watching Theo drive the boat as the first hints of dawn start to break.

By the time we reach the first trap location, the sky has softened to shades of yellow and blue, casting a gentle light over the water. It's quiet and serene, and for the first time in a while, my mind is completely quiet.

Theo slows the boat and turns to me, pointing towards a buoy bobbing in the water as the crew jumps into action behind us, getting things set up on the deck.

"These are our trawl lines," Theo says. "Everyone in our fishing area paints their buoys, so we know whose is whose. Each licence has an area where we can set traps, which is determined on trap setting day at the beginning of the season." He flips a switch, and the boat shifts into neutral, rumbling softly as we drift towards the buoy. He grabs a long hook from behind him, smiling as he looks back at me. "And we always get the best spot."

"Damn right we do," Mitch says, stepping up beside me with a grin.

I watch Theo as he hooks the buoy and pulls it up onto the deck. There's a quiet confidence in the way he moves, and I can see why he's torn about this life. It might have been chosen for him, but it's obvious he loves it too.

He lifts the buoy, showing it to me. "Ours are blue and red. Sarah paints them every year." He gestures to the faded paint, revealing an octopus with big eyes and a smile. "And she tends to put adorable little sea creatures on them as well," he says with a roll of his eyes.

Sarah beams as she opens the hatch to the holding tank. "Each year they get even better."

Mitch groans. "They're going to have like... glitter or something next year, aren't they."

"Who knows." Sarah shrugs. "Maybe googly eyes."

Theo shakes his head as he secures the line to a hydraulic winch. He flips a switch, and the system starts reeling in the trap line.

He leans in closer to me as he points at it. "This brings the line in, so we can pull the traps up to the side of the boat where we unload, re-bait, and set them again." He then turns to face me, and his expression turns serious. "Feet flat on the floor at all times, and keep your eyes down. If rope is moving on the floor, always step up to the wheelhouse. If you feel a tug on your foot, drop to the ground immediately and point your feet to the stern."

I nod, taking in the intensity in his eyes. "Got it."

He holds my gaze for a moment longer before nodding back. "Ok."

Mitch leans over the side of the boat as the first trap surfaces, and pulls it onto the ledge. Theo flips a switch to stop the hauler while Mitch opens the top, and him and Theo reach in.

Mitch holds up a large crab. "These fellas like to sneak in and eat all the bait. At least we're feeding the ocean floor." He chuckles, tossing the crab back into the water.

Theo pulls out a lobster, giving it a quick once-over before tossing it into the holding tank. "That's our job, really," he says, looking at me over his shoulder. "Feeding the ecosystem and keeping the fishery sustainable." He pulls another lobster from the trap and holds it up, then tosses it back into the ocean, glancing at me with a shake of his head. "Too small."

I nod, stepping forward, hanging on to every word he says. Seeing and hearing the confidence in him while he works has me completely hooked, and I'm fascinated by this process.

And him.

"Our job is to keep our traps full of bait to feed the young and breeders," he continues. "We only keep a small amount of what we catch. In our waters here in the South Shore, it can take a lobster seven to nine years to reach the minimum legal size, which is a carapace length of 82.5 millimetres." He holds up another lobster and runs his finger along the shell from the tail to the eyes to show me where he measures. "We can eyeball most, but if I think I need to measure it, then it's probably too small." He shrugs and tosses it back into the water. "So back in they go to keep eating and growing."

Once the trap is empty, Theo switches the hauler back on, sliding the empty trap down to Sarah as Mitch hauls up the next one on the line. Sarah loads the empty trap with bait, and Glen starts banding the lobsters in the holding tank. Everyone moves efficiently with a practised ease, like a well-oiled machine. This crew clearly works well together.

Theo reaches into the next trap and pulls out a large lobster. He turns it over to show me the bottom of it, where hundreds of tiny eggs cling to the shell. "Breeder," he says. "They hatch between June and September, so they tend to have a lot of eggs this time of year with only a couple weeks left in the season."

He pulls a tool from his pocket that looks like a pair of pliers. He places it over the tail of the lobster and notches a V into it. "We don't keep breeders. So if she's caught without eggs, other fishers will know and put her back." He grabs a small fish from the bait bucket and tucks it into her claw. The lobster latches on and he chuckles, glancing up at me. "I always throw the breeders back with a snack."

He then leans over the edge of the boat and places her gently in the water on her back, letting her float down undisturbed.

I can't help but smile as I watch him. Even with lobster, he is so caring, and has the biggest heart.

Mitch shakes his head with a chuckle. "Such a softie."

Theo shoots him a look as he reaches into the trap again. "Fuck off."

"And just like that, it's gone," Mitch says dramatically, tossing another lobster into the holding tank.

As the empty trap slides down the line to Sarah, Theo gestures for me to step forward. "You're up."

I smile, stepping forward as Mitch opens the next trap. I peer inside and reach for a lobster, pulling it out to inspect it.

"What do you think?" Theo asks.

I look it over, turning it to check out its underside and tail. "Decent size, no eggs, no tail notch..."

"Keeper?" he prompts.

I nod. "Keeper."

As I toss it into the holding tank, Glen looks up at me and shakes his head with a *tsk*. "Your first one, and it's the biggest in here. You're gonna replace one of us in crew, aren't ya?"

I laugh. "No worries, I've got another job. But..." I turn to Theo. "This is pretty great."

His soft brown eyes meet mine, and we hold each other's gaze for a moment, sharing something that feels warm and comfortable. His lips lift into a small smile, and my gaze immediately drops to take it in. But the clatter of the trap sliding down the deck snaps us out of it, and Theo turns the hauler back on, pulling up the next one.

I help Mitch empty the rest of the traps from this line,

while Theo looks over the catch to decide whether this spot is still viable. Once the traps are all baited, Theo flips the hauler to reverse and we toss them back into the ocean. He places a firm hand on my arm as the rope slides quickly over the edge, reminding me of the intensity behind his earlier warning. Watching the rope dangle and uncoil as the traps sink to the bottom of the ocean, I now understand exactly what he means by eyes down and feet flat on the deck.

Theo marks the trawl line location on the GPS, and we move to the next spot. We repeat the process for all two hundred and fifty traps, as we empty each one, then re-bait, and reset. Theo adjusts the locations of a few trawl lines where the catch was low, and marks these changes on the GPS.

When the last trap is back in the water, the bait bucket is empty and the holding tank is full, Theo turns to look into my eyes. "Good work, fisherman."

As I look into his eyes and take in his smile, I realize I've been wearing one of my own all morning. Being here with him, covered in dirt and salt water, watching him in his element and spending this time with him... it was perfect.

He's fucking perfect.

THIRTY-ONE

LIAM

THE SECOND we step into the house and the door closes behind us, our lips collide. I don't know who initiated what, but it doesn't matter. After spending the day on the boat with him, watching him work, and seeing the quiet confidence in every one of his moves... I've been craving this. And finally, my hands are on him.

He's just as frantic as his hands slide under my sweater and he pulls it over my head. I shrug it off and drop it to the floor, vaguely aware of Miss Bobber roaming around at our feet as I bring my lips back to Theo's. But when Theo's shirt falls to the floor and I hear a little scurry, I break away from him and look down.

Miss Bobber is staring up at us in wide-eyed horror as she sits among the discarded shirts and sweaters.

I push Theo's chest so he backs up a step, then bend over to pick her up. "You dropped it on her."

He scoffs. "Pretty sure that was you."

Ignoring him, I kick off my boots and carry her into the kitchen.

Theo follows with a chuckle. "Guess I'll just go shower then?" he says, amusement lacing his tone.

I look over my shoulder as I grab Miss Bobber's food and take her to her dish. My gaze lingers on his bare chest before I nod slowly. "Be up in a minute."

His lips tilt up in a smirk, then he walks over to give Miss Bobber a scratch behind her ears. I keep my eyes on him a moment longer as he disappears down the hallway, then I fill Miss Bobber's dish and leave her to eat.

I need to go finish what we started.

I hear the shower running as I make my way up the stairs, and when I push the bathroom door open, I'm met with a view of Theo… completely naked.

His eyes are full of heat as they land on me, and I'm across the bathroom in an instant, devouring him in a needy kiss. We pick up right where we left off as he quickly drops his hands and undoes my belt, pulling my pants open.

The second his hand lands on my cock, I'm moaning into his mouth and grabbing at him, desperate for every inch of his body. I step out of my pants as I walk him backwards into the shower and right up against the wall. The warm water sprays over us as I press my body into him, the taste of salt lingering on our lips from the day at sea.

I eventually pull away from him and grab the bodywash, his eyes following my movements as I pour some into my hands. As I tease him, running my hands over his chest and down his abs, creating suds and feeling his hard muscles, I can feel the anticipation bubbling up inside him. And it's growing in me too.

My soapy hand finally finds his cock, and I slide it along his length. His eyes close as he releases a breath and I bring my lips to his neck, softly sucking and pulling a moan from him.

"Oh my god..." he murmurs as his hands trail up my back, bringing soap suds with them.

My cock is aching with need as his hands roam my body and I continue to stroke him. But when the soap is washed away and I can't fucking take it anymore, my hand reaches behind him, and I run a finger over his hole.

He moans into my mouth, and I swallow it down, eager for more. As I continue to press and rub my finger over his ass, his breaths quicken and his hand drops to my dick.

But I step back and bat his hand away, shaking my head.

His eyes bore into me as I let my gaze roam over him, taking in his muscles, his freckles, his hard cock...

I want to make him see fucking stars.

"Turn around," I say, bringing my eyes back up to his.

They widen slightly, and he hesitates.

I tilt my head as I give him a little smirk. "Turn around, mo chridhe..." I step into him, and run my hand up his chest to grip the side of his face. "Let's see if you can take my tongue as well as you take my cock."

Theo draws a breath in, then turns around to face the shower wall. I reach up to angle the showerhead away, then drop to my knees.

My heart races as I palm his ass, wanting to do this just right for him. I've had so many firsts with him in the time we've known each other, and each one just keeps getting better and better. I want to do it all, and give him everything he's ever wanted... and then some.

I lean in and run my tongue over his hole as I squeeze his ass. Theo presses his forehead to the wall with a groan that comes from deep within his chest.

"Fuck, yeah..." he moans.

As I do it again, he grunts and I feel him tense. "Jesus, fuck..."

"Hm," I hum, licking him again and pulling his ass into my face to encourage him to take what he wants.

And he does.

He pushes his ass back into me as I continue to lick and suck him, his needy groans and desperate movements making me impossibly hard. And when I push my tongue into him, the sound he makes is absolutely fucking feral.

I grip him tight as I continue to fuck his ass with my tongue, not willing to stop until he wants me to.

"Fuck, ok," he says, turning around and releasing a deep breath.

But now his cock is right there, and it's fucking *leaking*.

So I take him into my mouth to taste him, and give him a long, slow lick up his length.

Theo grabs my hair and pulls me back with a shake of his head. "I'm not coming until you fuck me."

Next thing I know, I'm on my feet and taking him in a frantic kiss. With lips still locked, he reaches out to shut off the shower and push the door open. But as we step out, he gently pushes me away from him and lets out a long, slow breath as he reaches down to squeeze his cock and close his eyes.

I bite back a smile as I take him in and drop a hand to my cock as well. "Fuck," I murmur. "Tha thu bòidheach."

His eyes snap open as he releases a pained groan with a shake of his head. "That's not helping..."

Then he blows out another breath and walks out of the bathroom, into the bedroom.

I follow with a chuckle, but the second I reach him, he pushes me onto the bed and kneels on the floor between my legs.

And when he takes me into his mouth, I'm flooded with pleasure. My body seems to melt as he slides his mouth along my cock and the anticipation that has been building crashes with a sense of intense relief. He feels so fucking good, and it feels like every single one of my nerves is tingling and waking up.

Each time he takes me into his mouth, he takes a little bit more... and I feel that anticipation starting to rise again. His hand lifts to cup my balls, pulling a groan out of me as I sink my fingers into his hair.

Then he slides his lips down my cock once again... taking me to the back of his throat.

"Jesus Christ..." I mutter, gripping his shoulder tight as I stare down at him, feeling like I could come at any moment from the sight alone.

He gags slightly as he slides back off my cock, then takes me right back in.

"Oh my god," I pant as I chase my breath, unable to take my eyes off him.

But I need to be inside him.

Right now.

I pull him up to me as I fall back onto the bed, taking him in a fierce kiss. He grinds himself into me as my tongue slides along his, and I hold him tight against me.

But then he pushes back, and leans over to grab the lube from the bedside table.

I take it from him and place a hand to his chest to keep him right where he is, straddling my hips. He watches with bated breath as I coat my fingers in lube, then pull him back down to kiss him again.

And when I reach behind him to press my lubed fingers to his hole, he lets out a moan and drops his forehead to my shoulder. I hold him tight against me as I push a finger inside him, and he immediately rocks his hips to push back against my hand. When I push a second finger into him, he grunts and brings his lips back to mine.

Then he mutters against my lips, "Just fuck me already."

I chuckle, removing my fingers from his ass and pushing him back. He wastes no time grabbing the lube, and I just watch him, almost forgetting to breathe as he lubes up my cock and pushes onto his knees.

Theo's eyes stay locked on mine as he grips my cock and lowers himself onto it. My hands rest on his thighs as I let him control this, watching as his abs flex and his chest rises and falls with heavy breaths as he sinks onto my dick. His ass feels incredible, and the sight of him is even better. Once he's fully seated on my cock, he leans forward and presses his lips to mine.

"Guess I'm fucking you."

My hands grab either side of his face as I push my tongue into his mouth. And as he slowly moves his hips, we both groan. He does it again, and again, grinding harder each time. I start to rock my hips with him, and eventually he's riding me as I tightly grip his hips.

I watch him as he tilts his head back and closes his eyes, getting lost to the feeling and doing exactly what I wanted him to do.

To *take* what he wants.

To control me, use me, and *fuck* me.

And when his hand moves to his cock, I take it instead. He drops his head as I stroke him, and he groans. "Oh, fuck."

Tingles are quickly spreading throughout my body as I ride closer to the edge, and by the looks of him, I'd say he's almost there too.

His abs flex with every thrust of his hips, and his fingers dig into my arms as he pants, "I'm going to come."

I grunt, unable to say anything as I try to hold back my own release and wait for him.

Then his hips stutter and he lets out a beautiful moan, his cock pulsing in my hand as his cum decorates my abs.

And I need to come, *right now*.

I roll us over so he's on his back, pulling out of him to take my cock in my hand as I lean over him. But he uses the same move I did on him, and pushes my hand away so he can take it instead. A sudden rush of pleasure courses through my body as Theo strokes my cock and I come over his stomach. As I come down from my high, my heart beating fast and euphoria lingering, Theo meets my eyes and smirks.

His hand lifts to his stomach as he runs his fingers through my cum, and my gaze drops to follow the movement. Then, he does the same thing to his cum on me. And when his hand lifts to his lips, and his tongue runs over his fingers… I feel like I could come again right now.

He hooks his other hand around the back of my neck, bringing my mouth to his. His tongue pushes past my lips to give me a taste of us… and it's fucking perfection.

When he releases me, I roll onto my back beside him and let out a breath, waiting for my heart to settle.

We're silent for a moment, only our heavy breaths filling the room.

Until Theo speaks.

"Holy fuck."

I huff out a laugh and nod. "Yeah."

We lie in comfortable silence for a bit longer, staring up at the skylight as a warm, contented feeling settles over me. A peaceful feeling… like everything in the world has slowed down just for us.

When Theo turns his head to look at me, I meet his gaze and take in the way his eyes are sparkling.

I think mine might be too.

Because with him, everything else fades away. All the

confusion, hurt, and pain… it all takes a back seat, making room for so much more in my life. A soft smile pulls at my lips as I stare into his eyes, and let my gaze roam over his freckles.

He reaches up and gently pushes my hair back from my face. "I love seeing you smile," he says softly.

I nod. "Same."

His gaze lingers on mine, his expression turning thoughtful. "There's something I think I want to do… before you go back to work. If you're ok with it…"

"What?" I ask.

Theo takes a deep breath, his eyes flicking to my lips before meeting mine again. "Tell my family I'm gay."

I smile, leaning in to brush my lips over his.

"Let's do it."

THIRTY-TWO

THEO

LIAM STIRS in bed before I can slip out of the room, and I hear his low voice in the soft darkness. "Hey."

I cross the room and sit on the edge of the bed, leaning down to press a kiss to his lips. "Hey."

He rubs the sleep from his eyes, and I smile down at him and Miss Bobber, who is sprawled out in her usual spot in the middle of the bed.

"What's your plan for today?" I ask, tracing my fingers lightly over his arm.

His hand lands on my thigh with a gentle squeeze. "I'm going to put the baseboards in the sunroom now that the floor's done."

I smile. "Then it just needs a coffee table."

He smiles back at me, and I need to remind myself to breathe.

I nod, pausing for a moment. "What do you think about going to see my mom tonight?"

He tugs me down again, placing a kiss on my lips, full of

quiet reassurance. "Whatever you want, mo chridhe. I'm there with you."

I kiss him back, thankful for him and the strength and courage he gives me. I'm nervous to come out to my family, but I also know he's right. They love me, and I know it'll be ok. But to make things a little more manageable, I've decided to tell my mom first. And now that I've decided this is happening, I can't sit on it for too long and let the anxiety build.

"But," I say, pulling back from his lips, "we also need to find time to go fishing before you head back to work. I need to kick your ass once and for all."

He laughs, his breath warm on my lips. "You wish."

"It's happening," I say firmly, leaning down to give him one last kiss before I stand. "I'm starting to get a bit pissed off."

"Starting to?" he teases with a chuckle.

"Whatever," I mutter, heading for the door to hide my smile. "See you this afternoon."

"Have a good one," he says, his voice already fading into sleep as I gently close the door behind me.

Downstairs, I set the coffee to brew, and let my eyes drift towards the sunroom as the rich scent fills the air. A smile forms on my lips as a warm feeling settles over me and I think about spending time with Liam in there. In the room we built together. Lobster season ends in just two weeks, and usually I'm dreading this time of year because I need to keep busy to stay out of my head. But now... quiet, slow mornings sound pretty damn good.

With Liam.

I grab my coffee, taking that comforting feeling with me as I head down to the marina through the quiet, sleepy town. As I pull into the parking lot and hop out of my truck, I see Sheila just stepping out of hers as well.

"Morning, Theo," she greets me, bright-eyed and cheerful.

"You know, Sheila," I say, falling into step beside her as we head onto the dock, "you don't have to be here this early."

She waves a dismissive hand in the air as we walk. "And who would keep all you in line if I wasn't here?"

I glance around the quiet marina, seeing only John, one of the other captains, here so far. "I think we'd manage."

She raises a brow at me. "The day I'm not here is the day everything goes to shit." She turns towards her office, waving to me over her shoulder. "Have a good day, my boy!"

"Thanks, Sheila," I say with a chuckle, then head to the boat.

I fall into my usual routine getting everything ready, and Sarah arrives first, as always.

"Aw, one crew member down today, huh?" Sarah says with her usual cheery hop into the boat.

I nod as she pulls out her waders and slips them on. "Didn't want Liam showing you guys up any more than he already did. Especially Glen."

"Jesus Murphy," Glen exclaims, appearing on the dock with his hand dramatically over his heart. "I heard that. You've got some nerve."

I just smirk at him, then step into the wheelhouse to look over the coordinates for our traps. I want to start where we finished yesterday at the new locations I set, hoping they'll give us a better haul.

By the time we're prepped and pulling away from the dock, the air is warming up and the sky is starting to show the first signs of light. As I listen to the familiar hum of the engine and the laughs from my crew as we drive towards the first trap, my mind wanders.

To yesterday, with Liam here on the boat. His soft smile under the morning sun, and his crystal blue eyes sparkling with joy as he held up a lobster. To what we did after, and how we fell asleep in each other's arms after yet another shower that also ended up quite heated. And to tonight… when I'll finally tell my mom I'm gay.

I never thought I'd have the courage to be here, ready and able to do this. But Liam has helped me see exactly who I am, what I want, and has shown me how to do something about it. And I still can't quite believe that he wants to do it all with me.

I'm seriously, madly, in love with him.

And I plan to tell him that too.

He's been through so much, facing intense grief and pain every day. But over the past couple days, he's been working through it. And when he's ready to face it head on, I'll be right there with him.

When I pull the boat up to our first trawl line, the sky has lightened with beautiful, subtle hues of pink and orange. The water is still and the sky is clear, making for a perfect morning.

"Let's see what we got," Mitch says, moving beside me as Sarah and Glen take their positions. I reach out with the hook and snag the buoy, pulling it in to see a bright seahorse painted on it, with long eyelashes.

"Quite possibly my best work," Sarah says seriously, watching as I secure the line to the winch and flip the switch to start hauling the line up.

I shake my head with a smirk. "Honestly, I do think you're onto something with googly eyes."

Mitch groans and turns to me. "Oh fuck right off, don't encourage her."

I shrug as Sarah cackles with delight and Glen shakes his head, clearly on Mitch's side.

The first trap breaks the surface, and I lean over to haul it up, setting it on the edge of the boat to start emptying it.

"Think Liam will come back out?" Mitch asks as he reaches into the trap.

"He's heading back to work in a couple days," I say, my stomach dropping at the thought of not having him here for three weeks. "So, not sure."

"Tell him it's his last chance if he doesn't want to wait until November," Sarah says. "Season will be done when he gets home."

I nod, tossing a lobster into the holding tank. "Yeah, maybe he can get out again before he leaves."

"What's he up to today?" Glen asks as Mitch passes an empty trap down the line to Sarah for bait, while I pull up the next one.

"Doing some work on the house," I say, opening the trap.

Sarah looks down the boat at me. "What have you done to it so far? Sounds like you guys have gone hard on it the past couple months."

"A lot," I reply with a nod, pulling out my notcher to cut a V into a breeder's tail. "When he got here, I only had part of the kitchen done. He's been working on the rest, and I've been finding more time to put into it too." I place a herring between the lobster's claws, smiling as she latches onto it, then set her back into the water.

Mitch aims a wide grin my way. "I knew I liked him from the first day I met him. He actually got you to slow the fuck down! That's a goddamn miracle."

I huff out a laugh, hitting the switch to pull up the next trap. But I don't argue with him. Liam has been saying that to me since we first met... and I guess he did make it happen.

Not that I'm complaining.

A sudden warmth fills me as I look at my crew. They like Liam, and they're the kindest and most understanding people I know. And I find myself wanting to tell them about us. To stop hiding, and let them in.

I take a deep breath as I turn to continue emptying the

traps, knowing I need to tell my family first. But still, it feels good to have finally found the courage to share something that's been weighing on me for so long. And if things don't go well... I'll face that if it happens.

But I don't think it will.

We continue to empty and re-bait the traps, and when we finish this trawl line, Mitch lets out a low whistle as he eyes the holding tank. "Looks like you picked the right spot, Captain."

I nod, looking over the haul from the line. There's definitely more here than at our last spot.

At the next trawl line, I pull the buoy up and load the line into the winch, hitting the switch as I lean back against the wheelhouse wall. My eyes scan over the horizon as we wait for the first trap to surface, and I take a moment to just sit with this peaceful, easy feeling. This feeling I've been chasing for so long, and finally found.

But that peace is interrupted when the line suddenly pulls taut, and the winch grinds, telling me something's wrong.

"Shit," I mutter, stepping forward to shut off the winch. "I think a trap is caught on a rock."

But before I can turn the switch off, a loud, sudden snap fills the air. The line breaks under the tension, and time seems to slow as I watch the end of it coming right for me... straight at my head.

My arm lifts as I attempt to block the impact, and I close my eyes, unable to do anything else.

And all I feel is intense, searing pain.

THIRTY-THREE
LIAM

AS MY COFFEE BREWS, I gaze out the window at the peaceful morning and let the calm wash over me. The air is quickly warming up as the sun shines, urging me to get outside and take it all in. My eyes land on the firepit and I smile as I get an idea. Looks like I'll be doing some yard work after installing the baseboard today, and Theo and I can have a fire this evening. After we visit his mom.

I'm surprised at how calm I feel about it all. About supporting Theo as he tells his mom he's gay, and that we're together. I keep thinking it should feel bigger to me, and scarier... but it doesn't. I've never felt this strongly about anyone before, and the fact that he's a guy doesn't even seem to matter. All that matters is that I'm with him, and he's finally doing something for himself that he's worked towards for so long. I want this for him, and I want this for us.

And watching Theo find the strength to do what's best for him, makes me realize I can, and should, do the same. It's time I face my own fears and talk to my parents again. So I can stop running from the pain, and move past this storm. Just these past few days with Theo is proof that I can… and I'm ready to try.

When the coffee is finished brewing, I pick up the mug and glance down at Miss Bobber at my feet. She looks up at me expectantly.

"Let's get to work," I tell her.

I take my coffee into the sunroom where I've already stacked the baseboards. But before I start, I take a slow sip of my coffee, looking out the bay window as the sun shimmers over the ocean like millions of tiny crystals.

I can't wait to share these mornings with Theo.

As I set my mug down and kneel on the floor to line up the first baseboard, Miss Bobber rolls onto her back in front of me and grabs at my hands. I laugh and rub her belly as she wriggles around, trying to catch my fingers.

Then, there's a sudden, loud knock on the door and she jumps to her feet, frozen as she looks out into the living room.

"Who the hell is that?" I mutter as I push to my feet, and make my way through the living room and kitchen towards the door.

When I pull it open, Heather is on the other side, wide-eyed and frantic.

"I'm sorry," she says on a breath. "I don't have your number…"

My heart thumps and my stomach twists as I take in her worried expression. "What's wrong…"

She meets my eyes as emotion swirls in hers. "There was an accident on the boat this morning."

Her words hit like a punch right to the gut.

I can't move as I stare back at her, my entire body feeling frozen as my heart tries to beat right out of my chest.

"They took Theo to Halifax," Heather continues, her voice sounding like it's miles away. She runs a shaky hand through her hair and draws in a deep breath. "They're taking him into surgery now."

Panic takes hold of me as my vision goes fuzzy and my chest tightens. The only thing I can hear is my pulse in my ears as the world fades away, and the familiar wave pulls me under, hard and fast.

No... no, please, no...

"Liam?" Heather's voice breaks through the haze as her hand grips my arm.

I pull in a sharp breath, and shake my head, trying to pull myself together. My hand trembles as I push it through my hair. "I'm sorry... I..." I trail off, unable to latch onto any thoughts or words.

It's all happening again.

And this time, it's the man I've fallen in love with.

I feel paralyzed with fear as Heather stands before me and places her hand on my shoulder, her brow furrowed as she peers into my eyes. Then she tugs my arm, leading me through the house. And before I know it, I'm sitting on the couch next to her.

"Liam," she says, pulling me back to reality. "Liam?"

I blink as my gaze focuses on her.

And guilt hits me hard.

I'm a fucking asshole. This is her brother. She's been through this before with their father, and here I am, crumbling when *I* should be there for *her*.

"I'm sorry," I breathe out, trying to find my voice. "What... what happened?"

"A line snapped," she says quietly. "It hit Theo and wrapped around his arm and hand. I think... I think it's pretty bad." Her voice cracks as her eyes fill with tears.

My breath hitches as emotion swells in my chest and I do

everything I can not to break down right here in front of her. But I don't trust my voice, so I just give a small nod.

"Mitch called from the boat," she says, wiping her eyes. "Mom is with him in Halifax, and they took him right into surgery." She blows out a breath and shakes her head. "It could have been a lot worse..."

My mind races as panic settles in again, threatening to drown me.

"I need to grab some things for him," Heather says, pushing to her feet with a sniff.

And still, all I can do is nod stiffly, lost to the wave as I try desperately to stay afloat.

Heather eyes me for a moment before she turns, and heads upstairs.

My mind spins as I sit here, frozen, as panic rapidly grows and threatens to drown me.

I can't lose him.

My chest heaves as I struggle to breathe, memories crashing over me of another hospital, another waiting room, another loss. I hear the echoes of voices from just months ago, when I sat in a hard plastic chair, anxiously waiting for good news. But instead, they looked at me with sad, empty eyes, and said they were sorry.

Nick died.

A low, pained sound escapes me, and I drop my head into my hands, pulling at my hair. I can't go through this again. Not with Theo. Please, not with Theo...

Heather's footsteps return, stopping in the doorway to the living room. I lift my head to look at her, standing with a bag in her hand, and a sad look on her face as she watches me with understanding and compassion in her eyes.

And I know why.

She just went into Theo's room.

Our room.

Where my clothes mingle with his, and the bed is still rumpled from our sleep together.

She crosses the room and sits beside me, pulling me into a hug. I try to swallow the emotion, but it's too much. A tear slips out with a broken breath.

"It's ok," she whispers. "He'll be ok. It's his arm and hand... They're going to fix him up, and as long as there are no complications, he'll be home tomorrow."

I want to believe her, and I know she's right, but the fear continues to press down on me. It comes out in pained breaths and fallen tears, no matter how hard I try to stop them.

Heather pulls back slightly, looking into my eyes. "Do you want to come with me?"

A shock jolts through me at that question, and instantly my heart starts racing. The thought of stepping into the hospital, seeing the sterile white walls, hearing the beeping of monitors, and solemn-looking doctors... I can't go back there.

I want to. I *want* to be there when he wakes up, so I can tell him everything is going to be ok.

But I can't know that. I thought Nick was going to be ok.

Everything inside me is telling me to go, and screaming at me not to. The memory of soul-crushing pain is overwhelming, flooding me with fear so that I can't even speak.

And I can't break down in front of him, when he's been so strong for me.

Heather watches me as her eyes widen and she reaches out to take my trembling hand. "It's ok," she says. Then she lowers her gaze to Miss Bobber as she crawls over my lap. "You should probably stay here with this little one anyway." She looks back at me with a sad smile. "Can I call you when I hear how the surgery went?"

I nod, my hand drifting to Miss Bobber's fur, grounding myself in the softness of her.

"Ok," Heather says, handing me her phone. "Put your number in. I'll keep you updated."

I type it in with shaky hands, and Heather watches me carefully, her brow furrowed with concern. "Grandpa is with Mom, but I can get a friend to take the kids and Chris can come over?"

I shake my head, wiping my wet eyes. "No, it's ok."

"You sure?" she asks softly. "I don't want to leave you like this."

I blow out a frustrated breath, guilt gnawing at me because Theo needs her more than I do.

And I fucking hate myself that I can't pull it together enough to be strong for him.

My hand runs roughly over my face, and I exhale forcefully again.

Heather's hand rests gently on my back. "Liam?" she asks softly.

I take a deep breath, and bring my eyes to hers. "I just... I lost someone not long ago," I murmur, my voice trembling.

She nods in understanding. "You're not losing anyone else."

I nod as I feel the tears start to well again. "You're not either."

She smiles, her own tears falling as she pulls me into another hug. "It took me years to walk into a hospital again without feeling like I was going to completely lose it," she whispers.

I hold onto her tightly, finding comfort in her words and understanding.

When she gently releases me, she gives my arm a squeeze. "I'll let you know as soon as he's out of surgery, ok?"

I nod, the nagging guilt still present as I wish more than anything I could be there.

But Heather seems to sense it and shakes her head. "He'll be out of it all night. But he'll be so happy to see you tomorrow when he's home," she says gently.

"Thanks," I whisper.

She gives my arm another squeeze and stands, giving Miss Bobber a gentle pat. "Talk soon, ok?"

"Ok," I manage, my voice sounding far away.

Heather leaves, and I listen to the door closing behind her and the crunch of the gravel under her tires as her car heads down the driveway.

And I sit here, alone with my thoughts as I stare out at the water.

But as an image of wild hair, soft freckles, and a warm smile takes over, I latch onto it and try to keep my storm at bay.

THIRTY-FOUR

THEO

I SIT on the edge of the hospital bed, my arm in a sling and my hand and forearm wrapped in layers of bandages and a large splint. The doctor's voice drones on with final instructions, but my eyes stay fixed on the floor while Mom and Heather listen intently.

"The forearm fracture will take about three months to fully heal," the doctor explains. "But since both bones were fractured, plus the wrist, we could be looking at longer. We put three plates in due to the severity of the injury."

I bite back the urge to tune him out completely.

"Your hand, however, is more complicated," he continues. "Given the extent of the fractures and soft tissue damage, we may need another surgery in the future to improve functionality. For now, I'm referring you to occupational therapy to start early mobilization, manage scar tissue, and prevent stiffness." He pauses for a moment, but I still don't look up at him. "Progress will be slow," he continues cautiously. "It's going to be about six months to rehabilitate your hand. I'll be honest… it will never be exactly as it was before."

I close my eyes as my stomach drops and dread washes over me.

"But our goal is to get you as close to normal function as possible," the doctor says. "And achieving this has a lot to do with the therapy that comes after surgery. So, work hard, and it will pay off."

As he starts in on medications and pain management, I finally let myself zone out. Everything feels distant, muted by the haze of meds and the heavy weight of sadness sinking into my chest.

Until the bed dips beside me, and I glance up to meet Grandpa's eyes. He offers a small, sad smile, patting my leg while the doctor finishes talking to Mom and Heather.

The doctor then gives me a nod with a, "Good luck," and leaves the room.

"Ok, I think we got everything," Mom says, glancing around the stark, depressing room.

"I already got your prescriptions filled, Theo," Heather says, placing several pill bottles in my bag and zipping it shut. Then she looks at me with a forced smile. "Ready?"

I blow out a breath and push off the bed to stand, ignoring the fog in my head and the unsteady feeling beneath my feet.

"Wait," Mom says, quickly stepping forward. "You're supposed to use a wheelchair."

"I'm fine," I mutter, walking past her and forcing my body to cooperate. "Let's just go."

Mom and Heather murmur behind me as I leave the room, but Grandpa stays close as we make our way to the car.

When we get there, Heather places my bag in Mom's car and turns to me. "Hey, Teddy," she says softly.

I meet her eyes, and she offers a small, gentle smile. "You've got this," she says. "Liam's waiting for you at home. I told him to stay..." Her eyes flick between mine as they fill with some kind of emotion. "I called him yesterday after your surgery to fill him in on everything."

I nod, swallowing hard as I drop my eyes, my own emotion gently nudging at the fog in my brain.

"I drove myself here this morning," Heather adds, nodding towards her car parked nearby. "So I'll check in later, ok?"

"Ok," I manage with another nod.

She holds the door open for me as I slide into the back seat of Mom's car, wincing as I try not to bump my arm. Mom and Grandpa get in the front, and by the time we're pulling away from the hospital, sleep is pulling me under.

I don't wake until I hear tires crunching on gravel, and I open my eyes to the familiar sight of my house as Mom parks next to Liam's truck.

"Oh good, Liam's here," Mom says. "I should go over your meds with him."

"He's going back to work tomorrow," I mutter, awkwardly pushing the car door open. Grandpa holds it for me as I get out, then grabs my bag and follows me inside.

The first thing I see when I step into the house is Liam, standing near the kitchen, watching me with wide, worried eyes.

"Hi, Liam," Mom says warmly, placing a hand on his arm as she walks past him into the kitchen. "Theo won't let me stay here with him for some reason," she chuckles, "so I'm just going to run through his meds with you. He's still a little fuzzy."

I walk past them and head into the living room, ignoring the sound of their voices in the kitchen as I sit on the couch. Miss Bobber hops up with me, curiously sniffing my bandaged hand as I tip my head back against the couch cushion and close my eyes.

After a few minutes, a hand squeezes my shoulder, but I

keep my eyes closed. I know it's Grandpa, and I know they're leaving... but I just can't do it... any of it. Not right now.

"Take care, Theo," he says softly. "Talk tomorrow."

I hear the door close, and the house falls quiet. Except for the sound of Liam's hesitant footsteps as they approach me.

"I'm sorry," he whispers, his voice breaking.

My eyes open and I turn my head to look at him.

His eyes are wet with tears, and it looks like he's barely hanging on. I stare at him for a moment, taking in the dark circles under his eyes and the sleepless look about him.

"I... I should have been there," he says as a tear rolls down his cheek, and his hands shake.

And suddenly, I feel everything.

Every emotion I've buried since I woke up after surgery yesterday rushes to the surface. The anger, the sadness, the fear of what comes next... I've been holding it all back as I tried to stay in control. But now, with him, I can't keep it in anymore.

I feel everything.

And I need him.

I reach out with my good hand, and the moment he takes it, I break. A sob escapes me as he drops down beside me and pulls me carefully into his arms.

"Fuck," I mutter into his chest as my tears fall.

I fucking hate this, and I wish more than anything that I could go back to before, when everything was good. When we had plans to move forward with happiness and hope.

He kisses the top of my head as he holds me close, letting me catch my breath and let it all out. His breaths are shaky, but he remains calm and steady.

"Everything is fucked," I say.

I feel him start to shake his head, but I pull back to look into his eyes before he can say anything else.

"It is," I say, a wave of frustration rolling over me as I finally let myself realize what this all means. "It's going to be six months before I have any sort of use of my hand again, and even then, it will never be the same. It's the end of lobster season, my crew is left hanging, and I won't make it back for tuna season either." I shake my head as reality settles over me. "I may never fish again." My eyes drop to the floor as the weight of it all crashes down on me.

Liam slides his hand into mine and squeezes, drawing my gaze back to him as I blink back tears.

"It's not over," he says softly. "You'll take some time off to heal and then get back into it when you're ready." He gently rubs his thumb over the back of my hand. "I'll help you."

I stare into his eyes for a moment longer as his words hang in the air, and I want to believe him. But it's hard to see how this is all going to be ok.

"Everything can wait," he says. "Right now, you need to take care of yourself."

My eyes drop to my arm wrapped in heavy bandages, and a dull ache creeps in as the meds begin to wear off. My vision blurs with fresh tears, but before they fall, Liam pulls me into him again and threads his fingers gently through my hair.

"I wish I was there for you," he whispers.

"You are," I murmur, finding comfort in his touch.

He shakes his head. "I should have been there..." he says again, his voice breaking with guilt.

I'm quiet for a moment as I think back to when I woke up after surgery, searching for him even though I knew he wouldn't be there. But I know why he wasn't. And I understand.

"I froze," he continues, "and I couldn't make myself go... I'm so sorry." He holds onto me a bit tighter, like he's afraid to let go.

I look into his tear-filled blue eyes, and my heart sinks,

hating that he's carrying this weight. "I get it," I say. "It's ok. We're here now."

He nods as a tear falls. "I thought I was going to lose you." Then he takes a deep breath in and presses his lips to the side of my head. "But... we're here now," he says, repeating my words like he's trying to believe they're really true. "And you're going to be ok."

I drop my head to his chest again, letting my eyes travel out the window to the ocean. "I hope so," I say quietly.

THIRTY-FIVE

LIAM

THEO'S CHEST rises and falls with soft breaths as his bandaged and splinted arm rests on a pillow beside him. I clutch my bag tight as I watch him, not wanting to wake him after a restless night, but needing to say bye before I leave for work. My chest tightens as my eyes roam over his arm, hating that things have to be like this.

I quietly lean over and kiss his forehead, just like he's done to me every morning before he leaves for work. His eyes flutter open, and I set my bag down as I sink onto the edge of the bed.

"I have to go," I say, looking down at him in the stillness of the early morning, the first signs of light just starting to peek through the windows. But the ache in my heart grows the longer I stare down at him, urging me to stay and climb back into bed with him. "I don't want to."

His uninjured hand slides onto my thigh. "I know... I don't want you to either." He pauses for a moment and releases a breath. "But you have to."

A deep, resigned sigh escapes me as I nod. Last night, I almost called off my rotation to stay home with Theo, because the thought of leaving him for three weeks feels like a knife in my heart, twisting deeper with every passing second that brings me closer to leaving. But he told me I have to go, and I know he's right. If I bail on a rotation last minute, especially when it's only my second with this company, my career in oil and gas will be over. No one would ever hire me again if they can't rely on me.

It just fucking hurts to leave him like this.

He looks into my eyes and squeezes my leg. "I'll be ok."

I lean down to kiss him, lingering against his lips for a moment longer to take in every bit of him that I can, memorizing this moment so I can bring it with me. And when I pull back and meet his eyes again, the words are on the tip of my tongue.

I love you.

But I keep them in for now. Because even though the love I feel for him is overwhelming and those words are desperate to come out, I can't say them when he's hurting the way he is and I'm about to leave for three weeks. I want to be able to share that love with joy and happiness. Not sadness and pain.

My hand cups the side of his face as I run my thumb over his freckles, and stare into his warm brown eyes.

"Mo chridhe."

Sparks fly around me as I work, hanging by ropes underneath the platform of the rig. Waves crash loudly against the legs, nearly drowning out the sound of my welder. But I remain focused on the job before me as I reinforce the joint which is starting to show some signs of corrosion, worn down by the severe forces and relentless weather out here in the Gulf of Mexico. One bad weld can lead to devastating consequences, so I block out everything around me and keep my attention firmly on the job.

When I'm finished, I lift my shield and inspect the welds, satisfied with the result. But as I reach for the ascender to haul myself back up to the platform, my gaze falls to the ocean below me. The waves continue to forcefully crash against the rig legs, and I get lost in their hypnotic rhythm. As I watch the deep, dark ocean swirl and churn, I think of how much it could hurt me. The waves could easily pull me under, into its darkness, and never let me go. The same waves I've been riding through grief are right here before me, begging me to come join them, and promising to take my pain away forever.

But they don't control me anymore.

What I once wished would take me away and swallow me whole, I now want to fight. An urge rises inside me, but it's not the one I'm used to. It's the urge to rise above it, and wait out the storm.

Because I want to be here. I want to be strong.

For Theo. For my family.

And for me.

I pull my gaze from the water and hit the ascender, letting it pull me up. When I get to the top of the platform, Bryce, one of the safety guys, helps me up.

"All good?" he asks as he helps me unhook the ropes from my harness.

"Yeah," I nod. "Straightforward weld. Easy job."

He chuckles. "Easy," he says with a shake of his head. "Not the word I typically use for hanging on ropes over the ocean."

I shrug as I step out of the harness, and he laughs again.

"Welders are fucked," he says.

"Yeah," I say with a simple nod.

He snorts and shakes his head again, scooping up the ropes

and helmets. "Have a good one," he says as he heads off with the gear.

And I immediately shove my hand into my pocket to pull out my phone.

My heart flutters as I see Theo's name on my screen with a text, returning mine from when I checked in on him earlier.

THEO

Just woke up. These meds knock me out.

I rest my elbows on the railing as I tap out a response, the waves continuing to crash below me.

It's good you're getting sleep though.

Then I lift my phone and snap a picture of the sunset over the water. Fiery orange softens into golden yellow as it meets the edge of the darkening sky, and the water below ripples with its reflection, like fire dancing across the ocean. I send it to him, then watch as he types, the bubbles appearing, disappearing, and appearing again. He's typing one-handed so it takes a while longer, and a pang of guilt settles in my chest.

Not a bad view. You done now?

Yeah, just need to put my gear away.

He starts typing again, and I wait patiently, hating how hard it clearly is for him. But I can't help but chuckle when his response comes through.

Then warming up the ping-pong arm?

I shake my head, smiling as I tap out my response.

Saving that for tomorrow night. Gotta ease everyone into losing.

I hear some of the guys walking down the corridor as they wrap up their shift, so I shove my phone into my pocket, grab the welder, and head to the workshop. Luckily the shop is quiet, so I quickly put everything away and duck out before I run into anyone.

As I walk to my room, I pull my phone out again.

Very noble of you.

Once I'm in my room, and the door is closed behind me, I tap his name and hit call. I sit on the edge of my bed as it rings a couple times, then he answers.

"Hey," he says in a soft and tired voice.

"Hey," I reply, a feeling almost like relief flooding through me just at the sound of his voice.

"How was your first day?" he asks.

"It was ok," I say. "Busy right away. I was on the ropes for most of it."

There's a pause on the other end and my heart sinks. Because I know he's thinking what I've been thinking all day. We both take risks in dangerous jobs, every day. And one of those risks became all too real for him. Who's to say it won't for me someday too...

But I shake off that feeling and change the subject. "Did you see your family today?"

"Yeah, Mom and Heather were here this morning," he says. "And Grandpa stopped by this afternoon." He pauses for a moment, and his voice softens. "He took the crew out today. He's going to finish the season with them."

A lump rises in my throat. I know how much it hurts Theo

not to be out there with his crew, but I also know it's about more than the job. Jimmy stepping in is for Theo's peace of mind. To not only take care of what Theo can't right now, but to also take care of him.

"Let me guess," I say, forcing some lightness into my voice. "He brought in the biggest haul of the season?"

Theo lets out a breath of laughter, and the sound lifts my heart.

"Obviously."

I smile, happy they haven't lost their ability to rib on each other amongst this pain.

"He's a good one," I say softly.

"Yeah. He is."

We're quiet for a moment as I lie back on the bed and stare at the underside of the bunk above me.

"How's Miss Bobber?" I ask.

"She's asleep on my lap right now. I think she likes having someone to sleep with all day." He pauses for a moment. "She's been sleeping on your pillow beside me."

My breath catches in my chest as I close my eyes. "I wish I was."

I hear his breath through the phone as he lets out a soft sigh. "Me too."

I rub my hand forcefully over my eyes as I momentarily pull the phone away from my ear and let out a sigh of my own.

Fuck, this is hard.

But I draw a breath in and push it all aside, knowing I need to stay strong for him.

I bring the phone back to my ear. "I feel like you've set me up for failure here, by the way."

There's a long pause on the other end, and I just wait.

"What?"

"You were all talk about challenging me in ping-pong," I say. "But because you never did, I'm rusty now."

An incredulous breath of laughter escapes him, making me smile.

"And I was supposed to do that anyway, when you told me to fuck off every time?" he asks, but I hear the smile in his voice.

I chuckle. "Who can't take the challenge now?"

"Still you," he says, not missing a beat. "Because you could be playing right now, but you're hiding away in your room instead."

Both fire and laughter rise in my chest. "*Hiding*?"

"I mean, yeah. Sounds like you're scared."

I huff out a laugh. "I'll report back tomorrow after I win."

"And if you lose?"

"Fuck off."

We both laugh again, but then fall quiet as the comfortable silence settles between us.

"Tha mi gad ionndrainn, mo chridhe," I say softly.

I hear him release a soft breath. "Do I get to know what that means yet?

I smile as I close my eyes and picture his face. "Soon."

We're silent for a moment longer, before I reluctantly check the time.

"You should get some more sleep," I say. "And I should too."

"Yeah," he says with a sigh.

But neither one of us makes a move to end the call, as we just listen to each other's soft breaths through the phone.

Eventually I find the courage, knowing he really should get more sleep.

"Talk again tomorrow?" I ask softly.

"Yeah," he says again. "Night."

"Night."

I pull the phone away from my ear and hit *end*, gripping it tight in my hand as I run my fingers through my hair.

Then it buzzes, the screen lighting up with Theo's name.

I tap his text, and smile down at the photo of Miss Bobber, curled up on his lap with the white tip of her tail tucked in against her little face.

Our nightly routine while I'm away, where he sends a photo of her before we go to sleep.

While life may feel uncertain right now... we don't. We're going to get through this together, and I'll be with him every step of the way.

He's going to be ok.

We're going to be ok.

THIRTY-SIX

THEO

I DRAG Miss Bobber's toy across the couch for her and she pounces on it, pulling it to her mouth to bite it. As she falls over to furiously kick at her catch, I let the toy go and my gaze drifts to the ocean out the window as a sigh escapes me.

I am so fucking bored.

It's been a few days now since I got home from the hospital, and I haven't even left the house. I can't drive because of the meds I'm on, not to mention how hard it would be with my arm. But if I could, I'd try. Not that I know where I'd even go or what I'd do.

As I stare at the ocean, my mind wanders to my crew and Grandpa, who are out there right now. Grandpa didn't have to come out of retirement for this... but I appreciate that he did. He's looking after my crew and letting them finish out the season so they get paid, which was one of my biggest worries.

I tear my eyes away from the ocean, trying to keep the regret and sadness from growing any more than it already is. But as my gaze then lands on the sunroom door, it flows in anyway.

I haven't stepped foot in there since I got home, and I don't want to. Not without Liam. It was supposed to be finished by now... our spot to relax and just be together. But now it's left unfinished, with baseboard piled in the corner and a half-finished coffee table in the workshop. And Liam isn't here, while I'm stuck with a mangled arm, watching the days slip by.

I push to my feet with a frustrated sigh, needing to move and find something, anything, to keep my mind from spiralling. All I've been doing is sleeping and waiting to talk to Liam when he's free, and I think I'm going to go crazy soon.

But I don't know what to do.

My phone buzzes in my sweatpants pocket as I stand in the middle of the kitchen, and I eagerly pull it out, expecting a text from Liam.

But it's not him. It's Caleb.

CALEB

Hey, up for a visit?

He's been checking in ever since he heard about my accident, but I haven't seen him since he was here a couple months ago, when I brought Liam to the pub to watch him and his girlfriend play. So I feel a stir of excitement that he's going to be coming into town again soon.

Yeah, when?

Right now. I'm here.

My brow furrows as I look towards the door and head over, pulling it open to find Caleb standing on the other side with a big smile.

"Hey, buddy," he says

"Hey..." I trail off. "What are you doing here?"

"I came to see you. And I brought a shit ton of stuff." He

gestures to the bags at his feet, then picks them up and carries them into the house.

I close the door after him, watching him curiously.

"Uh... what is all this?" I ask as he sets the bags on the kitchen island.

Caleb looks around the kitchen with a low whistle. "Damn... this is a far cry from the shithole you bought." Then he winks at me and reaches into one of the bags, taking out a stack of cards and setting them on the counter. "Everyone has been dropping stuff off for you at the store. And I needed to come see you, so I'm delivering it."

I watch as he starts pulling out meals, gifts, and baked goods, piling them onto the counter. I step closer, pulling out a piece of paper from the pile of cards. It's a drawing from one of the kids in town... a picture of me with a cast on my arm and "Get well soon Theo" scrawled across it.

Caleb places the last of the meals on the counter and watches me for a moment as I silently take it all in.

"It's time we take care of you," he says.

I bite back the overwhelming emotion that rises as I just nod, my eyes scanning the counter covered with gifts from everyone in town.

He leans on the counter, catching my eye. "So... how are you doing?"

I rub a hand over my face and blow out a breath. "Been better."

His gaze drops to my arm as sympathy fills his eyes and voice. "I'm sorry, man. This sucks."

"Yeah..." I agree with a nod.

He reaches out and squeezes my shoulder on my good side. "I'll get this stuff put away for you."

"Thanks," I murmur, sinking onto a stool at the island.

Caleb opens the freezer and starts stuffing it full of lasagna and casseroles. "I've been given very specific instructions on each of these meals, from everyone who made them. And all of them said to freeze them if you're not going to eat it right away." He glances over his shoulder at me. "You know how it is. The moms are momming."

I let out a tired laugh, having been getting quite a bit of *momming* from mine the past few days. "Oh, I know."

He smiles at the drawing on the fridge as he grabs another dish for the freezer, the one Mason drew with "To Uncle Theo and Liam" on it.

"Liam still here?" Caleb asks, glancing over his shoulder.

I nod. "He's at work."

"Ah." He nods. "Rig life."

As he continues to arrange the meals in the freezer, I watch him... and wonder what he would think...

"Caleb," I say, his name coming out of my mouth before my brain can catch up and stop me.

He turns to look at me, eyebrows raised as he waits.

My heart pounds in my chest as I stare back at him. I wanted to tell my family first, but... he's my oldest friend. We've been through a lot together, and even though he doesn't live here anymore and I don't see him as much, every time we talk... it's like no time has passed. An urge is rising, and a voice inside me is getting louder, telling me to just do it. Try it. He'll understand.

And suddenly, I can't hold it in any longer.

"I'm gay."

His eyebrows lift as he nods slowly. "Oh." He turns around to place the last dish in the freezer. "Ok, cool."

My pulse roars in my ears as I continue to sit here in silence and fear, and wait for everything to fall apart.

But when he meets my eyes, his brow furrows. "What?"

All I can do is stare back at him, unsure what's happening.

Panic starts to rise as I think maybe he doesn't want to talk about it. Because he is getting ready to bolt, and our almost thirty-year friendship is about to shatter.

But he studies me for a moment with curiosity. "Have you told anyone else?"

I shake my head, swallowing hard.

The corner of his mouth tilts up in a soft smile as he rests his elbows on the counter. "How does it feel?"

A rush of relief rolls through me, so strong it almost fucking takes me out. I release a large breath that I feel like I've been holding my entire life. "So fucking good."

He smiles widely. "Been holding that in for a while, eh?"

I nod with a huff. "You could say that."

He watches me for a moment with soft and understanding eyes. "Liam?"

"Yeah." Then I quickly add, "But I haven't told my family yet."

He brings his fingers to his lips in action to lock them and throw away the key.

A small smile tugs at my lips, but then I sigh, knowing there's still so much left in this journey. "I just don't know what everyone will think..."

Caleb drops his gaze, scanning the cards and gifts all over the counter... the tokens of care and support from everyone in town. Then he meets my eyes again with a small smirk. "I think you'll be just fine."

I watch the sky darken through the skylight as I lie in bed, Miss Bobber lying beside me as she falls asleep. My arm hurts as the meds are starting to wear off, and I should take more... but I want to talk to Liam first so I'm not drowsy.

The second my phone buzzes, I answer, putting it on speaker and setting it on my chest.

"Hey," I say.

"Hey," his tired-sounding voice comes through the speaker. I hear a door close in the background, like he might just be getting back to his room.

"How was your day?" I ask.

He hesitates for a moment, and I hear rustling like he's removing a jacket. "It was ok... fucking long. I had to get up twice last night for emergencies on the pipe, and it was nonstop today."

I feel a wave of sympathy for him, wondering how he manages to do this for three weeks straight, working twelve to fourteen hour days and being on call all night. "Just over two weeks left..." I say, trying to give him some hope.

"It can't come soon enough," he sighs.

I run my fingers through Miss Bobber's fur beside me. "Caleb stopped by today," I tell him.

"The guitar player?" he asks.

"Yeah."

"How was that?"

"It was good..." I take a breath, my heart pounding. "I told him I'm gay."

There's a brief silence. "And?"

"It was fine."

"Would you look at that..." he says slowly.

I huff a laugh. "Fuck off."

He laughs, and I can't help but smile at the sound.

"I'm happy everything went well with him," he says. "I know that was probably really hard to do."

I stare up at the ceiling for a moment. "It actually wasn't as hard as I thought it was going to be..."

He chuckles. "Even better."

"And..." I take a deep breath, "When you're home, I still want to tell my family."

"Of course," he says softly.

I smile, already feeling some weight lifting.

"I've... actually been thinking about family a lot lately," he adds hesitantly.

"Yeah?" I ask, unsure of where he's going with that.

"Yeah..." His voice grows quieter. "I want to go see mine when I get home."

Well, I wasn't expecting that. I don't know what to say because I have no idea what prompted this. So I stay quiet as he continues.

"I think... I think your injury, and..." a frustrated sigh escapes him, like he's trying to find the right words, but can't. "It's just... I need to do it. I need to stop running."

I feel like there's more, and like there's something he's trying to get out. So I stay quiet, letting him work through his thoughts.

"Nick died in an explosion at camp."

My heart feels like it stops as those words settle over me.

He pulls in a shaky breath. "He was working on an oilfield steel skid that I was working on the day before."

I stay silent, not even moving as he slowly lets it all out.

"Nick and I were the only two welders on shift that day, so when our supervisor said one of us needed to go finish it, I convinced him to go." He pauses for a moment. "I didn't want to do it."

My heart races as I take in the pain in his voice.

"The acetylene cylinders needed to be switched out because they were low from the day before," he continues slowly, like each word is heavy and hard to get out. "The foreman switched them out... but something went wrong, and too much was released." He's quiet for a moment, then his voice breaks. "It should have been me."

My heart fucking breaks for him.

He's said that before, and I didn't know what he meant.

He was supposed to be on that job...

"Liam," I say softly, hearing him sniffle on the other end.

"I shouldn't have told him to go. It was my job, and I should have been there. I should have checked the levels the night before, I should have—" His voice catches, and I hate that he's been blaming himself for this.

"But you wouldn't have been the one replacing the cylinders anyway," I say gently.

"Doesn't matter," he murmurs. "I still should have done the job myself. I shouldn't have convinced him to do *my job*."

"Liam," I say adding strength to my voice, "none of this is your fault. You didn't know the equipment would fail. How could you?"

There's a long silence, his sniffles the only sound coming through the speaker.

I think of everything he's told me since we've known each other, and all the pain he's been carrying, and suddenly, everything comes into focus. The distance from his family, the guilt, the running... the self-harm... it all stems from this moment.

"Your family doesn't know this, do they?" I ask gently.

"No," he says, his voice so quiet I almost don't hear him.

"Do you think they will blame you?"

I hear him pull in a breath. "Yes," he whispers, and the pain in his voice crushes me.

I close my eyes as my chest aches. "Do you think if it had been the other way around, they would blame Nick?"

He doesn't answer, but I let the question sit with him.

"I'm so sorry you lost your best friend like that," I say gently. "But there's no way you could have predicted that would happen. And if it had been you... you know Nick would be thinking the same thing. How would you want him to feel?"

I hear him take a deep breath.

"Some things are just out of our control, no matter how shitty they are," I add, glancing down at my arm resting on the pillow, the dull ache growing stronger.

"Yeah," he says, his voice raw and fragile.

"I'll go with you to see your family," I say. "Whenever you're ready."

There's a quiet beat. "Thank you," he says.

While there's a deep sadness in his voice, and I know that was hard for him to say... I swear I can also hear a hint of relief in there too.

I know how hard it is to keep something inside for so long.

And today, we both finally let that out.

"Are you ok?" I ask.

He sighs deeply. "I will be."

"Yeah... you will," I say softly.

Silence falls over us for a moment, but I don't let it last for long.

"Now," I say, "tell me all the latest ping-pong gossip."

He chuckles softly, and I smile. He's pulled me out of my own darkness so many times these past few days, it's time I return the favour.

"Besides Raúl almost breaking the table last night, there's not much to report," he says.

I laugh. "Sore loser?"

"No, he won," Liam replies. "He's just a big guy who doesn't know his own strength when he celebrates."

I laugh, trying to picture big, burly oil rig workers getting so into ping-pong. "And when you win?"

"I accept my victory with grace," he says simply.

"Oh, of course," I say with another chuckle.

As we fall into another quiet moment, I let this one sit a bit longer. I take in the sound of his soft breaths on the other line and wish more than anything I could reach right through this phone and hold him.

But the pain in my arm is growing quickly, and it's starting to throb.

"I need to go take my meds," I say reluctantly.

"That's ok," he says softly. "I'm just going to go to sleep. Give Miss Bobber a pat for me."

I reach down and run my fingers through her fur as she yawns and stretches. "Already am."

"Have a good sleep," he says.

"You too."

When we hang up, I open the camera on my phone, snap a picture of Miss Bobber and send it to him.

But before I can lock my screen, he sends a reply.

Liam: Thank you, mo chridhe.

I stare at the words as my eyes trace each letter. It's the first time I've seen them written out, as I've only ever heard the beautiful, rolling sound of them on his lips.

Mo chridhe...

I type them into a search engine, and I'm suddenly filled with an overwhelming love for him as the translation appears before me.

My heart.

THIRTY-SEVEN

LIAM

THEO

Mason wants to know if the shark tried to climb onto the metal island.

I LAUGH with a shake of my head, leaning against the platform railing as I tap out a reply. Sending a photo of a shark in the water didn't seem like it would be such a big deal, but... with Mason, I should have known better.

He still can't quite figure out the rig, can he...

I've even showed him pictures. I don't know what else to do.

I huff out another laugh as I picture Mason at Sunday dinner, just losing his mind over the shark and the metal island while everyone is trying to eat. I sent the photo over an hour ago, and he's still going. But I can only smile, because I'll have more pictures of marine life to show him at Sunday dinner next week when I'm home.

Maybe we should just let him think it's a floating metal island.

Probably for the best.

I smile and lift my eyes, staring out over the open water as I take a deep breath in.

Ever since I told Theo what really happened with Nick… everything feels just a little bit lighter. I know I'll forever carry this guilt, but… even just saying those words out loud shifted something in me. And it's not as heavy anymore.

His words echo in my mind as I watch the waves roll and listen to them crash against the rig. When he told me it wasn't my fault… and asked me how I would want Nick to feel if it was me, and not him.

I'd want him to remember everything good that we had.

I'd want him to *live*, keeping me with him to show me how good this life can be.

I'd want him to love, grow, and be happy.

And that's what I'm working on.

I unlock my phone and open my messages with Mom. I stare at it for a moment before I take a deep breath, and type out a message that has been a long time coming.

Hi Mom. Just wanted to let you know I'm coming to visit soon.

My heart thumps as she immediately starts texting back.

MOM

Oh Liam, I am so excited to hear this! We miss you so much, mo mhac.

Let us know when, we can't wait!

I swallow hard, blinking back the tears forming in my eyes as I tap out my reply.

I will. I miss you too.

Love you.

Gu bràth.

I release a long breath as my eyes close, then fill my lungs with the fresh, salty air. And I imagine being at home. With my parents, with Theo... and I let that image sit for a moment, finding comfort in their love.

I can do this...

Then I push off the railing and head back inside, where the guys are all playing ping-pong.

Of course.

"Listen here, fucker," Keegan points at Russel across the ping-pong table. "That was absolutely a foul, and you know it."

"Oh," Russel tosses his paddle onto the table and tosses his hands in the air. "You're just making up the fucking rules now, are you?"

Keegan huffs and shakes his head, glancing at me. "Liam. Tiebreaker, because none of these assholes are any help." He gestures to everyone else sitting around the common room, watching this all unfold with smirks on their faces. "If a player *accidentally*," he shoots a look at Russel, "moves the table while playing, that's a foul, right?"

I draw my brows together, looking around the room as everyone watches me expectantly... waiting for my ruling.

"Uh..." I shrug, "I mean, I guess it technically would be, but—"

"Ha!" Keegan points at Russel.

"No, no!" Russel shouts, pointing a finger at me and then to Keegan. "The table moved because this bastard didn't hit his side of the table first, so I had to scramble to get it, so *he* had the foul."

I throw my hands up, shaking my head as I step back. "Nope. I wasn't here to see it, not my problem."

"Ok, guys, just... start over," Dylan says, standing up and approaching the table. "Let's move the fuck on."

As they all fall into another argument about why they should or shouldn't do that, I slip out of the room and down the hall, towards my room.

I pull my phone out on the way and text Theo.

Home yet?

I'm just dropping onto my bed when he texts back.

Yeah, Grandpa just dropped me off.

I tap his name and hit call.

"Hey," his voice sounds through the speaker, immediately putting a smile on my face.

"Hi," I say. "How's your arm today?"

"My arm feels ok, but my hand is sore," he says. "At least this new splint I got the other day in therapy is lighter, so it's not so big and awkward."

"How are the exercises going?"

"They hurt," he admits. "But the scars are the worst part right now. Now that the stitches are out, they've put silicone strips on them. My whole arm and hand feels tight and uncomfortable. Sounds like it's going to be months of scar tissue management."

"You're doing all the right things," I say in a reassuring tone, knowing how frustrated he's feeling with the amount of therapy he has to do. "With all the work you're doing, you'll have the best possible outcome."

He sighs. "Yeah. I just wish 'best possible outcome' was returning to normal."

"I know." I release my own sigh. "But you'll be able to get back to what you love. It's just going to look a little different."

"Yeah..." he murmurs.

"Where are you right now?" I ask.

"I just laid down in bed."

I pull the phone away from my ear and hit video call.

Theo answers with a curious expression. "Hey."

But there's a small smile on his lips, and my eyes immediately drop to them.

"Hm," I hum. "I can't wait to kiss those lips..."

He lifts an eyebrow, and the corner of his mouth twitches. "And what else?"

I huff out a breath of laughter. "You know what else."

He chuckles and I soak in the sound.

There's been a new sense of ease for both of us this past week, since we each stepped out from under the weight that's been pressing down on us. And while there are still hard steps we need to take, knowing that we can face them together and get through it... it feels good.

And I want to make *him* feel good tonight.

"Set your phone up on the bedside table," I say.

His brow furrows. "Why?"

I just smile. "You know why."

Theo cocks an eyebrow at me with a playful smirk. "What about your roommate?"

"He's on night shift."

"And if he decides to come back to the room for some reason?"

"Then he'll get a show." I shrug.

He chuckles, but then leans over and sets his phone on the

bedside table, angled towards the bed so I can see his entire upper body.

I take a deep breath in as I run my eyes over him. "Shirt off."

He sits up so he can remove his shirt awkwardly with one arm. What I wouldn't give to have my hands on him...

After he tosses it on the floor, he nods his head towards me on his phone screen. "Your turn."

I momentarily set the phone down so I can take my shirt off, and I chuckle at his grumbles. But when I pick my phone up again and angle it so he can see me, he draws in a breath with a nod.

"Fuck yeah..." he says.

I slide my hand down my stomach and slip it into the waistband of my pants, moving my phone so he can watch. I'm hard already at the sight of him, and let out a soft moan as I grasp my cock.

"Push them down," he says, and I do as I'm told.

He groans as he watches me push my pants down and grasp my hard cock. As I stroke it for him, he reaches down to free his dick as well, and I can't take my eyes off him.

He runs his hand along his hard length as he watches me, and the feeling of his eyes on me is enough to drive me wild. But when he moans and starts stroking himself faster, I can hardly fucking stand it.

"Fuck... sin an rud as teotha a chunnaic mi riamh," I breathe out.

He lets out a guttural groan. "Fuck that's hot."

"Exactly," I say with a huff. He doesn't know what I told him, but he basically just agreed with me... because this *is* the hottest thing I've ever seen. And I love how Gaelic gets him so riled up.

Another moan escapes him, and I bite my lip while I watch

him, letting pleasure flow through me as I jerk myself to the beautiful sight and sounds.

"Fuck I wish your mouth was on me..." Theo pants.

A rush of air leaves me and I let out a groan as he tips his head back and closes his eyes, the muscles of his arm and abs flexing as he rubs his cock.

"What do you want me to do to you when I get home," I ask, barely hanging on as I tip closer to the edge.

His eyes open, and he turns his head to look at me. "Fuck the cum out of me."

My breath hitches, and I release my cock, swallowing hard as I try not to bust just at the sound of those words.

But he shakes his head, staring right at me. "Come."

The second my hand is on my cock, pleasure crashes over me. I try to keep my moans quiet as I stroke myself through it, coming over my abs as I watch Theo's muscles tense. He grunts, his cum spilling over his stomach as his chest rises and falls with heavy breaths.

Fuck...

We both lie still in our beds as we catch our breath, and I watch him with a soft smile.

"Mo chridhe..." I say slowly.

His own smile spreads across his face as he looks at me through the screen, and he gently taps his chest.

The love I feel for him spreads through me, and I place my own hand over my chest. Now he knows exactly what he means to me.

He's my entire heart.

THIRTY-EIGHT

THEO

MY FOOT TAPS restlessly on the floor as I sit at the kitchen island, staring out the window as my untouched coffee grows cold in front of me. Anticipation stirs in my stomach, coiling tight like a spring ready to release at any moment, while Miss Bobber watches me curiously from her perch on a chair in the living room.

Then I hear it.

The sound of tires crunching on gravel grows louder, and my heart leaps as I push to my feet.

Liam's home.

My pulse races as his truck door slams, and his footsteps sound on the porch as he approaches the door. And when the door pushes open and he steps inside, I finally take a breath.

Without a word, he drops his bag and crosses the room, his arms wrapping firmly around my waist as he pulls me into him. When our lips meet, it's like a flood of everything we've been unable to share while we were apart. The need to touch him, taste him, devour him, make up for lost time... it's overwhelming, and we hold each other tight as we stay locked in a needy kiss and give each other everything we can.

The kiss he left me with was tinged with sadness and pain, but this one... this one is full of relief, happiness, and hope.

His hands slide up my body to either side of my face, and I place my good hand over his, resting my splinted hand against his hip as my tongue slides against his. I can't get enough of him.

Until he chuckles softly against my lips then looks down at the floor, where Miss Bobber is standing at his feet, her tiny paws resting on his boot as she lets out a delicate meow.

"Hey, little one," he says, smiling as he bends to pick her up.

I watch him scratch her behind her ears as she purrs against him, and I can already see the shift in him from when he left three weeks ago.

His eyes lift to meet mine again, before they travel down my arm and his gaze settles on my splinted hand. The full bandage is off now, and the thick, red, raised scars across my hand and forearm are on full display. He reaches out and gently places his hand under the rigid splint running from my elbow to the tip of my fingers, and lifts it up.

As he runs his gaze over the scars, I try to swallow down the fear that he might not like what he sees.

But he gently lowers his lips to kiss my knuckles, then presses his lips to mine again.

I hold onto him, keeping him tight against me as Miss Bobber purrs in his arms, happy to be a part of this moment with us.

Then he pulls back, just enough to look into my eyes.

"I love you," he says softly.

My heart skips and my stomach flips as I stare into his beautiful blue eyes, letting those words settle over me. Those words I've been wanting to say to him, and have been feeling for longer than I think I realized.

But I don't say them back. Because there is one word that encompasses everything I want to say to him. One word that has bonded us in understanding from day one, and that we have said so much with, despite its simplicity.

"Same."

Our lips meet again, and I feel like I'm fucking soaring. I breathe him in, and he fills every empty space inside me as the intense love I feel for him somehow grows even stronger.

I'm so happy he's finally home.

My eyes slowly open to the dim bedroom, and I turn my head to look at Liam beside me. But the bed is empty, with only rumpled sheets and a vacant pillow on his side of the bed. My brow furrows as I take in the quiet space around me, then I lean over to check the time.

It's 5:00AM. Guess I sleep in now.

I push myself up to sit on the edge of the bed, rubbing my eyes as I yawn. Miss Bobber hops into the bed with a little meow, then rubs her head into my knee as her little motor starts up.

"Where is he?" I ask her as I give her a scratch behind her ears.

After I pull on a pair of sweatpants and a t-shirt, I head downstairs, expecting to find him in the kitchen making coffee. But the house is quiet as the early morning light filters through the windows, casting everything in a cool, blue-grey glow. The air feels still as I make my way to the kitchen, but I pause when I pass the patio doors. A faint light catches my eye, coming from the workshop.

I push my feet into my sneakers and open the door, crossing the driveway as the sound of a drill comes from inside the barn.

Liam looks up as I step through the door. "Morning," he says softly.

My eyes land on our coffee table before him, and my heart skips a beat.

He's cut the top, since I wasn't able to finish it, and he's screwed the edges in place.

I meet his eyes and immediately step forward, pressing my lips gently to his. When I pull back, he smiles and lightly brushes his thumb over my bottom lip.

"I figured we need our coffee table if we're going to start using the sunroom," he says.

I smile and rest my forehead against his. "Yeah. We do."

He brings his lips to mine again, kissing me slowly in the quiet stillness of the morning, with nowhere to go, and nothing to do. It's just us, and we have all the time we want and need.

And that feels pretty damn good.

When we part, Liam gestures to the table with a nod. "I just need to attach it to the base. Then we can stain it?"

Excitement stirs inside me, knowing that's a part of this I can participate in. I nod eagerly and he chuckles.

"Want some coffee?" I ask.

He nods seriously and I laugh, heading back in the house as the drill hums behind me while Liam gets back to work.

I brew us each a coffee and awkwardly tuck one mug between my arm and body, balancing them as I walk carefully back to the workshop.

Liam looks up as I enter and rushes over to grab a mug from me. "I could have helped."

I give a little shrug. "I'm only wearing some of it." I glance down at the coffee stain on my shirt where it was jostled out of the mug, and Liam shakes his head with a soft chuckle.

He reaches out, lightly tugging at the wet spot on my shirt to pull me closer as he presses a kiss to my lips.

Liam has the table assembled, so we settle in to start staining. Which is the final step before it's all done, and ready for the sunroom.

Peaceful silence surrounds us as we work, the swishing of our brushes on the wood mixing with the soft chirps of the birds in the trees outside.

Eventually, I look up at Liam, and hope this question doesn't disturb his comfort.

"So," I start hesitantly, "when do you want to go see your parents?"

He glances up at me as he drags the brush along the tabletop with slow, thoughtful strokes and he inhales deeply. "This week?"

I smile, feeling the confidence in him, growing stronger among the lingering uncertainty. "Yeah."

He watches me as I dip my brush into the stain. "And when do you want to tell your family about us?"

I meet his eyes, and think on that for a moment. "Well... I did want to tell my mom first but... I actually think I'd rather talk to everyone at once. So... tomorrow, at Sunday dinner?" I ask, some nerves still fluttering at the thought.

Liam smiles, nodding in quiet agreement. "Yeah." He studies me for a moment, looking thoughtful. "No one... mentioned anything to you about... anything?"

I furrow my brow in confusion. "What? Who?"

He shakes his head with a shrug. "I don't know." But before I can decipher what that means, he looks up at me again. "I'm proud of you."

My heart swells as a smile spreads across my face, and I stare into his beautiful eyes.

"I'm proud of you too."

THIRTY-NINE

THEO

MY PULSE THUNDERS in my ears as Liam pulls the truck onto Mom's street, and her house slowly comes into view. I've been building up the courage for so long to face this moment, and now that it's here... that courage seems to be slipping away under the weight of my fear.

Liam's hand slides onto my thigh and he gives me a gentle squeeze. He smiles softly when I look at him, and immediately some of the anxiety eases, just knowing he's here with me.

I just hope tonight won't be the moment where everything crumbles, and my truth hurts my family.

Liam parks in front of Mom's house, and I feel like I'm moving on autopilot, just floating through the air as I walk to the front door. But as I stand before it, looking into Liam's eyes, I take a deep breath and know there's no turning back now.

The scent of dinner cooking greets us as we enter the house, and Grandpa smiles widely as we step into the living room. Heather, Chris, and the kids aren't here yet, so it's quiet as Mom bustles around the kitchen.

But the second she sees us, she rushes forward to wrap Liam in a tight hug. "Welcome home!"

"Thank you," he says, hugging her back as his eyes meet mine over her shoulder.

A smile forms on my lips as I watch them, and the usual feeling of comfort I have with my family slowly pushes away the uncertainty.

"Come in, come in," Mom ushers us into the living room.

Grandpa steps forward, offering Liam a firm handshake and a smile. "How was the rig this time?"

Liam takes his hand with a nod. "Good. Long as always."

"I'd imagine."

"Hey!" Heather's voice sounds from the front door, and Mason zooms into the room, breathless and wide-eyed as he stops in front of Liam.

"Did you see the shark again?" Mason asks, excitement literally oozing from him.

Liam chuckles. "I don't think I saw that one, but I did see some other cool animals."

Mason's eyes somehow widen even more. "Tell me!"

Heather grins as she enters the room and reaches out to squeeze Liam's arm. "Welcome home!" She then turns to me, her smile still impossibly wide. "Hi, Theo."

I cock an eyebrow at her. "Why are you so happy?"

She shrugs, moving into the kitchen. "Just am."

Mom brings Liam and I each a beer, and as we sit on the couch opposite Grandpa and I take a sip, I almost groan with delight. I'm finally off my pain meds, and haven't been able to have a beer in almost a month... it tastes like fucking heaven.

Mason immediately plops down next to Liam, stuck to his side like glue. "Did you see a stingray?"

Liam pulls out his phone with a smile. "I saw a manta ray, actually. Want to see a picture?"

Mason's jaw drops and he looks at Chris as he sits next to Grandpa. "Dad! Did you hear that? A *manta ray!*"

"I did," Chris laughs, taking a sip of his beer. "Careful, Liam, you may have just made a new best friend. Little dude loves sea life."

Liam smiles at Chris, then pulls up a photo of the manta ray floating in the water below the rig. Mason, as expected, loses his mind and demands to see every picture of every animal Liam saw. As they flip through the pictures and Mason asks a million questions, Grandpa pulls my attention back to him.

"So, Theo," he starts. "Are you doing the end-of-season dinner with your crew this week?" Then he adds carefully, "Or, do you want me to?"

I nod thoughtfully, having been thinking of this. Every year, I take the crew out to thank them for the season, which is something my grandpa and dad have done ever since they started this business. And even though my season was cut short with them, I still need to celebrate the success we did have, and thank them for being the best crew I could ever ask for.

"I'll take them," I say, and Grandpa nods with a smile. Then I lean back on the couch and cock an eyebrow at him. "You're retired anyway, and it's time you get back to the porch with *your* crew. Your tales are getting a little too far-fetched."

He smirks at me. "You're just upset you didn't take in the biggest haul of the season."

I roll my eyes. "Conveniently, I've yet to actually see that slip. So I'll believe it when I see it, old man."

A chuckle escapes him as he shakes his head. "You're just going to have to bring it harder next season."

I nod. "I will."

His smile softens, and he nods back at me.

Because I *will* be back next season.

My gaze wanders around the room as I take in my family. Isla and Chris are looking at a book on the couch next to Grandpa, Mason still has his eyes glued to Liam's phone, and Heather is sitting on the arm of the couch next to him, intently listening as he rambles on about the sea creatures in the photos.

Mom sets a salad on the table and wipes her hands on her apron as she looks around to ensure everything is ready. But before she can call us all to the table, I take a deep breath in, knowing I need to do this now.

"Hey, Mom?" I say, my voice tight with nerves as she turns her attention to me. "Can you come sit for a minute?"

She eyes me curiously as she steps into the living room. "Everything ok?"

"Yeah," I say, glancing at Liam. He gives me a soft smile and an encouraging nod. But my heart is *rioting*.

Mom sits on a chair, concern flickering in her eyes. Everyone stares back at me, waiting... and the weight of their silence presses down on me until my hand trembles and I rub it on my knee with a shaky breath.

"Honey, what's wrong?" Mom asks, leaning forward.

"Nothing's wrong," I say, my voice quiet and breathy. "I just... uh..."

I feel frozen as I sit here, with everyone's eyes on me as I hold onto a secret that is desperate to get out... and may be one they don't want to know.

But Liam subtly presses his leg against mine, lending me the strength I need to just do this.

I drop my eyes to his leg pressed against mine and pull in a deep breath. "I'm gay."

The words hang heavily between us all, and everything seems to still. I force myself to look up at my family and meet their gazes, knowing I need to face whatever outcome is coming my way. Mom and Grandpa both stare at me with raised eyebrows, while Chris nods slowly, and Heather smiles softly. Isla still has her nose deep in a book, and Mason is looking between everyone with confusion etched on his little face.

The silence is unbearable.

"What's gay?" Mason suddenly asks, breaking the silence.

The question lingers in the air for a moment until Heather bursts out laughing, and everyone follows suit.

But I can't join them. Because something just opened up deep inside me, ready to be filled in with either regret and pain, or love and freedom.

And I can't even move until I know which one it's going to be.

Liam's hand squeezes my leg, and I turn my head to look at him. His eyes sparkle with warmth and reassurance, reminding me to breathe.

"Theo," Mom's voice is gentle, drawing my attention back to her. "Why do you look so scared?"

"I... I didn't know..." I start, unsure how to explain the thoughts swirling around in my head. The same ones I've had for so long, longer than I've even realized, that were created out of fear. They've played out every possible scenario for how this was going to go... and now that I'm actually in it, I have no idea what to do.

"Didn't know if we'd still love you?" Grandpa finishes for me, tilting his head as he observes me.

I swallow hard and nod. "Mostly though... I was worried it would hurt the store, or any of you, if people knew..."

Mom scoffs. "Theodore MacKinnon, stop that." She gives me a scolding look. "If anyone has an issue with you, they're not welcome in our store."

"Damn right," Grandpa adds, raising his beer. Chris holds his up in agreement, and Heather just smiles.

But my gaze lingers on Heather, who has been unusually quiet.

"Why aren't you saying anything?" I ask.

"Oh," she waves a hand in the air, "I already knew."

"What?" I ask, my pulse picking up its pace again.

Her eyes dart between me and Liam. "Liam didn't tell you?"

Liam winces as my gaze lands on him. "I wanted you to be able to tell your family how you wanted to..."

Confusion is quickly muddling my thoughts as I try to make sense of this. "How though..."

Mom sits forward on her chair putting a hand up to stop us. "Wait, you two are together?"

I nod in response to Mom's question. "Yeah." But I keep my eyes on Heather. "How?" I ask again.

Grandpa huffs out a little laugh as he takes a drink of his beer, and I see Chris out of the corner of my eye, his head whipping back and forth between me and Heather.

And she just shrugs.

"When I went to pick up your clothes for the hospital, I went into your room..." she says slowly. "And it was very obvious there were two boys living in there. With one unmade bed in the entire house..."

Heat rushes to my face. *That's* how she had to find out?

"And..." her gaze shifts to Liam. "Liam was so worried about you, it just... it all clicked."

Liam squeezes my leg again and smiles softly at me. I stare into his eyes for a moment, getting lost in the clear blue as everything inside me seems to finally settle.

"And yes," I nod, finally tearing my eyes away from him and looking at Mom. "Liam and I are together."

Her eyes flick between us, then a big smile spreads across

her face. "Well, isn't that the cutest fucking thing I've ever seen."

"Mom," Heather breathes out a laugh, reaching forward to place her hands over Mason's ears.

Mom waves her off. "He'll live."

Chris lifts his beer to his lips and mutters, "He's heard worse," and Isla gives him a knowing look.

Laughter bubbles up from somewhere deep inside me, and a rush of relief flows through every part of my body. The last bit of weight has lifted, and for the first time in my life... I feel completely free.

Mom pushes to her feet and motions for me to stand up. She pulls me into a tight hug, and I hold onto her as emotion wells up in my throat, threatening to spill over.

"You know we love you, honey," she whispers. "And everyone in this town does too. We just want you to be happy, and to be exactly who you are."

Tears sting my eyes as I nod. "Thanks, Mom."

She gives me one last squeeze before turning to Liam. "I guess it's time to *officially* welcome you to the family."

Liam smiles as he stands, and Mom wraps her arms around him in a loving hug. My heart swells as I watch them, and I see the emotion written all over Liam's face too.

When she releases him, Mom looks around the room and gestures to the table. "Come on. Let's eat."

As everyone files out and towards the table, Chris and Grandpa clap me on the back with a smile, offering the quiet acceptance I've been longing for, and Heather pulls me into a hug. But before we can follow everyone, Mason stops in front of us, looking up with wide, curious eyes.

"So... you sleep in the same bed?" he asks.

Liam and I exchange a glance, then I nod. "Yeah."

"And… you kiss?" his eyes dart between us.

Liam bites back a smile. "Yes."

He nods seriously. "So, you're in love," he says, more as a statement than a question.

I smile as I look down at his curious expression. "We are."

Mason tilts his head as his brows draw together, and I try to prepare myself for questions I have no idea how to answer appropriately for a five-year-old.

"Weren't you already?" he asks simply.

A laugh escapes both me and Liam, and Mason just watches us, waiting for his answer.

Liam slips his arm around my waist and nods at him. "Yeah, I think we were all along."

And when his lips press softly against mine, right here in front of my family, I feel like my heart could burst.

Everything is fucking *perfect*.

I sit at the kitchen island, resting my arm on the counter as I carefully begin undoing the Velcro on my splint.

I fucking hate this part.

Liam walks into the kitchen, having just changed into sweats after getting home from Mom's, and his eyes drop to my arm. I pause as the weight of vulnerability settles over me. I also hate that he has to see this.

"I need to massage the scars every night," I say, gesturing to the silicone strips and the compression bandage lying on the counter. "Then cover them with these."

Liam nods and sits on the stool beside me. And I hesitate with the last Velcro closure on the splint. I don't even like looking at this mess myself.

But before I can say anything, he reaches out and gently

takes my arm, undoing the Velcro himself. His movements are calm and careful as he removes the splint and places it aside, and I keep my eyes on him the whole time.

His gaze runs up the length of my arm, over the deep scars across my hand, and the long, thick scar on the underside of my forearm. The skin is uneven, puckered in places from the injury, surgery, and lack of use. It looks fucking hideous.

But when I meet Liam's eyes, they're steady and soft. "Battle scars," he murmurs with a small smile. He picks up the lotion and squeezes some onto his fingers. "Tell me what to do."

My throat tightens as I watch him, feeling more exposed than I expected. "Firm pressure with circular motions. All along the scar."

He nods, then starts working his fingers over the length of the scar on my forearm first, doing exactly as I instructed. I watch him as we sit here in silence, and his words echo in my mind.

Battle scars.

I glance down at the deep, jagged lines etched into my skin, and inhale deeply. As ugly as they are, they are also a reminder that I survived. And not just this injury, but so much more. They're proof that I've faced my biggest fears, and came out the other side, stronger than ever.

And through it all, I also found the love I've been looking for my whole life.

Liam continues to massage my scars, loosening the tight tissue under each one. When he finishes, he places the silicone strips on them, helps me wrap the compression bandage over my arm and hand, and secures the splint back in place.

"Thank you," I say quietly as I lift my eyes to his.

He nods, then leans in and brushes his lips against mine. "Tha gaol agam ort."

A breath escapes me as a smile tugs at the corners of my lips.

I know that one.

"I love you, too."

FORTY

LIAM

"HEY," I whisper as I shake Theo's shoulder, and he stirs awake.

"Hm?" he looks up at me with sleepy eyes. "Do you not sleep anymore?"

I chuckle, glancing at the clock. "It's 5:30AM." Then I look back at him thoughtfully. "Is sleep all you do now?"

His eyes narrow and I smile. "Come on, get up."

"Why?" he groans, rolling onto his back as Miss Bobber stretches out lazily beside him.

"We're going fishing."

He stares blankly at me for a moment, then lifts his splinted arm. "How?"

I just smile, rising to my feet. "Let's go."

I head downstairs with a chuckle as I hear Theo get out of bed, asking Miss Bobber if she thinks I've lost my mind. I brew two coffees and pour them into travel mugs, screwing on the last lid as Theo walks into the kitchen, dressed for fishing despite his earlier protests.

He takes the coffee I hand him, and I lean in and press a kiss to his lips.

"So, I'm just going to watch you fish then?" he asks, lifting his coffee to his lips to take a sip.

I shrug. "I mean, usually that's what you do anyway."

His jaw tightens as he glares at me, but I flash him a smile and head towards the door. He follows me down to the dock, where I have the boat ready to go. When he stops beside me, his eye catches something on the edge of the boat near one of the seats. He furrows his brow as he inspects it for a moment, then his eyes lift to meet mine.

"You... made that?" he asks.

I nod, stepping into the boat and picking up a fishing rod. I place it into the metal rod holder I welded and clamped to the side of the boat. "You can rest the rod in here so you can hold it with one hand. And *if*," I glance up at him, "you get a bite..." I reach forward and flip a spring-loaded clamp over the holder, which snaps down to keep the rod in place, "you don't have to hold it. You can reel it in with one hand."

Theo stares down at it for a moment, before he steps into the boat and pulls me into him. His lips crash against mine, and I feel the weight of his gratitude behind his kiss. I wrap my arms around him to give him everything I can before he eventually pulls back and looks into my eyes.

"Thank you," he says.

I nod and press another kiss to his lips. "Let's go fish."

I untie us from the dock and move behind the steering wheel so I can drive us to Theo's favourite fishing spot. Which has now become our favourite fishing spot. When we get there, I flip on the trolling motor and grab Theo's rod, putting a worm on his hook while he watches. It's quiet and peaceful out here, as a soft fog rolls off the water in the early morning light, and waves gently lap against the side of the boat.

Theo takes his rod as I pass it to him, and I watch as he clamps it in the holder, so he can use his good hand to release his line, and his lure drops into the water. I smile, grabbing my own rod and getting it ready.

As we sit in the peaceful silence, listening to the breeze rustling in the trees on shore and the seagulls hunting around us... I can't keep my eyes off him.

It's been a couple days since he told his family he's gay, and the shift I see in him is unlike anything I could have imagined. It's like a dark cloud has lifted, and now all his days are sunny.

I'm so proud of him for doing what he needed to do to find shelter from his storm.

And now I need to do the same.

"So..." I say slowly. "How do you feel about a drive to Cape Breton tomorrow?"

Theo turns his head to me, and his eyes flick between mine for a moment. Then he nods with a soft smile. "Yeah."

I smile back at him as I swallow down the fear attempting to push through. But something else churns inside me, growing stronger beneath everything else.

Excitement.

Because tomorrow, I'll finally see my parents for the first time in months.

But before I can say anything else, the end of Theo's rod bends.

You're fucking kidding me...

He quickly reaches forward, closing the clamp to hold the rod in place, and starts reeling it in with his good hand. Moments later, a large mackerel is pulled to the surface and Theo leans forward, grabbing the line and pulling it into the boat.

I help him unhook it, and open the livewell for him so he

can toss it in. And once he does, he turns to look at me with a smile.

I just shake my head. "I shouldn't have made that for you."

He tilts his head and gives me an assessing look. "Lost your edge, Fraser?"

My eyes narrow as I push the bait box towards him with my foot.

Oh, it's fucking on.

"Five-one."

"Yeah, I know."

"Just wanted to remind you."

I close my eyes with a sigh and turn to face Theo as he steps out of the shower. "No need. I remember."

He smiles as he heads into the bedroom, and I just shake my head as I watch him go.

He caught five fucking fish this morning.

And I caught one.

I follow him into the bedroom, my eyes trailing over him as he sits on the edge of the bed with a towel wrapped low around his waist. As he starts removing the plastic covering from his splint, I can't help but smile.

As much as it sucked losing by such a drastic number today... he deserved this one.

But next time, it's going to be me.

I push my damp hair back and sit beside him on the bed as he pulls the plastic off his arm. When he lifts his eyes to mine, I lean in and kiss him.

His lips part as I push my tongue past them, and let my hand slide over his abs, down to the edge of the towel around his hips.

He pulls in a breath, and I smile. "We have time before we need to be at the pub to meet your crew..." I say, my fingers lingering as they trace along his skin, just above the towel.

Theo chuckles softly against my lips. "Yeah, we do."

I pull his towel, letting it fall open as I take him in a heated kiss.

We fall back against the bed as I run my hand over his hardening cock, and he moans as he pulls me closer against him, my own towel falling away.

His good arm is trapped underneath me as I lie on my side beside him, stroking his cock and letting my lips trail down his neck to his chest. And as I take his nipple in my mouth and suck, his fingers dig into my back as a groan escapes him.

"Fuck," he pants.

I suck his nipple again, pulling more moans and groans from him as I slowly run my hand up and down his length, taking my time to just feel him, appreciate him, and worship him like he deserves.

He takes a deep breath in as I run my lips back up his chest to meet his mouth again, and kiss him deeply and slowly, savouring every moment.

When I pull back, I let my gaze trail over his freckles, then stare into his beautiful brown eyes. I can't believe this man is mine.

"Tha thu foirfe, mo chridhe."

His lips tilt up in a soft smile, then he lifts his splinted arm and gently rests his hand against my chest. "My heart..." he says softly, and my breath catches.

My lips meet his again and we fall into a desperate kiss as he wraps his good arm around me, holding me tight.

But as I sit back and stare down at him, my heart races and my cock twitches with need.

A need to make him feel *so* fucking good.

FORTY-ONE

THEO

LIAM STARES down at me with so much heat in his eyes, I think the room is going to light on fire.

His hand trails down my stomach. "I need to taste you, mo chridhe."

Anticipation swirls in my stomach as I nod, keeping my eyes locked on his.

"Can you roll over?" he asks, his eyes dropping to my arm.

I nod again and roll over, wincing as pain flares in my arm when I put too much weight on it. I grit my teeth and shift, trying to ignore it.

But Liam watches me carefully, then grabs a pillow and slides it beneath my chest and arm. I can't help but breathe out a laugh, appreciating the quiet way he's always looking after me.

Then he settles between my legs, and his warm, wet tongue glides over my hole, lighting up everything inside me. My head drops and I bury my face in the pillow, letting out a loud moan.

Holy shit.

He gently bites the flesh of my ass before he licks me again, and the feeling of his rough stubble against my skin and the soft warmth of his tongue over my hole nearly has me whimpering. As he continues to lick and suck my ass, I find myself pushing back into him, both begging for more and needing him to stop so I don't come before he's inside me. But when he shoves his tongue into my ass and moans, the vibration is overwhelming, and a shock rolls up my spine.

"*Fuck*," I mutter.

He does it again, and again, and before long I'm panting and moaning into the pillow, barely hanging on.

"Fuck, Liam," I grunt as I finally try to roll over, needing him inside me. But I struggle to push off the bed with my arm and hiss in pain.

He immediately pulls away from me and reaches up to help me roll over onto my back. Once I'm there, he leans over me with a soft look in his eyes as they dance over my face.

My good hand lifts to his chest, and I trail my fingers down his abs. A breath escapes him as I grasp his hard cock and stroke him, and he lowers himself to place a soft kiss on my lips. But after a few more strokes, I push him back onto his knees.

I follow him and kiss his stomach, lightly trailing my lips down his skin until I reach his cock. When I take him into my mouth, a groan escapes him as his fingers slip into my hair, tugging just hard enough to let me know how good this feels.

And that's all I want, to make him feel as good as he always makes me feel. He's always taking care of me, steady and strong despite his own pain, and the gratitude I have for him is too much to hold inside. I want to give him everything, to pour myself into him and return just a fraction of what he's given me. His touch sends electricity through my body, igniting something deep within me that builds and surges back to him in waves of love and need.

His moans grow louder as I take him deeper into my mouth and taste his precum on my tongue. His sounds are urging me on and I'm desperate for him as I grip his ass with my good hand and take him to the back of my throat. I lift my eyes to meet his as I do, and his throat bobs as he stares down at me, an intense heat in his gaze. I hold him deep in my throat and he groans as his grip in my hair tightens. He watches intently and his stomach muscles contract as I pull back and do it again, until he pushes me back.

He shakes his head as he blows out a breath. "You're going to make me come."

I smirk at him, settling onto my back and opening my legs for him. "Then come."

He falls over me, pressing his lips to mine as he shoves his tongue into my mouth. I take everything he gives me as he kisses me fiercely and grinds his cock against mine. But as he reaches for the lube, my heart rate spikes.

I watch him as he kneels between my legs and rubs the lube on his cock, then lowers his fingers to swipe over my hole. Anticipation rolls through me as he lines himself up to push into my ass. But just as the tip of his cock presses against my hole, he looks up and meets my eyes.

And I smile. "Fuck me."

His lips tilt up in a devilish smirk, and he pushes into me. A shiver ripples through my body as the pressure in my ass increases, and my breaths come quick and heavy. And when his hips meet my ass, and the pressure morphs into a feeling of intense fullness and pleasure, he drops to place a gentle kiss on my lips.

Liam holds himself over me as he slowly moves his hips, thrusting in and out of me in a slow and gentle rhythm that feels *so* fucking good. He slides against my prostate, over and over in a steady and tortuous pace that sends continuous streams of tingles up my spine and moans to my lips.

I grab at him as he kisses me again, and I need everything I can get. I need him to devour me, take me, and *fuck* me.

He seems to know exactly what I need and he increases his pace, thrusting into me harder and faster. I place my hand on his chest and feel his heart thundering as his breaths come quick and frantic.

And as soon as he sits back and takes my cock in his hand... I'm fucking done for.

"Oh my god," I mutter as I feel everything in me tense.

"Hm," Liam mutters, stroking me as he fucks my ass. "Come for me, mo chridhe."

Those words alone are all I need to tip over the edge, as overwhelming pleasure surges through my body and my muscles tremble as I come, harder than I think I ever have before.

Liam falls over me, dropping his head to my chest as he continues to fuck me.

"I'm coming," he pants.

But as he starts to pull back, I wrap my arm around him to keep him right where he is.

"Come inside me."

I feel his body go rigid under my touch as he groans, pressing his forehead into my chest as he comes. His cock pulses in my ass, and I sink my fingers into his hair to pull his head back and press my lips to his.

He pants against my mouth as he catches his breath, then pulls back to look down at me with a heavy exhale.

"Ready for dinner?"

"Well, Captain's payin' and I got pretty near 'bout half left, so..." Glen looks at his half empty beer and nods to Allison. "Yeah, I'll take another."

I chuckle as Allison's gaze shifts to me, and I nod. "Bring another round."

"Fuck yeah," Mitch holds his beer up. "Cheers, crew!"

We all raise our glasses as laughter and clinking fills the air.

Liam adds a, "Sláinte," and Sarah's eyes light up as she turns to him.

"Oh, I like the Gaelic," she says with a smile.

Liam gives me a sly side smirk, and I huff out a small laugh.

You have no idea.

"Well, here's to another great season in the books," Mitch says, pushing his empty plate aside. "And another good meal."

Glen nods, finishing off the last bite of his meal. "Thanks, Cap. Appreciated as always."

"My pleasure," I say, with a smile.

Mitch leans forward, eyeing my arm. "So, how's the healing process going?"

"It's ok," I say. "I meet with the hand therapist a couple times a week now. I guess it's progressing as it should be, but the doctor was right. It's fucking slow." I blow out a breath. "And painful."

Sarah gives me a sympathetic look. "Any timeline for when you can come back?"

I shake my head with a sigh. "I don't know. I definitely won't be back in time for tuna season in August. There's no way I could haul one of those onto the boat." I shrug. "If I get enough strength in my hand by November to start lobster season... maybe. But to manage the winch and pull up traps... I'm not sure I'll be able to by then."

Liam shrugs slightly beside me. "I could weld you new switches for the winch so they're easier to manage."

I smile at him. "You'd do that even after I kicked your ass so hard this morning?"

He huffs out a laugh. "That victory won't be lasting long."

A chuckle escapes me as well as I look into his sparkling eyes… and I get lost in them. I love that he's here with me, helping me celebrate my crew, having a good time, and is just… *happy*. My hand drifts to his knee as I smile at him… until I'm suddenly very aware of where we are, and that there are eyes on us.

I keep my hand where it is as I slowly glance around the table, where Mitch, Glen, and Sarah are looking between me and Liam curiously.

Shit.

I was going to tell them eventually, but hadn't exactly planned on it tonight.

My heart starts racing as I try to figure out what to say, but Sarah beats me to it.

"I…" she starts, then claps her hands together with a wide grin. "*Knew* it! Well, I didn't *know* it, but I knew *something* was going on with you guys, and this is even better than anything I could have imagined."

Mitch and Glen both look at her in confusion.

"Huh?" Glen grunts.

She rolls her eyes and waves a hand at them in dismissal. "You're men, you wouldn't get it."

But I just stare back at her, waiting for an explanation.

"Please," she says with a shake of her head. "That day on the boat? Fucking obvious." Then she pops a fry in her mouth.

"What was obvious?" Glen asks, then looks at me and Liam, pointing between us. "You knew about this?"

"Like I said…" Sarah sighs. "Men."

Glen just shrugs. "Well, congrats boys." He holds up his beer and takes a swig.

Mitch just smiles with a soft, approving nod as he raises his glass to both of us.

"Alright, here we go..." Allison approaches the table and sets the tray down with our drinks on it and starts passing them out. But when her eyes land on my hand, still on Liam's knee, they quickly snap back up to me.

But I take a deep breath and accept that this is all going to be a bit hard for a while. Despite feeling confident and comfortable with my choice to be fully out... I still need to take those uncomfortable steps to do that.

But her eyes soften, and she sets my beer down in front of me with a smile. "Here you go." Then she does the same to Liam.

I smile back at her. "Thanks Allie."

"So, Liam," Sarah says as Allison leaves the table.

Liam's gaze follows Allison for a moment longer and I chuckle, giving his leg a gentle squeeze to bring his attention back to the table. And selfishly... I kind of love the jealous possessiveness.

"You joining the crew next year?" Sarah asks him.

He huffs out a little laugh with a shake of his head. "As fun as it was... I'm a welder." He pauses for a moment, taking in a deep breath as he looks out the window at the water. "It was mine and my best friend's dream to be welders... and he's not here anymore." I slip my hand into his, and he shifts his gaze back to me. "So, I'll keep doing it, for him. And me."

I smile softly as I stare into his eyes, feeling the quiet strength radiating from him, and I'm filled with pride for how far he's come.

"But," he says, turning back to the table with a smile, "I'll definitely come out whenever I'm home."

"Cheers to that," Mitch says, holding his beer up.

I keep my eyes on Liam for a moment longer, savouring the

happiness in his expression, then I pick up my beer as well and clink it to everyone else's.

"Sláinte!"

FORTY-TWO

LIAM

THE CEILIDH TRAIL stretches out ahead as the road brings us closer to Inverness. We've been driving for almost five hours, but now we're just minutes away. Theo sits quietly beside me in the passenger seat as I grip the wheel a little tighter and try to keep my breathing under control.

But it's too much. The weight of everything catches up to me, and I pull off onto an old dirt road. As the truck comes to a stop, I just stare blankly ahead.

"Liam?" Theo asks cautiously as I just stare out the windshield, my hands tingling, and my heart pounding in my chest.

I shake my head. "I don't know if I can do this."

Theo turns to face me, reaching over with his good hand to rest it gently on my arm. "Hey."

I force myself to meet his gaze, swallowing hard.

He gives me a soft, reassuring smile. "They're not going to blame you," he says gently. "You had no control over what happened. And if it wasn't Nick..." he hesitates, but then continues, "they'd be mourning you. But right now, you know they're just excited to see you."

I nod slowly as his words sink in. He's right. I've replayed his words in my mind a thousand times since he first said them. It was always going to be one of us. And if it had been me, I wouldn't want Nick to be feeling the way I have been.

And Mom was so excited when I texted her yesterday to let her know I was coming... I don't want to let her down.

"Ok," I say, exhaling a long, shaky breath. I squeeze Theo's hand before pulling back onto the road, and try to keep my breaths slow and even as we near my parents' house.

But when I pull into the driveway, my hands are trembling again. I cut the engine, staring at the front porch as the door swings open. Mom steps outside, hand over her mouth as she tries to hold back tears.

Theo stays quiet, his gaze on me as I unbuckle my seat belt and step out of the truck. Mom rushes down the steps, and my body moves on its own as I walk towards her, and wrap her in a tight hug.

The sound of her cry shatters something in me, and it's like a dam opens. Everything floods to the surface as I bury my face in her shoulder, releasing everything I haven't let out yet.

"It's ok, baby," she whispers, her breath catching as she holds me.

I hear Dad's footsteps coming down the stairs, and when I lift my head, he's standing before us with glassy eyes.

Mom pulls back just enough to look at me, wiping a tear from my cheek. "Oh baby... mo mhac."

Dad steps forward, wrapping me in a strong, quiet hug. I hold on tight, taking a deep breath as I try to pull myself together.

"Let's go inside," he says, gesturing towards the house.

But Mom peers around me, and we all turn to face Theo as he stands back, giving us space.

He steps forward with a small, almost shy wave. "Hi… I'm Theo."

"Hi, Theo," Mom replies, her gaze flicking between us with curiosity.

I step towards Theo and hold his gaze for a moment as I reach out for him. Then I turn back to my parents. "This is my boyfriend."

Both my parents raise their eyebrows in surprise, but then Mom laughs softly, wiping away her tears. "Well, let's get inside. We have a lot to catch up on."

My heart is still pounding as I follow my parents into the house, and Theo places a reassuring hand on my back.

As we step through the door, memories immediately come flooding in. The familiar scent of home wraps around me as I sweep my eyes over the space, finding comfort in this place I grew up in. The old wood banister I used to slide down every morning while Mom yelled at me that I was going to break my neck, the creaky hallway from the backdoor that always gave me away when I tried to sneak in late, and the photos lining every inch of wall space.

I stop just before the kitchen, my eyes landing on one of my favourite pictures of Nick and me as kids, sitting on the bridge over the Margaree River as our legs dangle over the edge, wearing big smiles after a day of swimming.

Theo's hand slips into mine, and he gives it a gentle squeeze. I turn to meet his eyes, which are warm and comforting.

We head into the kitchen as Mom pulls out mugs and sets them on the table. "Coffee?"

I nod, unable to trust my voice, and Theo smiles. "Please."

We take a seat at the table as Mom starts preparing coffee and I rub my hand on my thigh as I take a deep breath.

Dad watches me with sadness in his eyes, then blinks it

away and leans forward with a soft smile. "Did you fly in this morning?"

I glance at Theo, then shake my head. "No, I..." I pause for a moment. "I've been living in Nova Scotia since April."

Mom stops pouring coffee and both her and Dad just stare back at me.

And I *hate* that I see hurt in their eyes.

This is exactly what I didn't want to do. I didn't want to hurt them.

I pull in a shaky breath. "I'm sorry. I just, I couldn't stay in Alberta any longer." My eyes drop to the table so I can focus on getting these words out. "I couldn't live there, or work there anymore. I got a new job, offshore in the Gulf of Mexico." I hear Mom sit down next to me in her chair. "I just started driving to get out of Alberta... I kept going until I got to Nova Scotia, but... I couldn't come home." Tears blur my vision as I hear Mom sniff and Dad shift in his seat. "I kept going until I ended up in Torrin Cove..."

Mom's hand covers mine, and I look up to meet her tear-filled eyes.

"I'm sorry," I say, my own tears falling. "I'm so sorry."

"It's ok, baby," Mom says softly.

Dad nods from across the table. "Liam... we know you're hurting. And we understand that you needed time."

I nod. "Yeah, but... I didn't tell you everything."

Theo leans forward, and I glance at him to steal strength from his soft, encouraging eyes.

I inhale deeply. "I felt too guilty to come home."

Mom squeezes my hand tighter. "Why?"

"Because of the job Nick died in..." I say, the words feeling thick and heavy, like they're coming out in slow motion.

The room is quiet, and I slowly shift my gaze to Mom and Dad.

"What about it?" Dad asks carefully.

"It was my job," I say, my voice cracking as emotion rolls over me. "It was supposed to be me in there, but I asked him to do it."

Mom covers her mouth with her other hand and a small sob escapes her.

"I didn't check the gas levels, so the cylinders needed to be replaced and..." My breath catches as the tears fall faster. "If I had just—"

"Liam," Dad says, his voice firm, but gentle. I look at him and prepare myself for whatever he's going to say or do. But he just shakes his head and leans forward, resting his forearms on the table. "Nick's parents received the accident report a few weeks ago."

My heart skips a beat as I stare at him.

"The cylinders had a faulty valve. It doesn't matter when they were replaced, or who did it... this would have happened anyway." He pauses as I just stare back at him, unable to move. "The company who produced them was found responsible. And the cylinders you used the day prior had the same faulty valves." He shakes his head slowly. "It wasn't supposed to be you."

My head goes fuzzy and my heart thumps as those words sink in.

"It's not your fault, my love," Mom says, bringing my attention to her. "You've both asked each other to do jobs, switch shifts, and so much more over the years. And you both always did it, because you love each other. This was no different."

A sob escapes me, and I drop my head to her shoulder as she wraps her arms around me. And having her here, feeling her touch and hearing her words... I think it's the piece I've been missing, to finally pull my head up and really start healing.

"I miss him so much," I say through my tears and Mom kisses the side of my head.

"I know," she says softly, and just continues to hold me as I let it all out.

When my tears slow, Mom gently pulls back and looks down at my arm, tracing her fingers over the Triquetra tattoo I got for Nick. "Bòidheach, a bhobain," she says with a smile.

I nod, lifting my eyes to meet hers.

"I'm so happy you're here," she says softly.

"Me too." And I am. I *really* am.

Mom's eyes then shift to Theo, and he gives her a soft smile. I slide my hand onto his thigh as I look into his eyes, my love for him overflowing as I appreciate him for being so supportive, steady, understanding, and patient.

"So, when do I get to hear this story?" Mom asks as she smiles between us.

I turn back to her with a nod. "Soon." Then I take a deep breath and look around the table. "I just need to go do something first."

I push to my feet and lean down to press a kiss to the top of Theo's head. "Will you be ok here for a bit?"

He looks up at me with a simple nod. "Yeah."

Dad meets my eyes, giving me a gentle nod, knowing what I need to do.

I step out the front door and down the steps, feeling strangely calm as I reach the edge of the yard. I step onto the worn path through the tree line, pushing back the overgrown branches which show it hasn't been used in years. Not since Nick and I grew up and moved away. But as I walk through the familiar path, I can still hear Nick's laughter as he ran through it from his house next door, and my soft footsteps as I snuck over to meet him at night so we could go to the beach and throw rocks in the water.

Soon, I'm standing on the other side, staring at Nick's parents' house. I hesitate for a moment before I walk up the front steps and knock on the door.

I hear footsteps on the other side, then it swings open and Leah, Nick's mom, is standing before me.

Her eyes widen as her hand flies to her mouth, and she gasps. "Liam," she whispers, rushing forward to pull me into her arms. "Oh my god, sweetheart, I've missed you."

Tears sting my eyes as I hold her tight. "I've missed you too."

"Liam?" Nick's dad, Phil, rounds the corner, and his face lights up as he sees me. "Oh my god, Liam!" He pulls me into a tight hug when Leah lets me go. "Oh my god," he says again. "How have you been?"

I nod as he releases me and wipe my eyes. "Getting better," I say. "And you?"

He nods, his expression softening. "Getting better."

"Will you come in?" Leah says gesturing inside the house. "I want to hear all about what you have been getting up to."

"Actually..." I glance back towards the path leading to my parents' house. "You want to come over? There's... someone I want you to meet."

Leah's eyes light up and she steps forward. "Oh?"

I chuckle, holding my arm out for her. "Yeah."

I grew up surrounded by love, in a home that made me feel safe and warm no matter what. And now, I know that same love in a different way, from the man who found me when I was broken. He picked me up, quietly putting me back together again, while showing me that life is worth living. Having my family meet him, with the most important people in my life all gathered at one table, is a feeling I can't even describe.

And Nick is here with us.

We sit around the kitchen table late into the night, talking, laughing, and sharing stories about Nick so Theo can get to know him, and we can remember him.

Finally, the weight in my chest is lifted, and a feeling of warmth settles deep into my soul.

And as I slip my hand into Theo's and gaze into his eyes, I'm so happy to have my heart here with me.

FORTY-THREE

THEO

THE SCENT of fresh coffee fills the air as the morning sunlight streams through the windows, bathing the kitchen in a warm, golden glow. I close my eyes as I take a deep breath in and feel the warmth on my skin, letting this peaceful feeling wash over me.

Gentle hands slip around my waist from behind me as soft lips press against my neck. I smile, tilting my head as Liam trails kisses over my skin.

"Morning," he murmurs against my neck.

"Morning," I say, opening my eyes.

I turn in his arms and meet his icy blue eyes as they sparkle in the sunlight, so bright they almost look translucent. But my eyes drop to his smile, and my heart skips. I press my lips to his as he holds me against him, kissing him soft and slow, just like the peaceful morning that surrounds us.

Miss Bobber weaves between our legs, purring loudly until I chuckle against Liam's lips and glance down at her. "Someone needs attention."

Liam nods. "I do." Then he gently grabs my face and kisses me again.

I laugh against his lips, returning his kiss before kneeling down to give Miss Bobber some love too.

Once the coffee finishes brewing, we each take our mug and just like we've done every morning this week since returning from Inverness, we head into the sunroom.

Miss Bobber jumps up with us as we settle onto the couch, and I smile, setting my mug on the coffee table we made so she can settle on my lap.

The view of the ocean is beautiful this morning, with barely a ripple on the surface, and the pale blue sky is clear, painted with soft yellows of the early morning light. These quiet mornings with Liam have become my favourite part of the day, and I want to soak in every moment with him before he goes back to work next week.

Liam turns his head to me. "What should we do today?"

I stare thoughtfully out at the water. "I don't know," I say slowly, then look at him. "Fishing?"

He cocks an eyebrow as a playful challenge sparkles in his eyes. "In the mood to lose?"

I scoff with a shake of my head. "After all you caught was seaweed last time? I'll take my chances."

His eyes narrow slightly, and I smile at the reminder of him pulling in endless clumps of seaweed, while I brought in three fish.

"It's on," he says.

I laugh, reaching over with my good hand to grasp the side of his face, my thumb lightly brushing over his cheek. "But first... let's just stay here a little longer."

He smiles as his eyes flick between mine, then he leans in, and our lips meet. I hold him in a gentle kiss as we melt against each other, knowing there's nowhere we have to be, and nothing we have to do. It's just us and Miss Bobber, and the home we made for ourselves.

I rest my head against his shoulder as I scratch Miss Bobber behind her ears, and her soft purrs fill the quiet space. Liam's hand slides onto my thigh, and we sit in the comforting silence as we gaze at the calm ocean outside.

Before we met, we were both navigating the rough waters of grief, guilt, and pain, running and hiding in a desperate attempt to tide over the relentless waves of what we couldn't confront.

But now, the peaceful scene before us is a complete reflection of the peace found within us both.

Our storms have finally passed.

LIAM

EPILOGUE

ONE YEAR LATER

THE SOFT BREEZE rustles my hair and tugs at my shirt as I stand on the dock, letting the sun shine down on me. It warms my face as I look out at the water, watching the gentle waves roll into shore, and the salty air fills my lungs with every deep inhale.

But a smile forms on my lips as footsteps approach behind me. And when I turn around, I see soft freckles and warm brown eyes.

I reach for him as he steps closer, and he takes my hand so I can pull him against me. His lips are soft against mine as my hair swirls around us in the breeze, and the sounds of birds chirping and water lapping against the dock all fade away in his presence.

I breathe him in before I release him, and he keeps his eyes locked on mine as he smiles softly. "Everything is ready."

My gaze shifts to the house, but I just nod as I bring my attention back to him.

Theo starts to turn, but I hang onto his hand and keep my feet planted, keeping him right here with me. I let my eyes fall to his hand in mine, tracing the pale scars that tell the story of his strength. This hand that has hauled countless lobster traps, built homes for our town, and has cared for so many. And even with these scars, he continues to do all of that... while also caring for himself.

My thumb rubs over the metal band on his ring finger, a promise we exchanged just hours ago that marks him as my husband. I lift his hand to my lips and press a kiss to his knuckles.

His lips tilt up in a gentle smile. "Tha gaol agam ort."

I step into him, lifting my hand to brush my thumb over his cheek. "Tha gaol agam ort, mo chridhe."

He leans in and kisses me again, before I let him lead me back up to the house, where our families and friends are gathered around a long table overlooking the water.

Mason immediately bounds over to us, looking excited and... dirty.

"Uncle Theo, Uncle Liam!" He stops before us with wide eyes and a dirt-streaked suit. "Guess what?"

Theo cautiously looks down at him. "What?"

He glances over his shoulder at Heather, who is in deep conversation with my mom. Then he leans in closer to us, opening up his suit jacket pocket, revealing about five squirming worms.

"Can we fish with them?" he asks excitedly.

I chuckle with a nod. "Yeah, just... make sure they stay in there for now."

He nods seriously, closing up his pocket. "I will."

Theo shakes his head as Mason takes off around the corner of the house, probably to look for more. "Well, the suit was nice while it lasted."

I smile, holding his hand a little tighter as I look around at everyone who came here today to be with us. Mine and Theo's parents, Theo's crew, Phil and Leah, and friends from in town are all here.

I married the man I love today, standing on the dock where we shared our first kiss in the rain. And we get to celebrate with the most important people in our lives, in the home that started this all.

As everyone takes their seats at the long table, Theo and I sit in the middle, leaving two empty chairs at the ends.

One for Theo's dad, and one for Nick.

I take a moment to look at each of them, imagining them here with us. Theo's dad being the strong and steady support I know he always was for Theo, and Nick bringing laughter and light to the day, just like he always did.

Theo's hand slips into mine, and I shift my gaze back to him so I can look into his eyes.

This perfect man, who makes all my days sunny, and is the port in my storm.

Mo chridhe.

THE END

SCOTTISH GAELIC

Mo mhac – My son

Gu bràth – Forever

Mo chridhe – My heart

Tilg a-mach air mo shon, mo chridhe. Tha feum agam ort – Come for me, my heart. I need you

Tha thu bòidheach – You're beautiful

Tha mi gad ionndrainn – I miss you

Sin an rud as teotha a chunnaic mi riamh – That's the hottest thing I've ever seen

Tha gaol agam ort – I love you

Tha thu foirfe – You're perfect

Sláinte – Cheers

Bòidheach, a bhobain – Beautiful, my darling

THANK YOU

Thank you so much for reading Tide Over! I hope you fell in love with Theo and Liam as much as I have! And thank you so much for allowing me to share a piece of my home with you all.

If you found yourself curious about a certain awkward bird-watcher in this story, you're in luck! We're heading to Newfoundland next on our journey through Atlantic Canada, where this guy will introduce us to the world of bird-watching, along with more of the breathtaking beauty that Atlantic Canada has to offer.

I want to send a big thank-you to all of my Alpha, Beta and ARC readers! I'm always blown away by the support you all send my way, and I can't even begin to express how much I appreciate you all.

And I have to give a special shout-out to Melissa, Liza, and Cait. Thank you to the best ever Alpha team and friends a girl could ask for. You're all the absolute best, and I love you!

Tapadh leibh!

ALSO BY EVE HOLMES

No Holds Barred

An MMA MM rivals-to-lovers romance duet

Book 1: Hooks In

Book 2: Choke Hold

Songs of Freedom

An MM Rockstar romance trilogy

Book 1: Silhouette

Book 2: Details

Book 3: Remastered

ABOUT THE AUTHOR

Eve is an avid lover of coffee, getting lost in fictional worlds, crafting, and ducks. She lives in a small town in Nova Scotia with a bunch of animals and plans to get many more, much to her family and friends' dismay.

When she's not writing or trying to get ducks to love her, she can usually be found fantasizing about living in a tree house, riding her horses, and exploring Nova Scotia.

Eve enjoys a challenge, and will gladly turn the strangest writing prompt into a book. There's much more to come, we're just getting started!

Facebook Group: Eve's Elites: Eve Holmes' Reader Group

facebook.com/eveholmesauthor
instagram.com/eve.holmes.author
tiktok.com/@eveholmesauthor